BURN
MARK

BURN MARK

LAURA POWELL

BLOOMSBURY

LONDON BERLIN NEW YORK SYDNEY

Bloomsbury Publishing, London, Berlin, New York and Sydney

First published in Great Britain in June 2012
by Bloomsbury Publishing Plc
50 Bedford Square, London, WC1B 3DP

A CIP catalogue record for this book is available from the British Library

ISBN 978 1 4088 1522 9

Typeset by Hewer Text UK Ltd, Edinburgh
Printed in Great Britain by Clays Ltd, St Ives Plc, Bungay, Suffolk

1 3 5 7 9 10 8 6 4 2

www.bloomsbury.com
www.laurapowellauthor.com

This book is for Benedict Whitehouse,
who shared the author's early adventures
as a pirate, bandit, deity and witch.

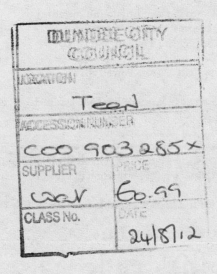

PROLOGUE

The walls of the Burning Court were high and white-tiled, its ceiling one giant chimney. If the young witch at the stake had been able to look up the funnel, she might have glimpsed a distant pane of sky.

Instead, she stared ahead. There was a glass panel in front of her, and the shadowy shapes of the inquisitors behind. One of them would have his hand on the switch, ready to light the fuse.

She couldn't speak or move. Her body had been frozen rigid by the drug they'd given her so that she would be numb and immobile throughout her execution. Her reflection in the glass was calm. Everything was quiet and orderly, exactly as it should be.

In which case... should she be aware of the coarse material of her prison shift, or sense the chill coming off the shining tiles? Propped up in the centre of the pyre, she was newly conscious of the weight of its wood.

The witch's heart began to stammer. This wasn't right. Something must have gone wrong. The drug wasn't working properly. She had to let them know before it started. She had to tell them, she had to explain –

But her tongue didn't move. Her eyes were locked open, her mouth was locked shut. The fear was suffocating, but she couldn't gasp for breath. Her face in the glass gazed peacefully back, while every nerve, every muscle, every pulse of her heart and brain screamed STOP.

The wood sparked.

No, wait, please wait –

A thin yellow flame wriggled into life, then danced upwards. Smoke rose with it. Heat blossomed, intensified.

Behind the blurred glass, the unseen audience was waiting.

Somebodyhelpmeohgodpleasestopstopstop

Tendrils and coils of fire. Her eyes stung from its smoke. Her pale hair was already rippling into flames. At any second they would be eating into her flesh. She was screaming and screaming now, soundlessly –

CHAPTER 1

In bed, Glory was screaming too, her body thrashing into wakefulness in the moonlit room.

A tall shape blundered through the door. Light flooded in after him.

'It's over,' her father said, coming to the bed, wrapping her in his arms. 'Hush now. You're safe; it was just a dream.' He pushed a sweaty strand of hair off her face as she shuddered and gasped.

'Was it the Burning Court again?'

Glory nodded. She was eight years old and had been having the same nightmare for as long as she could remember. 'I'm sorry,' she whispered. Thumps and grumbles could be heard through the walls as the building's other residents resettled themselves.

'There's nothing to be sorry for, baby-girl. Nothing to be frightened of either. I'll chase the bad dream away.'

But in the end it always came back. As Glory got older, she learned to control her waking outbursts and no longer disturbed the house with her cries. The terror didn't diminish though. The dream was so vivid; immediately afterwards, she could swear the scent of smoke clung to her hair.

Her father believed she'd grown out of it. In the early years, he tried to get her to describe it properly, and talk about what might bring it on. But even as a little girl, she was embarrassed by her weakness, refusing to revisit the panic of the night. And the Burning Court dream was bound up with two secrets that her father mustn't know.

The first was the image in the glass panel. In the dream, Glory was the witch at the stake, yet the face she saw reflected was her mother's. She recognised her from photographs, not memory, for Glory's mother, Edie, had disappeared when she was three.

Edie Starling's farewell to her husband and child had been a single line on a postcard, dropped on the doormat the morning she walked out of their lives – and perhaps her own – for ever. I *love you, but it's better if* I *go. Forgive me.* That was the last they or anyone else heard of her. 'She'll have run off with some fancy-man,' the neighbours speculated. 'Done herself an injury,' said others. 'Too flaky for family life,' declared the rest. Any of this could be true, but whatever else Glory's mother was, she was also a witch. The illegal kind: unregistered, unlicensed and hunted by the Inquisition.

For this was Glory's second secret fear: that the dream of her mother's burning felt so real because her mother had been caught by the Inquisition, because it was true.

Yet despite this, once the nightmare was over, after she'd been soothed and petted and her tears had dried, she'd wait until the house was quiet again. Then she would climb out of bed and go to her attic window. She would look over

London's jumbled rooftops, the ghostly glow of the street lights, the darkness above. And Gloriana Starling Wilde would lift her chin, take a deep, defiant breath, and say the same prayer she had said ever since she could remember.

Please, God . . . when I'm grown-up, make me a witch.

CHAPTER 2

The first time Lucas saw a witch burn, he was ten years old. Britain hadn't held a public burning for over three years, and the case dominated headlines for weeks on end. 'Disgusting rabble-rousing muck,' his father had muttered, sweeping yet another lurid newspaper supplement off the breakfast table.

As Chief Prosecutor for the Inquisitorial Court, Ashton Stearne had been instrumental in bringing the guilty witch to justice. Lucas had looked forward to saying at school, 'You won't see it in the news, but my dad says . . .' However, his father remained tight-lipped about the details. The case had taken its toll on everyone involved. Death by balefire was reserved for the worst witchcrimes (first-degree murder, treason, terrorism), and this was a particularly horrific one. Bernard Tynan had used witchwork to lure a young school-girl into his house, where he'd murdered her.

Ashton Stearne was one of the officials who would oversee the burning at a secret Inquisition prison. It would be filmed so the public could watch it live on open-air screens. Even though his father hadn't forbidden Lucas from watching it, Lucas knew he wasn't supposed to. This wasn't because Ashton thought his son was too young or too delicate, but because he disapproved of public executions on principle. They pandered to the worst of the mob, he said.

It was true people queued for hours to get a viewing space. Balefires weren't televised and were only shown in the cities, on a limited number of screens. Their audiences were heavily policed. Of course, almost as soon as filming started, somebody would manage to upload an illegal video of it on to the web. But watching some fuzzy pirated version would be cheating, Lucas felt. If he was going to witness a balefire, he wanted it to be as part of the official event, with all the sense of occasion attached.

And when his friend Michael invited him to watch it in Trafalgar Square, in a prime spot on the roof of his father's office, the opportunity was too good to resist.

A car picked the two boys up from school on Friday afternoon. Both were excited and nervous, and trying to hide it.

Michael hadn't invited anyone else from their class. He and Lucas weren't especially close but when a secretary led them up to the insurance firm's rooftop terrace Mr Allen welcomed him like an old family friend.

'Aha! Master Lucas!' he boomed. 'Here you are!' He turned round to his assembled colleagues and guests. 'It's his father we have to thank for today's burning, y'know. This is Ashton Stearne's boy.'

The other men looked admiring. 'Your old man deserves a knighthood for this,' one said. 'You must be very proud,' said another.

Mr Allen clapped Lucas heartily on the back. 'He'll soon be following in the family footsteps, I'll be bound. Eh?'

Lucas nodded. He was going to be an inquisitor one day, just like his father and his grandfather before him, and every man in his family before that – all the way back to the seventeenth century and John Stearne the First, Cromwell's own Witchfinder General.

It was flattering how attentive they all were, these grown men with their expensive suits and important, well-fed faces. They asked Lucas questions about the case and his father's job, and although he didn't have anything new to tell them, they still seemed interested in what he had to say.

'Well, I'm sure you'll make a grand witch-burner,' said one of the few women present.

'Bloody hags,' said somebody. 'Burning's too good for them.'

'Here, here,' said somebody else, raising a glass.

This made Lucas uncomfortable. 'Hag' was a word you weren't supposed to use – like 'harpy' or 'hex'. His father got very cross if he ever heard him saying it. Lucas thought how strained and irritable his father had been the last couple of days, almost as if he wasn't looking forward to the balefire.

He left the grown-ups to it and found Michael with his twin sister, Bea, looking over the edge of the balustrade. In the late July afternoon a dull film of heat lay over the city. Lucas felt all the privilege of being up here, away from the dusty crowds and the traffic fumes. In front of them, Nelson's Column reared upwards, dizzyingly high. Nelson had used witches to fight the French; they'd learned about it in Witchkind Studies at school, and one of the square's plinths had a statue commemorating witches in war. The abstract sculpture had only been unveiled last year, but now Lucas saw someone had daubed it with red paint, a bloody spatter across the bronze.

Every inch of steps and paving was covered with people. They were perched on the great lions beneath Nelson's monument and packed tightly along the edges of the switched-off fountains. The National Gallery, with its ranks of columns and creamy grey dome, made a stately backdrop for the screen in front of its portico. At the northwest corner of the square, close to the vandalised memorial, a little group of Witchkind Rights protesters had assembled. They were within a police cordon and carrying banners and placards: One Law for All, Burning for None, and Ban the Balefires. Nobody paid them much attention.

For a while, Lucas, Michael and Bea amused themselves by dropping bits of canapé on to the heads of the crowd. Bea tired of this before the boys did. She was a thin, serious-looking girl, and her eyes kept flicking restlessly towards the screen. 'I've got butterflies,' she said.

Lucas kicked at the wall. 'I wish they'd get it over with. The wait, I mean.'

At quarter to five, the countdown began. A digital clock appeared on screen to mark the fifteen minutes till burntime. Several groups broke into the National Anthem and began waving Union Jack flags. Mr Allen's guests moved to the edge of the terrace, drinks in hand, their faces bright with anticipation. One of the secretaries was clutching a newspaper poster with a picture of the dead schoolgirl.

The singing and talk faded as the seconds blinked

away. When the clock reached the final minute, the crowd sent a collective bellow echoing round the square. 'Ten – Nine – Eight –' The party on the terrace joined in too, cheering and whistling. But when the countdown stopped, and the screen flashed up with the particulars of the condemned man and the sentence passed, the silence was absolute. Then the name of his victim appeared.

'Poor wee angel,' sighed the secretary with the poster. She wasn't the only person with tears in her eyes. Several people crossed themselves.

It was a solemn moment. But just as the waiting began to be oppressive, the screen returned to black. There was a fizz of static, and the interior of the Burning Court appeared.

The condemned witch was already in place, strapped upright on to the board that rose from the centre of the pyre. By now, Bernard Tynan's features were intimately familiar: the thinning hair, the fleshy nose, the soft pouches under his eyes. *The Face of Evil*, the tabloid headlines had screamed, but he looked wholly unremarkable really. That was what was so frightening.

Little could be seen of his surroundings. The Burning Court was just a plain white space. Behind a glass panel in the wall facing the balefire, Ashton Stearne would be sitting with his fellow High Inquisitors, the Home Secretary, a medic and a priest. But the camera didn't show any of this. Its lens was fixed on the witch.

Bernard Tynan stared back impassively, frozen stiff by the anaesthetic they'd given him. Britain was a civilised country after all. In plenty of other nations witches were burned alive in just the same way they'd been for the last thousand years or more.

Fat bundles of wood were neatly stacked around the man's feet and up to his calves. An electric fuse led from under the pyre back to the room where three prison guards were preparing to press three separate ignition buttons. Only one switch would light the fire, but nobody would know which of the three was responsible.

Michael pointed and giggled. There was a damp patch on the crotch of the witch's white shift; as they'd slid the needle in for his injection, or perhaps before, when they came for him in his cell, he must have wet himself. Lucas smirked dutifully. But he felt anxious somehow, breathless, and his palms were sweaty; he was worried people might know. The next moment, the unseen switch was flicked, and a spark leapt out from the wood.

The witch waited, inanimate as the poppet he'd made to bind the dead girl to his will. His eyes were wide and unblinking as the fire licked upwards. The burning wood made a muttering, scratching sound. Flames began to writhe through the man's flesh.

Beside him, Lucas could hear Bea crying softly. He didn't turn to her, he didn't look away. He stared at the screen as stiffly as Bernard Tynan stared out. The witch's anaesthetised death would be more merciful than that of his victim, he told himself. Yet though the man might feel no pain, his living mind knew his body was cracking and blistering; he would be able to smell the stench of charred meat and oily black smoke. He would hear the fatty hiss and spit of fire as his flesh melted from his bones.

In the old days of burning, it could take two or more hours for a condemned witch to die. In these enlightened times, a prisoner's clothes were treated with flammable chemicals so that they would be overwhelmed by fire in minutes. Already, billows of smoke obscured the blazing body. At six minutes past five, the show was almost over.

People began to clear their throats and fidget. For the moment, there was an embarrassed sense of relief; celebration would come later. As the screen went blank for the final time, the bells of the church of St Martin-in-the-Fields began to ring, along with all the other church bells in London.

Lucas was not the squeamish sort. He put the images of the burning man away, and if he chose to remember them, he did so slowly and carefully, like somebody examining broken glass. Afterwards, he and Michael never directly talked about the balefire. At school, they were as they'd always been: casually friendly, no more. Sometimes, at sports matches or speech days, or while waiting to be picked up from a party, Lucas would see Mr Allen. He always greeted Lucas as if they were long-lost friends. 'Aha! It's my young witch-burner!'

And Lucas would smile obediently. He couldn't account for why his stomach always clenched at the greeting. Or why the world should seem to slip, just for a second, out of joint.

CHAPTER 3

Clearmont's school colours were green with a gold trim. When they saw Lucas and Tom get off the bus, the girls at the stop across the road hooted and catcalled. 'Ooh,' one of them shouted, 'it's the Frog Princes!'

Lucas and Tom ignored them loftily. Now they were in Year Ten, they were supposed to be above responding to this sort of thing. They set off at a brisk pace; the Senior School was having a careers talk from one of the Inquisition's Recruitment Officers that morning, and their bus had been late.

'Hop along now!' cried the loudest of the girls, the one with big hooped earrings and bare legs mottled with cold. The others made croaking sounds.

'Chavvy little hags,' muttered Tom.

Lucas glanced back and accidentally caught the earring-girl's eye. She blew him a kiss, to more screeches of laughter. 'Hideous,' he agreed, as they went through the school gates.

It was gone nine and most people were already inside the building. On their way to the hall, however, they passed Ollie Wilks standing outside the senior common room. He was enjoying a leisurely smoke.

'Aren't you coming to the presentation?' Tom asked.

'Not eligible, am I? My first cousin's a witch.'

Tom and Lucas exchanged looks. Ollie had said it quite naturally, but it was still embarrassing.

'I didn't know that,' Lucas said at last.

'Yeah. Sarah used to do fae-healing for the NHS. She's non-practising now; she got herself bridled once she was married.'

Fae was the common term for a witch's abilities, the so-called Seventh Sense. It was reckoned that one in a thousand people would develop it, and since the fae was practically always hereditary, anyone who'd had a witch-relative within the last three generations of their immediate family was barred from working in the Inquisition. 'Fae runs thicker than blood, quicker than water', the saying went. And the strict background checks worked: in the last twenty years, only two inquisitors had turned witchkind after joining the service.

Ollie, however, didn't seem bothered by his exclusion. 'You should bunk off and join me,' he told Lucas. 'It's not like you're going to hear anything you don't already know.'

'Ah, he just wants to chat up the lovely lady inquisitress,' said Tom.

Lucas grinned, and swung ahead to the hall. 'Try and stop me. You know how those uniforms turn me on.'

An air of ritualised boredom hung over the assembly hall whose stained glass and odour of wilting flowers gave everyone who entered it the feeling of being at church. A projector screen had been set up in front of the stage curtains, and a woman in the scarlet and grey inquisitorial dress was waiting to one side. The school's career advisor and Year Heads were seated on the other, together with a slim fair-haired boy. He was the real focus of interest in the room. Gideon Hale had left Clearmont last summer, and was taking a year out before university to join the Inquisition's Accelerated Development Programme.

Tom and Lucas slipped into their seats just as the Recruitment Officer got up from hers. Her face was sunny and dimpled, her smile determined, as she began her introduction. The screen next to her displayed the image of an eye, drawn in black, with the iris quartered by a red cross. It was the emblem of the British Inquisition.

'Now then,' she said, 'I'm sure you're all familiar with the work we inquisitors do. However, it's still important to challenge the mythical image of our organisation being full of mean old men in black robes, getting their kicks out of persecuting innocent witches.'

The inquisitor gave a cheery laugh. Her audience stared back with blank politeness. Clearmont always had a strong showing at the Inquisition; the school had a proud tradition of preparing its students for public service.

'Over the years,' the inquisitor continued cosily, 'the Inquisition has made great progress in developing good relations between ourselves and the witchkind community. We have a duty of care to the witches under our surveillance and we take a lot of pride in finding fulfilling work for them within the State. Public safety is our priority, but the personal welfare of law-abiding, registered witches is an important aspect of our service.'

'Yeah, right,' whispered Tom. 'Next she'll say, "Some of my best friends are witches."'

'. . . In fact, I myself am proud to have made several good friends within the witchkind community . . .'

The boys' shoulders shook with silent laughter.

'However, as I'm sure you know, national security is our principal responsibility.' The inquisitor's face grew grave. 'The main challenges faced by the Inquisition are the use of witchwork in organised crime – the gangster societies known as covens – and witch-terrorism practised by extremist groups such as Endor. Thankfully, Endor hasn't been active in Britain since the late 1990s, but this does not give reason for complacency. Witchcrime prevention, detection and punishment is what the Inquisition was created for.'

There was a solemn pause. Then the dimples and twinkles returned.

'That doesn't mean we only recruit people interested in law enforcement, of course! We also offer exciting opportunities in sectors as diverse as technology and research, education and PR. And it's *my* job to tell you all about them . . .'

The rest of the presentation lasted about forty minutes. By the end, her listeners were shifting restlessly. It was Gideon Hale they had come for, and the Accelerated Development Programme.

This involved recruiting students into the Inquisition while they were in their final year at school. They would spend a year before university on an intensive training scheme, which they would continue part-time while studying for their degrees. In return, trainees got their tuition fees paid, and would join the inquisitorial officer class once they graduated. The programme had only been running a few years and was somewhat controversial. It had been established partly because witches usually developed the fae in their early twenties, and it was therefore thought useful to have inquisitors within the student body. It was a deterrent too, to the Witchkind Rights campaigners and protesters who targeted university campuses. However, since the student inquisitors were not undercover – in accordance with the agency's new policy of 'outreach and transparency' – there were grumblings that the surveillance benefits were limited.

Gideon Hale would be putting this to the test once he took up his place to read Law at Oxford next year. As he came forward to talk about his experience of the programme so far – the parts that weren't classified, that is – the audience visibly revived. Gideon was tall and tanned with dusty fair hair and an easy smile; his speech was focused yet relaxed, calculated to charm.

Lucas watched Clara and Daisy, two girls in his class, smirk and flick their hair about in an effort to catch Gideon's eye. They weren't the only ones. As Head Boy, Gideon had always had girls sigh over him and younger boys hold themselves straighter in his presence. Now he'd left, even the crabbiest teachers spoke of him with pride. Lucas's own feelings were mixed. In time, he would be following in the older boy's footsteps, and although the Inquisition was a vast organisation, once inside, it was a surprisingly small world. No doubt they'd run into each other on a fairly regular basis. In light of their previous encounters, however, Lucas wasn't entirely sure this was a good thing.

His first encounter with Gideon was in his second year at Clearmont, when he was twelve and Gideon fifteen. Because of a dental appointment Lucas was late for games, and when he went to the locker room to change, he found Gideon there with two other older boys, huddled over a laptop.

The way they looked up when he entered, both shifty and excited, made him wonder if they were watching porn. The sound coming from the laptop was muffled, but then he thought he heard a scream.

'Come and have a look at this, Stearne.' Gideon beckoned him forward. He smiled conspiratorially. 'You'll find it quite an education.'

Lucas understood he was being granted a favour.

He approached the computer screen. It was showing a film of a balefire. The location was somewhere in rural Africa, he thought, from the hot dusty square, and colourful robes of the assembled crowd. The picture was grainy, shot by a shaky hand-held camera, but you could see what was going on right enough. Three women in white shifts were being dragged to the stake.

'Look at them,' said Gideon with slow, soft relish. 'Look at the dirty harpies.'

One of the witches was very young, maybe even in her teens. She was dumb with terror, but the others were crying and pleading. There were no drugs administered here. The wobbly camera swung round to the crowd, who were singing and dancing. Lucas, who had seen no burnings since Bernard Tynan's, remembered the gathering on the roof terrace above Trafalgar Square. The clink of glass and fizz of tonic, the party chatter.

The other two boys sniggered furtively. The women were naked under their thin shifts, which clung to their bodies, slick with heat and fear. A man danced forward with a burning brand.

Lucas leaned over and pulled the top of the laptop down.

'We shouldn't be watching it,' he said.

Lucas had already got used, without quite noticing it, to leading other people's opinions. But that was among his peers. It was only in the ensuing pause – seeing the two older boys tense up, ready for Gideon's cue – that the enormity of his presumption hit home.

'A delicate little flower, aren't you,' Gideon remarked pleasantly. 'What would Daddy say?' From underneath the lid of the laptop, they could hear the crackle of flames, and screaming.

'At a guess, that foreign balefire films are classified,' Lucas replied, as lightly as he was able. 'And that distributing and viewing them is illegal.'

Gideon regarded him coolly. His grey eyes were very pale. Lucas kept his own face neutral.

'Then we'd better listen to Daddy,' Gideon said at last. He opened up his computer again and pressed a button to send the screen blank. 'Out in the bush, they do things the old-fashioned way. No red tape.'

*　　*　　*

'. . . And what's so nerve-racking as well as exciting about this scheme,' Gideon was saying on the stage, 'is that right from the start, you're dealing with highly sensitive, classified material. There's a lot of regulatory stuff to get through, but most of it's interesting and all of it's important . . .'

Throughout the rest of his time at school, Gideon was always perfectly agreeable to Lucas, though both maintained a certain watchfulness in the other's presence. And although the second thing about Gideon that stuck in Lucas's mind was also to do with witches, it was so trivial he didn't even know why it had left an impression on him.

It happened last summer, one sun-drowsy evening near the end of term, when Lucas and a couple of friends were on their way back from the park. Along the High Street, they became aware of people stopping to stare, exclaiming and pointing upwards. Two sky-leapers were moving along the roofs, skimming over the gaps between buildings and swooping over chimneys with dizzying ease. They were dressed in the blue uniform that WICA, the witchkind division of the security services, wore when engaged on public witchwork. It seemed to be a training exercise, for their progress was leisurely. Gliding between the shadowed bricks and gilded sky, they were remote as angels.

Lucas had seen footage of sky-leaping on the news and as part of Witchkind Studies but never in real life. Even among witches, the ability was rare. Flying dreams were, of course, a common childhood nightmare, and though Lucas hadn't had one for ages, seeing the real-life equivalent gave him a shiver of dread. The fluid, graceful movements were so *wrong*. Defying gravity, defying the solidity of bricks and mortar, and the frail human bonds of flesh – it went against nature. *But*, thought Lucas, *all the same . . . how bold, how beautiful it must be to skim above the city in golden evening air.* And, for a fleeting moment, he knew the other people gazing at the sky thought so too.

Suddenly self-conscious, Lucas let his eyes drop. It was then he saw Gideon standing in the entrance to a bar across the street. He too was staring at the sky-leapers. As they vanished into the horizon, his face twisted. Unnoticed by the other bystanders, he spat into the gutter.

'. . . and I'm really looking forward to liaising with witch-agents in law enforcement and the intelligence services. It might sound pompous, I know, but to be able to engage with different people from all kinds of backgrounds, in service to your country, is such an amazing privilege . . .'

Gideon's speech ended in warm applause. Lucas joined in, taking care to look as animated as everyone else. He was conscious of a slight pressure in the back of his head, which had been there since he got up this morning and was probably the start of a headache. It would be good to get out of the stuffy hall.

He saw Bea Allen in the lobby outside. Michael had left for boarding school in Year Nine but his twin had stayed at Clearmont. The solemn little girl who'd cried at the bale-fire had grown glossy and self-assured, with a rosebud mouth and hair like dark treacle. Now she stopped and smiled at Lucas. Was she waiting for him?

'So . . . does the Inquisition have a new recruit?' Lucas asked.

'Maybe if they changed the uniforms.' Bea pulled a face. 'Grey's *so* not my colour.'

'That's a shame,' Tom said from behind. 'Because Lucas was just saying how he's hot for girls in inquisitorial dress. Or was it the "old men in long black robes" you meant?'

Lucas gave him a friendly shove. Tom shoved him back and moved on, with a theatrical wink.

Bea pretended not to notice.

'Have you really never thought of doing anything else but the Inquisition?' she asked.

'Like what?'

'I don't know. Becoming a racing driver. Astronaut. Rock star.'

He laughed. 'You wouldn't say that if you heard me sing. I'll have to leave the pop-idol-astronaut stuff to you.'

'I wish. I'm thinking about medicine, actually. Like Mum.' Bea gave a half smile, half grimace. 'So I guess I'm destined for the family business too.'

They came to the foot of the stairs, ready to go to their different classrooms. She fiddled with a strand of hair. 'Are you . . . will you be going to Nick's party tomorrow?'

'Should be.'

'I'll maybe see you tomorrow, then.'

'Sure. See you there.'

It seemed that Lucas had known Bea for ever, yet lately it was as if they had become different people; working each other out afresh. It felt new, exciting. He returned home in a buoyant mood, even though the pressure in his head had moved behind his eyes. Now he came to think about it, the tension had been building for a couple of days. He hoped the headache would work itself out before the party tomorrow.

Paul, the guard at the gate, who had been with the family for nearly ten years, gave his usual smile and waved as Lucas entered his access code into the keypad. Security was tight at the Stearne residence, a handsome Regency town house set well back from the road. Its enclosing walls were monitored by CCTV and visitors had to present ID to gain admittance. Biometric ID cards were issued to all UK citizens from the age of twelve, partly to prevent witches who'd altered their appearance with a glamour from gaining access to places they shouldn't.

The house also had the usual witchwork defence of bells encased in perspex boxes over the outside doors. They were wired to a central alarm system, in order to give a warning if a witch hexing a bane approached. Banes were any kind of witchwork that caused harm to living things and so emitted a particularly strong kind of fae, a malignant radiation that the iron in the bells reacted to. 'Bells warn, iron prevents, water reveals', the maxim went. As a High Inquisitor, Ashton Stearne took his and his family's safety very seriously. He had learned the hard way.

Once inside the house, Lucas followed the sound of voices to the drawing room, where his father and step-mother, Marisa, were having a drink with a neighbour. Lucas was surprised to find his stepsister there too. Philomena was rarely home on a Friday evening. Although she and Lucas went to the same school, she was two years older than him and took considerable pains to lead as separate a life as possible.

'Lucas!' Marisa waved him in. She was looking even more elegant than usual, in a cream silk cocktail dress, and Lucas remembered that she and his father were going to dinner with Sir Anthony Brady that evening. Sir Anthony was the Witchfinder General, head of the UK Inquisition, and it was widely expected that Ashton Stearne would be his successor when he retired. 'Come and say hello to Mr Pettifer.'

Lucas went over to shake hands. He had met Henry Pettifer, a plump and cheerful civil servant, on a couple of occasions before.

'Philly's been telling us about your careers talk this morning,' Henry said. 'How did you find it?'

'Predictable. A lot of warm fuzzy stuff about witchkind welfare.'

'Hug a harpy,' Philomena put in, with a snort.

Ashton Stearne raised his brows. 'It's easy to mock, but community relations are important. You don't want to bully people into cooperating with the authorities – the results are never as good, particularly when it comes to intelligence-gathering.'

Lucas settled into the chair beside him. 'I know, Dad. But the way that Recruitment Officer was going on, you'd have thought "inquisition" was a dirty word.'

'Political correctness gone mad,' said Henry, shaking his head.

'Even so, some of the persecutions suffered by witchkind

24

have been very regrettable,' Ashton remarked. 'And there's no denying the contribution that witches have made to our society over the years.'

He stared down at the whisky in his glass, and took a meditative sip. 'However, the stark fact remains that most of the work that law-abiding witches do is simply counteracting the damage that other witches inflict.'

'Quite right, quite right,' Henry agreed. 'Which is why I so admire you chaps for working alongside them when the occasion demands. Jack Rawdon might be flavour of the month, but he needs watching. No doubt about it.'

Jack Rawdon was the Director General of WICA, the office of Witchkind Intelligence and Covert Affairs. It had been established after the Second World War but its work was controversial. Its witch-agents were not trusted to run their own operations, and were instead assigned to assist MI5 and MI6 officers on a short-term, case by case basis.

According to the statistics, witches made up less than one per cent of the population, yet their work was connected to twenty-five per cent of all crime. Officially, the police only dealt with ordinary law-breaking and if they or anybody else found evidence of a witchcrime, they were supposed to bring it to the Inquisition. In particularly complex cases, or those relating to national security, the Inquisition's Witchcrime Directorate would work in partnership with the secret services. The increasing involvement of WICA agents in such operations was something many inquisitors found hard to accept.

However, during Endor's terrorist campaign in the late 1990s, the notion that witchcrime was best defeated by witchwork had gained new ground. It was an idea that Jack Rawdon was keen to promote. As a young witch-agent, he had helped dismantle Endor's network in Britain. He was the first director in WICA's history whose name was publicised on appointment, and one of the UK's most high-profile witches. It helped that he looked like a man you could trust, with the rugged, square-jawed appeal of an old-fashioned action hero.

'Rawdon's highly able,' Ashton acknowledged. 'Charismatic too – which some of my colleagues find troubling. But I suspect that increased collaboration with witch-agents is inevitable.'

'And an "amazing privilege", if Gideon Hale's to be believed,' Lucas said drily.

'Gideon . . . hmm . . . yes, I remember. He came and introduced himself when I gave a talk to your sixth-form last year. I was glad to hear he's on the fast-track scheme. Rather an impressive young man, I thought.'

'Oh, Gid's a sweetie,' said Philomena.

'"Gid"?' Lucas was amused. 'I didn't know you were on nickname terms.'

'There's no reason you should. You're not a High Inquisitor yet.'

'Darlings . . .' Marisa shot them a reproving glance. 'Now, what I find so objectionable,' she continued, smoothing her coil of blonde hair, 'is this trend towards giving the fae some kind of spurious *thrill*. There's even a witch-character in that dreadful soap, for instance – what's it called? EastEnding? Apparently he's terribly popular.'

'Mummy! Since when do you watch *EastEnders*?'

'My manicurist was telling me about it. She's worried her daughter is taking an unhealthy interest in the fae. As a kind of teenage rebellion, you know.'

Henry laughed, but Ashton looked thoughtful. 'In some respects,' he said, 'I suppose we're all attracted to the darker, more primitive aspects of human nature; the parts that civilisation can never entirely control. The Seventh Sense can't be rationalised by science or social theories. That's always been part of its allure.'

'Yes, but from the way some people talk,' his wife replied, 'you'd think that witchwork was the same as any other unusual skill. Like writing poetry or . . . or . . . being able to stand on one's head. They seem to entirely disregard the *moral* dangers.'

'It's just as well, then,' said Henry jovially, 'we've got the Stearne boys on hand to keep witchkind in their place. Just look at them now! What a picture the three of them make, eh?'

Lucas and Ashton were sitting under one of several family portraits in the house. This was the 'third' Stearne Henry was referring to: Augustine Edgar Stearne, the nineteenth-century reformer responsible for modernising the Inquisition and supporting the recruitment of witch-officers within the police. The resemblance to his descendants was striking. All three had the same black hair – silvering, in Ashton's case – springing from a peak. The same high foreheads, the same dark blue eyes and pale English skin. Furthermore, in the face of unexpected scrutiny, both father and son had unconsciously assumed the portrait's air of calm hauteur.

'*So* handsome,' said Marisa fondly.

Lucas grimaced. A flash of pain had struck across his eyes. It was very peculiar: for a moment, the room seemed to warp and shiver. From the shadows, he heard a low hiss.

CHAPTER 4

Today, thought Gloriana Starling Wilde, *is going to be a lucky day*. She tilted her head to the pale sunshine, enjoying the way her new gold hoops tugged comfortably at her ears. On a fine spring afternoon even a dump like Rockwood wasn't so bad. The weeds sprouting from the cracked concrete were still young enough to have a freshness around them. The graffiti on the underpass had a splurge of new colour. The litter swirled with a jaunty air.

The East End borough of Hallam had a rough reputation for several reasons, and Rockwood Estate was the main one. The place was a maze of interconnecting walkways and ramps lined with dilapidated terraces and maisonettes, with one tower block in the centre. It was all too easy to be lead astray into a fistful of dead ends and dark corners if you didn't keep your wits about you. For Glory, its rat-runs were as familiar as the lines on the palm of her hand. As she sauntered into the forecourt, with its shabby huddle of shops and boarded-up community centre, the boys loitering outside the bookies wolf-whistled.

Glory gave them a flash of smile. Auntie Angel might lament how the neighbourhood had changed (waves of immigrants who didn't know or care about the Old Days and Old Ways of doing things; feral kids running riot) but the Cooper Street Coven had good working relations with the gangs on the estate. Besides, even though its muscle wasn't what it was, Cooper Street's connection to the Morgan family ensured respect. Nobody messed with the Morgans. Their Wednesday Coven was the biggest under-world outfit in London, and it looked after its own.

Nobody messed with Glory's great-aunt Angeline either. Once, when Glory was six and playing in the street, two older boys with bony heads and scabbed knuckles came and snatched her dollies for a kick-about. Glory's wails brought Auntie Angel storming from the house. She clipped the boys round the ear.

'Hexing old hag,' the older one spat.

'Damn right I am. And I've got fae enough to melt the flesh from your bones.' Auntie Angel's pointed creased face and snapping eyes belonged to a witch in a fae-tale. She gave a throaty hiss. 'You try any more of your tricks on me and mine, and I'll rot your crotch with green maggots.'

The younger boy, who must have been about eight, started snivelling. The other one tried to stare her out, but in the end his nerve broke and they both slunk off down the road.

Later that evening, the older kid returned with his mum. Her face was as flinty as her son's, but she was bearing a carton of cigarettes and a tin of shortbread. An offering.

'Heard this little bastard's been giving you grief,' she

said, pinching the boy's arm. 'Don't take no mind of him. Here's something to make it up to you anyways.' Then she straightened her scrawny shoulders, and looked Auntie Angel in the eye. 'Me dad still talks about the days when them sisters of yours called the shots. They got things done proper, he says. Times was better then.'

Her words gave the six-year-old Glory a tingly feeling inside. She knew that once upon a time Auntie Angel had been the big sister of the famous Starling Twins, and that was one of the things that made her special. Because Lily and Cora Starling didn't just look as alike as two peas; they were identically powerful witches too, and their coven had as good as run the East End during the 1960s and 1970s. Glory had heard the stories of how they went to parties with film stars and had their pictures in the papers, and only did witchcrimes that helped people. But the Inquisition got Granny Cora in the end, and Great Aunt Lily died of a broken heart, and Glory's mum Edie went and vanished three Christmases ago. Being a Starling girl was a dangerous business.

Auntie Angel patted Glory's hair. 'Maybe those days will come again. Fae runs thicker than blood, quicker'n water . . .'

. . . *and wild as wind.*

That was the final part of the proverb, but Auntie Angel had left it out. People generally did. *Fae runs wild as wind.* It was the most troublesome aspect of witchwork, not being a hundred per cent certain of which way the fae would blow. Where it would go, and to whom.

*   *   *

Thinking of this, Glory – fifteen now, and tough enough to take on any number of scabby skinhead boys – felt a chill creep into her day. She still dreamed of the white-tiled Burning Court, of the witch on the pyre with the locked mouth and the frozen scream. And she still said the same prayer, night after night. To God, just in case there was one, and also to Mab and Hecate, witchkind's guardian spirits. So far none of them seemed to be listening.

Granny Cora and Great-Aunt Lily had turned witch-kind at the age of thirteen. Her mum Edie had been the same. Was her time running out?

She shook her head impatiently, sending the gold hoops dancing. Candice Morgan, Lily Starling's twenty-three-year-old granddaughter, had only got the fae last year. Auntie Angel's arrived when she was nineteen. Most witches, she knew, had to wait until well into their twenties. She had plenty of time . . . The problem was, the younger you were when the fae developed, the stronger it tended to be.

For Glory wasn't planning on being just *any* witch. Her fae would be her fortune, and her coven's too.

Cooper Street, like the coven which took its name, had seen better days. A run-down Victorian terrace, it was one of the few survivors of a Blitz bombing raid that had flattened most of its neighbours. The houses behind it were modern boxes of cheap brick; in front was the murky sprawl of the Rockwood Estate. Other nineteenth-century leftovers had been snapped up by city workers on the hunt for period charm and the edgy cool of an East End postcode. Cooper Street, however, had resisted the trend towards gentrification. Peeling paintwork and grimy windows were the order of the day. Only one house, Number Six, boasted a smartly-painted door over a well-scrubbed front step – Auntie Angel's step.

The coven owned Numbers Seven and Eight too. Doors knocked through walls and an eccentric arrangement of stairs and hatches had made the three separate, small houses into a rambling warren of one. That wasn't to say there weren't territorial divisions, though. The ground floor of Number Six was Auntie Angel's lair, with Glory and her dad, Patrick, living in the top of the house. Number Eight was home to Joe Junior, the coven boss (his late father, Joe Braddock, had married Auntie Angel after his wife, Mary, died) and his son, Nate. The middle house, Number Seven, was the coven's official HQ. The upper floors were used for storage or else as dormitories for passing cronies and contacts, while business took place in the basement. The lounge functioned as a general common room.

This was where Glory was headed. She planned on spending the rest of the afternoon doing her nails in front of the telly. However, as soon as she let herself in she knew there was no hope of having the place to herself. The hallway was blocked by a stack of microwaves, still wrapped in poly-thene, and a spill of shiny white trainers. Hip hop pounded through the walls.

She found Nate and two of his sidekicks, Chunk and Jacko, sprawled on the battered leather sofas around the TV. On screen, a group of semi-naked girls were writhing against the rapper in their midst. He was making gun signs with his hands, spitting out a monologue about blood and bullets, pimps and hos, as the spectators in the lounge nodded along appreciatively. Glory thought this pretty funny. The younger coven crew liked to play at being proper villains, but it was all front, as fake as the bumping and grinding of the girls in the music video.

Nate greeted Glory's arrival with a belch. He was only a couple of years older than her and they'd grown up together, but there wasn't much love lost between them. Nate liked to throw his weight around as the boss's son, and resented Glory's rival position as Auntie Angel's pet.

'You seen the gear we got?' Jacko asked.

'Could hardly miss it. Nearly broke my ankle clambering past.'

'Nice little job, that,' said Chunk complacently.

The way he and Jacko told it, their staged break-in at the depot (whose security guard was in coven pay) might as well have been a gold-bullion bank heist, Hollywood-style. Glory had been hearing such stories her whole life.

There'd been a time too when she would have lapped it all up, wide-eyed. But she had known for a long while that Cooper Street's criminal activities didn't involve much skill or daring, and hardly any witchwork. In spite of Auntie Angel's local reputation, her fae had always been small-scale, good for scrying and elusions and minor banes, but not much else, and her involvement in coven business was in decline. She was seventy-eight, after all. And a coven's reputation rested on its head-witch.

Thinking of this, Glory's mood sank another notch. It sank further when she went to get a Coke from the fridge, only to find a partially-eaten kebab crusted to the top shelf, and chow-mein noodles splattered down the sides. The surrounding floor was littered with cigarette butts. Glory knew that if she didn't clean it up, nobody else would. She slammed the fridge shut.

'This *place*. It's a pit,' she said. 'It stinks.'

'Then go somewhere else, girlie,' Nate advised, scratching under his T-shirt to reveal a slab of toned stomach. He worked out obsessively – the basement of Number Eight bristled with gym equipment – and was capable of a slouching, sulky sort of charm. This wasn't something he bothered using on Glory.

Glory gave him the finger. She decided to stay for a bit, even if it was only to piss off Nate. But she couldn't relax. Her senses were oddly heightened, too strong to be comfortable. The air was thick with beery male breath and the warm, green-brown pungency of hash. Fleetingly, she seemed to taste the pulses of music – metallic; like blades, like blood – and hear the flavour of Coke zing through her mouth. But she shook her head, and the muddle cleared.

Thuds and curses from the hall announced the arrival of Patch and Earl, two older coven members who, from the sounds of it, had come to grief among the microwaves. Patch came through the door rubbing his shin.

'Now then,' he said, his pock-marked face splitting into a grin, 'you lot heard about the Wednesday's latest? Charlie Morgan's only been and met the PM's missus!'

Charlie Morgan was boss of the Wednesday Coven. His brothers Frank and Vince were the financier and enforcer respectively, and his wife Kezia was head-witch. Their coven wasn't just big and brutal, it owned legitimate businesses too, including a fashionable restaurant and several nightclubs. And now, apparently, they'd moved into the arts – the tabloid paper Patch was holding up showed Charlie's tough, fleshy face staring out beside the Prime Minister's wife. The setting was a VIP-studded gala for the Royal Opera House. Charlie was name-checked as an 'entrepreneur and investor'.

Shouts of laughter followed the paper around the room. When it was passed to Glory, her arm got jogged so that she slopped her drink down her top. 'Hexing hell! Can't you slobs watch what you're doing?'

'That PMT's getting the better of you again,' Nate drawled.

It wasn't, but the mood-swings felt like a more extreme version. All this week, Glory was either flying high or soaked through with gloom. Like today – irrepressibly cheerful at the sight of weeds blowing in the breeze, and now black as thunder because of a stupid splash of Coke. It was about time she got a grip.

'Post Moron Tension sounds about right,' she said to Nate, chucking her empty can in his direction. 'I'm outta here.'

Glory's quickest route home was through a sliding door on the first floor landing of Number Seven. It led to a make-shift kitchen containing a microwave, hotplate and mini-fridge. Her dad was there, heating a mug of soup. He looked startled to see her.

'No, er, school this afternoon?'

'Teacher Training.'

'Ah . . . again?'

'Yeah.'

'Hmm.'

Her father rubbed his thinning brown hair in an anxious sort of way. He knew as well as Glory did that nobody could make her go to school if she didn't feel like it. Sharp as a knife, that one, Auntie Angel said. She don't need any certification to prove it.

As a matter of fact, Glory was bunking off less than she used to. Her second cousins, Candice and Skye Morgan, liked to put on airs about their fancy schooling and educated ways, and though lessons might bore her stiff, she didn't plan on being lumped together with the bimbo dropouts who hung around making eyes at Nate and Jacko and the rest.

Either way, her dad was in no position to lecture. He kept out of coven business, except for doing the accounts, and spent most of his time in his room, playing computer games in which kick-boxing inquisitors armed with fabulous gadgets had to thwart an array of witch-criminals and their evil schemes. He collected the illegal, black-market versions too, in which the witches were the good guys, but the quality of the graphics and game-play was always poor.

'How's it going with *Deathstar Enigma*?' Glory asked. 'Cracked level five yet?'

Patrick's hands cradled the mug, thin wrists poking out of his fraying jumper. He smiled his vague, sweet smile. 'Not yet. Tricky. But onwards and upwards, y'know.'

'A shadow of his former self,' that's what people said about her dad. Never been the same since his wife walked out one Sunday morning twelve years ago. It had been a long time since Glory had thought of him as her protector, the night-time comforter who, in the end, hadn't been able to keep the bad dreams away.

She ran a dishcloth round the soup-speckled microwave. *Nobody* in this place cleaned up after themselves. 'Speaking of moving up in the world . . . You hear about Uncle Charlie?'

'He's not your uncle.'

'OK, cousin.'

'First cousin once removed.'

'Whatever.' Glory was not interested in the finer points of genealogy. 'Well, he's only in the paper schmoozing the PM's wife. One of these days he'll be taking over Downing Street himself, I shouldn't wonder.'

Patrick's brow creased doubtfully. 'I hope I'm not around to see it.'

'C'mon, Dad. I'm no fan of the Morgans' methods – you know that. But it's still *funny*, right? A coven boss hobnobbing with heads of state! Proves how far the likes of us can go, if we put our minds to it.'

'"The likes of us" . . . and what does that mean? Mm?' Her dad shuffled slowly away towards his room. 'Careful what you wish for, Glory.'

CHAPTER 5

Lucas slept badly that night. Twisting around in a knot of sheets, he was oppressed by a sense of foreboding, of something he hadn't prepared for or had left undone. Eventually, he drifted off, only to start awake a few hours later. His head was bubbling with heat, swamped on all sides by a darkness that seemed full of strange flittings and whispering. And although he should have been afraid – he had a fever, he was ill, he was hallucinating – Lucas was instead filled with a strange exhilaration. In a waking dream, he rose from the bed and reached into the vast seething dark with his arms outstretched. Whatever he was waiting for, let it come. Let it consume him –

But the next thing he knew, there was sunshine on his pillow, and music on the radio. In the light of an ordinary Saturday morning, the night's strangeness soon seeped away.

His stepsister, Philomena, and her mother were having breakfast in the kitchen, their every mouthful droolingly scrutinised by the family Labrador, Kip. In the four years since Marisa had married his father, Lucas had never seen her appear without perfectly positioned hair and a perfectly polished face, even while in her dressing gown. Philly, meanwhile, was in her jogging kit, and picking moodily at a rice cake. 'You look r-o-u-g-h,' she informed him.

'And good morning to you too.'

'Dear me, Lucas – you *are* looking rather peaky. Are you feeling all right?'

'Fine, thanks.' He shook his head to clear the faint buzzing in his ears, and went to pat Kip. The dog bared his teeth and backed away, and Lucas looked at him in surprise. 'Er . . . I just didn't sleep that well.'

'Well, make sure you don't overdo it at this party at the Charltons' tonight.' Marisa took a delicate sip of green tea. 'Though I suppose Philly can keep an eye on you.'

Both Lucas and Philomena stiffened. 'God, Mummy. I'm not a babysitter. It's bad enough that Sophie's parents are forcing her to let Nick's little friends tag along.'

'Oh, but, darling, I think holding a joint birthday party is a lovely idea. So inclusive. We should think about it for when you and Luc—'

'Is Dad around?' Lucas interjected hastily.

'He got called into the office half an hour ago. Another crisis with the Goodwin trial, I imagine.'

Ashton was prosecuting the case of Bradley Goodwin, a witch accused of freelancing for the Wednesday Coven. The Inquisition was pressing for the death penalty on the grounds that one of his banes had resulted in a police officer's death. They hoped to use the threat of balefire to frighten Goodwin into cutting a deal. If he could be persuaded to inform on his former associates, the coven would be badly hit.

So far, however, the trial had been beset by problems. Evidence had been tampered with, one of the witnesses had disappeared, and another had retracted their statement. Witch trials didn't use ordinary juries, but a tribunal of judges drawn from a pool of retired inquisitors and serving military officers, civil servants and magistrates. All of the tribunal members were under inquisitorial guard.

Marisa sighed. 'Why these emergencies always seem to happen on the weekends, I really don't know . . . Anyway, I suppose it's time I got dressed.'

As soon as her mother was gone, Philomena looked at Lucas through narrowed eyes. 'Seriously, you'd better not tag after me tonight. Gid will probably be there, and the last thing he'll want is to be cornered by some fanboy banging on about the bloody Inquisition.'

Lucas stretched and yawned. 'Don't you think I'll have better things to do than spend my time cramping your style?'

'It hasn't stopped you before.'

Philomena shared her mother's expertly applied hair colour and expensive tastes, but her sturdy frame and heavy features were her father's, the banker Rupert Carrington. She was well-groomed and fashionable enough to pass for attractive, well-connected and intimidating enough to pass for popular, but neither came naturally. It was different for Lucas. The fact that he was younger, and a boy, and therefore shouldn't be any kind of threat, was a thorn in her side she refused to acknowledge.

At some level, Lucas was aware of this. It made him

slightly more tolerant of Philomena than he would otherwise have been.

However, his tolerance had its limits.

Eyeing Philomena's rice cake, Lucas moved towards the fridge. 'Now, what I *really* fancy,' he said gloatingly, 'is a nice, fat, juicy bacon sandwich. Mmm . . .'

The real cause of Ashton Stearne's summons to work became apparent quarter of an hour later, when Marisa called out to Philomena and Lucas to turn on the news. A witchworked storm (or 'whistle-wind') had been raised in the office of Helena Howell, MP – smashing windows, toppling furniture, scattering documents. Although the building should have been empty in the early hours of Saturday morning, a cleaner coming off the night shift had been struck on the head by a light fitting and killed. The motive for the attack was clear enough: Howell was introducing a controversial Private Member's bill to limit the state benefits available to witchkind.

The three of them watched the latest report on the television in the drawing-room.

Jack Rawdon, director of WICA, was being interviewed in the studio. Would his agents be assisting the Inquisition in bringing the perpetrator to justice? the journalist asked. Rawdon's face was solemn as he addressed the camera.

'Crime is crime, whoever commits it. And justice is justice, whoever deals it – whether that's a witch or an inquisitor. Both WICA and the Inquisition bring unique skills to the fight against witchcrime. The Inquisition's commitment and expertise are justly celebrated. It is my hope that WICA's contribution will also come to be recognised. The more work we're enabled to do, the safer our country will be.'

Opportunistic git, thought Lucas. He didn't even answer the question.

The interview was followed with a recap of the story so far, and reaction from the father-in-law of the dead cleaner, who left behind two small children. 'That poor family . . .' Marisa murmured, pressing her hand to her heart. With her other hand, she reached for Lucas's.

Philomena's eyes darted to the pen and ink portrait of Camilla Stearne above the mantelpiece. It had been done the year before Lucas's mother was killed by the witch-terrorist group Endor.

As soon as he could, Lucas politely extricated his hand from Marisa's. He was careful not to look towards the mantelpiece either. Lucas had never especially liked the drawing; he knew his mother had been a pretty woman, but the artist had given her a dreamy wistfulness that was at odds with other accounts of someone both lively and determined. Though Lucas had only been a baby when Camilla died, he resented the portrait's power to create a memory that was pure romance, and fateful melancholy. It was something he tried to resist, following his father's example.

By the time Lucas arrived at the party, celebrations were well under way. He had always liked the Charltons – a loud, jolly gang – and he liked their house too. Large and rambling, the grandeur of its scale was mostly obscured by a tide of family clutter. All of the ground floor rooms were already spilling over with guests and music from competing sound systems.

He found the noise level hard to take. As the day wore on, the tension in his head had returned; a hot, heavy pulse in his skull. Though it didn't hurt, exactly, he struggled to exchange the usual banter with his usual crowd. He wondered if Bea was here yet and how long it would take to find her in the crush. Tom was trying to tell him something, but the thrumming in his head meant he missed most of it. '– downstairs in the den,' Tom repeated, beckoning. 'Come and see.'

It was much quieter in the basement. Fairy lights twinkled cosily around the room, illuminating a sagging sofa and widescreen TV, and the layer of film posters and concert flyers that obscured the walls. Gideon was there, holding court in the centre of a group of five or six people. They were admiring something he had on display. A helmet or muzzle of some kind. It was a witch's bridle.

As Lucas drew closer, Gideon looked up and met his eye. He smiled. 'Come and have a look at this, Stearne. You'll find it quite an education.'

And Lucas knew that Gideon had not forgotten the incident with the balefire film any more than he had.

As a matter of fact, Lucas had seen such contraptions before. The bridle was a kind of iron cage for the head, with a metal curb fitted to project into the mouth and hold down the tongue. On this example the curb was plain and flat, but some came studded with spikes, so as to draw blood if the wearer attempted to speak. For many years, people thought witchwork was primarily accomplished through the spelling out of words. They knew better now, but the real point of the bridle was its material. Iron constrained fae. Nowadays, iron cuffs were worn by witches who chose to renounce their fae and live ordinary lives. But in times past, the bridles were used as ready-to-wear, portable prisons.

'This one's an early nineteenth-century model,' Gideon was saying, 'and what's unusual is the way wrist restraints have been incorporated into the design.' He held up a chain attached to the back, which ended in a pair of handcuffs. Although the bridle was opened and shut by a simple clasp, the imprisoned witch would not be able to reach up to use it. 'It would have been state of the art in its day. And just look at the decorative work.' He gestured to the iron bands, which bore a patterning of birds and flowers. 'Must've been made by a true craftsman.'

'A higher class of torturer,' Lucas agreed.

Gideon's pale eyes were almost colourless in the dim light. 'People did what they had to do. It was a harsher world back then.'

'And not much has changed since,' said one of the girls, to murmurs of agreement. 'Look what happened today with that MP's office.'

'We might face the same threat,' Lucas replied, 'but at least we've got better tools.'

'"*We've* got better tools?"' Gideon drawled. 'Funny – I didn't know you were already an inquisitor, Stearne. Unless there's an alternative fast-track scheme I don't know about. Something Daddy's running, perhaps.'

Lucas could tell from the ripples of amusement that

this was one occasion when he didn't have the room on his side. Even Tom kept quiet.

'Now,' Gideon continued, briskly marking the end of the exchange, 'who'd like a go in the bridle? Any budding witches want to be my victim?'

People looked round at each other, a little uncertainly. Several girls giggled.

'I'll try it,' Nell Dawson announced. She was normally a rather quiet person, but she had just downed a glass of wine, and was tossing her hair about in what was no doubt intended to be a reckless manner. When Gideon looked her way, she blushed violently.

'Good girl.' He touched her cheek, and Nell blushed again. Slowly, she lowered her head in submission.

The room was very still as Gideon put the bridle on.

'Open wide,' he said.

Nell opened her mouth and Gideon slid the metal curb on to her tongue. Then, less gently, he pulled her arms behind her back, clamping her wrists into the manacles. She made a small muffled sound.

'How's it feel, Nell?' various people asked, and she managed a lopsided shrug.

'Haunted, I expect,' Gideon remarked. 'Think of all the witches it's silenced.'

'Careful, Nell,' said someone. 'You wouldn't want to catch anything nasty.'

'Yeah,' said someone else. 'Maybe she'll come down with the fae.'

'Oooh – any harpies in the Dawson bloodline we should know about?'

46

'Is that a freckle on her arm, or the Devil's Kiss?'

'I always *thought* Nell had something spooky about her . . .'

"Ware the witch!'

Laughing, they began to pelt her with screwed-up napkins and beer bottle tops.

Lucas watched and waited. Anger had intensified the hot throb in his head.

Perhaps Gideon had been right to challenge his remark about torturers. It wasn't always fair to judge the past according to modern sensibilities. The witch's bridle was a defensive weapon as well as an instrument of oppression; a relic of a war that hadn't yet been won. But the Inquisition had worked hard to become an institution that could be respected and trusted as well as feared. And for all the care of its construction, the bridle was a crude, ugly thing, which belonged to more primitive times. To make such an artefact part of a drunken party game . . . It was like ogling a pirated balefire film. It was like those men sipping gin and tonic as Bernard Tynan burned.

Meanwhile, Nell sat alone on the sofa, as the merriment and missiles rained down. Her head was bowed awkwardly under the weight of iron. Lucas saw her eyes darting about inside. She made another muffled sound, and her shoulders twitched.

'I think she wants to get it off,' he said, abruptly cutting into the fun.

'I'm sure she does. But that's not the way it works, I'm afraid,' Gideon replied. Taking hold of the chain behind Nell's back, he pulled her off the sofa. Caught off balance, she fell on to her knees. Gideon pushed a hank of fair hair off his forehead and moistened his lips, staring down at the muzzled girl. He gave the chain another tug. 'First she has to learn her lesson.'

He's *turned on*, thought Lucas, with a shock of disgust. 'And what lesson is that?'

Gideon smiled blandly. 'That witchcrime doesn't pay.'

Lucas hardened his face. He walked swiftly over to Nell and felt for the catch at the back of the bridle, releasing the cage. After a bit of fiddling, he managed to open the manacles too. Nell gulped and coughed, moisture filming her eyes.

'Are you all right?' he asked.

The next cough was more like a retch. Nell's hands fluttered to her throat. There were red marks around her wrists. Then, 'Sure,' she said, over-brightly. Her voice was hoarse. 'I'm fine.'

Nobody even looked at her. They were all watching Gideon watch Lucas.

Lucas found the bridle heavier than he'd expected. It felt colder than metal should, the iron bands biting icily into his skin. The heat in his skull flickered and faltered. He felt extraordinarily tired.

'You look a little green, Stearne,' Gideon observed. 'Maybe it's time to lighten up, hmm? Life shouldn't be all work, no play.'

Lucas put the bridle into the other boy's hands. 'Trouble is, I don't much like your games.'

It was only then he realised that Bea was there. She

must have come down the stairs behind him. He wondered how much she had seen and what she had thought, but went past her regardless. He needed some air.

Lucas was immediately regretting his intervention. He'd come across as a pompous, humourless bore. And Nell was a silly little bimbo anyway, trying to suck up to Gideon like that. She didn't need rescuing. *What's* wrong *with me?* he thought, as he sloped moodily through the conservatory and into the garden beyond. But the question was unsettling. Of course there's nothing wrong, he told himself quickly. It's just one of those days. I'm getting ill and it's making me cranky. God – if only my head would just *keep quiet*...

Several people, mostly Sophie's friends, were smoking on the patio among a scattering of tea-lights. One of the boys was tunelessly strumming a guitar. Even so, the night air and relative peacefulness were a relief. The garden's growth was luxuriant, blurry with spring. Lucas walked across the lawn to the pond and frowned down at his reflection.

Someone said his name. 'Hello,' Bea said, a little breathlessly.

'Hello.'

'I liked what you did back there,' she told him. 'You were right to intervene; it was getting out of hand. Though Nell should have known better. She's got this ridiculous crush on Gideon, you see.'

'Doesn't everyone?'

'Oh-ho – that sounded a touch bitter.'

Bea's smile had a mischievous slant. He liked that. Lucas approved of girls who were confident without being too assertive about it. He also liked her thin gold top, and the way the droplets of her earrings had got tangled in her hair.

He tousled up his own hair and grinned back. They sat down together on the raised stone rim of the pond.

'I think people are generally on edge today,' Bea remarked. 'About witchwork, I mean. It's because of the attack. Dad was saying that coven witches keep clear of capital offences, and so only fanatics like Endor could be responsible. He said normal witch-criminals wouldn't risk the Burning Court. Is that right?'

'Well, it's true that covens keep their witches behind the scenes. They tend to do the groundwork rather than committing the actual crimes. But the . . .' Lucas paused. Though his reflection looked as pale as ever, waves of heat had begun throbbing through his body. The sensation wasn't entirely unpleasant but he plunged a hand into the water, hoping the coolness would steady him.

'Yes?' Bea prompted.

'Uh . . . the death of that cleaner was clearly a mistake. Creating a whistle-wind is one thing, controlling it quite another. That storm was meant to scare people, not kill them. That's not Endor's style. And Endor hasn't been active in the UK for over twelve years.'

'Do you ever wonder . . .' She hesitated. 'I know about the Oath of Service, and how inquisitors are legally bound to respect witchkind rights. But do you ever wonder how you could . . . what you would do . . . if some atrocity happened, and you found yourself face to face with the witch responsible?'

'Like the one who killed my mother, for instance?'

Her cheeks went pink. 'Sorry. I didn't mean to be insensitive.'

'It's OK. It's something I've thought about. I'm sure Dad has too. I hope I'd do the right thing. One has to bear in mind that witches . . . well, they're subject to impulses that normal people can't understand. There's something primitive – unnatural – inside them.'

'You're saying we should make allowances?'

'No. I'm saying we have to remember they're not like the rest of us. If I found the witch who killed my mother, I'd want to do the right thing because it would prove I was better than him or her. Better than *them*.'

'More humane?'

'Or more human . . .'

A motorbike revved noisily in the road. In the glinting wrinkles of the pond, the imagined scene of his mother's murder swam up at him. The swerve, the jump, the downwards fall – the crumpling of metal and crushing of glass. The sheet of flame.

It might have been written off as just another road accident, if it wasn't for a witness who had seen his mother struggling at the wheel, her face frozen with horror and her movements stiff and jerky, as if not her own. Since a witch had to be in view of his or her target to hex a bane, a second onlooker would also have been present on that bend. There they would have watched and waited for the car, holding a poppet of Camilla Stearne in their hands. Somewhere in the background, this witch would have wound the shadow-strands of fae through the manikin and into its human counterpart; spooling their darkness through his mother's blood and brain, binding her limbs to their will.

The car crash had come at the height of Endor's campaign, after the Southampton bombings and the assassination of the Home Secretary, before the sabotage of HMS Thrace. The authorities said that the murder was intended as a warning for Ashton Stearne. But Camilla came from an old inquisitorial family as well. For Endor fanatics, that would be justification enough.

Lucas looked at Bea's hand, resting on the stone beside his. However close they became, they would always be two different bodies, two separate souls. So how must it feel to invade another person's consciousness, like some witches did? To tether another soul to yours and move their body to your command? *Maybe that's why Gideon's so enthralled by the bridle*, Lucas thought. He doesn't just fear the power that witchkind has. He envies it.

The motorcycle revved again, matching the buzzing in his ears. Although he remembered little of last night, he dimly recognised the surge of feverish disorientation. Waves of pins and needles had begun prickling through his skin.

'Lucas, are you OK?' Bea was frowning in concern.

'I'm fine – I –'

I'm going mad.

But no, no, he wasn't. Bea could see that. Bea would make sure he was all right. Her soft touch would soothe the itch in his blood; her rosebud mouth would hush the rising din. All he needed to do was keep his focus. He smiled, and leaned towards her.

'Lucas!'

Philly was marching across the lawn. Her make-up was smeared and her hair dishevelled, and she was clutching a bottle in one hand. 'What's this,' she said belligerently, 'what's this I hear about you causing a scene with Gid?'

Lucas and Bea drew apart. 'It's got nothing to do with you,' said Lucas curtly, over the drumming in his ears.

'Yes, it bloody well does if you keep making an idiot of yourself in front of my friends. Gid—'

'Gideon's never going to look twice at you whether I'm around or not.'

There was a nasty pause.

Then, 'You pompous *arse*,' Philly exploded. 'You know what your problem is? You're so damn pleased with yourself the whole hexing time. You –'

Her voice joined the buzzing in his skull, the hissings in the shadows. Both increased to a new intensity.

'Be quiet,' he said, keeping his voice low, so as not to add to the uproar all around. For some reason, one of Philomena's hairgrips was in his jacket pocket, and he grasped it savagely. He couldn't hear himself think.

Philomena ignored him. She ignored the whispers and nudges of the group outside the conservatory. She ignored Bea's hostile stare. Philomena's evening had not been a success, and its assorted frustrations had now come to a head.

'I'm warning you, if you carry on acting so superior –'

On and on. Lucas closed his eyes, trying to concentrate on the dewy balm of the night garden. He envisaged scooping up its peace and pressing it against Philomena's jabbering mouth. Tightening his grip around the hairgrip, he bent back its thin metal as he begged for silence. A curb of iron, a cloud of numbness. Be quiet, be quiet, he mouthed, like a prayer. *Quiet . . .*

'The thing is, Lucas, what you fail to appre—' Philomena coughed. 'You fail –' She made a retching sound, like Nell after the bridle. 'You –' Her voice died to a rasp, then a whisper. Then, nothing. She blinked woozily.

One of her friends, who had been hovering near by, came and put her arm around her. 'Come on, Phil,' she coaxed. 'Let's go inside. We'll get you some water and you'll be absolutely fine.'

They set off towards the house, Philomena croaking in faint protest, her hand around her throat.

'H*ex*,' Lucas swore.

'She's off her face,' Bea told him. 'Don't worry about it.'

Lucas was, in fact, feeling better. The pressure had lifted and heat retreated. 'All the same, I'd better check she's OK.' He got up, slightly unsteadily.

'That's funny,' said Bea, and pointed. 'Look at the bells.'

The conservatory door, like all entrances to the house, had a row of boxed iron bells over the threshold, ready to sound the alarm if a witch hexing a bane approached. All three had begun to quiver.

Bea was more intrigued than worried. 'Weird. I wonder what's set them off? Still, it's not as if they're actually ringing.'

All the same, the threat of their chime was near, as close as an echo. Lucas seemed to feel the metal reverberate in time to the tingling in his head. Whatever happened, and for whatever reason, he knew he must not take a step closer to the bells. He must not pass under that threshold.

Meanwhile, the crowd on the patio continued laughing and smoking and drinking. The tea-lights flickered in the breeze. Yet the night had lost its peace, just as Philomena had lost her –

Her voice. Philomena's lost voice.

How strange and abrupt, the way the noise had been choked out of her. It was almost as if she . . . as if he . . .

My God, Lucas thought wildly, *we've been bewitched*. He stared round at the rustling depths of the garden. Who knew what could be lurking here? With the fear, the throbbing heat returned, with a force that made him gasp. Bea looked at him curiously.

'I'm s-sorry,' he stammered. 'I'm feeling really – uh – ill. I have to go. Sorry.'

'Wait,' she called, but he was already stumbling away from her, towards the door in the wall at the bottom of the garden.

He had to get away.

The taxi driver eyed him suspiciously but Lucas told himself that it was perfectly natural; as far as this man was concerned, he was just another binge-drinking kid who might be sick in his cab. And Lucas really did feel sick now. Sick with shame. Leaving Bea, leaving Philly and the rest like that – what if there was indeed some evil-doer on the prowl? He'd fled, abandoned them. Abandoned everything . . . Deep down, however, he knew his fearfulness for the others was misplaced. It wasn't even true. It had been fabricated to distract him from the other, unacknowledged dread. Because instinct told him that whatever threat had whispered in the breeze, and set the bells quivering, had already left the house.

The taxi pulled up almost before he knew it. Lucas thrust a twenty-pound note in the driver's hands and stumbled out without waiting for change. The night-time guard, Andy, was on duty at the gate, and it took all of Lucas's strength to look into the CCTV camera with his customary smile as he typed in the code for the main entrance. He approached the front door with a dry mouth and clammy hands, and when he passed through without alarm, was only partly reassured. Bells didn't warn of all witches, only of those hexing banes.

The house was empty. Philomena was still at the party, Ashton and Marisa were out too. The silence was only broken by the throaty tick of the grandfather clock in the hall. Yet the familiarity of home did not welcome him. Like an intruder, he avoided the portraits' eyes.

Something dark moved in a corner. He paused, uncertain, and heard a long, low growl. 'Kip? It's all right, boy, it's me.' The growl intensified. But the next moment, there was a scrabble of paws on polished wood, and the dog had gone.

Lucas squared his shoulders. Then he went up to his bedroom and started pulling things out of the cupboard he used to store old books and files. He forced himself to make his haste orderly: there must be no panic here. He pulled out an essay from last term, Identifying Witchkind and Witchwork, and stared at his own writing, how the brisk black ink flowed confidently across the page.

It is estimated, the opening paragraph announced, *that approximately one in a thousand people become witchkind.*

Less than 0.1% of the British population. Lucas already knew that, of course. He already knew all the information he was searching for. He just needed to see it committed to paper, by his own hand.

> *Of these, female witches outnumber male ones by about three to one. The Seventh Sense ('fae') is usually developed between the ages of twenty and thirty . . .*

So statistically speaking, his personal odds were much greater than a thousand to one. His mind raced to do the calculation.

> *. . . although in exceptional cases, it can emerge earlier, in the teens or sometimes even in childhood.*

Exactly how exceptional, though? At this point, Lucas would have welcomed some proper data. Lists, charts and graphs, like those scattered through the research papers in his father's study. But never mind, because

> *The fae nearly always runs in families.*

Nearly always. Nearly, nearly, nearly.
But not one hundred per cent.
Not infallibly, continuously and for ever.
Lucas gritted his teeth and turned the page.

The emergence of the Seventh Sense affects people differ-
ently. Symptoms can include ringing in the ears,
synaesthesia (sensory cross-over), night-time hallucina-
tions and a burning or itching sensation. These discomforts
are only relieved by a witch's first act of witchwork.

'No,' said Lucas aloud, though his voice shook. Enough. His blood had cooled, and the echo in his head had gone, but he had not committed witchwork. For God's sake! Philomena had simply had too much to drink and choked on her own indignation. It was a coincidence, that's all. It had to be.

Meanwhile, his own words marched relentlessly on.

A witch uses his or her Seventh Sense by channelling
mental powers (similar to telepathy, mind control,
psychokinesis and precognition) through or into people,
animals and objects. The practice of fae also draws on
normal physical faculties, such as sight, touch and
sound.

Hard as he tried to block them, the memories came thick and fast, in a kaleidoscope patterning of sight, touch, sound. The image he'd created in his head of black silence, muffled against Philomena's mouth. The clenching of his hand around her hairgrip. Those whispered pleas for quiet. The shiver of bells.

For the first time, he remembered waking in the night, and the strange sense of exaltation he'd felt as he opened his arms to the darkness. Exaltation, and . . . power.

But there remained one final test. One last hope.

. . . The so-called 'Devil's Kiss' is the physical mark of the fae, borne by all witches, that waxes and wanes according to the witchwork done . . .

Lucas carefully put the essay away (*Really excellent work!* his teacher had scrawled on the covering page). Then he went down to the utility room and found the housekeeper's sewing kit. Methodically, he searched for the longest, thickest needle he could find. Calmly, he went back upstairs and into his bathroom. Slowly, deliberately, he began to undress.

Lucas stood and regarded his naked self in the mirror. His appearance rarely troubled him but tonight it felt as if he was scrutinising his body for the first time. He started with his hands, making a precise examination of each crease and fold of flesh. He knew what he was searching for. A new and unexplained mark, bigger than a freckle or mole, but not by much. Something like a bloom or bruise under the skin.

Yet the longer he looked without finding anything, the more frightened he became. Hope was unbearable. He grew obsessive, then frantic. He began pinching and twisting lumps of flesh, raking the stretched skin with his nails.

Then –

Could it –?

There.

A small unfamiliar blot under his left shoulder blade. It was purplish-black, dark as sin. Lucas touched it and felt a soft throb bloom in his head, like an echo.

Where the Devil had kissed, people said, the body died. The mark of the fae was numb. A person could put the tip of a hot poker against it and the bearer wouldn't flinch. The witch-prickers of the Inquisition, however, used needles.

Blindly seizing his needle, Lucas stabbed it into the blot. The metal pierced the skin and slid through to the bone of his shoulder blade. There was no blood, no twinge. No trace of hurt. Nothing. He carried on viciously thrusting with the needle: arms, neck, chest, until he was blood-speckled and whimpering. He flung the needle away.

Lucas crouched naked on the floor as the tears burned from his eyes and blurred the bloody flecks on his skin. He barely noticed them. For how long he stayed there, rocking back and forth, he didn't know. Crisp black letters marched through the blankness in his head.

My name is Lucas John Augustine Stearne. I am fifteen years old. My father is a twelfth-generation inquisitor. My mother is dead.

I am Lucas Stearne.
I am fifteen years old.

I am Lucas.
I am a witch.

CHAPTER 6

Glory was often exasperated by her dad but after their last encounter she just felt depressed. She had a sudden urge to celebrate Friday night, to join a crowd and go dancing. In the end, she made peace with Nate and gatecrashed a club night he'd scammed tickets for.

The doorman was a mate of Earl's, so getting in wasn't a problem. But it wasn't Glory's kind of place: an overpriced basement dive full of scruffy hipsters and the kind of public school type who likes to slum it in style. Nate had got their tickets from one of the latter – a trust-fund brat who wanted to play gangsters, and was dumb enough to think that Nate was the real deal.

It was a strange night. Glory felt tearful and panicky, yet laughed the loudest and talked the most. Her senses tingled all over, black flecks and bright sparks dancing before her eyes. She got home just before dawn and didn't get up until lunchtime, when she was woken by a row in the room next door. Jacko and his on-and-off girlfriend were yelling blue murder. By the sounds of it, she'd just chucked her phone at his head. Then a door slammed, and it was quiet again.

Same old, same old . . . Glory stumbled out of bed with a groan. The pale yellow duvet ached against her eyes. The brush of a curtain rasped on her skin. A child crying somewhere outside scraped, monotonously, inside her skull.

Her window looked over a clutter of rooftops that widened out to London's smoky rim. It was a view she loved. Today, however, the city didn't seem to stretch out in all its possibilities, but appeared to box her in. Cooper Street showed few signs of spring. Since Auntie Angel had a theory that nature attracted germs, their own back garden was mostly concrete and plastic flowers in pots. The garden to Number Seven grew mud, beer cans and nettles; Number Eight's was a barbed-wire prison camp for Joe Junior's bull terriers.

This is it, Glory thought. *My life, my world. Scams, squalor and stupid bickering . . . I should be better than this. Mab Almighty – I have to be.*

Like Lily and Cora: self-made women, and head-witches worthy of the name. Style with substance. And unlike Lily's thuggish sons, who'd made the Wednesday Coven a byword for viciousness and greed, they'd kept their integrity. That's why people still talked about them with respect. Glory thought of the other coven women she'd known over the years, who'd grown pinched and sour from always coming second best to their man's latest con or newest fling. Even Auntie Angel, for all her toughness and wiliness, hadn't escaped. Married at nineteen to a bully who'd used her fae when it suited him, and blown everything she'd saved on drink and gambling . . . What were Glory's chances of beating the odds? She leaned against the window frame, resting her hot cheek against the glass.

On the fence at the back of the concrete garden a tabby cat was licking its paws. Glory remembered she'd been petting it yesterday afternoon, even though it was a mangy old thing. Now it looked up towards her, ears pricked. And in that brief moment, the world changed.

Everything was suddenly washed-out, almost colourless, and blurred at the edges, though even the smallest of specks seethed with life. But it wasn't just the quality of Glory's vision that had altered. Her view had gone into reverse. She was outside the back of the house, looking up from the garden towards the attic window. For a second, Glory saw herself through the cat's eyes.

Glory gave a stifled cry. She screwed her eyes shut, then stared out again. The view was back to normal. Yet all her senses were heightened and confused, sparking with fierce, hot energy.

Animals were more sensitive to witchwork than humans. It was why they made good familiars. It was said they could detect the onset of fae; some people thought they had a fae of their own, and that they used it to commune with witches.

Is it –? Is this how –?

No. *Don't start*, she told herself, in a kind of panic. *Don't think about it, just* do.

The cat, unconcerned, had gone back to its grooming. This gave her an idea. Light-headed, she went to find the jumper she'd been wearing yesterday, when she had stroked the cat. Sure enough, the front was covered in cat hair. Her trembling fingers raked over the wool until she had gathered a small, greyish-brown clump. The activity calmed her, giving her a focus for the gathering pressure in her head.

Thank Hecate. The animal was still there when she got back to the window. It was stiff and watchful. Listening, as if it had been called . . . Glory pulled out a couple of hairs of her own, and entwined them with the cat fur. Then she spat on it. Like everything else, this was pure instinct. But although she hadn't seen anyone else do what she was attempting, her trembles had gone, and she felt strong and sure.

She kept the cat in view as she rolled the spit-dampened twist of hair and fur into a thread across her palm. Carefully, she looped it around her right forefinger, like a collar or ring. Then she held her hand up to the window, and beckoned.

The cat flicked its tail, but its unnatural stiffness did not change. Something was missing.

Glory thought back to their first encounter, and the crooning, kissing noises she had made when cuddling the cat. She made them again. In response, the animal opened its mouth in a soundless hiss. Still crooning, Glory beckoned it down from the fence. This time it obeyed. Her finger circled the air. The cat circled on the ground. She pointed left, and the cat followed. Right, and it came back again. She laughed delightedly.

All the while, she had glimpses of a second view, colour-bleached yet impossibly vivid, teeming with movements sensed rather than seen. Her own nose twitched at scents of blood and earth. As she drew the cat across the garden, she felt the coarse scratch of concrete under its paws.

The animal drew closer. Dark stars danced at the edge of her vision. The world reeled and sparkled, and Glory fell to the floor.

When she awoke from her faint or sleep or whatever it was, it was late afternoon and the house was quiet. She was a little stiff, but otherwise fine. No heightened perceptions or shooting stars.

Could she have dreamed it? Or exaggerated and confused what she thought she'd seen? There'd been a mortifying occasion when she was eleven and got the flu, and bragged to everyone that her overheated state was the onset of fae. The memory still made her wince.

She didn't really doubt herself, though. Whatever she had felt, and seen, and done, was *true*. It was imprinted on her soul. Its aura still hung in the air around her.

Glory went to the drawer in her bedside table, and took out the photograph she kept there. Now that everything had changed, she wondered if she would find a resemblance to the stranger in the frame . . . the face that haunted her visions of the Burning Court. The woman's eyes were guarded, distant, even though she was smiling. It was the same in every other photo of her mother, even the ones from her wedding day. Edie Starling, thought Glory, had always had the look of someone who was preparing to leave.

Perhaps Edie had been raised that way. Her mother Cora had been the wilder of the Starling Twins; Edie's father could have been any one of the assorted celebrities, politicians and crooks Cora was partying with at the time. When Edie turned eight, Cora had had some kind of breakdown, quarrelled with Lily, and disappeared, taking her daughter with her. Nobody heard from them for five years. When Cora finally got in contact with her sisters, it was too late. Before the three of them could meet, she was arrested by the Inquisition, and died in the course of her interrogation.

By then, Edie was thirteen. Lily adopted her and raised her in the Wednesday Coven. Edie never spoke about the five years she'd spent on the run, but Glory sometimes wondered if it had given her mother a taste for escape. All those fresh starts and disappearances, disguises and false names . . . How many lives had she lived? Could she be living a different one now? Perhaps one day Glory would dream of it, instead of the Burning Court.

Yet although Glory did not look like the wide-eyed blonde behind the glass, today she felt closer to her mother than she ever had before. The fae that sang through her body had once leapt in her mother's veins, and those of her grandmother and great-grandmother before that.

Carefully, Glory placed the photograph on the floor. She sat beside it, cross-legged, in front of her mirror. Her ordinary brown hair was dyed to match the Starling Twins' white-blonde and her eyes were brown too; soft in some lights, black in others. She had her father's slightly hooked nose, but her strong brows and wide curved mouth were her own. Perhaps these features were too strong for prettiness, but if people remembered her face, it was for the right reasons.

Glory took a deep breath. Then she pulled down the neck of her T-shirt. Again, instinct took her directly to what she sought. Nestled underneath her collarbone was a small bloom the colour of midnight. It was velvet-soft, perfect; a true beauty spot.

For many hours longer, Gloriana Starling Wilde sat in front of the mirror, hand resting on the seal of fae. Her birthright and destiny.

CHAPTER 7

Glory woke up early the next day and for a few groggy seconds, it could have been any old Sunday morning. Then the memories hurtled back and it was like being a little kid again, getting up on her birthday or Christmas. She fizzed all over with glee.

When her cousin Candice Morgan turned witchkind in November, her parents Charlie and Kezia had thrown a party that lasted three days. Never mind that her fae was a pretty low-grade affair, and the girl was unlikely to put it to much use – she was currently undergoing her second stint at a private rehab facility in Arizona. Candice had always been a daft bimbo, and now she was a daft druggie too.

Glory was already looking forward to her own celebrations, complete with champagne and sucking-up. Ha. Even Nate would have to treat her with a bit of respect.

Because a head-witch-in-waiting should look the part, she got dressed and made-up with extra care. Base, bronzer, thick black eyeliner, hot pink lipgloss. Gold hoops and spiky boots. Her red top had a low neckline, but by stroking the mark under her collarbone, and visualising the darkness shrinking into her skin, she was able to reduce it to the size of a pinprick. She slung on a scarf anyway, just in case.

This was the first of many precautions she would have to take. Life was about to become both risky and restricted, and she needed to be prepared. Yesterday, her secret had been too new, too private, to share. Today she longed to shout the news from the rooftops – Inquisition be damned. But Auntie Angel had made her swear that she would be the first to know if Glory got the fae, and she wasn't going to break her word.

So when, at half past nine, she tapped on her great-aunt's door and got no response, the disappointment was crushing. She felt cheated. Where the hell had the old lady gone? There was no point asking her father, who rarely got up before lunch, and though Glory could hear laughter from the lounge, she wasn't ready to face the rest of the coven.

As the wait stretched out her excitement began to seep away, to be replaced by frustration. She wanted action and purpose. She wanted the delicate, dangerous thrill she'd felt as her fae reached out and touched another living creature for the first time . . .

She wanted to commit witchwork.

Glory had seen Angeline at work often enough to know the ways and means of practising fae, and knew she should start with something small and tricky to detect, that wouldn't backfire too badly if it went wrong. But she wanted to be useful too. Coolly, she considered recent coven business, looking for a gap to be filled or problem solved. Then she remembered Jimmy Warren.

Jimmy was a fence who made a living from selling

stolen jewellery. Cooper Street took a cut of his profits in return for sending business his way. But last week he'd absconded, leaving the coven among his many creditors. He'd also left behind his sister, Trish. She claimed she had no idea where he'd gone. Nate, however, was planning some serious aggro to refresh her memory.

Glory liked Trish and had babysat her little girl on several occasions. She didn't want the coven thugs to come over all heavy on her. How much better for everyone concerned, then, if she could get the information some other way . . .

An hour later Glory faced Trish Warren across the table, warming her hands on a mug of tea. Trish usually had a faded prettiness but today her face was blotchy and drawn. This was going to be easy.

Searching the household rubbish had been unpleasant, but it got results. Glory was holding the pink plastic casing of a false nail. Now she rested it on the empty packet of headache tablets in her pocket, nodding in sympathy as Trish talked about the failings of her no-good ex, and the pressures of her new bar job. She seemed glad of Glory's company and had welcomed her into the flat without suspicion. The row of bells over the building's entrance had been smashed up long ago; on an estate like Rockwood, witchcrime wasn't something you bothered the authorities with.

The grubby tablecloth bore a design of yellow flowers and pink polka dots. Perfect. Under Glory's scarf, nestling by her collar bone, she could feel the Devil's Kiss begin to warm. She thought of its mark, purple-black, beating beneath her skin.

Glory concentrated on the tablecloth. In her mind's eye, she recast the polka dots, so they were hot and red. She visualised gathering them up and pressing them, one after the other, into Trish's forehead.

Trish put her hand to her brow, grimacing.

'You all right?'

'Bit of a twinge. I get these migraines sometimes.'

I *know*, thought Glory, her finger scraping Trish's false nail against the plastic tray from which the pills had sprung. *Pop, pop, pop*, she thought, in time to the movement of the red spots.

'Oof. Come out of nowhere, they do.' Her victim got up and went to fetch herself a glass of water. 'The doctor says it's stress. Too much on me plate. But what can I do about that?'

'Mm. You must be worried about Jimmy too.'

Trish stiffened at the mention of her brother. However, the approaching migraine made it hard to think. 'I s'pose,' she mumbled.

The time had come for Glory's other find in the rubbish. Shreds of torn-up bills, typed in red. She would use their text to spell out the bane.

Behind Trish's back, she mouthed *Final Demand, Last Warning*, sending the words, like the red-hot polka dots, into her target's head. The painkillers' plastic and foil packaging crinkled against her fingers.

'About Jimmy,' she said gently. 'We're all very anxious to find him.'

'And like I told the coven, I don't know where he's gone,' said Trish faintly.

'But you must've some idea,' Glory murmured.

Final Demand . . . red spots . . . popped foil . . .

Pop spot pop spot pop spot.

'I need a lie-down –'

Yet somehow Trish could not move from the sink. She wanted to tell Glory to go away, but the pressure in her head was making her sluggish.

'You'll feel better soon,' the girl soothed. 'You just need to get it off your chest.'

And suddenly, Trish felt that, yes, it *would* be a relief to tell. Family loyalty was well and good, but it wasn't as if that waster Jimmy had ever come through for her. She didn't owe him anything.

'Jimmy's got a bird down Bermondsey way,' she said woozily. 'She works at a chippy there – The Hungry Bite. Could be he's hiding out with her.'

Glory smiled. 'I see.' A bubble of pleasure rose deliciously up her spine. 'Ta very much.'

After texting Jimmy's whereabouts to Earl, his coven handler, Glory's triumph began to cool. She couldn't avoid the fact that she had inflicted pain on someone for her own ends, and although she had not taken pleasure in Trish's discomfort, she'd definitely enjoyed the process. Now she felt ashamed. The next time she used her fae, and revelled in its giddy rush, she wanted the witchwork to be for something clean and bright. Uncompromised.

The fae wasn't like she'd expected. In some ways, it was

like her first period or first kiss, or even when she'd got drunk for the first time: the experience wasn't quite what she was prepared for, but once it had happened, it was impossible to imagine any other way.

A touch of headache was a lot better than getting slapped around by Nate and co., she reasoned. As for Jimmy Warren's fate once the coven caught up with him . . . well, that wasn't Glory's concern. He'd ripped off a lot of people and now he'd have to pay the consequences. Jimmy knew the rules. So did Trish. So did everyone.

By the time she got home, Glory had talked herself out of her misgivings. Even better, the lights were on in Auntie Angel's living room, and the door was ajar. Glory slipped in to wait for her return.

It was a room where every object competed for attention. The surfaces were higgledy-piggledy with lace doilies and china ornaments; the lamps were beaded, the cushions were tasselled and the curtains fringed. Press cuttings and photos from the Starling Twins' career papered the walls. Glory's favourite was an early black and white snapshot of Cora, Lily and Angeline walking down a street arm in arm. Angeline looked so like her younger sisters in this photo that they could almost have been identical triplets. All three had platinum blonde Sixties bobs, black-rimmed eyes and nude lips, and their expressions were bright with mischief. They looked young and carefree, invincible.

She noticed that Auntie Angel had got out the glass bowl she used for scrying, and wondered who she'd been snooping on this time. Surveillance technology was so easily available these days there wasn't much call for this kind of witchwork but, as her great-aunt said, gadgets broke, fae didn't. Glory picked up the bowl, and was swirling the water around speculatively when its owner returned.

'No messing with that,' the old lady said tartly, 'or you'll get slops on my furnishings. I don't remember inviting you in neither, Miss Nosy-beak.'

Then she took another look at Glory's face. And Glory found that now the moment of revelation had arrived, she didn't need to say anything at all.

'It's come, hasn't it?' Angeline whispered. 'God's own balefire, it's *come*.'

Glory nodded, breathless.

Angeline's old fierce face didn't soften, but tears began to slide quietly down her cheeks.

'All these years . . . These years of waiting and watching, hoping . . . But I always knew. In my blood and my bone, I knew. You were one of us.' She closed her eyes. 'It's all paid off,' she murmured, as if to herself. 'The sacrifice, the suffering. Yes, it's come good at last.'

She let out a long, wavering sigh. Then she went over to her great-niece and clasped her solemnly by the hand, like somebody making a pact.

'A life lived through fae is the best and bravest in the world. I never had a chance to fill my potential, nor did your darling ma. But it will be different for you. I'll make sure of it.'

Glory tried to smile back. Her eyes welled, she was ready to laugh and shout and cry all at once. But Auntie Angel was already tidying her emotion away. Briskly, she sat down on the chintzy sofa and patted the space by her side.

'Right then, sit yourself down and tell me all about it. Every last detail, mind.'

This was what Glory had been waiting for. When she came to the cat, Auntie Angel's breath hissed. 'You summoned a familiar? Hecate help us! Don't you know how dangerous that is? There's been witches as have gone mad that way – merged their minds with some dumb beast's and never got 'em back.'

'It happened so quick I didn't have time to think.'

'Hmph.' Auntie Angel pursed her lips. 'Well, summoning's a rare skill. Chances are you'll be a powerful witch. Which is just as well, seeing as those pyros at the Inquisition will've had you on their watch-list since the day you was born.'

Glory glanced at the three smiling girls on the wall. Their exploits had been her bedtime stories, but she'd always known that, just like in the old fae-tales, witches often met unhappy ends. Legend had it that the persecutions suffered by her own family had started back in the seventeenth century.

Denouncing a witch to the authorities remained the greatest taboo in the coven world. Two years ago, a freelancer who'd done some witchwork for Charlie Morgan was shopped to the Witchcrime Directorate. The man who informed on him was found dead three days later with every inch of his body pierced through with rusting pins. It was coven tradition to punish witch-snitchers with tortures derived from Inquisition techniques. The deterrent worked, for despite vigorous campaigning by the Inquisition, denouncements remained few and far between.

Thinking of this, Glory said, 'At least I'll have the coven watching my back.'

'The coven mustn't know. Not yet.'

Glory stared. 'What?'

'You heard me. This has got to stay between the two of us.'

But what about her party, and the presents, and swanking around Nate . . . 'You mean I can't tell *no one*? Not even Dad?'

'Not one solitary soul.'

'I don't understand. The coven needs me. *You* need me. I thought I was going to help, to learn alongside you, and –'

'And so you shall, my girl. But if you're even half the witch I think you are, it's not only the Inquisition you'll have to watch out for. The Wednesday Coven will be after you just as quick.'

Glory frowned. 'The Wednesdays don't need no more witches. They can afford the best. 'Sides, Kez is already training up Candice to be head-witch after her.'

'The only training that girl is capable of is the quickest way to snort white powder up her nose. Besides, her fae's even weedier than her ma's.' Angeline sniffed. 'Kezia Morgan may be a smooth operator but she's a workaday witch.'

'What about Candice's brother and sister?' Glory tried. 'Skye's only nineteen. She could still get the fae. So could Troy, for that matter.'

'They could. But it's a long shot, and Charlie Morgan ain't a gambling man. No, once he knows you're witch-kind, he'll want you on his books, doing his bidding same as the rest.'

'I ain't going to be no one's hired help, specially not for that crowd. They lord it over us enough as it is.'

'For good reason. Cooper Street's only allowed to operate on the Wednesday's say-so. Without their backing, we're finished.' She looked at Glory slyly. 'There's another thing too. Breeding witches is a risky business, but Charlie Morgan plays a long game. My guess is he's already fixing to set you up with his son and heir. Troy's got a brain on him; ambition too, unlike those daft sisters of his. Give it a year or two, and he'll have you popping out witch-babies for the Morgan bloodline.'

'*Eurgh*. No, I bloody won't!'

'You might not have a choice, missy. If you won't be one of their assets, then you'll be a threat. And you know how the Morgans deal with those.'

Glory went pale and cold, then hot again. 'They wouldn't. We're not just allies – we're family, for Christ's sake. I don't believe it.'

'Then you've as much to learn about families as you do about fae. Look how they shafted your ma.'

Lily Starling had adopted Edie with the intention of bringing her up to be head-witch after her. But when Lily died, the other members of the Wednesday Coven decided that twenty-one-year-old Edie was too inexperienced to take her place, and Charlie Morgan's wife Kezia became head-witch instead. That was when Edie came to Angeline. If it hadn't been for Angeline, she would have been out on the streets.

'Charlie Morgan's been watching you, and waiting, same as I have. Same as those witch-prickers at the Inquisition.

Lucky for you, I've kept one step ahead of both.' Angeline lit a cigarette, squinting at her through a cloud of smoke. 'Now, I've got us a plan but there's still some things what need putting in place. So in the meanwhile, we sit tight and we keep quiet. Business as usual.'

'Plan? What kind of plan?'

'All in good time.' She patted Glory on the knee, then laughed at her stormy expression. 'And no sulking! First things first: you sure nobody could've seen you messing with that cat?'

'Positive. But . . .'

'But what?'

'There was . . . there was one other thing. You see – I, uh, did a bit of extra witchwork earlier. Just to test things out.'

'Testing like how?'

Glory described her encounter with Trish. 'It's fine, though,' she wound up. 'Trish didn't suspect a thing.'

But now she wondered if this was true. She remembered the searching look Trish had given her as the pain began to recede, and the way the woman had shrunk away from her as she went to the door. She felt another stab of shame.

'It were only a little headache,' she added lamely.

'That's not the point,' her great-aunt snapped. 'Mab Almighty! Don't you know where Trish Warren is working these days? That bar in Cannonby Street: The Angel. The one managed by *Felton Cobbs*.'

That brought her up short. Felton was an informant for the Wednesday Coven. 'Oh . . . OK. Still, I don't reckon there's any cause for her to –'

Somebody rapped on the door.

'Piss off,' Angeline called. 'I'm busy.'

'It's for Glory,' Nate's voice replied sullenly. 'Charlie M's on the phone. He wants to see her, pronto.'

CHAPTER 8

'Can I have a word, Dad?'

'If it's a quick one.'

From behind the stack of papers on his desk, Ashton Stearne gave a slightly tense smile. He was due at a colleague's memorial service that afternoon, and so was in his ceremonial dress uniform: a military-style affair of silver-grey and scarlet, adorned with his service medals. It was what he wore in court, Lucas noted grimly.

'I, er . . . It's rather important.'

'Then you'd better come in.'

Lucas closed the door behind him and advanced to the desk. He was unsure whether to sit down or remain standing. The frenzied horrors of the night had passed; at this point, he was conscious only of blankness. He felt light-headed and unreal. Everything was unreal. This moment of confession in the study was certainly too theatrical to be true. He stared stiffly ahead, like a bad actor in a worse play.

Ashton's hands fidgeted with his pen. He saw Lucas noticing the fidgeting and put the pen down. He tried an encouraging smile. 'Right then, old chap. Speak up. What's this all about?'

Lucas cleared his throat and said, too quickly, 'There's something you need to know about me, and I'm afraid it's going to be a bit of shock.'

His father waited, but all the other scripted, rehearsed, impossible words had died in Lucas's throat.

'Are you in trouble?'

He gave a half nod, half shrug.

'Have you done something wrong?'

'Not on purpose. The trouble – the problem – is . . . personal.'

'A problem with your friends? Or with a girl?'

Lucas felt a wrench of comic bitterness. He almost laughed. He took a deep breath. 'No, the problem's me. There's something I've discovered about myself, you see. A difference. It's hard to admit to, but I need to tell you what kind . . . what kind of person I am.'

His father looked down. For the first time, his hesitancy matched his son's. 'Is this about . . . boys, then?'

'Boys?' Lucas repeated blankly. Understanding dawned. 'No! No. God –'

'In that case,' said Ashton Stearne with heavy patience, 'what exactly are you trying to say?'

Lucas waited. His father waited. The words still wouldn't come. Dumbly, Lucas began to unbutton his shirt. He kept his head bowed, hatefully aware of the flush of shame flooding his skin. Once his shirt was loose, he turned around and tugged it down, exposing his bare shoulder blade. The small velvety blot.

He heard Ashton get up, muttering, and lean over the desk towards him. He felt the nearness of his father's warmth on his skin, sensed the lightness of his curiosity, followed by a sudden tightening of focus. The sharp indrawn breath.

'Is that . . . is it . . . ?'

'Yes.'

Ashton did not touch the mark. His back was very straight and his face was very still. In the silence, Lucas straightened his shirt and redid the buttons, but awkwardly, because of the trembling of his hands.

'How long have you known?' his father asked eventually, as if from very far away.

'Since last night.'

'And have you told anyone else?'

'No.'

'Soon you must. You must inform the Inquisition. Within twenty-four hours, that's the rule.'

'Yes. Yes, of course.'

More silence.

'You're very young.'

'I know. It should be impossible. The whole thing should be impossible. It –'

His father didn't seem to be listening. 'You are so very young,' he said again, quietly. He closed his eyes, and his own face grew old.

But when he opened his eyes again, his gaze was steady and his tone brisk. He put his hand on Lucas's shoulder and gave a resolute smile.

'I am sure you'll deal with this very well. Admirably, in

fact. There's no point pretending this won't change a great many things, but together we will stand firm and do whatever has to be done. Of course, you have my full support. You always will – I hope you know nothing can change that. No doubt Marisa and Philomena will be entirely supportive too.'

He did not say that everything would be fine. He did not say, I'm sorry, and, I love you, and neither did Lucas. They both knew the other wanted to, though. For the moment that would have to be enough.

The rest of the day was the loneliest of Lucas's life. He stayed shut in his room, dazed by a bewilderment so heavy it was as if he'd been drugged. Occasionally he would be overcome by panic. His thoughts would hop and sputter manically. Then he would have to get to his feet, wrapping his arms around himself, and pace back and forth until the shaking stilled.

The house was deathly quiet. Philomena was still in bed, nursing her hangover; Marisa was at the tennis club. Ashton had left to attend the memorial service as planned. Everything else, he said with uncharacteristic vagueness, would be settled on Monday, after the weekend. He would 'drop by the office' on his way home.

By this, he meant that he was going to break the news to the Witchfinder General. Afterwards he would set up an appointment for Lucas to be registered.

Lucas knew the registration included a test of his witchkind abilities, but not exactly what this would involve. Inquisitorial techniques were not publicised; he had learned about them in general, not specific, terms. He would have to exchange his ID card for a new version stamped with a 'W'. Then there was the bridling itself. The iron cuffs would remain until he left school and found a public-sector job as a practising witch. Even then, he would be monitored to ensure he only committed witchwork as part of authorised government business.

So these were his last hours of freedom. Lucas looked at his wrists, picturing the metal bands that would soon circle them. A bridled witch was like someone with a disfigurement. The civilised, polite thing to do was not to look. You always noticed, of course, but you and the witch both pretended you hadn't. If you weren't civilised then it was a different matter. People would spit and jeer; Lucas had seen it. There were beatings too.

When it came to his friends, he wasn't sure what would be worse – their pity, or disgust. He remembered the raised eyebrow he and Tom had shared when Ollie told them about his cousin. It had seemed admirably restrained of them at the time. He tried not to think of Bea's face, flushed and hopeful, leaning towards his by the pond.

Instead, Lucas kept returning to his single act of witchwork. Obsessively, he went over every detail of Philomena's bane. It was like picking at a scab: revolting yet pleasurable.

He also brooded on what Ashton Stearne would be saying to his colleagues. Decisions were being made and processes set in motion that Lucas had no control over. *If only*, he thought, I *could know what they all really think. If only I knew what's going on behind the scenes. I need to be prepared.*

But you can be, said a small treacherous voice. You

have other resources now. And another inner voice, a voice Lucas didn't even admit to hearing, whispered, *it's your last chance*. There was an itch in his blood that was still unacknowledged, and unsatisfied.

As the afternoon wore on, he kept coming back to a discussion he'd heard between Ashton and a colleague about the use of the fae in surveillance operations. Maybe it was time to put his insider knowledge to the test.

At about four o'clock, Lucas heard Philly stump along the corridor and down the stairs. The front door slammed. A moment or so later, and before he could think better of it, he was making his way into his father's study.

Lucas surveyed the room, and realised he was past the worst of his shock. Everything was easier now he had a task to work on. He assessed the challenge with the cool recklessness of someone with nothing to lose.

A witch with a scrying-bowl filled with water could see through walls and across cities. It was a building's entrance and exit points that made it vulnerable. The bowl was usually made of glass because windows were made of glass, and this enabled the fae to work through the panes. A wooden or steel bowl would let a witch see through a wooden or steel door.

But scrying was one of the few witchworks that could be stopped with iron. (It was usually only the witch, not their work, which was blocked by the metal.) People with something to hide or protect installed iron shutters over their windows and fixed an iron panel to the centre of their doors. Ashton's study was iron-proofed. And in any case, you couldn't hear anything in a scrying-bowl.

Lucas had tried to listen through doors before. When his father first got involved with Marisa, he had even attempted the glass-held-to-the-wall trick. The theory went that the wall picked up the vibrations of sound in the room, and the glass helped channel them. It had not worked when Lucas was eleven. But things were different now.

Ashton's study was next to the dining room. From the cabinet there, Lucas took out a pair of crystal wine glasses. His pulse was speeding up in anticipation, and he could feel the blot on his shoulder blade begin to warm.

A talisman was any kind of witchworked object; an amulet, by contrast, was a witchwork device made from scratch. From what Lucas could remember of the spying trick his father had described, he needed to cast his fae into the two glasses so that they became talismans to transmit and amplify sound. There were no exact rules for using the Seventh Sense and the fae often required the use of bodily substances as well as physical props. Lucas was of the popular opinion that witchwork was too makeshift, too *grubby*, to be considered a craft.

Here goes nothing, he thought, as he held one of the glasses at the base of its stem. He had no option but to make things up as he went along. Grimacing slightly, he ran his forefinger inside his right ear, feeling for the whorls of bone and flesh, the warm hole of the drum. After spitting on his finger, he rubbed its wet tip round the rim of the glass.

As the motion of his hand set up a wave of vibration travelling through the crystal, it began to hum, then sing. It was something he'd done in a science lesson on sound waves, back in prep school. But this time the fae in his head echoed in answer: a darker, richer note.

Even when he lifted his finger from the rim of the first glass and moved to the second, the first kept up its thin whine. For a few moments the two sang together, their crystal bowls vibrating slightly. Once silence returned, and he ventured to pick the glasses up again, they hummed at his touch. Recognising him, welcoming him.

The walls of the study were lined with books. Lucas placed one of the witchworked glasses on the empty section of a lower shelf. With a bit of luck it would be unnoticed there. He took the other glass back to the dining room, and hid it behind the curtains. As the fae subsided, his nerves shivered and hummed, as if his body was made of crystal too. He felt at peace for the first time that day.

Half an hour later, Ashton Stearne returned. When Lucas heard his father's tread along the corridor, he quickly moved from his bed to his desk, opening up a school text book at random. Ashton entered the room to see his son apparently deep in study.

'How was the service?' Lucas asked, as casually as he could make it.

'It was fine, thank you. How . . . how are you?'

'Fine.'

'Good.' Ashton nodded towards the desk. 'Business as usual, I see. Very sensible.'

'Did it go all right at the office?'

'Fine.'

'What did they say? Have you spoken to Sir Ant—'

'I said it was fine.'

Lucas looked away. 'Right. Sorry.'

'No need to apologise. I've made you an appointment for Monday, by the way. We'll leave here at nine.'

'I should go on my own.'

'Oh.' A shadow crossed his father's face. 'I thought . . . I thought you might like some support.'

'Thanks,' said Lucas awkwardly. 'It's just that it will be easier to keep a low profile if I'm alone. Though I suppose you'll have to release an, er, official statement . . . ?'

'Mm. For the moment, I've been asked to keep matters confidential until we know exactly what we're dealing with.'

Lucas took this to mean it hadn't yet been decided whether or not his father would have to resign. He was at a critical stage in the Goodwin trial; if he had to pull out now, the case might well collapse.

'Of course, Marisa needs to be informed. It's probably better if she explains the situation to Philomena herself.'

'OK. Sure. And then we can talk things over properly. I mean, there's so much to discuss. So much to sort out. I need to know how –'

'One thing at a time, old chap.'

Marisa returned soon after her husband. From the top of the stairs, Lucas listened to the usual bustle of her arrival, and the point at which it was cut short by Ashton's calm interjection. 'A word, Marisa, if I may . . .'

Lucas felt surprisingly little guilt at the betrayal he was about to make. His father had made it clear that the less Lucas knew about arrangements for his new life the better.

Besides, everyone knew that witchkind were deceitful to the core. He was just reverting to type.

He gave Marisa and Ashton a few moments in the study before putting his ear to the door. Not even a murmur could be heard within. Then, his mouth very dry, he shut himself in the dining room. He collected the wine glass from behind the curtain, and went to the section of wall behind which he'd placed its mate.

Would his talisman work? He reassured himself by stroking the glass, and heard the hum in the crystal answer the hum beginning in his head. His next worry was that using the glass in the dining room would set the one in the study singing. From here on, everything was guesswork.

Lucas sat on the floor, his back against the wall. Breathing deeply, he ran his fingertip inside his ear, wetted it on his tongue, and began to circle the glass's rim. He pictured the discussion in progress on the other side of the wall and the glass on the shelf, vibrating silently in answer.

As his finger circled the glass in his hand, the fae in both called to the glass in the other room. A thread of sound stretched between the two, then looped round the crystal rim, up through his finger and into his ear. There, the voices in the study spoke to him.

'Perhaps you should sit down,' his father was saying. 'You've had quite a shock.'

So Lucas had missed the moment of revelation. He found he was relieved.

There was a choking, gasping sound. When his stepmother did speak, her voice was faint. 'Have they . . . have they asked you to resign?'

'I'll remain where I am until after the Goodwin trial. There's a chance some kind of arrangement might be made. A move to a more administrative role, perhaps.'

'Even if the Inquisition supports you, the press will be out for blood. The humiliation! After everything you've done for this country! I can't bear it.'

'You must. We have other priorities now.'

Lucas, trance-like, stroked the glass. The fae pulsed at his skin. There was another effect too. When he closed his eyes, the two voices – or rather, their separate sounds – were coloured. Marisa's was dark red, exposing an anger that wasn't expressed in her tearful words. Ashton's colour was also at odds with his calm manner. A whirling, grainy black. Could it be . . . panic?

'How could it have happened?' Marisa asked at last.

'There's always a chance.'

'But your *family* – it's biologically impossible – unless Camilla's –'

'No. Absolutely not. I did the usual checks: her pedigree was impeccable.'

His father's sigh reverberated through the glass. Lucas saw it as watery grey, like rain.

'The fae isn't simply a rogue gene. Yes, it runs in families, but that's only part of the story. Look at the War. The Nazis purged not just Jews but whole communities of witchkind. The British Empire did the same in some of its colonies. And yet when a new, so-called 'purified' generation was born in these places, witchkind were still part of the mix. The fae is an aberration, but a natural one. It will always be with us.'

'So I'm beginning to see.' His wife's tone was crisp, but the green of the emotion behind it was acid. 'Very well. Where do we go from here?'

'It's been agreed that Lucas's condition should not be disclosed until the Goodwin business is over. There may well have to be a press conference. In which case, the four of us appearing together would be a great help – a "family united" and so on. Do you think you could face it?'

There was a pause. Then, 'Of course.' Marisa's voice had strengthened into a theatrical purple. 'Of course. Whatever you think best. Together, we can survive this. We can survive anything. My darling –'

Lucas let the glass fall into his lap. It wasn't as if he'd learned anything new. An *aberration, but a natural one*. Exactly how much of an aberration, he'd find out tomorrow.

CHAPTER 9

Ashton Stearne had arranged for his son to be privately assessed by a colleague in an office on the other side of London. The need for secrecy had spared Lucas the indignity of a public processing centre, and the stares and whispers that would follow him through the corridors. 'You know who that is, don't you? The Stearne boy. Yes, turns out the Chief Prosecutor's son is a hag! What a shock. What a scandal . . .'

That would come later. But as Lucas turned down the alley at the side of a dingy office block, and pressed the buzzer of an unmarked door, it was hard to feel the privilege of his situation. All this sneaking around was just a different kind of humiliation.

His father's contact met him at the door. He introduced himself as Dr Simon Smith. He had greying hair and blandly smooth features, and his manner was both efficient and impersonal. Lucas determined to act the same, as if none of this business was actually to do with him, and he was merely going through the motions on somebody else's behalf.

In a windowless basement office, Dr Smith took his statement about Philomena's bane and the onset of his fae, and photographed the mark on his shoulder blade. Copies of Lucas's school and medical reports were already in the inquisitor's file.

Making the statement took over an hour. Afterwards, Lucas was given a thin grey cotton shirt and trousers to change into. An armed guard watched him all the while. Lucas knew this was to ensure he didn't smuggle any witchworked devices into the test, but as he was escorted down the corridor, walking barefoot in the flimsy uniform, he felt cold and exposed. Though he would have hated his father to see him like this, a small scared part of him wished he was there.

The assessment room was bare and cell-like. There was a CCTV camera in the corner, a box on the floor, and a table with an iron bell hanging from a frame. Lucas and Dr Smith sat down on either side of the table. The guard took up his position by the door.

'As you know,' Dr Smith began, 'the fae is inhibited by iron.' He pulled out a drawer, in which pairs of iron wristbands were displayed. They were all of the same thickness but of varying widths. 'I'm going to ask you to wear these bands while performing a small act of witchwork. Each time you successfully complete the task, I will give you a new and wider band, until we reach the point at which you are no longer able to perform witchwork at all.'

'And then you'll know what it will take to bridle me.'

'Exactly. The greater your fae, the greater the quantity of iron needed to curb it.'

Lucas looked at the bell. *Bells warn, iron prevents.* Iron was one of the most abundant elements of earth; there was a chemical trace of it in almost all living organisms. The fact that witches were allergic to it was further proof of their unnaturalness. Yet iron was sensitive to witchwork in turn. Made into a bell, the wrought metal picked up the energy of harmful fae, which caused its parts to reverberate, then ring. The process was something that Lucas had thought he might like to research once he was an inquisitor . . . He shook himself back into the present. 'Why do we need the bell?'

'Your task is to hex a minor bane. The bell should chime continuously as soon as you start. It follows that if you only make a pretence at witchwork, the bell will remain silent and I'll know your attempt is fake.' Another bland smile. 'Now for your victim.'

Dr Smith took out a metal tray from the box by his feet, together with a woven straw doll. It was about twelve centimetres high with a clear cellophane pouch in its middle. This contained a tiny black spider.

He placed the doll in the dish in front of Lucas.

'I would like you to use witchwork to set this alight.'

Like a balefire. How appropriate. Unbidden, the image of Bernard Tynan flared into his head. The oozing, blackened flesh, the spitting flames . . . Fire was often a key element of witchwork. Maybe that's why people wanted witches to burn.

'I – I don't know how.'

'I'm sure you'll think of something. Take your time. We won't bridle you for the first attempt.'

In its cellophane cell, the spider stirred minutely. Of course it had to be alive: banes needed living things to work on.

Lucas clenched his jaw, aware of Dr Smith's impersonal gaze, the guard's stare, the camera in the corner. He wondered who else could be watching.

He picked up the spider-doll, still thinking of the burning witch. Though he didn't want to, he knew it would help to visualise the flames. A wave of pity went through him: for himself, and the spark of life he was about to extinguish. He pulled out a strand of straw.

Lucas rubbed it between the palms of his hands, never taking his eye off the straw man with the spider heart. The Devil's Kiss began to warm, its mark visibly expanding under his thin shirt, and as it did so the bell softly chimed. What did fire need? Heat, fuel, oxygen. Lucas blew lightly at the brown strand twisting between his hands, and hissed between his teeth, echoing the hiss of flames. The strand smoked, then sparked, as the doll and its prisoner combusted in a hot bright flash.

Dr Smith's expression gave nothing away. He simply nodded once, and reached for one of the pairs of iron bands in the drawer. They were about two centimetres wide, and only a couple of millimetres thick. Once clipped around Lucas's wrists, they were fixed in place by a small lock and key.

'Again, please,' said the inquisitor quietly. He brought out another doll from the box. Another spider.

The iron was unpleasantly cold on Lucas's skin, but it was only a slight distraction. Though the second blaze was not as dramatic as the first, the process was still over in a matter of moments.

Another spider-doll, another pair of iron bands. This time, it took longer for the strand of straw to smoke and for the doll to be consumed by fire. It was more tiring too.

The third wristbands were six centimetres wide. The metal felt unnaturally heavy as well as cold, and when Lucas lifted his hands, dizziness swilled through his head. He struggled to attend to his task, and it took nearly three minutes for the flame to catch.

The next pair of bands was the last. Lucas put them on with a surge of nausea. Wearily, he plucked out another piece of straw from another doll. He felt too cold and sluggish to do anything, let alone witchwork. But he could still feel the unsteady pulse of his fae. After five long minutes, the doll began to smoke, then smoulder. There was a frantic twitching before the spider too was burned to ash. Lucas closed his eyes in exhaustion.

'It seems more bands are required,' said Dr Smith neutrally. 'Excuse me a moment.'

He got up and left the room. The guard stared at Lucas. Lucas stared at his wrists. The bridled witches he'd come across had never worn bands of more than a couple of centimetres wide. He was already wearing six-centimetre cuffs and there was more to come. Now he understood the point of the bell. How tempting it would be to stop trying, to go no further, and so avoid the penalty of an even larger restraint.

I *must be a powerful witch*, he thought. Dangerous, too, though he felt so feeble the idea was laughable. Presumably this was the after-effect of his fae fighting against the iron. If he stopped trying to perform witchwork, he'd feel better. But then the bell wouldn't ring and Dr Smith would know he was trying to cheat. Unless . . .

Unless he hexed a different bane, one unconnected to the spiders and dolls. Something secret, that neither the inquisitor nor the guard would detect.

The only possible subject was himself. Could he create a new blemish or wound? But his thin cotton clothes might not be enough to cover its appearance, and when he changed back into his own things the guard would see. *Come on*, he thought feverishly, *think*. The inquisitor could return at any second.

His gaze fell on Dr Smith's suit jacket, which he had taken off during the last test and hung over the back of his chair. The chair's back was rounded and narrow, and as Lucas watched, the jacket slid off and puddled on the floor. In one smooth swift movement, he bent down to pick it up. At once the guard started forward and snatched it out of his hands. He eyed Lucas and the garment with equal suspicion, before shaking the jacket out and carefully replacing it on the chair.

Lucas sat back with a shrug of apology. He had made his move almost too quickly for thought. And yet he had something all the same: a short silver hair. His hand had brushed it up from the lapel. Lucas's two pulses – his heart rate, and the throb of fae – began to speed up in anticipation. Maybe, just maybe, it would be enough.

The next moment Dr Smith returned, carrying another three sets of iron cuffs. The largest was at least fourteen centimetres wide.

'I'm sorry for the delay. We'll start you on the ten centimetres, if you're ready?'

Lucas nodded, taking care to keep his expression wan. Though he was still a long way from coming to terms with his condition, there was a small, bitter satisfaction in the idea that his was an unusual power. Better to be a force of fae to be reckoned with than some small-time harpy amateur. Outwitting his assessor would be proof of this. It would also be in breach of the law; an act of rebellion against the entire inquisitorial system. But Lucas wasn't ready to think about that.

Another doll was placed in the tray. There must be an assembly line somewhere: junior inquisitors bagging up spiders, and inserting them into dolls. Maybe that was how Gideon and the rest of the fast-trackers spent their time. A bubble of hysterical laughter rose in his chest. Lucas coughed it back and ran his hands through his hair, before picking out the dullest, most brittle piece of straw he could find. He began to rub it between his palms, as before, but this time it was twined with the silver hair of the inquisitor, and a black one from his own head. As the three strands rubbed together, the fae twisted into them too.

It was hard. Very hard. The effort of drawing his Seventh Sense out through the iron left him with sweat running down his face, and chills running up and down his body. It was difficult, too, to keep his eyes on the doll. Yet the bell was ringing, to warn that a bane was being attempted, even though there was no smoke or spark from the straw. This time, the only heat Lucas had created was in his fingertips. He slumped back in his chair, as if in defeat, and brushed his hot fingers over the hair just above his ear.

The soft young hair coarsened at his touch. At once, he let his head droop and a flop of hair fall over his forehead. That way, he hoped the small silvery streak he'd put in it would go unnoticed by his audience.

'I can't do it,' he mumbled. 'I can't do it any more.'

Dr Smith nodded. The doll's straw body was cool and dry, its spider quiet. Lucas, on the other hand, looked a wreck: sweaty and dishevelled, with bloodshot eyes.

'Very well,' said the inquisitor. 'We'll stop here.' He made no comment on the outcome of the test, but behind the blank screen of his face, Lucas sensed the calculations still in progress: measuring, speculating, judging.

Lucas was bridled with the ten-centimetre cuffs. He was allowed to change back into his own clothes afterwards, under the scrutiny of the guard. The indignity of this hardly mattered any more; the only thing he could think about was his hair. He'd rumpled it up to cover the grey patch – the dead patch, as he thought of it – and it took all his willpower not to keep touching it.

The iron felt less cold and heavy than when he'd been using his fae, but the cuffs still dragged at his arms. They were a temporary set he would wear until he could be fitted with a custom-made pair. They'd be part of his life until he turned eighteen and found a witchworking job for the State.

The bridle's dull black metal was thin as a sheet, and treated with a protective substance to make it waterproof.

As long as he didn't raise or stretch his arms they were hidden by his shirtsleeves. He tried, and failed, to picture himself casually strolling around in a T-shirt, cuffs glinting in the sun. There was a photograph of a male witch doing just that on the cover of a booklet called *Living With Fae*. It was one of several brochures in the information pack Dr Smith had given him. The witch in this particular picture, a catalogue-model type with a fake tan and even faker grin, was holding hands with a pretty (and non-bridled) blonde. Section One of the booklet was entitled *Friends, Family and Relationships*. Lucas didn't read any further. He knew that if he starting thinking about Tom and Bea and the rest, the paralysing panic would return.

'. . . ideally, he or she will be appointed in the next couple of days, and the two of you will meet soon after. It's not just about monitoring your activities, but providing support in a range of . . .'

Dr Smith must be talking about his warden. Through his daze, Lucas remembered the dimples and twinkles of the Recruitment Officer who'd given the talk at school. *If I get someone like* her, he thought, *I'll die*. I'll hex us both into oblivion. I know I will. He only realised the session was over when the inquisitor got to his feet and reached out to shake his hand.

'Thank you,' Lucas said, rousing himself. He must remember he was obligated to this person. 'I appreciate your help, and I know my father does too.'

Dr Smith nodded. For an embarrassed moment Lucas thought he was going to extend his sympathies, or commiserate. But all the man said was, 'It's for your own good, you know.' His gaze moved to Lucas's sleeves, pulled down over the iron. 'For everyone's good. Remember that.'

Lucas managed to summon a taxi without revealing his bridled wrists, but it was an anxious ride. Every movement he made had the potential to expose him. He was exhausted; his mind felt beaten and raw. It would be no hardship to stay hidden at home until the end of his father's trial, he decided. There was no one he wanted to see and nowhere for him to go.

At least the session at the Inquisition had finished earlier than expected. With luck, he would have the house to himself, and some time to organise his thoughts before his father returned. But as he stepped into the front hall, a nerve-shredding shriek came from the drawing room.

'Ohmygodohmygodohmygod. He *hexed* me. I've been *bewitched*. Ohmygodohmygod.'

No need for witchworked eavesdropping here. The door wasn't even shut.

'Pull yourself together.' Lucas had never heard Marisa sound so brusque. 'You're perfectly fine.'

'I'm in *mortal danger*! We all are. *We're not safe.*'

Philomena began to wail; on and on, louder and louder. There was the smack of hand on flesh, and a shocked silence.

Marisa's voice snapped through it. 'Hysterics won't help. No, the real threat we face is to our position. And after the time and work I've invested in this family, not to mention Ashton's career, I'm not giving it up without a fight.'

'But Daddy –'

'Your father has a new life and a new family now. He's made that perfectly clear. And if you breathe one word of this to him or anyone else, witchwork will be the least of your troubles. Understand?'

'But –'

'*Do you understand?*'

'Yeah-sure-fine-whatever.'

Philomena flung herself out of the room. She did a double-take at the sight of Lucas, and at once put her hands protectively around her throat. Her lip quivered.

'Witch,' she whispered in a trembling voice, eyes stretched wide.

'Drama queen,' Lucas retorted. At that she gave her trademark head toss, and flounced up the stairs.

Marisa emerged soon after. If she was embarrassed to find her stepson there, she didn't show it.

'Well,' she said to him calmly, 'this is quite a pickle, isn't it?'

He gave an awkward nod. 'I'm . . . sorry.'

'I'm sure you are.' She gave a brief, tight smile, before continuing down the hall. 'And I'*m* going to have a drink.' Her voice was back to its brightly social best, as if they were at a cocktail party.

A drink sounded like a good idea. The traditional response to disaster – to get steaming, roaring, crashingly drunk. Maybe he should try it.

But Lucas didn't even have the energy to move. The hall mirror showed him a stranger, with shadowed eyes, and a streak of old man's silver in his hair.

CHAPTER 10

'Just a family supper,' Uncle Charlie had said in his phone call on Sunday, while Glory grasped the phone so tightly her knuckles turned white. 'Kez has been nagging me to get you over. It's been too long.'

Now it was Monday, and Glory was on the bus to Hampstead and the Morgan lair. This time, it was her handbag she held in a white-knuckled grip.

When she was little, visiting her Morgan relatives had been like going to Disneyland. Everything at their mansion was sparkly-new. The two girls had a room each just for clothes, and more toys than anyone could ever play with. There was a cinema and a swimming pool, and dinners that didn't come from the microwave or tins. What did it matter that Candice used to pull her hair, or that Skye laughed at her hand-me-down clothes? Their brother Troy would give her piggyback rides round the garden, and Uncle Charlie would slip ten-pound notes and sweeties into her pocket when Auntie Angel wasn't looking.

The best visits were the special occasion ones, like Christmas and Easter or Balefire Night, when the house was draped in black and they said prayers for Guy Fawkes and the other witch martyrs, while outside the coven world, people burned the martyrs' images at garden parties and let off fireworks. Witchkind's own celebration was All Hallows' Eve. It was as secret as the Balefire Night gatherings but much more fun. There was a big dinner with coven witches and their families, followed by dancing and competitive fae-tricks.

But Glory had had enough of being the poor relation. Last All Hallows' she'd stayed in Cooper Street, playing drinking games with Nate's crowd. She'd gone to bed before midnight, sodden with self-pity. And dreamed of the Burning Court again . . .

Since she'd come into her fae, everything had changed. She wasn't a little girl to be petted and patronised and then forgotten again. Nor was she going to be bossed about like a coven drudge.

What did Charlie want? Did he know her secret? Even if Trish Warren had blabbed about the migraine, it was just a vague suspicion. And it was notoriously hard to prove someone was witchkind – even the Inquisition struggled. The first thing a witch learned was how to shrink the Devil's Kiss to the tiniest of dots, and witch-ducking only produced results on someone who'd used their fae within the hour or so. If they had, prolonged and violent ducking in cold water would result in a telltale stain around the eyes and nose and mouth, as if the Devil's Kiss was seeping out from under the skin. Auntie Angel and Kezia Morgan had both been witch-ducked by the Inquisition, emerging unstained and triumphant to tell the tale. Granny Cora, though, had not been so fortunate. She was one of those who drowned.

Thinking of the witch-prickers' needles, and the long plunge under icy water, Glory shivered. These days, the Inquisition's methods were supposedly constrained by law. Coven techniques were not.

Stop it, she told herself as the bus wheezed along the final stretch of road. *You're being paranoid.* Even if – and it was only *if* – Charlie had his suspicions, he wouldn't try anything at this point. He'd watch and wait, send out his spies. Meanwhile, Auntie Angel had a plan. She'd told Glory to trust her and not to worry. All she had to do this evening was act the innocent, and buy them some time.

Cardinal Avenue was home to a Premiership footballer, a couple of film stars and a Russian oil tycoon. Behind spiked electronic gates, a carriage drive swept up to the Morgans' Palladian-style modern mansion, its columned portico glaring white against the bright red brick.

A maid let Glory into the marble-floored foyer. It was two storeys tall, the walls hung with mirrors, and lit by a star-burst chandelier. A wide staircase dominated the far end, with glass double doors on either side. The entrance was the only part of the interior that hadn't changed dramatically since Glory was a kid, when the decor had had quite a lot in common with her Barbie Dream Castle. Since then, the pink satin drapes and gold statuary had been replaced by a minimalist vision of brushed steel, black leather and blond wood.

The maid informed her that Mrs Morgan had had to

take a telephone call and would be with her shortly. In the meantime, Miss Skye was in the family room, and would she like to go through?

Glory passed through the doors to the left of the stairs, and into the least formal of the three living rooms. Like Cooper Street, the lounge was dominated by a black leather couch and widescreen TV, but there the similarity ended. This couch was soft as butter, and as big as a limousine. The white carpet looked as if it had never been stepped on. A pair of sliding doors at the end of the room led to a glistening indoor pool. Someone was doing laps; the echoing slops of water were muffled behind the glass.

Skye was painting her nails in front of the TV. She glanced up at Glory's entrance and narrowed her eyes. 'What're you doing here?'

'Your dad invited me.'

'Oh. Well, I'll be going out.'

So much for a family supper. Skye's older sister Candice wouldn't be here either; she would be locked up in her American 'health retreat' for the next two months.

'Shame.'

'Mm-hmm.' Skye yawned. 'It's been an age since I saw you. Up to much?'

'Not really. The usual.'

Her cousin looked both pleased and pitying. Aged nineteen, she had finished her expensive education without much in the way of qualifications, but plenty of contacts, and described herself as 'in the fashion/film/music industry' depending on who she was dating (model/actor/DJ).

Small talk over, Skye went back to her nails. They were

sparkly-gold to match her pout. Her bronzed skin was one shade lighter than her hair and nearly as glossy. She was wearing a tangerine mini-dress, cut low to display her bulbous plastic breasts.

Glory had also dressed with care. Warpaint, she'd thought, making her eyelashes bristly black, her lips brave red. Next to Skye, however, she felt underdone. Drab. She had worn a polo-neck as a safeguard; already on edge, she could feel the Devil's Kiss begin to expand under the clingy purple fabric.

I've got what you haven't, she told Skye in her head, *and it's all I'll ever need.* This thought would have been more satisfying if she could believe that Skye actually cared about the fae. Why would a girl like her ever want to be witchkind? It would only cramp her style. No wonder her sister had ended up in rehab.

There was a sloshing noise as the swimmer pulled himself out of the pool. Glory realised it was Troy. He opened the sliding doors and stood dripping in the entrance of the room. The water behind him rocked gently in its shining basin, impossibly blue.

'Hey, cuz. Long time no see. You're looking good.'

To Glory's fury, she felt a flush starting. She was remembering Auntie Angel's words about breeding witch-babies.

When they were younger, Troy had been kinder than his sisters. There'd been a time she wished he'd been her big brother too. It was difficult to imagine now. His angular features, large frame and dark russet colouring weren't unattractive, but both his face and manner had hardened. Other coven men liked to swagger; Troy was reserved. Edgy, and watchful. He seemed older than his years – and twenty-one, Glory thought, was already quite elderly enough.

'Can't you go and drip somewhere else?' his sister huffed. 'There *is* a changing room, you know.'

'Yeah, and it's full of your crap.'

Troy knotted a towel around his waist, then sauntered slowly across the room, leaving a trail of damp footprints. As he reached the door, his mother and father came in; at the same moment, Skye's phone rang with the news her taxi had arrived. Everyone was caught up in a flurry of arrivals and departures and explanations. In the midst of it, Glory felt the weight of Uncle Charlie's arm around her shoulder. Before she knew it, she was being ushered towards his office. 'A little pre-dinner chat,' he said cheerily.

'We'll eat in fifteen minutes,' his wife called after them. Wiry and hard-bitten, Kezia could be formidable when she wanted to be. She was of Romany blood, and it was common knowledge that gypsies had above-average rates of fae. Tonight, although her tone was light, her expression was calculating. Glory looked back across the foyer to see Troy and his mother standing together, watching her.

Charlie Morgan's office was majestically oppressive with its heavy dark wood and velvet furnishings. Family photos crowded the walls, including several of his yacht – the *Queen Kezia* – and his villa in Spain. There was even a rare picture of his father Fred, a minor hit-man who had spent the last ten years of his life in prison, for the most part forgotten by both Lily and her children.

Charlie opened a drinks cabinet. 'What's your poison?'

'Nothing for me, ta.'

Glory sat down on one of the overstuffed chairs. She was careful not to fidget, to appear agreeable and unsuspecting. As a distraction, she fixed her eyes on a nineteenth-century painting of a water nymph that hung above the desk. The girl was bathing in a pool, her pearly nakedness offset by the dark bloom of the Devil's Kiss over her left breast. It was a sentimental picture but, as with pornography, artistic depictions of the fae were banned from public display. Even private collectors risked censorship by the Inquisition's Council for Cultural Integrity.

Meanwhile, Charlie poured himself a whisky and raised his glass to her in salute. 'Nice to have you in our clutches again.' The teeth displayed by his smile were as brilliantly white as the columns on the portico. His thinning hair was reddish, his eyes chilly blue. Glory looked straight into them and gave her best smile back.

A man like Charlie Morgan didn't need the fae. His Seventh Sense was one that honed in on other people's fears, their greed and hopes and desires . . . all the things that made them vulnerable, and which he could exploit. That was the true source of his power. Now, of course, he had wealth and influence to back it up. Charm too, though his face had grown mottled and fleshy from good living, and his once muscular frame was softening to flab.

'So . . . tell me the latest,' he invited. 'Boys, school, family – what's new?'

'Not much. Same old, same old.'

'Stuck in a rut, eh? Well, things'll change sooner or later. Any day now you could turn witchkind.'

'Yeah, and I'm getting sick of the wait.' Glory tried to turn her nerves to her advantage, putting on an anxious, unhappy expression. 'Sometimes I worry . . . as time goes on . . . it's not *definite* the fae'll come to me, is it? Not for sure.'

'Don't you fret. Even if I haven't been blessed with the fae myself, I reckon I can sniff it out as well as any pricker in the Inquisition.' His eyes met hers, and held them. 'I got all my instincts telling me you'll turn out witchkind to the bone.'

She swallowed. 'Fingers crossed.'

Uncle Charlie settled back into his chair. 'You're a clever girl, Glory. Gutsy too, just like your mother. And you know how fond my ma was of yours. Like her own daughter, Edie was.'

Yeah, thought Glory. *And when your mum died, you kicked mine out of the coven.* But all she said was, 'Families should stick together.'

'Exactly! Family is all. That's why me and Kez were so proud when our Candice came into her fae, and so devastated for her when she fell ill. There's a chance her disabilities will stop her from ever putting her gifts to use.'

Disability, thought Glory. *So that's what they're calling it.*

'Lightning does sometimes strike twice. Or three times even – in the case of the Starling girls. But I've gotta face facts. Skye and Troy could still get the fae, but more than likely, they won't.'

Glory had a nasty feeling she knew where this was leading.

'Troy's got enough on his plate anyhow. He's shaping

up to be a fine coven boss. Which is just as well, since neither of my two princesses have much of a head for business.' He shook his own head indulgently. 'I've spoiled them rotten and that's a fact . . . How about you? Do you get involved much in Cooper Street operations?'

His casual tone hadn't changed but Glory's nerves were on high alert. 'I like to know what's going on,' she said carefully. 'Auntie Angel includes me in as much as she can.'

'I'm glad to hear it. It's a crying shame Angeline's witch-working days are nearly done. It'll be the end of an era when she goes.' A regretful sigh. 'But I got a feeling you're destined for bigger things than Cooper Street – whether you're witch-kind or no.' He leaned forward. 'That's why I'm asking for your help.'

So they were coming to the point at last.

'How d'you mean?'

'Takings are down at your coven, and I want to know why.'

The Wednesday Coven took a percentage of Cooper Street profits in return for a share of contacts and territory, and the prestige of their alliance. It was an unequal partnership in every way. The Wednesdays made millions from money laundering, racketeering, drugs trafficking, extortion and heists. Cooper Street, meanwhile, scraped a living through the likes of pirated DVDs, email scams and identity theft.

Glory managed a shrug. 'Our head-witch is an OAP, our boss is a drunk and his son's a waster. Business ain't what it used to be.'

'Hmm. What about the Bishops Green depot raid,

then? And those designer watch knock-offs that did such great business round Christmas? They should've been prize jobs for your piggy bank. But the numbers don't show.'

At the mention of numbers, Glory felt a new fear. 'My – my dad does our accounts. And he's not crooked.' Her face grew hot. 'I'll burn before I believe it.'

Uncle Charlie held up his hands in a placating manner. 'Your dad's straight as they make 'em. But Patrick only makes a record of what cash and so on comes his way. If a slice of the pie is missing, he's not going to know about it.'

'You're sure someone's skimming the profits?'

'Frank is. He's the one who showed me the books. I haven't mentioned it to Vince, mind. Not yet.'

Frank and Vince were Charlie's brothers. Frank took care of the coven's financial affairs. Vince was the one who threatened and maimed and killed to order, the one even the coven toughs talked about in whispers. He was also the only Morgan brother to have done time. Glory hadn't seen him for a long while.

She understood the threat his name implied. Nobody wanted Vince Morgan looking into their business. She also understood that the issue wasn't really about money. Whatever cut of Cooper Street's earnings the Wednesdays took, it was small change to a man like Charlie Morgan. It was his reputation that was at stake. To cheat him was to disrespect him, and respect meant everything in the coven world.

'I'm a busy man,' Charlie continued. 'The Inquisition's over us like a sack of fleas, I got Bradley Goodwin's trial to contend with, and ten other types of grief beside. That don't mean I'm going soft. Far from it. So if there's something rotten in Cooper Street, I want you to be the one to sniff it out.'

'You want me to be a snitch.'

Uncle Charlie looked pained. 'I wouldn't put it like that. This is a very special relationship we've got here. Our covens are bound by blood-ties as much as business and, like you said, families stick together. Right?'

'Right.'

'That's my girl. I've got faith in you, Glory. Plans too – big plans. Now's the time to show me what you're capable of.'

His teeth flashed brilliantly.

Since it was an informal supper, they ate in the kitchen, a sterile expanse of black marble-topped counters and cabinets of frosted glass. When Glory arrived, Kezia and Troy were standing by the stove. He'd said something to cheek her, and she'd dabbed sauce on his nose. It was a small mother-son moment that gave Glory a stab of envy. She turned away, and concentrated on resenting the state of the art kitchen gadgets instead.

Although Kezia's position as head-witch was a full-time job, and she had an army of domestic staff at her disposal, it was part of her cover to play the part of a traditional housewife. The four of them sat down to roast pork with all the trimmings followed by home-made trifle. Charlie was on fine form: booming out crude jokes and coven gossip, topping up everyone's glass.

It was impossible for Glory to relax. The conversation

in the office had been such a slippery mix of flattery and veiled threats she hardly knew what to think. As for the task Charlie'd set her . . . Maybe someone at Cooper Street really was dumb enough to try to rip him off. Or maybe he'd made the whole thing up, to stir trouble.

Every rich, heavy mouthful lodged indigestibly in her stomach. She didn't like wine and this one tasted sour, even though the bottle probably cost as much as what most people spent on a crate. She was too hot and her head was aching.

At last it was over. When she stood up to say her thanks and goodbyes, Troy got up too. 'I'll give you a lift home. I'm going your way anyhow.'

Glory found this hard to believe. It meant she wasn't escaping just yet.

The mansion's garage housed a vintage Bentley and several sports cars that looked like fighter jets. Troy's Mercedes was relatively low-key in comparison.

They spent the first few minutes of the drive in silence. She had been aware of Troy's scrutiny during dinner, and when they waited at the traffic lights by the Blythe Hill roadworks, she realised he was looking at her again.

'What? Is there snot on my face or something?'

'Prickly kid, aren't you? Maybe I'm just enjoying the view.'

Glory didn't know what to resent more – being called a kid, or the remark that followed it. But he'd said it so drily she decided to let it pass.

'How's it going at uni?' she asked, partly to change the

subject, and partly because she was genuinely curious as to how Troy combined life as a final-year Economics student with that of coven boss-in-waiting.

'All right. It's stuff at home that's the hassle. Mum's tearing her hair out over Candice. Dad reckons this latest detox will straighten her out but . . .' He shrugged. 'He's in denial. When Candy got the fae, she went on a bender that lasted three weeks. It wasn't as if she was celebrating either. She's never wanted to be a witch. Too much like hard work. Anyway, Dad won't even admit she's got a problem, and that makes Mum mad.'

Interesting. Auntie Angel said Kezia's abilities were only average, but that she was a clever manager. She needed to be, for a head-witch directed all fae-based operations in a coven, from hexing banes and crafting talismans to more complex works such as glamours, which disguised a person's appearance, and fascinations, which were used for smuggling and forgery. The big restriction on coven witches was that they didn't use their fae for violence. An ordinary criminal convicted of murder would go to prison. A witch would get the Burning Court.

It was probably more of an arranged marriage than a love match. Kezia had done well for herself; a head-witch was a powerful figure in the coven, and in many outfits was equal to the boss. But coven wives always deferred to their husbands. When she wasn't witchworking, Kezia was at home being the loyal wife and mother. Meanwhile, Charlie gave the orders, met the contacts, made the deals . . . and played away with his string of girlfriends. Was Mrs Morgan content with the bargain she'd made?

'Mum still hopes me or Skye will get the fae,' Troy went on, 'though, as a girl, it's more likely for Skye. It'd only cause trouble for me. The boss should be the front-man; the head-witch, the power behind the throne. You need a division of responsibility. Combine both roles, and life gets complicated.'

'Your gran Lily managed it.'

'Things have changed since her day. Anyhow, Gran was a special case.'

Glory thought of the three blonde sisters in the photograph and smiled in spite of herself. 'That's 'cause she was a Starling girl.'

'Yeah . . . I wonder where I can get one of those?'

She sensed, rather than saw, his eyes on her again. She was certain now that Angeline was right about Charlie Morgan's plans for his bloodline. He and Troy and Kezia had probably already discussed it. Her guts twisted in anger and disgust.

At least they'd reached the turning to Cooper Street. 'Home sweet home,' Troy announced as the car pulled up at the kerb. 'God. I'd forgotten what a dump this place is.'

'Well, it's *my* dump, all right?' Glory felt for the door.

But Troy had taken her by the arm, pulling her back into her seat. His narrow green eyes fixed intently on hers.

If he tries anything on, she thought, *I'll nut him.*

However, it seemed Troy had other things on his mind. 'Listen. I know Dad's asked you to keep an ear to the ground. I also know he's not the easiest guy in the world to deal with. So if you turn up something you're not sure about, you can always run it by me first.'

'Very kind, but I'm sure I'll manage.'

'I hope so,' he said seriously. 'These are tough times, Glory. The Inquisition's upped its game and we're facing a new kind of challenge. Dad won't admit it, but if the Goodwin trial doesn't go our way, the Wednesday Coven will take a major hit.'

'Ain't my problem.'

'Don't kid yourself. The two –'

She opened the door. 'I know, I know. Blood-ties plus business equals A Very Special Relationship.'

'You take care, Glory.'

It wasn't so much a goodbye as a warning.

Auntie Angel's light was on but Glory was in no mood for a debrief. She decided to slip home via Number Seven instead. It was only ten, but she was dog-tired. Her feet ached in their spindly stilettos.

'Hello, girlie.' Nate was sitting and smoking on the steps of Number Eight. 'Had fun with your rich relations, did you?'

'Not really.'

'Should've been here then. Dad got rat-arsed in the Anchor and started raising hell with a couple of punks from the estate. Me and Earl only just managed to drag him off before the filth arrived.'

'Is he OK?'

'I guess. Probably collapsed in a pile of his own puke somewhere. It's not like anyone here gives a toss.'

Nate's mum Lola had lost patience and left around two years ago. She only visited when she needed to cadge money or coven favours. Thinking of this, Glory felt a pang of sympathy. 'Maybe we should get him on one of them detox thingies.' Like Candice Morgan – though she knew better than to mention her to Nate. 'Rehab and such.'

'What's the point?' Nate sucked on his joint broodingly. 'The old man's past it. Your Auntie Harpy is on her last legs too. It's about time they let someone else take over, and kick this place into shape.'

'There's more to running a coven than chasing girls and getting high.'

'Oh? So what's *your* game plan? Sleeping your way to the top? 'Cause I gotta say, you and Troy looked pretty cosy in the car back there.'

'Hex off, Nate.'

Glory jerked open the door of Number Seven. 'One of these days, you're gonna have to decide where your loyalties lie,' he called after her.

In the narrow hallway, the pent-up tensions of the evening finally caught up with her and she started to shake. Her breaths came fast and light. Getting the fae had been all she wanted. Her dearest wish had come true. And yet she'd never felt so trapped.

CHAPTER 11

The four principal departments of the Inquisition were the Witchcrime Directorate, the Witchkind Assimilation Bureau, Intelligence Command (for surveillance) and the Office of the Inquisitorial Court. In spite of its size, everyone knew the Witchcrime Assimilation Bureau was for inquisitors who weren't clever or ambitious enough to work anywhere else. Otherwise, Jonah Branning's steady rise through the bureau ranks from junior clerk to Senior Witch Warden might have attracted more attention.

Hug-a-harpy jokes aside, Jonah liked his work and thought it important. His secret – which he knew was a shameful one – was that as a little kid, he'd actually *wanted* to come down with the Seventh Sense, until his dad caught him trying to make an amulet and gave him a clip round the ear that made him howl. Even now, he sometimes worried that his interest in witchwork wasn't entirely professional. Within the Inquisition the fae was referred to as a 'facility', not an ability, and certainly not a gift. But Jonah hadn't grown out of his wonder at it all the same.

And then came the telephone call late on Monday

evening, and the summons to his department head's office. 'A strictly hush-hush business, this,' his boss warned, just before he dropped the bombshell about the Stearne boy.

Jonah greatly admired the Chief Prosecutor. His courtroom skills were legendary, as were the cases he'd won. The tragic killing of his wife had given him an added authority, and dignity, that even his opponents had to respect. And now the boss was telling Jonah that Ashton Stearne's only child, the heir to twelve generations of inquisition royalty, was a witch. A powerful one too: Type D. He'd been assessed that morning.

This news was followed by the second shock of the evening. 'We'd like you, Jonah, to be his warden.'

Jonah stammered out something about his own youth and inexperience. His boss waved it away.

'I've already discussed it with Ashton. He feels, and I agree, that Lucas would benefit from having a supervisor who is relatively close to his own age. What's more, your record in this department is exemplary. You're shaping up to be a damn fine officer.' The boss nodded impressively. Jonah blushed. 'There's no denying this will be a difficult case. Lucas's age is as unusual as his facilities. Then there's his family's history and position . . .'

The boss explained that Lucas Stearne would be registered in the restricted-access section of the National Witchkind Database. His records would be stored with those of witch-agents in the secret services and other classified or sensitive cases – but under a different name. Until the Goodwin trial was concluded, they couldn't risk his condition being leaked. 'Only four people know about this besides ourselves and the Stearne family. Sir Anthony himself, Commander Saunders from the Witchcrime Directorate, the inquisitor who conducted Lucas's assessment and the guard who provided the security. And for the moment, we intend to keep it that way.'

This was all highly irregular. For one thing, there should have been two inquisitors present at the boy's assessment. Jonah wondered what other bits of protocol had been ignored. 'I'm afraid I, er, don't quite understand –'

'I'm sure you're aware of the importance of the Goodwin case in our fight against coven witchcrime. Nothing can be allowed to undermine Ashton's role as prosecutor or to disrupt the trial. It's therefore been agreed that we should withhold his son's condition from the public until the trial is concluded. At that point, Ashton will announce Lucas's fae along with his resignation, and normal procedures will apply.'

Jonah wasn't entirely reassured. 'Won't the timing look suspicious, sir? We could still be accused of a cover-up.'

The boss shrugged. 'As long as the tribunal secures a conviction for Bradley Goodwin, no one's going to cause trouble in that respect. Sadly, I fear the fall-out from Ashton's departure will be a different matter . . . But you needn't worry about that, Branning. Your only concern is to ensure the Stearne boy matures into a law-abiding and well-adjusted witch.'

'Yes, sir. Of course, sir.'

The boss clapped him on the shoulders. 'Good man. No doubt young Lucas will be very grateful for your support.'

⁂ ⁂ ⁂

Jonah tried to keep these words in mind as he made his way to the Stearne household on Wednesday morning. According to the file, Lucas was intelligent, high-achieving and personable. But the boy would be in a traumatised, potentially unstable state. Jonah would take things gently.

The house was as imposing as he'd expected, with a self-important guard at the gate. He wondered, somewhat apprehensively, if the Chief Prosecutor was at home. Ashton Stearne represented the officer-class elite that Jonah aspired to while slightly mistrusting. Most inquisitors of Jonah's rank and above were privately educated, and had the easy confidence that privilege brings. Jonah did not have the same confidence but he wasn't without ambition. He knew a case like Lucas Stearne's could make or break his career.

This didn't make it any easier to keep his cool when the Chief Prosecutor himself answered the door. Jonah stumbled over his introduction. 'I've heard good things about you, Officer Branning,' the prosecutor cut in, fixing him with that famously steely blue stare. 'Come on through. My son's waiting in the library.'

Lucas Stearne was lounging in an armchair by the fireplace. He half rose when Jonah entered the room, and offered him a languid hand. As he shook it, Jonah glimpsed the cuffs under the boy's shirt. Ten-centimetre, as befitted a Type D. Lucas's eyes flicked over Jonah, taking in the blunt freckled face, the sandy hair and wide jaw. There was a stain on his tie, where he'd spilled some coffee that morning. Lucas looked at the stain and his lip curled.

Jonah lowered himself cautiously on to the spindly

chair that had been set out for him. It was probably an antique. The room was lined with faded prints and leather-bound books with gilt on the spine. A sad-eyed woman gazed down from the mantelpiece.

'My mother,' Lucas informed him. 'She was murdered.'

'Yes. I'm sorry.'

'Are you? It's not as if you knew her . . . Witches make good assassins. Have any of your cases gone on to a life of witchcrime?'

'No.'

He raised a mocking brow. 'Let's hope I won't spoil your record.'

'I'm sure you won't.'

Jonah started on the official script, the one about Responsibilities, Regulations and Rewards. Lucas barely covered his yawns. 'How old are you?' he interrupted.

'I'm twenty-three.'

'And already a Senior Warden . . . Were you on the fast-track scheme, then?'

'No.'

'So you didn't go to university?'

'No.'

'Tunny. I rather thought you hadn't.'

Jonah's mother had fallen ill when he was sixteen. With his dad having to take extra shifts at the car plant, Jonah had cut classes to stay at home to look after her. His mother recovered, his grades did not. He had joined the Witchkind Assimilation Bureau at eighteen, with a couple of AS passes and a letter of recommendation from the school head. But none of this had anything to do with Lucas Stearne.

He leaned forward. 'Well, it's never too early to think about careers. Using your fae in service of the State can be very rewarding. There's the police, of course, and someone with your facilities could even consider WICA. The armed forces are active recruiters too. Then you may have heard the Department of Agriculture is increasingly investing in witchwork-supported crops and livestock, as an alternative to GM –'

'A career in a cowshed. Inspiring stuff.'

'Or there's the health service. Medical advances have reduced the need for witch-healers, but many hospitals still employ them. The fae's often used in the easing of death and childbirth, I understand.'

'You think I'd make a good midwife?'

'Then again,' Jonah pressed on, 'you can choose to remain bridled. A non-practising witch is eligible for most jobs. Except for politics or the church, of course.'

'Or the Inquisition.'

The tone was still mocking, but Jonah could hear the bitterness underneath. He tried a different tack.

'How do those feel?'

He pointed to the iron cuffs. The skin around the edges looked red and sore.

'Fine.'

'And you yourself?'

'I'm fine too.'

'Really? You have grey in your hair.'

Lucas raised a hand to his head, then let it fall. He shrugged.

'Girl trouble. It'll send me to an early grave.'

In spite of the glib answer, it was the only point in their meeting when the boy looked ill at ease, Jonah thought. Shifty even. But the moment passed, and for the rest of Jonah's visit, Lucas was as smoothly insolent as before.

Lucas had been determined to dislike whoever was appointed as his warden and everything about Officer Branning was irritating. Those childish freckles, his patient expression . . . the way the man was so obviously in awe of his father.

Lucas knew he'd been behaving like an arrogant brat. He'd enjoyed it. If the warden had had any guts, he'd have risen to the bait and told him where to go. He was supposed to be the one in charge. He had all the power. But no, he just sat there asking his quiet questions, pretending to be interested and on the level, while they both knew the whole set-up was a farce.

Although he knew his real troubles would start once the Goodwin trial ended, by the end of the first week Lucas was boiling over with boredom and resentment. The prospect of another month under virtual house arrest was unbearable. It didn't help that he wasn't sleeping properly, kept awake by the discomfort of the iron cuffs as much as his thoughts. The custom-made set he'd be getting on Monday would be a better fit; polished smooth, with rounded edges to reduce chafing. But a permanent bridling was hardly something to look forward to.

Clearmont had been informed that Lucas had glandular fever, resulting in a stream of get-well-soon emails and texts from people at school. A lot were from girls: Bea sent a card with 'xxx' by her name. Lucas ignored them all. He also ignored the home-study programme provided by Officer Branning, and spent the long days and nights watching junk TV and reading detective novels. At least he had Kip for company, for the dog had got over his initial reaction to the fae and was back to his usual droolingly devoted self.

He saw little of the rest of the household. His father was mostly in court or his office; Philomena kept away as much as possible. Whenever their paths crossed, she went into the teary-eyed, trembling-lip victim routine. Meanwhile, Marisa was pleasant but watchful. *Busy calculating*, Lucas thought. He'd always suspected she was tougher than she looked. Well, good for her. She'd need to be. They all would.

Sometimes he would sit alone, stroke the thread of silver in his hair, and wonder if he'd ever dare try his fae. He knew the iron around his wrists wasn't enough to imprison it; the two glasses he'd witchworked were still in place, and awaiting his touch. But he had had enough of listening-in. It was true, after all, that eavesdroppers never hear any good of themselves.

On one of his flying visits, Ashton announced he would be home early on Friday and that he was looking forward to dinner with all the family. Lucas wondered if his father meant to hold a conference. Maybe the four of them would finally get the chance to discuss what had happened, and how best to deal with it. United We Stand . . . Or, more likely, it would be an hour of painful small talk and long silences, as everyone avoided the witchworked elephant in the room.

Only ten minutes after coming home, his father had a visitor. It was just after six: Marisa was starting preparations for dinner, Philly was watching television in her room. Lucas was in his room too, brooding by the window. From there, he saw Commander Saunders arrive at the gate.

Josiah Saunders was head of the Witchcrime Directorate, and one of Ashton's fellow High Inquisitors. His department was working alongside the prosecutor's Office of the Inquisitorial Court throughout the Goodwin trial. Lucas knew he was due to retire shortly for reasons of ill-health. He certainly looked unwell: thin and sallow-faced, and moving with the painful stiffness of a far older man.

Curious, Lucas went to wait in the shadows at the head of the stairs, from where he could look down over the hall. The guard must have announced the visitor via the intercom in the study, for Ashton came to the door before the bell could be rung. 'Josiah,' he said. 'This is unexpected.'

'I'm sorry to intrude on your evening. But I was in the neighbourhood, and I'm afraid this can't wait for the office.'

'Sounds serious.'

'Yes.' He lowered his voice. 'The situation we discussed earlier has come to pass.'

Ashton glanced around the hall. 'Come into the study.'

Lucas didn't hesitate for more than a minute. He went straight to the dining room and picked up the witchworked glass. Sweating and shivering, he fought his way past the iron to the faint quiver of his fae. It took all his strength to draw it out and into the talisman, and the thread of sound he picked up was much thinner than before. The colour of the sound was weak, and the effort to make sense of it made his teeth chatter and bones ache. But the longer he listened, the harder it was to tear himself away.

CHAPTER 12

'. . . I suppose it was inevitable,' the Commander was saying. 'Bribery can't be detected by bells or suppressed by bridles. In some ways, fighting witchwork would be simpler. At the moment, we don't even know which of the six tribunal members has been got at. But the tip-off came from a reliable source.'

'Someone within the coven?' Lucas's father asked.

'A police informant. So far, all our attempts to infiltrate the Wednesday Coven have failed.'

Ashton gave an exclamation of disgust. Behind closed eyes, the sound came to Lucas as phlegm-coloured. 'The trial only has another month or so to run. We have no solid evidence that someone on the tribunal has been bribed, and without an informant within the coven we're unlikely to get it. Game over.'

'Not . . . necessarily. There are still options to consider, and choices to make. None of them will be easy.' The Commander cleared his throat. 'In fact, I should warn you that what I'm here to discuss goes above and beyond matters of protocol.'

'Then perhaps you'd better explain things from the beginning.'

'It's rather a long story –'

'I get used to those in court.'

This time the Commander laughed briefly. 'True enough. As you know, although the Inquisition leads the fight against coven activity, in recent years my officers have been working increasingly closely with MI5. It was they who suggested we turn our attention to a small neighbourhood outfit known as Cooper Street. It's a coven in little more than name, but it shares a family connection, as well as business interests, with the Morgan brothers. We even have an asset there, though her resources are limited. She's an elderly lady – practically housebound.'

'I see. You think this place could be a back door into the Wednes-day Coven.'

'Placing a mole within Cooper Street is certainly an easier proposition. And it was to this end that I and my colleagues formed a task force with the agents of WICA. Operation Echo is its name.'

'Not a popular move, I'd imagine.'

'Naturally, there was some hostility to the idea at the start. As you know, I've come to believe that there are circumstances where witchwork can be a useful weapon against witchcrime – fighting fire with fire, as it were. But I have to respect that others feel differently.'

'Silas Paterson among them.'

Colonel Silas Paterson was Saunders's deputy. Lucas saw that his father's voice, neutral in tone, had a greenish-brown taint of dislike.

'Silas will have to accept that times are changing. WICA has proved the doom-mongers wrong so far. With Jack Rawdon at the helm, further expansion of the agency seems inevitable. In fact, it was Rawdon himself who proposed the mole's cover. He suggested that it should be that of somebody young, inexperienced and previously unconnected to the coven world. A schoolboy, in fact.'

'How is this possible? A glamour can transform a person's looks. But isn't using it to alter age highly unreliable?'

'It is. In such cases, the witchwork never holds for long. We would never have attempted the operation if Rawdon hadn't had a specific candidate in mind. Agent Andrew Barnes turned witchkind very young, at the age of eighteen, and was recruited by WICA soon afterwards. Now aged twenty, he is of small stature and slight build, and naturally appears younger than his years. As an added precaution, his features have been disguised by a glamour.'

The Commander sounded perfectly composed. But Lucas was watching the flickering yellow behind his speech. Josiah Saunders was a nervous man.

'So Agent Barnes created the role of "Harry Jukes", a young delinquent from a privileged background. His initial contact with Cooper Street was to purchase drugs; not for personal use, but for dealing to his friends. Since then, he's supplied the coven with information about his neighbours' security arrangements, resulting in several household break-ins, and has assisted in a fake charity fund-raiser . . . Naturally, all those affected will be suitably compensated.'

'Naturally.' Ashton's voice was silver with suspicion.

'And how will your teenage tearaway graduate from school to coven?'

'He'll get the fae, of course.' Lucas sensed a gingery tinge of amusement. 'Next week, phase two of Operation Echo will begin. 'Harry' will arrive at Cooper Street with the news he's turned witchkind. The story is that he's already been expelled from school, and has left home before his fae can be discovered.

'Morale is low at Cooper Street, and so is security. An unregistered witch of Harry's age and background would appear easy to exploit. Why wouldn't they want to take him in, and use him for their own ends? Even among criminals, a boy of sixteen or so is not subject to the same scrutiny as a mature adult. And of course this is only the first stage of the operation. Our coven asset assures us that if our young witch puts his fae to good effect, Charlie Morgan will hear of it and move to recruit him for his own outfit. He's used to taking his pick of underworld talent, and he won't want Cooper Street getting ideas above its station.'

'Sounds plausible. In fact, I don't quite see what the problem –'

'Agent Barnes was involved in the railway accident at Ealing on Monday. He'll be in hospital for the next six weeks at least.'

Ashton let out his breath sharply. 'Could witchwork be involved? After that whistle-wind . . .'

'At present it seems a mechanical fault was to blame. In any case, it was completely by chance our agent was on the train at the time.

'We have reviewed Agent Barnes's fellow officers in

the hope of witchworking one of them to take his place, and none are suitable. Our respective organisations have spent over a year working on this operation. It has taken months of preparation.' There was a pause. 'Agent Barnes's facilities are as remarkable as his youth. Exceptional, in fact. To come across another such person would be such an extraordinary stroke of luck, one might almost call it . . . fate.'

In the following silence, Lucas could feel his heart thudding, fast and loud. It seemed impossible they couldn't hear it in the other room. But the stillness was absolute.

When Ashton did speak, his voice and its colour were ice-white.

'Be very careful what you say next, Josiah.'

'I think you already know what I'm asking.'

'And I think you should stop now before either of us says something we'll regret.'

'Ashton, if you would just consider –'

'He is fifteen years old.'

'Lucas isn't a child. He's a young adult. A Type D witch, whose status has been kept secret and records classified. He is uniquely positioned –'

'I'm sorry, Josiah. This conversation is now at an end.' Then, in a final explosion of feeling, that showed itself as red and black bursts in Lucas's head, 'And don't think I'd react differently if this wasn't about my son. Christ! There have to be some lines we don't cross. Otherwise what the hell do we stand for?'

'All right,' Commander Saunders said gently. 'All right. I understand. I'm sorry to have put you in this position. We'll talk no more of it.'

'Let me show you out.'

In the room next door, Lucas put down the glass with a shaking hand. As he got to his feet, his vision went black, and he thought he was going to pass out.

But this was no time for weakness. He straightened up, wiped his clammy face on his sleeve and smoothed down his hair. It was important to appear controlled. He went into the hallway just as his father and his guest were reaching the door.

'Commander Saunders,' he said. 'I'm Lucas.'

Both men stiffened. The Commander's gaunt face, however, gave nothing away. 'Of course. It's good to see you again.'

'I was listening at the door while you were in the study.' Lucas went on quickly, before he could be interrupted or lose his nerve. 'I know it was wrong. But a lot of decisions are being made for me by other people, and I want to be involved.'

'Stay out of this, Lucas.'

Lucas had never seen his father afraid and in his own fearfulness, he only saw Ashton's anger: hard and cold. He pressed on.

'I can't. I'm sorry. For the first time since all this –' he raised his bridled wrists '– stuff has happened, something makes sense. I'm needed for what, as well as who, I am.' He turned to the Commander again. 'My father and I have to talk. But this isn't over, and I'll hope to meet with you again.'

The Commander smiled tightly. 'I'll look forward to it.'

*   *   *

134

Back in the study, Ashton leaned against the door. His knuckles drummed the wood. Lucas was ready for an outburst, but all he said was, 'You can't have heard anything through this.'

'No. I used witchwork.' It felt good to confess it.

'And how did you get past the bridling?'

'I cheated in the assessment. But that isn't the issue here. We need –'

'Don't you dare tell me what the issue is.' His father was still talking quietly, but the words cracked like a whip. '*You broke the law.* The officer who conducted your assessment did so as a personal favour to me. He could face disciplinary action over this. Meanwhile, I'm going to have to have the house inspected for hostile witchwork committed by *my own son.* You have been criminally irresponsible in every way.'

Somehow, Lucas held his father's gaze. 'I'm sorry. Especially if I've got your colleague into trouble. But I had to find out what was going on. You don't talk to me. Nobody does. You all –' He heard the whine beginning in his voice, swallowed hard, and suppressed it. 'Anyway. That doesn't matter now, because I know what I'm going to do with my life. I want to join WICA.'

Josiah Saunders had done what Jonah Branning could not. He'd shown Lucas his true calling. He couldn't be an inquisitor, but he could still hunt down and punish witch-crime. He could atone for his fae.

'A worthy ambition. I'll look forward to discussing it once you turn eighteen.'

'But it's *now* that counts. If you don't find out who the

Wednesday Coven's been bribing, all your work on the Goodwin trial will be for nothing. It's the most important prosecution of your career. It will be your last prosecution too once my condition is made public. We both know that. And I actually have the chance to help. If you won't let me do this for you, then let me do it for the cause itself.'

'For God's sake, Lucas! This isn't the time to play the hero. The only "cause" you should be furthering is your education.' With visible effort, Ashton softened his tone. 'I can understand why you might not want to return to Clearmont. Perhaps you'd like to spend some time studying abroad. Marisa has been looking into it. There is an institution in –'

Lucas laughed. 'A secret boarding school for teen witches? No thanks.' He tried a different tack. 'Look. I'm only asking for a chance to weigh up my options. If it turns out I'm not right for Commander Saunders's operation, or if I decide I don't want to get involved after all, then fine. But I'd like the opportunity to find out. And who knows what WICA is looking for? I might be able to join a training programme, or get a desk job I could do alongside my studies. That way I won't have to be bridled, and I'd be working towards a proper career.'

'You're a schoolboy, not a spy. And . . .' Ashton cleared his throat, looking Lucas straight in the eye. 'And you are my only child.'

'Dad . . .'

'Listen to me. You have no idea of the risks involved. The dangers, the complexities. *You're not ready for this.*'

'Then I must learn to be. Because I'm not an ordinary

witch; I'm a prodigy. No, Dad – I know it's true. There's a heat and strength inside me that I've never felt before . . . I didn't ask for it, and I don't want it, but that's how it is. And sometimes it feels that if I can't find a way of using it I'll go mad.'

Ashton Stearne studied his son, and it was as if he stood before a stranger.

'Please,' Lucas said quietly. 'You have to let me find my own way.'

CHAPTER 13

In the days following her visit to the Morgans, Glory concentrated on practising witchwork. With her great-aunt to guide her, she was shown how to hex banes that would give someone stomach cramps or buzzing in the ears. She was told the best way to rot food and poison water, and how to staunch a wound and calm a fever just by touch. She practised scrying in bowls of water to see visions of people elsewhere. She learned how to cast a glamour that would change her looks, and a fascination that would bedazzle people into seeing what she wanted them to . . . How to craft talismans and amulets . . . How to make animals do her bidding, find lost objects, whistle up a wind . . .

Auntie Angel couldn't do many of these things herself. But she told Glory how she'd seen others accomplish them, and gave famous examples from history and legend. There were some things Glory didn't want to try, like making poppets to enslave a person's will. Or casting the so-called black banes, the irreversible kind, which could break the heart and blind an eye. But Angeline taught her the principles nonetheless. In fact, the only thing they didn't go into was sky-leaping. It was just too risky to try in London. Auntie Angel promised her a day out in the country, where they'd find a nice deserted wood or empty farm for her to have a go, away from prying eyes.

It was all just as Glory hoped. Her instincts were on the mark, she could do everything she put her mind to, and each new act of witchwork filled her with delight.

Her great-aunt's pleasure in her gifts was almost as great as her own. Sometimes the old lady would get sentimental, though. 'Of course,' she'd say, 'it oughter be your ma teaching you this. Just like my own dear ma should've been there to teach me and the twins.'

Angeline's mother had been imprisoned at the end of the Second World War, and died a year later in an Inquisition prison. The Allies had employed witches in the conflict – it was one of their advantages against the Nazis – but this had been a secret strategy, and the penalties for civilian witches remained harsh. Mrs Starling had been caught using witchwork to try to contact her husband in the navy. In fact, his ship had been torpedoed and he was already drowned, so his wife's death left thirteen-year-old Angeline and ten-year-old Lily and Cora orphans. Cooper Street had been a proper neighbourhood outfit then, and they were looked after by various coven families. But it had been a hard life.

Glory never forgot how lucky she was. Now and again she'd look at her slim, strong wrists and wince at the thought of iron clamps around them. The Inquisition was the bogeyman of her childhood, and she knew all the horror stories. Most began with a midnight raid: fists on the door, boots on the stairs, brutal hands dragging you from your bed. Then came the descent to the underground cells with their vats of ice-water, the iron muzzles that tightened around the head, long needles spiking into the body's softest hollows . . . Of course, the Inquisition pretended things were different now. The secret trials and death squads had been plastered over with glossy leaflets and smiley mission statements. But Glory knew – everyone in the covens knew – that nothing had really changed. Inquisitors still treated the fae as a disease that needed to be burned out of the human race.

Cooper Street's members were used to Glory spending time with her great-aunt but as a precaution many of their sessions were held early in the morning or late at night. Angeline secured the room with iron shutters and protective amulets. Meanwhile, Glory put in enough appearances at school to keep the truant officer off her back. It was an exhausting schedule, especially since the problem of who was ripping off the coven was never far from her mind.

The obvious candidate was Nate. He was surely the only person stupid and cocky enough to try it. His dad, Joe Junior, wouldn't have the nerve – these days, he spent most of his time in the local boozer. Everyone knew he was boss only in name. It was old-timers Patch and Earl who really kept things going. Glory herself had little or no say in coven management. If they'd known she was a witch, it would be a different matter, of course. As it was, she was only on the fringe of things, and to get proof of Nate's deception she'd need to access all areas.

She'd told Angeline about the task Charlie Morgan had set her, but whenever she tried to properly discuss the issue her great-aunt waved it away with a wink and a smile.

'There's more than one way to skin a cat. Just you wait and see.' What could the old lady be up to?

Glory got the answer on Saturday afternoon, a week after turning witchkind. She and Auntie Angel had arranged to practise scrying together. Most of the coven were out, touting fake tickets to the football game at the local stadium, and Number Eight was quiet except for the *bleep . . . bleep . . . bleep-bleep*s of the computer in Patrick's room.

Auntie Angel had recently entrusted Glory with a key to her room. After fifteen minutes of waiting, Glory went in and decided to have a go at scrying by herself. It would be the perfect opportunity to spy on Nate.

Like all witchwork, scrying was time-sensitive. You needed a personal token of your target to do it, but the longer this token had been away from its owner, the less effective it would be. It worked best if your target was in the open air, and within walking distance of your own location. It didn't work at all if the room you were scrying on or in had iron shutters on the windows and an iron panel fixed to the door. Cooper Street's basement was iron-proofed, and so was Auntie Angel's living room. Glory had to fold back the shutters and leave the door open for the duration of her scrying.

Glory had filched Nate's lighter that morning. Now she placed it in a glass bowl full of water and sat on the floor. Humming helped her focus, and so she started a soft tuneless drone, feeling her fae swell with the swirling of the water as she swayed gently from side to side. When she sensed the fae begin to flow through her and into the bowl, she set it down, spat on her forefinger, and began to stir the water in a circular motion, still humming, and keeping the image of Nate in her mind. Minuscule bubbles began to rise from the bottom of the bowl. They were so tiny, and then so numerous, that the water grew silvery with them.

Once it was entirely clouded, Glory stopped stirring and sat back. The bubbles were like pinpricks, or pixels, forming an image on the water's surface. The picture was colourless and cloudy, no more than a few vague blurs, and would only last until the bubbles began to burst. The picture in Glory's head, however, was much clearer. This meant that Nate was relatively nearby. There was no sound unfortunately, but she was just watching Nate join two other people outside a pub when Auntie Angel returned.

'You and me got to talk,' the old lady announced.

'Uh-huh.' Glory was still peering into the bubbles.

'It's about them pyros at the Inquisition.' She locked the door behind her.

'What about 'em?'

'They need our help.'

Glory waited for the joke's punchline. It was then Angeline Starling broke the news that she had become an Inquisition informant, and she was helping them bring a government witch-agent into the coven.

Glory felt as if she'd been kicked in the stomach. She didn't even listen to the last part of whatever her great-aunt was telling her. It was like when she'd got back from dinner at the Morgans', and the walls of Number Seven's hallway had closed around her. She wheezed for breath.

Auntie Angel flicked water at her face. 'This ain't no time for hystericals. Pull yourself together, girl.'

'I don't understand,' she said hoarsely. 'After everything the Inquisition's done – they – you –'

'It's not likely I'd forget,' the old lady retorted. 'The Inquisition murdered my sister and took away my ma. They dragged me into their cells and poked at me with their needles, then ducked me till I half drowned . . . I wouldn't give those bastards so much as the spit from my lips.'

Glory took a steadying breath. 'All right. Then they're blackmailing you. They finally got proof you was witchkind and they –'

'An old crone like me ain't worth the bother. No, I'm more use as an informer than another witch-scalp on their wall. That's why I went to *them*. A poor little old lady, repenting of her sins. Ha! Those prickers couldn't believe their luck.'

'So . . . why . . . why're you doing it?'

'Cause of you.'

'Me?'

'You're the rightful heir to the Wednesday Coven. If your ma hadn't been kicked out of it, she might still be with us, and head-witch – just like Lily wanted.' The old lady sniffed a little, and wiped her eyes. 'It breaks my heart to see how Charlie and his brothers turned out. You'd never know they was Lily Starling's sons. If she and Cora could see what's become of their coven! There's times I think my poor sisters are better off dead.

'Well, never mind that. With fae like yours, you deserve real power; a chance to put things right, make your mark on the world. And the only way that's going to happen is if we bring the Morgans down.'

Glory shook her head dazedly. 'The Wednesday Coven's untouchable. The Inquisition and the police and MI5 ain't never got close.'

'Times are changing. Look at Bradley Goodwin – hauled up before the Inquisition, on trial for his life. And you know why? 'Cause he's got the dirt on every piece of witchery ever ordered by the Morgan clan.' Angeline smiled sourly. 'Now, Bradley's gifted but he ain't martyr material. If he's convicted, he'll squeal. Then, bit by bit, the whole damn empire'll come tumbling down. Which is when you'll step in, my duck, to pick up the pieces.'

Glory looked at the faded newspaper cuttings on the walls. Lily and Cora Starling: outlaws, celebrities, heroines. And Angeline, the sister who stayed in the background, and survived. The protector and schemer, keeper of the flame. All for Glory's sake.

'This witch-agent – Harry, you said? I remember Nate and Jacko talking about him. Some posh git who buys weed and pills off them. They think he's a joke.' It had been Harry too who had provided the tickets to the club-night last Friday.

'Well, he's going to have the last laugh.'

Glory didn't see the funny side. She knew, of course, that some witches worked for the police and other security services. Occasionally, they even assisted the Inquisition. But fighting crime was one thing, fighting fellow witches was another. And here she was being asked to break the same taboo.

Auntie Angel told her about the kind of information Harry Jukes was looking for, and what would bring him to their coven. 'I need you to act matey, show him round. We have to ease suspicion so he gets his invite to the Morgans'. That's the point, remember. Nobody's interested in Cooper Street.'

'You sure about that?'

'It's part of the deal: immunity from prosecution.' Angeline gave a crackly laugh. 'The Inquisition ain't what it was. There's rules and regulations these days. It's the only way they get those police witches and such to work with them. So don't fret – we're covered.'

Covered from the Inquisition's reprisals, maybe. If the truth ever came out, the coven's vengeance would be a different matter.

Glory thought of the Hampstead mansion, its luxuries bought with other people's blood and sweat. She thought of Candice and Skye's sneers; of Troy sizing her up like she came with a price tag; Kezia's slyness and Charlie's menace. She disliked the Morgans and everything they stood for. But she didn't hate them. At least, not enough to risk everything for the chance to bring them down.

'I . . . I don't know, Auntie,' she said at last. 'I'm not sure I can do this. It . . . don't feel right.'

Angeline watched her carefully.

'The law hasn't got anything on the Morgan kids, you know. They'll be OK. Nobody's facing the balefire neither; not even Kez.'

Glory looked away. 'Maybe I'm not as strong as I thought,' she mumbled. 'But however much I want to claim my rights, this ain't how I want to do it. I'm sorry. There's gotta be another way.'

Auntie Angel sighed. 'It's only natural you'd have doubts. I hoped it wouldn't come to this . . . but . . . No.' She gave herself a little shake. 'Hecate help me, I'm going to have to tell it to you straight. You deserve the truth.'

In spite of everything, Glory felt impatience as well as anxiety. She'd already had more than enough revelations for one afternoon. What's more, the old lady spent so long clearing her throat and twisting her hands that Glory came close to shaking the words out of her.

'You know,' Angeline began at last, 'that when the Morgan boys kicked your ma out of the coven, she came to me. My old man Joe – God rot him – had died a while back, but Joe Junior weren't shaping up to much, and we was all at sixes and sevens.'

Glory nodded. She'd heard all this before.

'There were some that said I ought never to have took Edie in. They said it would cause ructions with the Wednesday Coven, if it appeared Edie and me were setting Cooper Street up as a rival. When covens start fighting amongst themselves, lives get lost as well as business.

'But Edie kept a low profile when she came here. Very quiet, she was. After she met your dad, she even patched things up with the Morgans. You came along, and life got even better . . . It was then Edie went back to witchwork. And just as profits were up and the coven was making a name for itself again, Edie went missing.'

'She left,' said Glory in a low voice. 'That's different. We got a note.'

I love you, but it's better if I go. Forgive me . . .

'But there was no notes afterwards, was there?'

'What're you trying to say? Mum spent half her childhood on the run. She knew how to reinvent herself. Could be she's got a new life, another family.'

Auntie Angel looked at her sadly. 'You don't believe that.'

'No.' She bit her lip. 'I s'pose I don't. She'd have sent word, a sign. Something.'

"Course she would. I'm not saying Edie didn't have her troubles, or her low days, but she loved you and your dad more than life itself. And it's easy enough to forge a goodbye note. Ain't it?'

Glory closed her eyes. White tiles, frozen scream, flaming hair. 'You think the Inquisition got to her. It wouldn't have to be official. I've heard the rumours. The secret squads –'

'Somebody got to her, all right. But it weren't the Inquisition.'

'Uncle Charlie,' Glory whispered.

Perhaps part of her had guessed as soon as Edie's name was mentioned. The fact she'd suppressed this knowledge didn't lessen the shock.

'Uncle Charlie,' Angeline agreed. 'Not that he'd have done the deed himself. Giving orders is his speciality. But his brothers Frank and Vince would have been in on it – that's how the three of them worked back then; one for all, all for one.'

Glory pressed her hands, hard, against her eyes. The darkness ached. She pressed harder, as if to blot out the world.

'How did you find out?' she said at last. Her vision was blackness, her voice was dust.

'I had me suspicions from the off. But then a little bird came whispering...A witch had been buried, out in Dunstan Wood. If it hadn't been for the tip-off, I'd never have found the spot – there was no markings, except for a shroud. It . . . well, it contained a strand of your ma's hair.'

An ordinary shroud was a burial garment. A witch's shroud was an amulet used to hide something or someone – to 'bury' them from view. They were sometimes used to deter animals from disturbing a grave, and people from finding it. A rusty, wrenching sob forced itself out of Glory's throat.

'You're my own darling girl.' Angeline's cheeks were wet but her voice was firm. 'I hid the truth from you to keep you safe, but I can't protect you no more. You came of age, Gloriana, when you came into your fae. You came into danger too. Now you know what you're up against. It'll be a dirty fight, and a long war. But losing ain't an option. D'you see?'

Glory nodded. She had choked back the sobs. Her fists and jaw were clenched. 'I'll win or I'll burn. Whatever it takes.'

CHAPTER 14

In Jonah Branning's second interview with Lucas Stearne it was like meeting a different boy. Lucas was courteous, cooperative, frank. 'I know I have a lot to prove after my previous behaviour to you. In fact, I'm embarrassed just thinking about it . . .' An expert performance.

Of course he wanted something. Jonah could sense the impatience behind the charm. He himself was simply a tedious bureaucratic obstacle to be got around. As Lucas's witch warden, his authorisation was required if the boy was to apply for a WICA position. Jonah also knew that his agreement was no more than a formality. He'd been told as such by his boss, who'd had his own instructions.

'Lucas isn't the first young witch to be used in this way, and he won't be the last,' the boss had said, in another of their out-of-hours meetings. 'Juvenile witches can be a valuable asset as well as a potential threat.'

'Valuable to whom, sir?'

'To those in authority, of course. Well, under-age witches aren't like other kids, are they? The fae sets them apart. It hardens them in some ways, makes them vulnerable in others. Far better, then, to take advantage of their facilities while they're young and impressionable, and before they can be lead astray.' The boss smiled. 'We have to keep an open mind on these matters, Branning.'

Sir Anthony Brady, Witchfinder General, had established the policy of limited cooperation with WICA. Yet it remained controversial, especially in the Witchcrime Directorate. Everyone knew that Silas Paterson, the directorate's deputy head, was against it. And Paterson had many supporters.

Some were convinced that all witchwork was an instrument of the Devil. Others were against collaborating with any outside agency, witchkind or not, on the grounds that it undermined the authority of the Inquisition. Those in favour of the policy argued that the Witchcrime Directorate was overstretched. If the Inquisition's priority was fighting witchcrime, shouldn't they be willing to exploit whatever resources were available? Jonah himself had often made this point. However, Lucas Stearne's situation put the nature of such 'exploitation' in a different light.

'I can see how a child spy could be useful,' Jonah conceded. 'But . . . even so . . . if it was *your* child . . . ?'

He'd gone too far. A frown crossed his boss's genial pink features.

'Lucas's father respects, as we all must do, his son's courage and sense of duty.'

So Jonah agreed to process Lucas's application to WICA. He authorised the unbridling too. It turned out that there had been some muddle with Lucas's assessment, and he was actually a Type E witch – even stronger than previously thought. Jonah couldn't understand how the original assessment had gone wrong. There was no information about the mistake in the file. He remembered how Lucas had argued the case for his recruitment, impassioned yet self-possessed, blue eyes ablaze with conviction. Just like his father. This was not necessarily a good thing, Jonah thought. It seemed to him that Lucas had the makings of a formidable witch.

WICA had two internal departments: Unit A, which worked on domestic security, and Unit B, which specialised in foreign intelligence. They shared a centre for work and training. Jonah was going to meet Lucas there early on Monday morning – little more than a week after Lucas had turned witchkind.

Time was short. Lucas was only going to have a week's preparation before joining the coven. Jonah would be supervising him for most of this, and liaising with Lucas's Unit A handler during his period undercover. Ashton Stearne had insisted this would not go beyond the end of the Goodwin trial. But though Lucas didn't say so, Jonah knew that once this period ended he hoped to be taken on by WICA in a permanent role.

Their destination was a converted warehouse in the docklands. Much of the area had been redeveloped into a bright, shiny world of glass, granite and steel, and 'luxury river-view living'. WICA's HQ, however, was a grimy Victorian hulk on the edge of an industrial estate. The sign over the main door read: Avalon Atlantic Plc: International Shipping.

Beyond Avalon Atlantic's shabby foyer, and concealed

by a sliding screen, was the secure entrance to the rest of the building. Jonah, who was meeting Lucas inside, was directed by the fake receptionist through to the real reception. This one was both sleek and functional, and had a bust of John Dee in an alcove behind the switchboard. Dee had been a trusted advisor to Elizabeth I (an alleged witch and so-called 'Fae Queen'), and had set up a secret council of witch-spies to aid her war against Spain. WICA regarded him as their founding father, even though the agency had not been formally established until after the Second World War.

The Inquisition kept a close eye. Witchwork activities were monitored by CCTV, most of the offices and phone lines were wiretapped, and inquisitorial guards had their own station in the building. Jonah had to admit their presence was reassuring. He had never been in a place where so many witches were gathered together at the same time. Lucas, too, looked tense. His manner was distantly polite, like a well-bred guest arriving at a party he's not sure he'll approve of.

Lucas had not come through the main entrance, but via the so-called back door, an underground passageway whose entrance was located at the back of a computer repair shop round the corner. Apart from this and the fake reception, Avalon Atlantic showed little sign of being a centre of espionage. During the course of Lucas and Jonah's tour, they didn't see any computer suites or technical areas, just ordinary offices and a series of small windowless rooms. Most of these were empty except for a table with an object or two upon it. A glass bowl, a tangle of string . . . a feather tied to a finger bone. Jonah found them unsettling. But Lucas looked at them alertly. He must already be making connections, figuring things out.

The tour was given by a witch-agent named Zoey Connor, who – if everything went to plan – would be Lucas's handler. She was in her mid-twenties, small and wiry with a spiky dark crop, her features already marked with lines of decision and responsibility. She was welcoming to Lucas but when her attention turned to Jonah, he felt a distinct chill. He was a little disappointed but not surprised. Witches and inquisitors didn't mix well.

All discussions and activity involving Lucas took place in the few rooms that were free from Inquisition monitoring. These measures were to reduce the chances of his identity, and condition, becoming general knowledge at the Inquisition. Jonah's job was to observe where the cameras, wires and guards could not.

Throughout that long first day, Jonah watched Lucas embark on his training. Every witch worked differently but there were still principles to learn. Lucas and Zoey started by discussing the best ways to use fae in surveillance and defence. No gadgets or weaponry were involved, just a handful of household objects mixed in with more intimate material – an eyelash, a tear, a drop of sweat or blood. Jonah's task was to make a record of each act of witchwork, and observe Lucas's reactions. He needed to pick up on signs of recklessness, or frustration with authority. The other danger to look out for was, in the words of a training manual, 'an unhealthy and obsessive interest and/or pleasure in the practice of fae'.

So far, Lucas's behaviour was exemplary. He was calm

and collected, accomplishing each act efficiently and without any sort of show. Even so, Jonah sensed a suppressed excitement behind his restraint. It was almost as if Lucas wasn't learning something new, but drawing on a primal foreknowledge. Perhaps this knowledge was within all of them, thought Jonah, and most people had simply lost the means of finding it. This was heretical thinking, though, and he pushed the idea away.

At six o'clock, Lucas was told that he'd done enough for one day, and should go home. Jonah had to take a bus back to the office. He needed to write up his report, talk to the boss, and check on his other cases.

After being promoted to Senior Warden, Jonah had moved from his local authority branch to the Inquisition's headquarters. It was an independent enclave known as Outer Temple, near the Inns of Court and the City of London. Witchfinders had established a settlement there in 1401, after the first Act of Parliament against witchwork.

The church of St Cumanus was a rare fifteenth-century survivor. The catacombs below it were even older, but most of the buildings had been rebuilt or modified in the eighteenth and nineteenth centuries. They were set around a series of small courtyards and lawns. Boxed in by tower blocks and high-rise offices, the enclave had a somewhat hunched, narrow look, in spite of its grandeur.

There was a Library, Great Hall, the Inquisitorial Court itself, and head offices for all departments. Since inquisitors relied on technology to counteract witchwork, a complex of high-tech laboratories existed at basement level. There was an interrogation suite and cells too. But life above ground was, as the tour guides liked to point out, modelled on an Oxbridge college, with all the prestige attached. The Burning Courts had long been moved elsewhere.

The area was enclosed by a wall of wrought iron, crowned with bells. Jonah was just approaching the main checkpoint when he heard someone call his name. Lucas's handler, Zoey, was standing a little way down the street.

'Hello,' he said, surprised. 'Are you here for a meeting?'

'No. I wanted to have a word before you left, but got called away. So I took a cab here instead. I've been waiting for you to show.'

'Come on in, then. My office is just over there.'

'I haven't got clearance.'

Jonah glanced through the gates at the patrolling guards in their scarlet and grey. He should have known that even a WICA agent – an agent collaborating with the Witchcrime Directorate on a high-level assignment – would not be allowed in without all sorts of red tape to get through first. Entering the compound was almost as laborious as passing through airport security. Even High Inquisitors had to submit to a fingerprint test and iris-scan on presenting their ID.

'Besides,' Zoey said, 'what I've got to say is off the record. At least out in the street there aren't any bugs.'

A bus trundled noisily past and Jonah drew closer in order to hear her. 'Is there a problem?'

'Damn right there is.' She ran her hands through her spiky crop. 'I want to know what the hell you think you're doing, sending a kid into a coven.'

He realised she had been biting back her anger all day. 'I had concerns,' Jonah said quietly. 'And I did raise them. But this is Lucas's decision. And with his father's connections –'

Zoey gave a snort. 'Oh, sure. There's no network like the Old Boys' Network . . . Look, I like Lucas. He's bright and capable, and as near a prodigy as I've ever met. I'm only a Type C myself. But that's not the point: he's going to be sent into the lion's den undertrained, underprepared and – when push comes to shove – unprotected. Why the hell d'you think he'd volunteer for something like this? To make his dad proud? Or is it some kind of rebellious teen death wish?'

'Lucas is rising to the challenge of his condition, as well as embracing its opportunities.' Jonah despised his words even as he said them. 'He knows he'll always be different. This is his way of dealing with it.'

'You mean he'll always be expendable.'

Jonah tried to speak, but she talked over him. 'Never mind all that guff about civic values, and the Greater Good. That's all we are to you people,' she said bitterly. 'Cannon fodder.'

His encounter with Zoey left Jonah tired and depressed. Light was fading on the Inquisition's mellow stone walls and lofty windows. People were starting to make for home, calling out cheerful farewells as they headed into the London rush hour. As Jonah walked across the small cobbled square in front of the church – Kindle Yard, in times past the scene of countless balefires – his shoulders slumped. He knew he should file a report of what Zoey had said. Recklessness and frustration with authority . . . it was what he had been trained to root out. The trouble was in this instance he respected her for it.

The Witchkind Assimilation Bureau was on the far edge of the enclave, and overshadowed by Intelligence Command's towering surveillance block. Besides Lucas, Jonah was warden for a bridled housewife, a police witch-officer and a biology student. All three presented difficulties. The police officer was facing a malicious accusation of bane-hexing. The student was trying to decide whether to graduate as a bridled biologist, or join the Department of Agriculture's Farming With Fae programme. Meanwhile, the housewife's little girl was being bullied in school for being 'hag-spawn'. Thinking of the mound of paperwork waiting on his desk, Jonah's shoulders slumped some more.

'Hello there, Jonah.'

He looked around. A slim, tall figure was sauntering across the cobbles. It was Gideon Hale, one of the new intake of fast-trackers and already marked as a rising star. He had recently completed a placement in Jonah's department, where he'd been attentive and deferential but Jonah hadn't warmed to him. There had been times when he felt – and suspected he was meant to feel – that Gideon was merely playing along.

'Rumour has it you've been hanging out at Witch-spook Central,' Gideon said. 'Is it as much of a freak show as everyone says?'

Sometimes it seemed as if there was no such thing as

confidential information in the Inquisition. The whole organisation ran on gossip. 'You know I can't comment.'

Gideon tapped the side of his nose in a theatrical manner. 'I understand. It's all strictly hush-hush. But having a witch-agent to warden must be a step up from the bridled grannies and Constable Plods, right?'

'I'd best be getting on,' Jonah said curtly.

'Oh, I'm sorry. I thought you must be going to the meeting too.' Then, when Jonah didn't respond, he nodded in the direction of the church. 'It's the Hammers tonight.'

'They're not really my scene.'

The Hammers was a social club. The name came from a famous fifteenth-century inquisitors' handbook, the *Malleus Maleficarum*, or 'Hammer of the Witches'. Its members met in St Cumanus's crypt to dress up in old-style inquisitorial robes, re-enact famous witch-trials and play drinking games. The membership list read like a roll-call of ancient inquisitorial families: Altham, Balfour, Grindal, Paterson, Hopkins, Hale . . . You had to be invited to join, as Jonah knew Gideon was well aware.

'Ah.' Gideon looked faintly amused. 'Well . . . have a good night, then.'

They were just parting ways when a high and terrible scream shattered the evening quiet. It came from the street outside. Almost simultaneously the iron bells that topped the Inquisition's wall began to ring, a harsh clanging that was loud enough to make the air shudder.

Jonah and Gideon exchanged appalled looks, and hurried towards the gate. There was a bus stop a little way down the road – just a few metres from where he had watched

Zoey get into her taxi. A young woman was staggering away from the stop and towards Outer Temple, plucking at her clothes and crying. Her face was covered in oozing black pustules. She was followed by three or four others, all suffering from the same disfigurement. No sooner had they reached the gate than they stumbled and fell, crawling drunkenly around the pavement and mumbling gibberish.

In a matter of moments, a squad of inquisitorial guards hastened to form a protective ring around the victims. Someone shouted that a team from the medical block were on their way. Ambulance sirens blared in the distance. On the other side of the road, horrified bystanders were huddled together. A small boy wailed. Meanwhile, Kindle Yard filled with inquisitors, murmuring fearfully to each other as the news spread.

'It's witchwork, isn't it?' Gideon stammered. 'I never imagined – not here, not like this . . .'

A witch attack at the gates of the Inquisition! For the first time in Jonah's life he felt the full force of something beyond the usual human fears: the sense of an alien and malignant power, unknowable and implacable. His flesh crawled.

Gideon's eyes glittered feverishly. 'It's a sign from the covens. They must be trying to intimidate us because of the Goodwin trial.'

The medics had arrived, and though it was difficult to see what was happening, it appeared the symptoms of the attack were disappearing as quickly as they had begun. One of the victims was already sitting up and talking.

Jonah and Gideon were joined by more onlookers. A

woman shook her head grimly. 'That whistle-wind in the MP's office was only the start. You know the train that derailed in Ealing last week? Twenty injured, three critically. The investigators thought it was a mechanical fault. Now it turns out the train driver was under a bane. He'd been witchworked into seeing a giant black horse come charging down the track! It's all been coordinated.'

Others were saying the same thing. Fear was giving way to anger, and a new sense of purpose.

Gideon too had regained his self-possession. His face had set. 'If that's true, then everything changes. It's not about control and assimilation any more. This is war.'

Lucas did not learn of the attack at the bus stop – the 'plague of boils' as the tabloids called it – until later that night. After leaving WICA, he went straight home and shut himself in his room with the armful of files that Zoey had given him.

Apart from Zoey, he'd seen little of the other witch-agents, and nothing of the famous Jack Rawdon. He had expected to be met with an over-eager, slightly defensive chumminess, as among people who share some fetish or embarrassing hobby. But the few witches he'd been introduced to had been brisk and professional, no more. Lucas was relieved. He didn't want to feel like he belonged.

Besides, he needed to distance himself from the seething mix of energies and impulses the day's witchwork had woken in him. Tomorrow, he would learn more about Harry Jukes and the part he was going to play in the coven. Tonight, he must order his thoughts, make his preparations.

He began by looking at a family tree of the Morgan and

Starling clans. It was accompanied by reports on members of the Cooper Street Coven. Flipping through the file, he paused when he came to a slightly blurred photograph of a girl. Gloriana Starling Wilde, according to the memo. Fifteen years old. Two cautions for shoplifting, a record of truancy. Risk of turning witchkind: high.

It wasn't surprising. She was the granddaughter of one of the twentieth-century's most infamous witches. What's more, her mother, Edie Wilde nee Starling, was also possibly witchkind, though low-grade. The report stated that this was unproved, since she had never been registered. The Inquisition suspected her of turning witchkind around the age of twenty-three. At the age of twenty-four her daughter was born, and three years after that she went missing, presumed dead. The file said that she was the likely victim of a coven hit, the consequence of feuding with the Morgan brothers over a disputed will. This was why her daughter was collaborating with the Witchcrime Directorate.

Lucas took another look at the girl's strong beaky profile and bright blonde hair. Her ridiculous name made some kind of sense now he'd read Operation Echo's files. Gloriana had been an honorific title for the Fae Queen, Elizabeth I. The Stearnes weren't the only family with grand ambitions for their children.

CHAPTER 15

Glory and Angeline's first meeting with 'Harry Jukes' was scheduled two days before he was due to join the coven. It was a Saturday, and Glory had only known the full story for a week. She remained in turmoil about every aspect of Auntie Angel's revelations but accepted that, for the moment, coming to terms with them was impossible. *I'll think about it all later*, she kept telling herself, suppressing another of those hiccuppy little bursts of hysteria that kept catching her unawares. *Not now. I can't, I mustn't. I'll go mad.*

For events were out of her hands. Angeline had already got in touch with her contact at the Witchcrime Directorate to confirm that her great-niece was on board. Apparently she had insisted from the start that Glory's involvement was essential if Harry was to be accepted into the coven, and from there introduced to the Morgan clan.

So on Saturday afternoon, she and Angeline set off for the WICA safe house where they were to meet Harry Jukes, and be briefed on the task ahead. They told the coven that they were going to try to track down an old forger pal of Angeline's. Both carried an elusion amulet that Glory had made. She'd bought two cheap toy compasses, which she stamped underfoot. Then she knotted her fae into an intricately tangled web of string around the broken compasses, and put them in two small cloth pouches. The tradition was to bury them at a crossroads. Since it wasn't practical to dig up city roads, Glory had fixed them underneath a pavement grating instead. It would take a few hours of pedestrians tramping back and forth over the amulets for the witchwork to set.

Today, she had retrieved the amulets and they were wearing them tucked into their shoes. It was not comfortable but it was effective. If anyone tried to follow them, they would be caught in a web of confusion, unsure of their quarry, and mistaking right for left, north for south. No one could scry on them either. Even so, Angeline favoured a roundabout route on foot and bus. It made for a long journey, especially since she needed several rest stops along the way.

Their final destination was an unremarkable apartment building in an unremarkable residential street. They dismantled their amulets at the end of it, in case they were searched. They weren't of any more use to them anyway – an elusion only lasted as long as a single journey.

Glory's insides were bunching into knots as they turned into the road. The authorities knew Angeline was a witch, but her own status was secret – and at least one inquisitor would be present during their meeting.

'Bear in mind,' Auntie Angel had warned her, 'that we won't see what this Harry Jukes and his witch-friends actually look like. It'll be glamours all round, mark my words.'

Glory and Angeline's appearances were already known to the authorities. But Angeline underwent a physical transformation all the same. She'd left off her curlers last night, was without her usual coral-pink lipstick and rouge, and wore a shawl over a frumpy paisley smock. As they walked along the street, her upright figure slumped and shrank. It wasn't witchwork, just good acting. Glory watched her turn into a doddery crone before her eyes.

The door to flat 9a was opened by a tall, sandy-haired young man with an awkward smile. He introduced himself as Officer Branning. When he went to shake hands with Glory, it took all her nerve not to flinch. He was the first inquisitor she'd ever met. As soon as his back was turned, she wiped her hand on her leggings.

Officer Branning led them into the kitchen-living room. It was a little too clean and bare to feel as if it had ever been lived in. The inquisitor helped Auntie Angel into a seat at the table; Glory couldn't tell if her great-aunt's tremors were a pretence. Her own body clenched in sympathy. She put some gum in her mouth, as she often did when she was nervous. 'Tea? Coffee?' the young man asked, and she nearly gave a spurt of disbelieving laughter.

His pocket beeped and he checked a pager. The officer looked relieved. 'The others are here. I won't be a moment.'

The moment passed too quickly. In seconds, Harry Jukes and his handler were standing in the room.

Glory folded her arms protectively across her chest. No more handshaking for her. She chewed the gum mechanically, trying to soothe herself with the familiar rubbery motion. The boy pulled out a chair opposite her. He looked her up and down with cool interest and she stared boldly back. He had a thatch of dirty-blond hair and a fleshy pink face. The woman who accompanied him was a freckly redhead.

'I'm Harry,' the boy said. 'It's a pleasure to meet you.' The voice: smooth, rich, leisurely. Was that faked too?

'And I'm Anne,' said his companion. 'Anne Jones.' Glory nearly laughed again: the name was so obviously an alias. She'd bet 'Anne' was wearing a glamour too.

It went against every particle of Glory's body and soul to sit at the same table as an inquisitor but this pair must collaborate with the Inquisition on a regular basis. 'Harry' and 'Anne' had clearly been brainwashed into believing all the propaganda crap that said if they gave up their freedom to do the State's dirty work, they'd be given some kind of legitimacy. As if, after suffering centuries of persecution, witchkind still had something to apologise for. As if the fae was a handicap, not a gift!

But she remained curious. Whoever this Harry character really was, he couldn't be older than late teens or early twenties. If he was already a field agent, then he must be a strong witch.

Glory was thankful she wasn't called upon to contribute much to the discussion. Auntie Angel had already explained her task: to help get Harry accepted by the rest of Cooper Street, and to use her family connection to get him introduced to the Morgans. All this was gone through in more detail, along with boring stuff about protocol and procedure and the Chain of Command. Glory nodded from time to time to show she was listening, but was otherwise free to follow her own thoughts.

She paid more attention when Harry talked about how he'd first made contact with the coven, ostensibly to buy drugs, and how from there he'd formed a casual acquaintance with Nate and his crew.

Glory had only heard Nate mention Harry on a couple of occasions, and always in scornful terms. Even so, she suspected Nate was secretly proud of the connection. The Starling Twins used to party with aristocrats and playboys, and it was part of his mobster aspirations to hang out with posh dropouts who ought to know better. The Inquisition and WICA had exploited this. They thought Cooper Street and everyone in it was a soft touch.

Fools, thought Glory. *Just you wait.* The satisfaction must have momentarily shown on her face, for she caught Harry looking at her and frowning a little. His eyes were brown, slightly bloodshot. She stared back until he looked away.

It bugged her, the fact this person could look her in the eye yet keep his own hidden. Like a ghost. Somewhere there must be an amulet that contained the raw material of his illusion. There and then, she decided she would make it her mission to find it. His fae might be strong but she was a Starling girl, a prodigy – one in a million. There was no way he could compete.

The first time Lucas Stearne turned into Harry Jukes was Wednesday evening, three days after joining WICA. Since Agent Barnes remained in hospital, Lucas never saw what his predecessor actually looked like, though he studied his case notes as well as film footage of him in the role of Harry. As part of his cover, Barnes had spent the last month enrolled in a private school in North London, so Lucas also had to familiarise himself with Harry's teachers and classmates. WICA had already assembled various accessories – from an MP3 player loaded with Harry's music to a closet of Harry's clothes.

There was other research too. Harry could be expected to be fairly ignorant of coven life, but Lucas still had to swot up on names, places, faces, business dealings and family history. Getting to grips with all this took up more time than the actual witchwork. There was a lot of this to practise, though he was relieved to learn there wouldn't be time to test his ability to sky-leap. Of all the facilities witchkind had, sky-leaping was the most abnormal.

Crafting a glamour was his hardest task yet. Agent Barnes had originally created Harry's appearance from a computer-generated illustration. Lucas had a photograph to reference instead. Dark blond hair, brown eyes, plump cheeks. Otherwise, his looks were deliberately nondescript.

He began the glamour by drawing two small pictures: one of Harry, one of himself. He had no artistic ability, as the end result proved. It didn't matter. The point was to draw out his fae with each line of the pencil, every stroke of colour and shade, so that the crude image on the paper could channel the strength of the image in his head.

Under Zoey's direction, he placed his self-portrait on a mirror laid flat on the table, then set it alight. As the picture turned to ash, his reflection in the mirror became faint and blurred, as if his own features were dissolving. Zoey had already warned him of this: for onlookers, it was as if he'd suddenly gone out of focus. Jonah, who was watching from a corner, looked a little green.

Ignoring his own queasiness, Lucas stirred a wisp of fair hair, a tear from a brown eye and a sliver of fingernail into the ash. He didn't know where any of this had come from and he didn't ask. He was concentrating on the mental image of Harry Jukes he'd taken from the film footage and photograph. He spat on the ash mixture, working the fae into it through his fingertips, and using the mirror as a work-board.

Finally, he smeared the ash-paste on to his drawing of Harry – a glorified stickman, with small brown eyes, a round pink face and scribbly yellow hair. As he folded the grimy paper into a sachet about the size of teabag, the mistiness of his reflection began to clear. And after he'd squeezed it hard between his palms, whispering the name of Harry Jukes, the mirror showed him a face to match.

Zoey nodded. 'Nice work. Your nose is too blobby, though, and you forgot to make your eyebrows match your hair.'

Tentatively, Lucas touched Harry's nose. It felt as straight as usual. The contours of his face felt exactly as he remembered, yet the mirror showed his hands moving over the shape of another boy's cheekbones and chin. He could still feel the coarse grey streak he'd put in his hair on the day of his assessment. But when he pulled out a strand – using Harry's big soft hands – it looked blondish, and was longer than it should have been.

'Nothing's physically changed,' Zoey reassured him.

'You're still there; the glamour's just a veil you hide behind. That's why your identity can be exposed by biometric tests, though the technology for this isn't yet fail-safe. We'll create false records for your fingerprints and so on as a precaution.'

There was a knock at the door. It was Jack Rawdon. 'Very impressive,' he said. 'I couldn't have done it better myself.'

He came over to shake hands. 'We're delighted to have you on the team, Lucas. I've always had a lot of respect for your father, and I'm sure your work here will do him proud. After all, there are many ways to serve your country. My own path in life has taken some unexpected turns, but I don't regret any of them. I hope you'll come to feel the same.'

Though not a large man, Rawdon's presence filled the room. Even in a business suit he managed to look rugged. The grizzled hair and square jaw, the frank and manly gaze . . . Lucas was starting to see why Rawdon was the poster-boy for high-profile witchkind. He could almost have been one of the models in those hideous *Living With Fae* brochures.

'I'm glad you two finally got to meet,' Zoey said to Lucas after Rawdon had left. 'Jack's been closely involved in this operation from the start. He and Agent Barnes pretty much created Harry Jukes together.'

'You think he ever misses being a proper spy – out in the field, I mean?'

'Right now, Jack knows the greatest challenge is in the boardroom. It's still early days for this organisation, and we need a leader that the public can trust.' She glanced quickly at Jonah. 'There's a hell of a lot to prove, and a lot of people wanting to see us fail.'

In which case, thought Lucas, maybe Rawdon should cut back the press appearances and photo calls. His frequent proclamations that witchwork was the best answer to witch-crime might raise his and WICA's profile, but they raised hackles too.

He turned his attention back to the glamour. 'All right. How do I get rid of Harry?'

In answer, Zoey took a lighter and held it to the paper and ash amulet. As the little sachet burned, the air surround-ing Lucas rippled and blurred. In seconds, his reflection was his own again.

'See? Easy. The time you spend with the amulet close to your skin extends the life of the illusion. It's a bit like charg-ing a battery. So if you sleep with the amulet for eight hours, you can go without wearing it for another eight the next day, and still keep the glamour. We'll show you ways to hide it too. Andrew's was small enough to tuck in the band of his watch.'

By the time Lucas went to meet Glory and Angeline, he was much more at ease in his second skin. He could craft Harry's glamour in under fifteen minutes, and get the perfect image each time. Zoey also used a glamour for undercover work, but even though she'd had much more practice than Lucas, it took her considerably longer to complete. It left her tired and dizzy too.

'OK?' she asked as they stood outside flat 9a, waiting for Jonah to let them in. Lucas nodded. It was ironic, but disguised as another person – a person who didn't exist – he was starting to feel more like his old self. Maybe this sense of control was as much an illusion as his appearance, but he was determined to make the most of it.

They entered the kitchen-living room, Lucas using Harry's slouchy, rolling walk. There was a guard stationed in a corner and two people at the table, an elderly woman and a teenage girl. Lucas sat down in front of the girl.

Glory Wilde was pretty much as he expected. Too much make-up, badly dyed hair scraped back in a ponytail, a large and sulky mouth. She was chewing gum loudly, and as he pulled out his chair, folded her arms in an aggressive sort of way across her chest.

Lucas was more interested in Angeline. Here was a witch who'd successfully evaded registration all her life, but was now voluntarily cooperating with the law. Maybe the Inquisition's outreach programme was more successful than it was given credit for.

He already knew about Angeline's sisters. Everyone did. The Starling Twins had clearly had star quality, even though it was of a criminal sort. This hardly justified some people's attempts to rehabilitate them as folk-heroines, but it was still kind of sad to see what remained of their legend: a decrepit old lady and a hard-faced chav.

As the meeting wore on, he found that there was something naggingly familiar about Glory, and it wasn't just because he'd already seen her photograph. At one point she turned her head towards Jonah so that her hooped earrings swung, and he realised she was the same girl who'd shouted at him and Tom the day of the Inquisition's careers talk. It had been something about frogs. For a moment, her raucous laughter echoed in his ears . . . But she'd caught him scrutinising her, and now her glare had daggers in it. She didn't look stupid, at least. Lucas supposed that was a good thing.

CHAPTER 16

On Sunday, his last evening at home, Lucas attended a lecture at the Athenaeum Club. He had been off school for two weeks now, and since Clearmont had broken up for the Easter holiday on Friday, the official story was that he was going abroad to recuperate from his recent illness. In the meantime, his father decided it would be a good idea for Lucas to show up at a public event, just in case there were rumours of something amiss. For this one night, they would pretend that it was business as usual.

There was an additional reason for Lucas to attend. The subject of tonight's lecture was 'International Witchcrime: Causes and Consequences', and there would be a strong showing from the Inquisition. Two of the tribunal members suspected of being bribed by the Wednesday Coven were expected to attend. The event would provide a good opportunity for Lucas to observe them.

Besides, anything was better than having a condemned man's last meal at home. Philomena had been told that Lucas was assisting with a high-level government research project, and had been made to sign a confidentiality agreement regarding his fae. Her air of martyrdom hung over the house like a cloud. Marisa, on the other hand, had cheered up considerably. Lucas's stint at WICA was the ideal way to sweep her stepson's embarrassing condition under the carpet.

His father was resigned but not reconciled to the situation. He had not asked Lucas anything about his training beyond polite and general enquiries to which Lucas gave polite and general answers. They spent the taxi ride to the event making the smallest of small talk.

Lucas approached the row of iron bells over the club's door hoping he didn't look as furtive as he felt. When he saw Jonah waiting on the other side, this awkwardness was replaced by annoyance. He had not changed his original evaluation of the man. A well-meaning plodder, but a plodder all the same.

Thankfully, Jonah was only there to keep an eye on his charge, not play chaperone. There was a drinks reception before the lecture, and the well-heeled crowd in the ante-room had a sociable buzz. Ashton was immediately taken to one side by a journalist friend, leaving Lucas free to survey the gathering. So far, only one of the two tribunal members he was supposed to be observing, Max Holland, had turned up.

Max Holland was a criminal barrister who had lately gone through a costly divorce. The other suspect, Ruth Mackenzie, was a senior civil servant whose husband's business had recently been saved from bankruptcy. Mr Holland looked prim and prosperous, and was accompanied by his second wife – and her display of diamonds. Perhaps they had been bought with coven cash.

Lucas decided to move a little closer. But his next step brought him face to face with the last person in the world he wanted to see. Gideon Hale was standing in front of him, a very pretty brunette on his arm.

'Good to see you up and about, Stearne. I heard you were ill – you certainly looked a bit off at that party the other week. And if you don't mind me saying so, you're still a little washed-out.'

'I thought I'd try the pale-and-interesting look.'

'Well, I should've known nothing would keep you away from tonight.' Gideon turned to his companion. 'Other kids dream of being footballers or pop stars when they grow up. Lucas only wants to chase witches.'

The girl gave a bray of laughter, and reached for a drink from a passing waiter. In doing so, she jostled the person behind her, who turned around. It was Jonah.

'Now *here's* someone I didn't expect to see. Unless, of course, you're here on official escort duty.' Gideon gave Jonah a conspiratorial wink.

'Why would a witch want to attend an event like this?' asked Lucas, a little too quickly.

'There's one over there.' The girl pointed.

A woman in a low-cut dress was standing by the side of a much older man. She had a thin iron collar around her throat. Lucas had never seen anyone bridled in such a way. She was, he realised, very lovely, with her swoop of bronze hair and violet eyes. There was something familiar about her companion, but Lucas couldn't place him. He was squat and stooped, with a bald freckled dome of a head, and small pouchy eyes.

'That's Lord and Lady Merle,' said Jonah respectfully. 'He's some kind of media tycoon. I think she was a model, before getting the fae.'

Lucas knew about Lord Godfrey Merle. He was the founder, chairman and chief executive officer of the Cardex News Group. Marisa had been on one of the same fundraising committees as his wife. The charity was in aid of sick children – he thought he remembered something about Lady Merle having a disabled daughter.

'What an odd way of wearing a bridle,' the girl observed. 'Ugh. If it was me, I'd do anything to cover it up.'

'Maybe she's not ashamed of what she is,' said Jonah quietly.

'Well, it was brave of her husband to take her on.' The girl didn't bother to lower her voice. 'Mind you, an old man like that was probably all she could get.'

To Lucas's embarrassment, Lady Merle looked over. She didn't seem to have heard for she gave them a sweet, rather vacant smile. Her pink silk dress was a touch over the top for the occasion, and its low neckline meant the metal of the bridle showed up dramatically on the white skin of her neck. It must be uncomfortable. Did she wear it there as a mark of shame, or a brand of courage? Either way, the sight disturbed him.

Conversation turned to the recent witch-attack outside the Inquisition. Gideon and Jonah had been eye-witnesses, and soon the other guests were asking for their account. Even Lord and Lady Merle were drawn to the discussion. There were reports of reprisals too. A bridled witch who owned a newsagent's had been doused with petrol by a gang of teenagers and set alight. Dreadful, shocking, everyone agreed. And yet . . . one could almost . . . well, it was only natural that people were angry. Britain had always been remarkably tolerant of witches. Yes, indeed: the witchkind community should remember how lucky they were.

Lucas was surprised to find that Lady Merle was one of the most outspoken on the subject. She had a breathy, girlish voice, and a way of widening her eyes when she spoke that made her seem both flighty and fragile. 'Oh, it so upsets me when people say that bridling is a repression. Why can't they understand that my iron makes me feel *safe*? One day we might find a way of curing the fae, but for the moment, I'm just grateful the condition is manageable.'

'Decorative, even,' said her husband, running a thick finger along her collar and then, teasingly, around her throat.

'It's not as if you're suited to a witch-career, Serena,' somebody said with a laugh. 'Much as we'd like to see you in a police-witch's uniform.'

'Or army gear,' said somebody else. 'There's always the Marines.'

Lord Merle smiled. 'Serena knows her limits – don't you, darling?'

His wife hugged his arm and giggled. Her violet eyes were glassy. Lucas wondered if she was quite all there.

It was a relief to be called into the lecture hall. He settled down in his seat and tried to look attentive, even though the speaker, an American academic from the Salem Institute of Witchkind Studies, was not a particularly inspiring one. The only point of real interest was when Silas Paterson came on stage to say thank you at the end. So this was Josiah Saunders's second-in-command at the Witchcrime Directorate. Lucas thought he looked intelligent, if forbidding; a tall, silvery man with a dark stare and a stately manner.

Afterwards the audience was invited to ask questions or comment.

Gideon got to his feet.

'Religion has always been opposed to witchwork, and used to be our first defence against it. Does this mean that people in the secular West feel less of a moral imperative to limit witchwork than those in faith-based societies?'

'Hrm, hmm. An interesting question,' said the academic. 'Perhaps someone in the audience would like to respond –'

Before he could think better of it, Lucas was standing up too. 'You can use religion to justify whatever you want it to,' he said. 'Take Islam – the Koran forbids witchwork, yet some clerics argue that it's legitimate in some circumstances. Witches are often condemned in the Bible, but King Saul goes to the Witch of Endor for help, and Moses performs witchwork-like miracles before the Pharaoh. So we need to deal with the world's witchkind on a rational basis, not through faith or superstition.'

'By way of UN Declaration 192, you mean?' There was a sneer in Gideon's voice. 'Calling for the global decriminalisation of non-practising witches might be "rational", but it achieves nothing.'

'It would be more effective if people actually understood

what it was about,' Lucas replied. 'Or managed to get its name right. I assume it's *Resolution* 192 you're referring to.'

Somebody laughed. Gideon's face tightened with anger as the audience rustled and hummed.

The academic looked uncomfortable. 'Thank you both for your ... er ... thought-provoking contributions,' he said. 'I only wish we had the time to address them further. Now, if anyone else has a question –?'

Lucas sat back in his seat. He was almost as pleased with himself as when he'd first crafted the glamour.

His satisfaction didn't last. Leaving the lecture hall, he wasn't able to ignore the frown on Jonah's face. And during the ride home, his father was more than usually quiet. 'You shouldn't have tried to argue with Gideon,' he said at last. 'You need to avoid anything that might draw attention to yourself – attention from inquisitors in particular. And Gideon Hale is going to go far.'

Lucas felt his heart twist. His father was only trying to protect him. But at the end of the day, Gideon was the kind of son Ashton Stearne should have had, and they both knew it. *Thank God I'm leaving for the coven,* he thought. *It will be better for both of us once I'm gone.*

Harry Jukes made contact with Nate on Monday morning. Nate listened to a voicemail, frowned, then took his phone into the hall to listen to it again. Glory was careful not to look too interested when he came back and stood in the doorway to the lounge, chewing his lip.

'What's up?' Jacko asked. He and Chunk, with Glory's help, were packing up fake Chanel No. 5 bottles to sell online. The digitally-printed labels looked just like the original, and the perfume smelled pretty good as far as Glory could tell, though when she tried a spritz it gave her a rash.

'A call from Lord Snooty. Y'know – the kid who deals our party-pills. And gave us the tip-off for the Dalton Street job.'

'Has he got us another break-in?'

'Dunno. His message's all garbled. I'll give him a bell.'

Nate went outside to make the call. He came back looking troubled. After pacing around a bit, he went to talk to Auntie Angel. Half an hour later, and still frowning, he went out. Glory watched him go down the road, but couldn't quite work out if he turned right or left at the end of it. He must have asked the old lady to make him an elusion. Forty minutes later, he phoned Angeline, and she left the house too.

The two of them came back from their rendezvous with Harry mid-afternoon. This time, Nate had a swagger in his step. Earl, Patch and the boys were summoned to a conference in the basement stronghold. Auntie Angel might have insisted that Glory was included, but on this occasion she wasn't told a thing. Nate shot her a triumphant look as he and the others trooped down the stairs.

Glory went to sit on Number Seven's front steps. Several of the fake perfume bottles had faulty caps, leaking their sickly contents into the lounge, and she needed some air. There were traces of vomit on the pavement below. Joe Junior, presumably. As the coven's so-called boss, he should be leading the meeting to discuss Harry Jukes; instead, he was sleeping off his hangover. Nate probably reckoned that if he recruited a witch for the coven, he'd get to be boss for real.

Glory scowled. Sooner or later, Nate would mess up big time, and the others would see him for the flash prat he was. Then Nate would have to be put in his place. But that was her problem – not the Inquisition's or the police's or WICA's. Auntie Angel was adamant she'd fixed things up so that Cooper Street had immunity from whatever doom was heading the Morgan brothers' way. Glory wasn't entirely convinced. It wasn't just her own safety she had to worry about. Nate and the rest were her responsibility too.

Someone came out of the door and sat on the step beside her. It was her dad.

'Where is everyone?'

'Basement conference. I weren't invited.'

'Ah. Would you want to be?'

''Course. I'm a member of this outfit, ain't I? I shouldn't be hanging round like a spare part. I need to *do* stuff.'

Patrick stared down at his threadbare slippers. His big toe was poking out and he wiggled it reflectively.

'Yes. You're like your mum in that way.'

Her heart leapt. Glory had decided long ago to stop asking Patrick questions about Edie, because she saw how much it hurt him. Most of her stories came from Angeline. Now she couldn't stop herself. 'Am I? For real?'

'Edie was like no one I've ever known.' Patrick was still gazing at his feet. 'You're brave like her, and smart. Restless too. But your mum was a very private person. She'd been hurt, you see, in her past. It made her strong in some ways, fragile in others. I – I tried to look after her. But that wasn't enough.'

There was nothing Patrick could have done to save Edie. As soon as Charlie Morgan had her in his sights, that was that. Soon Glory would have to tell her father the true story. It was why she'd been avoiding him over the last few days – the prospect was too wretched to contemplate. Now, however, she wondered if he might find the news a relief. Closure.

'I know how important becoming a, er, witch is to you,' he said hesitantly. 'And I hope you get your wish. But it's a lot . . . a lot to deal with. The pressure and so on. I think your mum . . . well, she found it tough.'

'I'll cross that bridge when I come to it. *If* I come to it.' Glory tried to smile, feeling the weight of secrets inside her, an indigestible lump. 'I just have to make sure I'm prepared.'

'Prepared . . . yes . . .' Patrick nodded slowly. 'That reminds me – Charlie phoned. He wanted to know how you were getting on. Some research project, he said.'

Balefire and blast him. Phoning her dad was a special kind of warning. A pointed reminder of who called the shots.

It had been a long time since Glory had taken a problem to Patrick, but sitting side by side on the steps having a proper conversation for once, she felt the urge to confide in him. 'Frank had a look at our books,' she said. 'He told Charlie that someone in Cooper Street's on the fiddle.'

'So Charlie asked you to investigate?'

'Yeah. I'm pretty sure Nate's to blame, but I need to prove it.'

'Hmm.' He was quiet for an infuriatingly long time. Then: 'It wasn't Nate. It was Patch.'

Glory gawped at him.

'His kid brother has a gambling problem,' Patrick continued placidly. 'Owes serious cash to some serious people. Patch said he'd help. Times past, he could've gone to Joe and asked for an advance. In this case, it seemed easier to sort things himself. So he siphoned off some cash from the Bishop's Green depot job. It was only meant to be short-term, but when a debt someone else owed him didn't come good, he panicked. That's when he came to me: asked if I could fix the numbers, buy him some time. He's been paying the money back in instalments. I should've known Frank would spot it.'

'Damn right. You gone soft in the head or what?' Glory got to her feet. She was more worried than angry. She liked Patch. He used to perform card tricks at her birthday parties when she was a kid, and only last week had nicked a stash of glossy magazines for her. With effort, she relaxed her tone. 'Never mind. I'll phone Charlie myself and sort it out.'

Patrick scratched his unshaven chin. 'Um, maybe I should make the call,' he said uncertainly. 'Or Angeline. You should be out with your friends and enjoying yourself. Not worrying about coven business.'

'Somebody's got to.'

He looked at her with unfamiliar seriousness. 'I know you want to find a purpose, Glory, and something to work for. But I don't think it should be this place.'

'Why not?'

'Oh . . . well . . .' Patrick shrugged and blinked, his

moment of authority already fading. 'Nothing really changes here, does it? Same old, same old. It's too late for us. It could be different for you.'

No, *it's too late for me as well,* thought Glory. *I've agreed to bring a government spy into our home.* Whatever happened afterwards, she knew nothing in their lives would be the same.

Awkwardly, she bent down and kissed her dad's bald spot. 'I know what I'm doing,' she said.

CHAPTER 17

Lucas didn't arrive at the coven until nearly ten on Monday night. The walk from the tube took him past smart Victorian terraces and yuppie wine bars, but the closer he got to the Rockwood Estate, the more run-down the buildings and people became. At the turning to Cooper Street, two skin-head hulks on bikes that were too small for them drunkenly circled the road.

For a moment, he couldn't think what he was doing here. How had he got into this? It was impossible, absurd. Then he looked into a car's cracked wing-mirror and saw Harry in the glass. Oddly, it steadied him. He was playing a part. He was wearing a costume, not clothes: loose layers over baggy jeans, as sloppy-looking as Harry himself. Whatever he did, whatever happened, was Harry's problem. Lucas Stearne didn't exist in this kind of world.

The lights were on at Number Seven, and music thumping into the street. Lucas knew if he hesitated for any longer he might never go through with it. He pressed the bell.

Nate Braddock let him in. A tight white vest set off his

sun-bed tan and pumped torso. His hair was slicked back, his grin cocky, as they clasped hands in the hall. 'Er . . . all right?' said Lucas weakly. In his meeting with Nate and Angeline that afternoon, he'd had a script to follow. Adrenalin carried him through. But then he'd been in a public space, with Zoey close by. From here on, he was on his own.

The hallway was stacked with all kinds of stuff – crates of booze, shoeboxes, electronic equipment that looked expensive, and cutlery sets that did not. Before he knew it, Nate was leading him into a large room filled with people. Huge speakers pounded out drum and bass, shaking the door, the floor and the windows in their frames.

'Glory!' snapped Nate. 'Fetch Auntie A.'

The girl glowered – she did a lot of glowering, Lucas remembered – but did as she was told. Nate indicated Lucas should take her seat.

He sat down, sweating slightly. The room was stuffy and smelled of unwashed clothes and hash, with a weird floral undertone. Like somebody had been spraying a particularly sickly air-freshener. Most of the space was taken up with a greasy-looking leather suite, and the largest TV and stereo Lucas had ever seen. A grizzled black man handed him a beer.

Earl, Lucas thought, trying to match the faces to the photos in his case file. Earl was sitting by Patch, who was thickset and acne-scarred. There were two younger guys, one with a long, pimply face, the other darker, with a tattoo of a snake on his arm. They must be Chunk and Jacko, and Harry – when played by Agent Barnes – had met them briefly before. Lucas returned their nods of greeting. A middle-aged man, who in spite of his sagging jowls had a look of Nate about him, was propped up in a corner.

Nobody said anything while they waited. They just drank, smoked and stared. The music was only switched off when Glory and Angeline returned. Lucas was interested to see that the old lady didn't look as decrepit as before. Her wrinkly face was made up with childishly bright cosmetics, like a doll's.

She pointed at Nate. 'You checked him for the dubyas?' Her voice was firmer too.

The three Ws were witchwork, weapons and wires. Earl patted Lucas down and searched his clothes while Nate went through his sports bag. Although Lucas was expecting this, he still tensed up. The glamour's amulet was concealed in the strap of his cheap watch. But he had one more ready-made, hidden in the false base of a deodorant can.

The bag didn't contain much, since Harry was supposed to have left home in a hurry. Nate was thorough; squeezing out some toothpaste and uncapping the deodorant. Lucas held his breath. However, Nate soon moved on to more interesting objects – like the MP3 player that Earl had found.

'The latest model. Sweet,' Nate said, transferring it to his own pocket. Then he took out a switchblade and slit the bag's lining. It didn't take him long to pull out the grubby bundle of banknotes that had been hidden there.

'It's all I have,' Lucas said, trying to sound both indignant and dismayed.

'There's over three hundred quid here . . . You made this from dealing our pills, I'll bet.'

'I've sent business your way too, remember.'

'Well, bed 'n' board here don't come cheap. We'll take this as down-payment.' Nate set the wad of cash to one side. Harry's keyring was also confiscated, and passed to Angeline. 'A little something for your scrying-bowl, Auntie.'

'You're going to *spy* on me?'

'Auntie'll want to see how you're settling in . . . and what you get up to when we're not around.' Nate pointed the blade of his knife at his chest, only half jokingly. 'So mind you stay on the straight and narrow.'

'All right,' said Angeline, rapping her knuckles on the beaten-up coffee table. 'Let's get to the issue at hand. Everyone here knows who Harry is by now, and what he's about –'

'I'd still like to hear it from the horse's mouth,' Glory interrupted. She looked at Lucas unpleasantly. 'Go on. Tell us why you're here.'

'Because I'm witchkind, I'm unregistered, and I want to keep it that way.' Pause. 'And if I'm going to escape the prickers, I'll need help.'

'So you, what, just upped and left home without a word?'

'There was a note. I said I was going travelling. My sister'll be relieved to get rid of me. She's an uptight bitch and her husband's worse – they had to take me in after Dad joined his new family in the States. Mum ran off years back. I've been causing them hassle ever since.'

Did it sound too rehearsed? He assumed the coven would have already done the basic background checks. WICA hadn't taken any chances: there was even an agent posing as Harry's sister at an address in Fulham.

'I don' like it,' mumbled a voice from the corner. It was Joe Junior, the so-called boss. He belched. 'Another bloody kid who doesn't know his bootsh from his backshide.'

'Don't you worry, Dad.' Nate shot a sly look at Glory. 'This one can pay his way.'

Angeline leaned forward. 'Harry me boy, it's time the others saw what you've got. Go on – show 'em what you showed me.'

Lucas drew out from his pocket some blades of grass and a twig that had gone unnoticed during Earl's rummaging. Licking the grass, he twined it round the twig, and rubbed the twig between his hands so it twisted back and forth. He began to whistle tunelessly, funnelling his fae out with his breath. First it stirred the loose ends of grass, then sent the faintest breeze drifting across the room. The longer he whistled, the stronger the breeze, until both grass and twig were bending like a tree in the gale. Suddenly, a miniature whirlwind whipped through the room, catching up cigarette ash and bottle tops, and blowing Glory's bright hair around her head. It was a watered-down version of the storm that had wreaked such havoc on the MP's office.

His audience was enthralled. Patch laughed delightedly. Nate looked as smug as if he'd done it himself. The only people who didn't seem impressed were Joe, drinking in the corner, and Glory. She smoothed down her hair with a grimace of annoyance. Once Lucas had got his breath back, everyone looked to Angeline. Regally, she rose to address the room.

'Harry's come to us 'cause he's got nowhere else to go. He won't be the first nor the last. A witch is honour bound to help their kind because fae runs thicker than blood, quicker'n water. That's the rule my sisters and I lived by.

'He needs our help, yes, but that don't mean we're going to get nothing in return. I'm old and I'm tired, and the sooner I start training up a successor, the better for all of us. It's witchwork what raises Cooper Street up, and sets us apart. And though these are hard times, it's witchwork what'll pull us through.'

She turned to Lucas. 'I'll teach you what I can, but it's not just me you'll be learning from. There's a lot of experience in this room, not to say talent. You stay here, you abide by our rules and our way of doing things, and we'll see you right.'

It was quite a performance. When it came to his own response, however, Lucas didn't think Harry was the eloquent type. 'I'll, er, do my best,' he mumbled. 'Thanks very much.'

'Harpies,' slurred Joe. 'You're all the shame. Think you're better'n rest of ush . . . more trouble'n you're worth . . .'

Nobody paid him any attention. Their eyes were fixed on Angeline, who'd taken a cut-out paper doll and a needle out of her handbag. Solemnly, she passed them to Nate, who jabbed the needle into his thumb and smeared the blood on the doll. Everyone did so – even Joe eventually.

Lucas was last. Angeline placed the bloodstained paper doll on his palm and told him his lines.

'I swear loyalty to this coven and everyone in it . . .'

As he spoke, Angeline rubbed a witchworked-twist of paper between her thumbs. It was a similar technique to the one Lucas had used in his witchkind assessment, but left the old lady huffing and puffing with effort.

'. . . their blood is my blood, their bond is mine . . .'

The doll caught alight. Lucas winced, but managed to hold his hand steady.

'So may my flesh burn if I fail to keep my oath – *ah* –'

The little doll flared briefly and crumbled away. His palm was tingling but unscorched.

The men grinned and slapped each other on the back. Except for Joe, who merely belched. *Dumb hoods*, thought Lucas, as he dusted off his hands.

Then he met Glory's sardonic gaze. Superstition tugged at him. For a moment, it felt as if he really had summoned a curse.

Once Angeline left, the music was turned up again, more beer fetched from the fridge, and the older men began to play cards. Jacko went out for food. He came back with chips and a trio of slutty-looking girls, who proceeded to drape themselves over him, Nate and Chunk. 'Meet Prince Harry,' said Nate. 'He'll be helping us out for a while.'

The girls screeched with laughter. 'I'll sit on his throne any day,' cackled the fattest one.

Lucas smiled politely. It was a relief when Angeline reappeared. 'Our new recruit's dead on his feet,' she announced, before dropping an armful of sheets on Glory's lap. 'Time to show him to the penthouse. Go on – off you trot.'

Glory got up with a flounce. Lucas picked up his bag and followed her into the hall.

'So what's your role in this set-up?' he asked, trying to lighten the mood. 'Housekeeping?'

She thrust the bedding into his chest. 'Pest control.'

They climbed the narrow stairs up to the top of the house. What Lucas could see of the rest of the building was dark and ramshackle, and the attic was no different. It was furnished with a mattress, a sink and a stack of broken chairs. From somewhere outside, a dog howled.

'This'll be yours for as long as you're here,' Glory told him. 'The toilet and shower are back on the ground floor. Or you can always piss in the sink.'

Lucas managed not to shudder.

'I'm on the other side of that.' She pointed to the wall. 'So I'll give it a thump when it's time to rise and shine. Auntie Angel wants me to give you the grand tour in the morning.'

'OK. Um . . . thanks.'

'All part of the service.' Her eyes flicked over him. 'That were a fine trick with the wind and the whistling. Seems like you've got this coven eating outta the palm of your hand.'

'I'm just doing my job.'

Her lip curled. 'Well, don't get too cocky. Making pals with the Morgans will be a different matter.'

'Believe me, I don't underestimate the challenge.'

'Don't underestimate the people here, either.'

In the light of a bare bulb, her face was all bones and shadows. They were as different as it was possible for two people to be, yet he knew they had one thing in common. Her mother had also been taken from her at an early age – not by witchcrime, admittedly, but as a result of its legacy. Angeline had told the Witchcrime Directorate that Glory wanted justice for her mother, and the chance of a normal life. Looking at her now, Lucas wasn't so sure. Coven blood feuds were about the pursuit of vengeance, not the righting of wrongs.

After she left, Lucas stood absolutely still for a minute, letting the emptiness wash over him. Then he squirted shower gel all over the sink and turned on the tap. The sound of running water was calming. A compact mirror had been stuck above the sink with Blu-tack; this time, however, he avoided Harry's face. He wished he had something, anything, of his own. A book, a postcard . . . even his old watch.

Music was still pumping away downstairs. Lucas lay down on the sagging mattress and closed his eyes. He tried not to think about the last time he saw his father, their embrace made clumsy by the weight of things unsaid. From there, his thoughts moved to his mother. He wondered what kind of difference his fae would have made to her. He wondered what she would think if she could see him now. It was several hours before he fell asleep.

CHAPTER 18

On the other side of the wall, Glory also lay wide-eyed and wakeful. She imagined the Inquisition's witch prowling around next door, plotting his next move. He was a strong witch, that was for sure. As soon as he'd begun his witch-work, her own Seventh Sense had felt the fae leap and crackle in the air between them. She wasn't afraid of him – at least, not in the way she was afraid of Charlie Morgan. But he made her nervous.

As a result of her restless night, Glory slept through her alarm and didn't get up until mid-morning. Still, the extra sleep had done her good. She felt hopeful and alert. First, she decided, she'd sort out the mess with Patch and the accounting. Then she'd show Harry around. He might be more forthcoming once she got him on his own, away from the coven.

There was a secure line to Charlie Morgan's office in the basement meeting room. It was furnished with a tele-phone, computer and a battered conference table and chairs. She half hoped she could leave a message, but her call was answered with an irritable 'What?'

'Morning, Uncle C.'

Monster. Murderer. I'm gonna take you down . . .

Coolly, she explained the situation with Patch's brother and the gambling debt, and confirmed the money would be repaid at the end of the month.

There was heavy breathing from the other end of the line. 'So what next?'

'How d'you mean? I did what you wanted and I got you your cash. Patch never meant no harm. As for Dad . . . well, he's a soft touch. But he knew Patch would do right by him.'

Charlie made a scoffing sound. 'Your dad's head is so far in the clouds it's practically on Pluto. This is what happens when a coven loses its way – without discipline, people take advantage.'

'Maybe so. In which case, getting us back on track – and restoring discipline – is my problem. And Cooper Street's business.'

She sucked in her breath, trying to visualise the man on the other end of the line. The shrewd cruel eyes, the well-fed face. Had she gone too far? There was a long wait before he answered.

'If you're not careful, there won't be much of a business left. I need to see results, Glory. I'm depending on you.'

He hung up. Murderer, she mouthed at the phone. Bastard. Murderous treacherous bastard scum.

She had just got up to leave when Jacko and Earl pushed through the door. They were talking about Harry.

'. . . I only met him the one time,' Jacko was saying. "S'funny, though. He seems younger than I remembered.'

Earl chuckled. 'All the better for us. He's used to living soft too. Anyone can see.'

'Ain't you the early birds,' Glory remarked, before they could ask what she was doing there. 'What's up?'

'Gotta check on the online perfume sales,' said Jacko. 'The computer upstairs keeps crashing.' He turned on the PC. 'Chinese Dave phoned – said there's a problem with the latest DVD order. Nate's gone to talk to him, and taken Harry along.'

'You serious? I thought Harry was supposed to be lying low. Not being paraded about like a prize poodle. At this rate, we'll have the Inquisition sniffing round our doorstep before the week's out.'

In fact, Nate's recklessness made her own job easier. The Wednesday Coven would be on to Harry even more quickly. She couldn't believe no one else had considered the risks though.

Earl looked uncomfortable. 'I did tell 'em to be careful. And Nate swore not to say a word –'

But Glory was already hurrying up the stairs to Number Seven's attic. If Nate and Harry were with Chinese Dave, they'd be gone for at least an hour. It was the perfect chance to investigate Harry's glamour.

If Glory had wanted to publicly expose him, she would need to destroy the amulet he was using. She only wanted to see through his glamour without him knowing. This meant reversing the witchwork involved.

Glory knew a glamour's illusion could outlast its amulet for some time, depending on its contact with the witch who had crafted it. But to be safe, Harry would be wearing an amulet close to his skin. To be even safer, he would have a ready-made spare. She could work on that just as effectively.

Her search began with the various nooks and crannies in the attic. All she found was dust. From there, she went through the folded pile of clothes by the mattress, checking the seams. Then she moved to the sports bag. Its lining had already been searched by Nate, and she didn't find anything new.

She sat back on her heels and surveyed the room. What a neat-freak. The contents of the washbag were laid out as tidily as the clothes. Toothbrush and paste, shower gel, flannel and the rest were all lined up to one side of the sink. The one missing item was the deodorant, which was in a zipped-up side pocket of the otherwise empty bag. It struck her as odd because everything else was so carefully set out.

Glory gave the can a shake, and – feeling foolish – sprayed it out of the window. OK, so it worked. What now? She'd already spent twenty minutes on the search. She took out some of her irritation on the can, twisting it about with her hands in frustration. It was then the base popped open, and a fold of grubby paper fell out. Bingo.

Now the real work could begin.

Firstly, she had to cover her tracks. Best keep it simple: she'd make up some story about having to 'borrow' Harry's bag, and present him with a replacement later. Since he could hardly kick up a fuss about a missing deodorant, he'd just have to craft another glamour as soon as he could.

Secondly, she had to find a vantage spot for undoing

the glamour. She needed to have a clear view of her target, yet be out of sight herself. This was easier said than done. But luck was on her side. It was a sunny day, and when Nate and Harry returned at twelve, they went straight out into the scrubby patch of weeds that was Number Seven's back garden. Chunk followed, carrying pizza and beer. Glory could do the job from the safety of her own bedroom.

She pulled a side table over to the window and placed a mirror face down, to use as a work-board. If she was going to undo the witchwork, she needed to reverse as many of its components as possible. Very carefully, she unfolded the amulet. It was gummed together by a paste of ash and bits of unknown grit. She spread it out flat to examine the little stick man with his pink cheeks and scribbled yellow hair. As she touched it, she could feel the Devil's Kiss warm beneath her collar bone responding to the fae imprinted on the paper.

Glory brushed off as much of the ash mix as possible, before licking her index finger and rubbing it through the grit. Then she picked up her eraser. She was glad the picture hadn't been done in ink; working with Tipp-Ex would have been messy, and harder to control. Watching Harry out in the garden, drink in hand, she took the eraser and dragged it in slow strong strokes across the yellow-haired stick man. Her fae flowed through, rubbing out the fae worked into the lines and shading of the picture.

It wasn't easy. The pencil didn't fade like it should. The other witch's fae was resisting hers, and the effort sent pins and needles shooting through her hand. Her Devil's Kiss ached. Still, Harry was looking blurred. Like a watercolour painting that had got wet. Finally, she took his name – a false name for a false identity – and unpicked it. Backwards-speech was the language of reversals. *Sekuj Yrrah* she whispered, as the brown pencil eyes grew fainter and the pink pencil cheeks faded. *Sekuj Yrrah*.

Now her view of Harry was nothing but grey fuzz. Glory pressed the blank rag of paper between her palms. *Sekuj Yrrah*, she said for a third time, this time command-ingly. Her eyes stung and watered. And when the mist cleared, a pale slim boy with dark hair was staring up at her window.

In spite of herself, she started away in shock. He really was her own age, not just some under-grown twenty-year-old. A boy witch with powers near equal to hers! He must already be an important figure in WICA if they and the Inquisition entrusted him with undercover work.

Who was he and where did he come from? He was better-looking than his glamour but she didn't reckon that he and 'Harry' were too dissimilar in background. You could spot the public school type a mile off. Like those twits in green uniforms at the bus stop the other day. It was an air they had. A gleam and polish . . . Maybe that's why this boy looked slightly familiar. She'd bet he wasn't putting on his toff accent, or that haughty manner. *Believe me, I don't under-estimate the challenge.*

But Glory liked a challenge too. Seeing the witch's true face had only increased her curiosity.

CHAPTER 19

The girl's face at the window was a far-off smudge, but there was something about the way she was looking at Lucas that made him uneasy. Abruptly, she disappeared from view. Lucas went back to pretending to appreciate Nate's latest anecdote.

They were all more or less the same. The morning's trip to the DVD supplier had mostly been an excuse for Nate to talk up his 'international contacts' – as if he was some kind of jet-setting criminal mastermind. Now they were out in the scabby garden, standing among thistles as the wretched dogs whined and scrabbled on the other side of the wall. Lucas had only had a couple of hours' sleep and was feeling hollow with tiredness.

'Don't worry if Glory acts a bit sore, by the way,' Nate told him. 'She can be an uppity little cow. Auntie A's spoiled her – filled her head with tales of Starling-girl stardom. You coming here has put her nose right out of joint.'

'Whose nose is that?' said Glory, coming out from the house. 'And where's me ham and pineapple?'

'Pizza's for those what earned it,' said Chunk. 'We've been working all morning.'

'Exactly,' said Nate, through a mouthful. 'Shouldn't you be off learning your times tables or something?'

'And shouldn't you learn to shut your gob when you're eating?' She grabbed a slice of pizza from the box. 'Auntie needs me to do the rounds. She wants Prince Harry to come with me.'

'That's my bag,' Lucas said, frowning. Glory had it slung over one shoulder, and it appeared to be stuffed with packets of cigarettes.

'Yeah. I needed to borrow it,' she said breezily. 'Now, are you coming or what?'

'Ask nicely,' said Nate. 'He's not for you to boss about.'

'You're not boss yet neither,' Glory retorted.

Lucas went after her into the house.

'Er . . . perhaps I should carry the bag –'

'Ain't you the gentleman.' She adjusted the strap. 'Lucky for you, I'm no lady.'

He tried to reassure himself with the thought that even if someone discovered the amulet inside the deodorant can, there was nothing they could do with it. From what he'd seen of Auntie Angel's efforts to set the paper doll alight, she was a pretty low-grade witch.

'So tell me what we're doing exactly,' he asked as they set off down Cooper Street.

'Getting to know the neighbours.'

It turned out the bag contained packets of mince, tea and cheap chocolate, along with the cigarettes. Glory was giving out care-packages – bribes, Lucas thought – for the locals in Cooper Street's territory.

They were mostly visiting young mothers and the

elderly. It was a chance for people to moan about the trou-
blemakers on the estate, and list various small grievances (a
leaking tap, a broken lock) the council hadn't got round to
fixing. Glory wrote these down. 'Earl's good with the DIY
stuff,' she explained. 'He'll be round later.'

She didn't just hand out food and fags. There was
witchwork as well. Auntie Angel had crafted small amulets
for luck and health, or finding lost property. People paid
for these, between twenty and fifty quid. Lucas wondered
how they could afford this on benefits. They also gave
Glory the local gossip: the comings and goings, the feuds
and romances and shady deals. Everyone was interested in
Harry too.

'He's on work-experience,' Glory would say, with a
wink and a grin. Or, 'Auntie Angel's special project.' And,
'You'll be hearing a lot more of him.'

Several asked if he was the 'new boyfriend'. For the
younger ones, Glory would toss her hair flirtatiously. 'Can't
you see I'm out of his league?' For their elders, she'd give a
sigh of mock-regret. 'He's an uptown boy and I'm an East
End girl. You know it'd never work.'

Until now, Lucas had only seen two sides of Glory:
sulky or fierce. This was a new Glory altogether: cheerful
and patient with the old folk, matey with the young mums.
If nothing else, she knew how to work a room.

It came as a shock to see how accepting these people
were, not just of organised crime, but of witchkind in
general. A couple of the old biddies they visited had pictures
of the Starling Twins framed on their mantelpiece. There
had been a coven at Cooper Street for nearly a hundred

years, and it seemed that old habits – and loyalties – died hard.

Perhaps it was just that anyone living here was grateful for whatever help they could get. Some of the newer council buildings weren't so bad. There were a few scruffy but respectable terraced houses. But the mass of the Rockwood Estate was a concrete jungle of rusting balconies, weedy yards and dank corners, with one lone tower block in the centre. Its windows stretched from earth to sky; stacks of smeary eyes, watching.

Most of the residents had the same worn-down look as their surroundings. There were girls with prams and push-chairs, still kids themselves, and young men with angry stares who stood around on corners; leering, gobbing, swearing. If Glory was nervous of them she didn't show it. In her too-tight jeans and extravagantly fake fur gilet, she walked through this wasteland with her hips swinging and her head high.

In fact, the only local feature Glory commented on was a graffiti tag they saw sprayed inside a stinking underpass. A red S with a diagonal line slashed across it, like a crooked dollar sign. 'It's the badge of Striker's crew,' she told him with a frown. 'I ain't seen one so close to Cooper Street before.'

'A local gang, are they?' Lucas knew the stories about hoodies on the rampage: street battles with knives and pit bulls, sometimes guns. You didn't need to belong to a coven to cause trouble.

'Not exactly. Their leader's this crazy preacher guy. Got converted in jail apparently. He acts like he's got a direct line to God – going to put the world to rights, vigilante style.' She frowned again. 'But this ain't their territory. They should know better than to come to Rockwood.'

From the underpass, they went to the mini-mart on the estate's forecourt. Lucas had a couple of things he wanted to buy, including a new deodorant. After their final house-visit, Glory had simply chucked his bag into a weed-infested canal. 'It's had Auntie Angel's witchwork in it,' she'd said by way of explanation. 'We don't want it to be traced back to us.'

Lucas was left to fume in silence.

He was also fuming about his lack of funds. All his cash had been confiscated, though Nate had doled him out a tenner that morning. Pocket money, he'd said with a smirk. The rest you'll have to earn. It was a small thing, but Lucas had never had to count his pennies before.

Afterwards, they took cans of Coke over to a bench scrawled all over with four letter words. 'We did good work today,' Glory said, yawning. 'Ouff. If the local gossips don't get Charlie's spies pricking up their ears, I don't know what will.'

Lucas nodded. The groundwork had been done. But he wasn't in any hurry to return to Cooper Street, and it didn't look as if Glory was either. She had begun to tap out a series of messages on her mobile phone. Idly, he picked up a news-paper lying under the bench.

The front page had a picture of Helena Howell, MP, addressing an anti-witchkind demonstration outside the Houses of Parliament. An update on the Goodwin trial reported that a witness for the defence had broken down under intensive questioning by the Chief Prosecutor, and admitted using a false alibi. The journalist described it as 'a rare success for the Inquisition, in a case that has been dogged by disruption and confusion'.

All the news seemed to be bad news. There had been a break-out at a detention centre for illegal immigrants a couple of months ago, and group of Roma asylum seekers were still on the run, including a child of six. One of the group had been recaptured yesterday, and set himself on fire in protest. Lucas thought, as he always did when he heard news of this sort, of the burning of Bernard Tynan. Another article contained an interview with the wife of the train driver who'd been under the bane. Apparently he was still suffering from the hallucination that had caused the derailment. A monstrous black horse, charging towards him . . .

With a sigh, Lucas turned to the editorial column. Its title was 'Wave of Witch Terror', and its author called for 'an urgent reassessment of witchkind rights and responsibilities'.

Glory leaned over and gave the paper a flick.

'Here we go again. The first sign of trouble, and out comes the lynch mob.'

'People are frightened,' he said shortly. 'They feel under attack. And of course the media loves to whip everything up.'

'Too right. Any excuse to pile all witchkind on to a great big balefire and light the match.'

'In which case, coven witches are playing right into their hands.' He lowered his voice. 'You know as well as I do what this is all about. It's Charlie Morgan and the rest of his crew, using witchwork to derail the Goodwin trial.'

'Why'd they want to draw that sort of attention to themselves? Most likely it's some random nutter. Or foreign terrorists.'

'It's the same old vicious circle. Witchkind complain about being persecuted, so they hurt somebody or disrupt something in protest. Then they become outraged when there are reprisals. No wonder people think they can't be trusted.'

'"*They*"?' she repeated. 'Ain't you a witch too?'

He coloured. 'Yes. And I'm all too aware of the responsibilities. The fae is like carrying a weapon – something to be used as a last resort. The end must always justify the means.'

He sounded pompous, and they both knew it. The girl raised her eyebrows. 'For "Queen and Country" . . . I s'pose that's what they teach you at WICA. Shame not everyone has the luxury to be so high-minded.'

'Well, the fact is most of the work that law-abiding witches do is simply counteracting the damage that other witches inflict.' Lucas didn't realise he was quoting his father until he'd said it. 'Look at history. Look at the crime statistics.'

She gave a snort. 'And who collects the statistics and writes the history books, who chairs the bloody debates? You want numbers, fine. Take the Burning Times: sixty thousand witchkind men, women and children – *children* – burned and tortured to death in sixteenth-century Europe alone.

'Just because I don't speak posh, don't mean I'm pig-ignorant either,' she added.

The girl was obviously carrying several chips on her shoulder, but the main irritation was that she had a point. Lucas struggled to keep his tone level. 'Most human history involves suffering. But any cult of victimhood is dangerous. It feeds on bitterness and revenge, not to say myth-making.'

Glory's eyes flashed. 'Myths! My gran and great-gran died at the Inquisition's hands. How's that for a bedtime story?' She came to a stop, and took a deep breath. 'OK . . . maybe your family's been one of the lucky ones. But imagine if they wasn't. Imagine it was your granny who got killed 'cause of her fae. Or your mum. Would you still be telling witchkind to keep a stiff upper lip?'

Lucas thought of the dreamy portrait in the library at home. His father had had to identify Camilla Stearne's body, pulled from the wreck of her burning car. He looked at her with distaste. 'I'd know that getting hysterical about it wouldn't bring her back.'

It was probably just as well Glory's phone interrupted them with the *beep* of a new text message. For a moment, he'd thought she was about to hit him.

'It's from Auntie A.' She got up, her face set. 'Time to plan your first gig.'

'Arrogant little turd,' Glory muttered to herself. All high-class sneers and condescension. But as they walked back – Glory marching ahead, Harry Whoever-He-Was strolling along with his hands in his pockets – she forced herself to calm down. She'd come very close to giving herself away.

He must know she was already on the Inquisition's watch-list; no doubt he'd been trying to goad her into saying something incriminating.

They met her dad outside Number Seven. 'Who's this then?' Patrick said with a nervous smile. 'New friend?'

'Dad. I told you about this, remember. He's Harry. He's going to do some work for the coven.'

'It's good to meet you, Mr Wilde.' Harry put out his hand and Patrick, giving Glory a slightly baffled look, shook it. Harry moved past him into the house, where he was noisily greeted by Chunk and Jacko. He'd said he was going to put his shopping in his room before rejoining her and Angeline.

'The poor lad looks done in,' said Patrick. 'What kind of work is he doing, anyhow?'

Glory managed not to roll her eyes. They'd been through this before. 'He's a witch, Dad.'

'Oh yes, that's right. But . . . dear me . . . if you two are seen together, mightn't that attract trouble? From the authorities, I mean. You don't want to draw attention to yourself.'

'Auntie Angel's supervising. We'll be careful.'

'I see . . . But –'

'It's *fine*, Dad.'

'All right, love. If you say so.' Patrick's forehead wrinkled in thought. 'Well, he's got a nice way of speaking, I'll say that for him. Very gentlemanly.'

Ugh. Smarming up to her dad like that – it was disgusting. Harry might be an Inquisition stooge, but Glory resented how quickly he'd been accepted by the rest of the coven. He'd only been here five minutes, didn't look, talk or act like anyone they knew, and yet he was already one of the boys. A real gentleman crook.

Going to Auntie Angel's made her feel better. Among the lace and china knick-knacks, the pink candy-striped walls, the Starling girls still reigned supreme; bad, bold and beautiful as ever. When Harry arrived, she could see his eyes were drawn to their pictures too. Lightly, she touched the undone amulet (reduced to a scrap of dirty blank paper) in her pocket. His glamour's eyes had been muddy brown, but as long as she carried the amulet she could see their true dark blue. She supposed the shadows under them must be showing up on his glamour too.

'Are you a Starling fan?' she couldn't resist asking.

He shrugged. 'Their facilities were remarkable. I just think it's a shame they couldn't have put them to better use.'

Facilities! It was as if he was talking about a household appliance. Or a well-designed kitchen.

'Maybe they didn't have much of a choice.'

'There's always a choice. Like you choosing to help me.'

'True enough,' Auntie Angel agreed, coming in with a tray of tea and biscuits. She beamed at them over the china. 'Now, let's all sit down, and find ourselves the best way to go robbing. Milk and sugar, Harry?'

Stonily, Glory listened to her great-aunt outline the plan of action, allocate roles and discuss preparations. Afterwards, Angeline told Harry to round up the rest of the coven so they could get things started.

Once he was gone, she reached across and tugged Glory's hair so hard she yelped.

'Whatever happened to easing suspicion and playing nice? I've had enough of the sulks and the stroppiness. So has Harry, by the look of things. It's time to mend your manners, girl.'

Glory had been about to boast about undoing the witch-agent's glamour. Now she decided to keep it to herself. Lately she'd begun to wonder what would have happened if she hadn't got the fae, not ever, and an unknown witch like Harry really had been recruited for the coven. She'd like to believe that Auntie Angel would have continued to fight her corner, to fuss over her just the same, but she couldn't be sure. Maybe she'd have ended up doing the housekeeping, like Harry said.

It hurt that the old lady didn't seem to realise how difficult this was for her. Harry's coven debut was going to be a copy of one of the Starling Twins' earliest and most audacious scams. To add insult to injury she, Glory, was going to have to stand by and watch him flaunt his fae in triumph.

CHAPTER 20

The Starling Twins had been sixteen when they pulled off the House of Cleeve robbery, at a diamond merchant's in Bond Street. It was their first act of witchcrime to hit the headlines, for they'd used both glamours and fascinations to waltz off with over ten thousand pounds worth of gems.

Cooper Street's ambitions were more modest. Their mark was a small jeweller's in a quiet Islington street. The manager was a young woman, new to the job. She spent most of her days reading celebrity magazines and updating her Facebook account. There was one security guard and two CCTV cameras. The shop and its display cases were alarmed and there was, of course, the usual iron bell over the door.

The account the manager gave to the shop's owner and the police began simply enough. She and the guard had been alone in the premises on Friday afternoon, when a teenage girl came through the door. Her hair was long and dark, and she was wearing a little black dress and leopard print heels. There was perhaps something a little . . . *common* about her, the manager thought, but the outfit looked expensive. Her Gucci bag and oversized Chanel sunglasses certainly were. What's more, she had arrived in a BMW with blacked-out windows.

The girl said she was just browsing. 'It's s'posed to be for my birthday.' Her voice was a touch rough around the edges too. 'But Blake's fed up with shopping. We've been looking all morning.'

Glancing out of the window, the manager saw a teenage boy lounging by the side of the BMW. She did a double-take.

This was no ordinary teenager. It was Blake Gordon, star of the *Heretic Heart* film franchise. He played a heroic young inquisitor, fighting witches in sixteenth-century Spain. She'd read in her magazines that he was in London to promote the latest film, and here he unmistakably was. Scruffy, with warm caramel skin and dimples, just like in all the posters and pap-shots. The only difference was that he was a little shorter than she'd realised, and looked younger than eighteen.

In her statement to the police, the manager was careful to explain that her excitement at seeing him was purely professional. This was her chance to make a big sale, and gain some publicity for the shop. Her pulse quickened.

Meanwhile, the girl was trying on a heart-shaped sapphire and gold locket, pouting into the mirror. 'I'm not sure he'd like it on me,' she said.

'Perhaps,' said the manager, 'your . . . er . . . friend might like to come in and help you choose?'

The girl shrugged. 'He says he's shopped-out. You can try.'

The manager needed no further encouragement. She hurried out into the street, leaving the security guard to watch the girl. Deferentially, she invited Blake Gordon to join them inside.

At first, the celebrity was both grumpy and reluctant. But if he'd been charming from the first it really would have seemed too good to be true. He was accompanied by his minder, a muscular young man with a bald head and dark glasses.

Inside the shop, Blake went up to the girl and squeezed her around the waist. She put her hands on his, squeezed him back, and smiled. 'What do you think?'

She was trying to decide between two necklaces. One was the gold locket, the other a diamond necklace. 'Either one, whatever,' Blake yawned. Catching the manager's eye, he flashed the smile that millions of girls had stuck to their bedroom walls. Blake Gordon's powers were so much more alluring than witchwork. He was, after all, a *celebrity*.

It was then that someone else came into the shop. A middle-aged woman – the frumpy type. 'Oh my God,' she breathed. 'It's Alanzo!' Alanzo was the Spanish inquisitor Blake Gordon played in the films. 'I knew it. I saw you through the window. Alanzo. It's really you!'

The security guard shifted his feet uneasily. It was getting pretty crowded in there: the film star, his girlfriend, the minder, the manager – and now the fan. Blake Gordon gave the new arrival a look of weary scorn, before turning his attentions back to the girl.

She had returned the locket to its case, and was just taking off the diamond necklace. There was a slight problem with a catch, which had got tangled in her hair. Blake was helping her. Meanwhile, the fan grew insistent: telling him how much she admired him, asking for an autograph for her niece. The security guard was between her and Blake, but the situation was complicated by Blake's minder, who was getting aggressive. The manager tried to intervene. There was a moment of confusion, raised voices and a slight scuffle, before the fan was ejected from the shop.

Calm was restored, but the damage was done. Blake wanted to leave. At once. Impatiently, he hustled his girl-friend away, dropping the diamonds into the manager's hand. 'You're a star,' he murmured in his soft American twang. Yes, she'd admit it, she was dazzled – but not so dazzled that she didn't get a good look at the necklace. All was as it should be. She carefully returned it to the case and the security guard held open the door.

The disgruntled fan had already left in a huff; now the BMW pulled away and drove down the road. The guard resumed his post, the manager fanned her flushed cheeks. The excitement was over. It wasn't until at least twenty minutes later that she glanced at the case and saw the diamonds had turned into a cheap trinket of paper, ribbon and plastic.

Cooper Street had only had two and a bit days to arrange the scam, but preparations had been intense, and more disci-plined than Lucas would have thought possible. Glory's wig was real hair but her designer accessories were fake. So were the number plates on the BMW, borrowed from a car sales-man who owed the coven a favour. Only Lucas had a glamour. He wore Blake's over Harry's, which he still carried, so the original illusion would remain intact after Blake's was destroyed. The others had used the services of Earl's sister-in-law, a make-up artist called Val. Her most dramatic work was on Nate, who had a latex cap stuck over his head to turn him bald. Val had played the persistent fan, and Patch had been the driver.

Stealing a real person's identity was quite different to inventing a character like Harry, and Lucas felt a twinge of guilt on Blake Gordon's behalf. The Starling Twins, he knew, had impersonated Elizabeth Taylor in their heist.

His first task, however, was to craft the decoy necklace. A fascination was witchwork that changed people's perception of their environment or objects in it. The most popular use for this was to disguise illegal goods and fake valuable ones. Using an image of the diamonds on the jeweller's website as his reference, Lucas created a rough copy by threading his fae through a gold ribbon and plastic beads. It wasn't just the physical appearance he needed to mimic, however. The false jewels had to take on the aura of beauty and luxury that the real ones represented. As symbols of this, he took a glossy picture of a model from a magazine, and a rare fifty-pound note from the coven kitty. Moistening both pieces of paper with spit, he rolled and twisted them into thick threads, which he knotted in turn to the gold ribbon. He wrapped up the end result in a silk cloth.

The transformation occurred after Glory undid the wrapping. Lucas couldn't do this himself; a fascination was brought to life only when looked at with fresh eyes. To all intents and purposes, the diamonds and gold were genuine. Unlike a glamour, the object had been physically changed, not just people's perception of it. But it too was a short-term transformation, and needed to be kept close to its creator for the witchwork to hold.

Passing the fascination to Glory was the next challenge. That was the object of the waist-squeezing exercise. Glory orchestrated the final switch: using her long hair to disguise her hand movements, and her light fingers to draw up the false necklace from where she'd dropped it inside her bra. Meanwhile, Lucas helped shield her from view by pretending to fiddle with the catch. The first few times they tried the hand-over, they did it sternly and straight-faced; but as Lucas kept fumbling the pass, Glory got exasperated, then amused. When they graduated to the necklace-down-the-bra stage, they started to laugh – in guilty, embarrassed spurts that even Auntie Angel's scolding couldn't bring under control.

Glory was certainly acting more friendly towards Lucas, though he never felt she truly relaxed in his presence. He was reluctantly impressed by her sleight of hand. He remembered the caution for shoplifting recorded in her file. She'd probably been playing pickpockets ever since she was in nappies.

After the laboriousness of their rehearsals, the real thing seemed to be over in seconds. Trying to recall it was like watching a film-clip play at double-speed. Lucas was still getting used to the dark, sweet rush of fae, and still mistrusted it. But the exhilaration afterwards, as they bundled into the getaway car, was less complex. It was pure adrenalin.

Lucas tore up Blake's glamour, Nate pulled off his bald spot and Glory her wig. They were all gasping and giggling. In the front seat, Nate whooped and punched the air. Patch was singing.

Glory turned to Lucas, hair spilling over her face, and dangled the diamonds in front of him. For the first time he really took in how beautiful they were: moonlight on ice. 'Tell me that wasn't fun.' Her eyes were as bright as the glittering stones, her laughter teasing and triumphant. Lucas grinned back.

He told himself it was only a performance. A crime caper, like in the movies or a trashy detective novel. WICA had been forewarned of the escapade. He'd slipped away from the coven during a break in rehearsals, using an elusion to make his way to a public phone box. There was a special number to dial. Muttering down the line to the secret service operator, he'd felt as much as a phoney as the decoy necklace.

Twenty minutes after their getaway from the shop, Patch pulled into a deserted underground car park. He stayed to change the number plates and wipe the BMW clear of prints. The other three, still talking loudly and over-excitedly, headed for Cooper Street to show Auntie Angel their prize.

The gems were worth just over three thousand pounds, a tidy sum for three days' graft, but hardly worth the risk involved. That wasn't the point. The robbery had made the evening news and would be reported in all the papers tomorrow, adding to the frenzy about the spike in witchcrime. Nobody would miss the connection to the Starling Twins. And the Wednesday Coven would be as intrigued as everyone else.

CHAPTER 21

Cooper Street celebrated until the early hours of Saturday morning. Auntie Angel stayed up late too, pouring out bootlegged champagne along with tales of Starling triumph. 'You've got thieving fingers, I'll say that for you,' Nate told Glory, patting them with drunken approval. She caught Harry's eye and nearly laughed. For a moment there in the BMW, she'd almost forgotten what he was. Flushed with their success, the hauteur gone, blue eyes smiling, he'd seemed for a moment like a real person. From now on, maybe things would be easier between them.

Glory was only allowed a sip or two of champagne, thanks to Auntie Angel's beady eye and the need to keep a clear head. But she was on a natural high. It almost didn't matter that she hadn't got to do any witchwork herself. Their escapade had all the colour and daring she could have wished for. This, she told herself, was how it was going to be once the Morgan brothers were bang to rights, Harry Whoever-He-Was had gone, and she was free to claim her inheritance. This was only the beginning.

The morning after, Glory decided to prolong the festive

mood by buying everyone doughnuts for breakfast. Passing her dad's room, she could hear the inevitable bleeps from his games console. He had been more rambling and distracted than usual at the party last night, and only stayed for a short while. She knew he was unhappy about her involvement in the heist. He wouldn't even admit she looked pretty in the diamonds, however much Auntie Angel pestered him. Now he appeared to be the only other person awake. At half past eleven, the lounge was still full of prone bodies and bubbling snores.

The baker's was a ten-minute walk away. Glory was just leaving the shop when a silver Mercedes drew up outside. Troy leaned out of the window. 'Perfect timing – I was on my way for a visit. Hop in.'

He looked every inch the young entrepreneur in his sharp blue suit, laptop and leather briefcase on the seat behind him. Successful mobsters needed to be good businessmen. But Glory was ready for the next round of negotiations. Unlike the last time he'd given her a lift, all the cards were in her hands.

Feigning reluctance, she got into the front seat and put the greasy bag of doughnuts on the dashboard. Troy raised a brow.

'"A moment on the lips, a lifetime on the hips . . ."' he quoted.

Glory ostentatiously bit into one of the doughnuts, so that sugar crystals rained on to the car's leather interior. He winced. Good. With a bit of luck, she'd get some jam on there too.

Moments later they were turning into Cooper Street.

Troy parked at the end of the road, just like last time. Neither of them made any move to get out.

'Congrats on the bling,' he said.

'Thanks,' she replied mid-mouthful. She shook the bangles on her wrist. 'Talbot Road market. Five for a quid.'

'I reckon you can do better than that. Diamonds are a girl's best friend, after all.'

'Oooh . . . like on a ring? 'Cause I gotta tell you, Troy, I ain't the marrying kind.'

'Don't get cute with me.' His eyes narrowed. 'We all know that the Blake Gordon scam was Cooper Street's. Dad's steaming mad and Mum's worse.'

Glory shrugged, and brushed more sugar off her hands.

'Everyone agrees it's got to be one of the most pointless stunts on record. What have you got to show for it? A couple of poxy grand, and your very own witch-hunt.' He shook his head. 'We've already had a whistle-wind and a train crash, and now there's been an attack right outside the Inquisition. Witchcrimes, all of them. Before we know it, there'll be curfews and round-ups and lynchings. Just like the old days.'

'Lucky for me I'm no witch then.' She reached for another doughnut. Troy smacked his hand down on the bag.

'But you know a boy who is. Hexing hell, Glory – even if it wasn't for yesterday's caper, Cooper Street's new witch-kiddie would be the talk of the town. Your outfit leaks information like a broken sieve.'

'People need to know we've got assets.'

'Cooper Street's assets are the Wednesday Coven's liabilities. That's why new recruits need our approval: we do the checks, and we ask the questions.'

'Check away. Harry's got form. Auntie Angel's been scrying on him for weeks.' She tossed her hair. 'Me, I don't see what the fuss is about. His fae might be flavour of the month, but it ain't nothing special.'

She and Troy both knew that yesterday's job required witchwork of the highest level. That was why he'd been sent to sound her out. But the situation was more plausible if she talked Harry down, and let Troy see her jealousy and resentment.

'All fae's special. That's why it's dangerous. Are you sure this boy is what he seems?'

'Yeah. Worse luck.'

'Why's that?'

''Cause he's a pillock.'

Troy gave a grudging smile. 'Well, Dad and the uncles want to meet him. Tonight at the Gemini. You're to come too . . . Unless, of course, you've got another half-arsed heist to plan.'

She climbed out of the car and slammed the door.

'Hey – don't I even get a goodbye?'

She leaned through the window, and wiped her sticky fingers on the dashboard. 'You get to keep the doughnuts.'

From Number Seven's front window, Lucas watched Glory lean into the Mercedes. It looked like she was giving the driver a goodbye kiss.

Nate loomed beside him. 'Smarmy git. Should've known he'd be sniffing round before too long.'

'Who is it?'

'Troy Morgan.' Nate gobbed into an overflowing

ashtray. 'He and Glory are pretty tight. She reckons he's her ticket out of here.'

In the thick of his hangover, all yesterday's good humour had gone. He eyed Lucas balefully. 'You'd better watch yourself. I bet Glory's been whispering sweet nothings about you and your witch-tricks into his ear. Troy won't take kindly to competition.'

Lucas already knew that Troy was a force to be reckoned with. The heir to the Wednesday Coven was studying Finance and Business Economics at Imperial College. The perfect training for a career in extortion, racketeering, larceny and fraud.

There was something distasteful about the idea of Glory being with a slick thug like Troy. He was a lot older, and her second cousin too. But Troy might seem a good catch to a girl like Glory, Lucas supposed, remembering the weary teens pushing prams on the estate, and the leers and wolf-whistles that had dogged their own progress. Watching her from the window, he idly wondered what she'd look like if she scraped some of that cosmetic gunk off her face.

He wished he could scrape off Harry. At first, he'd been reassured by the protection of the glamour. After over four days and nights of it, it was as if his old self – his real self – wasn't just invisible, but unreachable. He felt the loss every time he made a gesture with Harry's hands, or responded to someone with Harry's frown or smile. Agent Andrew Barnes had lived undercover as Harry for a couple of months. Lucas wondered how he'd kept himself sane.

He missed other things too. A proper bed and a working

shower. Cleanliness. Quiet. Normal conversations and real food. Trying not to dwell on the big things made it harder to shake off the little.

This made his meeting with Zoey that afternoon all the more important. It was his only chance of contact with somebody who knew the real him. She would also have a message from his father. It didn't matter how brief or restrained. Just a few words would be enough. Something to hold on to, to make him feel a real person again.

Then there were the things he needed to talk to her about – like the unease he felt about Angeline. The old lady was much more alert and active than she'd first appeared. And now there was the Troy issue. Lucas distrusted Nate and his innuendos, but if Glory *did* have a thing for her cousin, could she be compromised?

He was back in the attic, trying to distract his thoughts with Jacko's football magazine, when Glory burst in. 'It's on,' she said. 'You and the Morgan brothers. Tonight.'

Excitement and dread swooped through him. He tried not to let either show. 'That was quick. I'd . . . well, I'd better let my handler know.'

They'd already pre-arranged for Glory and Auntie Angel to cover for him while he went to see Zoey. But Glory shook her head.

'We can't risk it. The Wednesday Coven'll be snooping and scrying like mad. Troy said they're doing full checks.'

WICA had laid a false trail of school reports, medical and biometric records and other documentary evidence for a mole or hacker to uncover. This was the real proof of Harry

Jukes's identity, and Lucas was all too aware that his own safety depended on its success.

Glory handed him a cheap mobile. 'You can phone to reschedule on this. It's prepaid, and we'll get rid of it afterwards. Now's not the time to take any chances.'

The Gemini Club was named after the Starling Twins' first legitimate business venture, a cabaret bar in Soho. This former hang-out of the rich and infamous was now part of a coffee chain. But the Morgan brothers continued to invest in London's nightlife, and had revived the Gemini brand in memory of their mother and aunt.

Lucas knew the place by reputation. A dilapidated Edwardian music hall, it had been converted into a live music venue and club about ten years ago. Unlike the other Morgan investments, it was in a rough end of town, near Talbot Road market. Even if he'd been old enough to get in, it wasn't the kind of venue he and his friends aspired to.

Plenty of other people did, however. At half past eleven on a Saturday night, the queue for entry was already snaking far down the street. Many of the punters were in fancy dress: according to the flyers, the theme of the night was 'Fears and Fantasies'. Lucas and Glory got dark looks as Glory sashayed straight to the top of the queue to exchange banter with the bouncer.

She turned to Lucas. 'Paul says to go straight through. He'll let Troy know we're here.'

In spite of the throng of people, the place felt cavernous, its sweeping stage, broad balconies and plush boxes a reminder of its former role as a theatre. The fact that the paintwork was peeling and the gilt chipped only added to its decadent air. So did the costumes on display, though it wasn't always clear which were the fears and which the fantasies: aliens, clowns, queens and soldiers mingled with men in drag and women in bondage gear. No one was dressed as a witch, in the fae-tale trappings of pointed hat and crooked staff. That wouldn't be daring, just dangerous.

Glory moved smoothly through the crowd, hips and shoulders swinging to the music's beat. Her eyelids were pasted in smoky black, her lips cartoon red, shiny as her nails. Her cheekbones were highlighted in glitter and her hair teased into a tousled blonde mane. In the dark heat of the club, she didn't look overdone, but exotic.

Then, unbelievably, Lucas saw a face he knew. They had gone through the main bar and were waiting to get on to the stairs down to the dance floor, when he caught sight of someone in the antique inquisitor's costume of a scarlet and black cape. Gideon.

Lucas craned to get a better look. Gideon was the last person he'd expect to see in a place like this; what's more, he was deep in conversation with a bony-faced, heavily tattooed young man in a white tracksuit. They were huddled together in one of the bar's velvet-lined booths. As if sensing Lucas's stare, Gideon turned around. Their eyes met, and Lucas backed away in confusion. For a second he had forgotten about the glamour hiding him. But Glory was tugging his arm. 'Come on,' she said. 'It's this way.'

They were making for the Stage Right exit from what

had once been the stalls and was now the dance floor. The door had a box of bells built into the lintel, and a burly bouncer in front of its 'Staff Only' sign. On stage, acrobats in black leather writhed through hoops. Lucas wouldn't have been entirely surprised if Charlie Morgan had popped up through a trapdoor in a puff of smoke, like the villain in a pantomime.

He came to a halt. If things went wrong with his own performance, there would be no smoke to hide in, no exit route . . .

Glory touched him on his hand. 'We'll be OK,' she said, warm breath in his ear. 'They're greedy murdering scum but we're better than them. I know you can do this.'

For once, the way she was looking at him was uncomplicated: no mockery or aggression. But for all her bravado, she was nervous, he could tell. Her hand had trembled.

In any case, it was too late to turn back. The bouncer was already muttering into his walkie-talkie. 'One at a time.' He pointed a stubby finger at Lucas. 'Him first.'

Another sentry was waiting in the holding area on the other side of the door, ready to check for the three Ws: witchwork, weapons and wires. He had a small LED device for detecting spy-cameras too. The search was both speedier and more thorough than Nate's. Lucas had to unbutton his shirt and take off his belt and shoes for inspection. But his glamour remained safe in his watch.

A pair of swing doors took him into a lounge area equipped with CCTV monitors showing the exteriors as well as the inside of the club. Troy Morgan was there, doing something with spreadsheets on a laptop.

In spite of the impressive CV, Lucas had pictured Troy as an older version of Nate. Face to face, however, Troy was intimidating in a way Lucas hadn't expected. He looked polished, astute.

'It's the boy genius,' he said.

Lucas did the Harry Jukes shrug. *Whatever.* Troy didn't say anything else, just continued to scrutinise him as if he was a glitch in the spreadsheet, albeit slightly more tedious. The silence lasted until Glory arrived, protesting about the indignity of the stop-and-search. 'Bleeding hell. If this is how you treat family, I hate to think what you do to your other visitors. Did Harry get a torch shone up his nose?'

'We'll save the body cavity search for his departure.' Lucas hoped that was a joke. Troy glanced at his watch. 'You might as well go in, Harry. Through there, then second on the left.'

'What about me?' Glory demanded.

'You're only the escort, princess. Sit down and have a cup of tea with your favourite cousin.'

She wrinkled her nose. 'I was hoping for something stronger.'

'Not if you want us to keep our licence. But if you play nicely, I'll let you have a biscuit too.'

They were still goading each other as he left. Lucas didn't look back at Glory. It wouldn't do to appear weak.

He was backstage, among the old dressing rooms. The sounds from the club were faint here, an echo of freedom from a distant world. The first door on the left was ajar, but as Lucas walked down the passageway, whoever was inside pulled it abruptly shut.

Lucas straightened his back, and knocked on the one next to it.

A jovial voice invited him in. 'Aha,' said its owner as Lucas entered the room. 'The Witch-King of Cooper Street.'

CHAPTER 22

Charlie Morgan and Lucas shook hands. Somehow he managed not to wince at the strength of the man's grip. The small shrewd eyes crinkled appreciatively, as if they were sharing a joke.

'Charlie,' he said. 'And these are my brothers, Frank and Vince.'

Lucas had resolved not to think of this as an interrogation, but as a job interview. It helped that the office was as impersonal as a boardroom, the table empty except for a couple of water glasses and a notepad. No windows. In scale and turnover, the Wednesday Coven was the equivalent of a big corporate company. And here he was before the Members of the Board. Charlie, the Chief Executive Officer. Frank, the Financial Director. Vince . . . Director of Operations.

Frank was balding and bespectacled. He leaned forward to examine Lucas, hands clasped as if in prayer. 'Interesting,' he said.

'So you're the joker who thinks a glamour belongs in a gossip mag,' growled Vince.

Their father the hit-man had been known as Ginger Fred, and both Frank and Charlie's hair had a reddish tint, but Vince's was darker, his colouring more like Troy's. His face showed the remains of craggy good looks in spite of the broken nose. Lucas tried not to think about his record. Grievous Bodily Harm. Assault and Battery. Wounding with Intent.

'Now, now,' said Charlie. 'Harry didn't pull that stunt on his own. Dear old Auntie A will have put him up to it.'

Frank pursed his prissy lips. 'Angeline always did have a theatrical streak. She's like her sisters in that respect.'

'But without the talent,' said Vince.

'Talent,' Charlie agreed. 'Exactly. Witchwork doesn't grow on trees – and nor do diamonds and movie stars. You're a talented boy, Harry. Question is, are you a stupid one?'

Lucas thought that Harry probably was. He tried the shrug again.

Charlie's tone was still tolerant. 'D'you take an interest in current affairs, for example? Read the papers? Watch the news?'

'Four witch-lynchings in the past seven days, one of them fatal,' said Frank in his light, precise voice.

'It's not just the usual yobbos,' Charlie continued. 'The God-botherers are getting in on the act. That witch beaten up in Bradford? It happened right outside a mosque. The Bible-bashing brigade are even worse – choirboys turned vigilantes. Those prickers at the Inquisition don't even have to lift a finger.'

'A bit of bashing sounds good to me,' Vince growled. 'We could all do without the plagues of boils and whistle-winds. If I get my hands on the hagbitch responsible, I'll set light to their balefire myself.'

Lucas was surprised. It sounded as if the recent spate of witchcrimes weren't connected to the Wednesday Coven, or the Goodwin trial, after all. Of course, the Morgans could be bluffing. Or else they didn't like to admit that their own witches were out of control.

'I, erm, didn't mean to cause trouble.' He shifted on his chair. 'Angeline and the rest of the coven have been good to me. Getting those diamonds was my way of paying them back.'

'Oh, you'll always pay,' said Vince. 'One way . . . or another.'

Lucas felt a trickle of fear slide down his back.

Charlie, meanwhile, was nodding benignly. 'I'm sure Cooper Street considers you quite a catch. My informant tells me you're not even on the pyros' watch-list.'

'I shouldn't think so. No. There haven't been any witches in the family, except an aunt on my dad's side – back in Victorian times. I heard Gran mention it once.'

'Ah yes . . . your sorrowing relations. Your sister's filed a missing person report, you know. But I'm sorry to say she doesn't seem particularly anxious to find you.'

The Wednesday Coven's investigations had been as thorough as WICA had suspected. They must have spies everywhere. 'Emma will be glad to see the back of me.'

'I don't blame her.' Charlie flipped through his notepad. 'Suspensions, expulsions, brawls . . . a little dealing here, an assault there . . .'

Frank tutted. '"A born troublemaker and a bad influence", according to my source.'

'Who's that, then?'

'Daniel Law. Your friend Richard's father. One of our associates had a chat with him after parents' evening.'

This was exactly the sort of attempt to catch Lucas out that Zoey had prepared him for. 'That ponce Rich is no mate of mine. And I thought his dad lived in Australia, anyway.'

And so it went on, back and forth with the questions and probing. It was the perfect demonstration of how the brothers worked as a unit: Charlie taking the lead, charming and bullying by turn; Frank supplying facts, figures and queries in support; Vince, exuding menace from the corner.

It was a test, but also a game – a game that Lucas was determined to win. He was nervous and fidgety, but if anything, the heightened risk sharpened his wits.

At last, the interview drew to an end. Charlie's pager beeped. He glanced at it and frowned.

'It's from Kez,' he said.

'Trouble?' Vince asked.

'Could be . . .' He sucked his teeth. 'This is a bad time for our kind of business, Harry. Nobody wants to get in the middle of a witch-hunt.'

'I can still be useful, can't I? My abilities –'

Charlie smiled humourlessly. 'You don't read the papers. I guess you don't follow the financial markets either. So let me tell you about toxic assets. They're resources that start off highly prized, then suddenly lose their value. They become a liability instead. And when an asset goes bad, it gets dumped. You understand?'

Lucas gave an uncertain nod.

'Hmph. Keep your head down and your hands clean.

Then maybe we'll see what kind of an asset you and your "abilities" really are.'

Charlie showed him to the door, and watched Lucas walk to the end of the passageway. The door to the room next door, which had been pulled shut on Lucas's arrival, was now open. Glancing in as he passed, Lucas saw a bare table with an empty glass. There was nobody there.

To his surprise, Glory was alone in the lounge. When she saw him, she got up so suddenly her tea spilled. 'All right?' she said anxiously.

'Fine. Where's Troy?'

'He had to take a phone call. Kez – his mum – rushed in just a moment ago, through the same door you did. They went off together.'

'OK. If they come back, tell them I went to see if I dropped my lighter.'

'What lighter? You don't smoke. What're you doing? Wait. It's not –'

Lucas poked his head round the door he had just come through and looked down the passage. It was empty. Charlie had rejoined his brothers in the interview room. Nothing could be heard from inside. Lucas slipped into the room to its left, and picked up the glass.

As he'd suspected, it was a match for one of the tumblers on the table next door. A Wednesday Coven witch, presumably Kezia Morgan, had been listening in. She would have been spying on the colour of the thoughts and feelings behind his words.

Treating the meeting like an ordinary job interview had been a good strategy. He had used it to neutralise his emotions. Maybe that had been enough to conceal his contempt for the Morgan brothers and what they represented. He couldn't be sure, though. As for the other feelings that Kezia might have seen – anxiety, hostility, self-satisfaction . . . Well, they were only to be expected, given the circumstances. Or so he hoped. This was not the time to worry about it. Kezia and Troy had clearly been called away on some emergency, but they might return at any moment.

Lucas had heard that using someone else's witchwork was nearly impossible without their consent. Now he saw why. The tumbler vibrated at the touch of his fae, not welcoming it, but resisting. He ran a finger inside his ear, then began to circle the glass rim. It was even harder than working through iron. His head was shot through with pain and filled with a noise like fingernails scraping on a blackboard. Fighting past the distortion, he could just make out a few words here and there. None of them were coloured.

The first speaker seemed to be Frank. '. . . meeting . . . tomorrow night?' he asked.

'. . . The Radley . . . nine . . .' answered Charlie's voice. '. . . just the two of us . . .'

'So . . . you don't . . . why . . .'

'. . . could be . . . trial . . . Stearne's prosecution . . . sounded bad . . .'

Lucas's eardrum felt like it was being scraped out with shards of glass. He couldn't have held out for much longer, even if the situation had been less hazardous. Ears ringing, he put the tumbler down and hurried back to Glory.

Troy Morgan returned moments later. He looked

round the room, and at the two of them, with obvious suspicion.

'Where's Kez?' Glory asked.

'Her brother's been arrested,' he said tersely. 'On a train out of Newcastle – suspicion of witchcrime.'

'God. I hope everything's OK.'

'We're dealing with it. Now, isn't it about time you kids got off home?' Troy had seen Lucas smother a yawn. 'Seems it's past the prodigy's bedtime.'

They didn't immediately return to Cooper Street. Glory wanted food, and so they stopped by at a burger van down the road from the club. Lucas was getting accustomed to the coven's timekeeping, where most activity took place late afternoon or at night, and the day was for sleep. He wondered how Glory managed during term time. She'd mentioned school and her mates there once or twice, so she must attend one. But it was hard to think of her as an ordinary schoolgirl, with homework and a uniform, and ordinary friends.

The chips were good: crisp and hot, glistening with salt. Lucas, however, didn't have much of an opportunity to enjoy them. Glory was too anxious to hear about his meeting with the Morgans. He found this second interrogation almost as exhaustive as the first one.

'Look, I didn't mess anything up,' he told her. 'But I'm a long way from winning them over. Charlie reckons now's a bad time for witchwork. I'm starting to think the Morgans really don't know who's responsible for the recent attacks.'

'I told you that already. The Wednesday Coven don't need witchwork to intimidate people. They've got plenty of other methods. It'll be some lunatic, like I said.' Glory licked ketchup off her fingers. 'All right. I think it's time you came clean about that lighter business. What did you really go back for? Because whatever you were up to, you took one hell of a risk.'

She was right. Just thinking about all the things that could have gone wrong was enough to give him a cold sweat. But when he explained about the glasses, she was evidently impressed.

'Isn't hijacking another witch's work dead difficult?'

'Yeah. Painful too. But I did find out that Charlie's meeting someone important tomorrow, and I think it's connected to the Goodwin trial. He mentioned –'

Lucas stopped, horrified at the mistake he'd almost made. He'd been about to say 'my father'. He gulped, and pressed on. 'Er, Charlie mentioned the Chief Prosecutor.'

'That pricker Stearne.' Glory spat in a puddle.

'Right. Well, um, he's meeting this informant, or whoever it is, at the Radley tomorrow night. Does that mean anything to you?'

'At the moment it ain't much more than a building site. North Hallam way.'

'That sounds like a good place for a secret assignation. Especially if it's with someone who shouldn't be anywhere near the Morgans – like a tribunal member, for example.'

'You don't know that. Charlie could be meeting anyone.'

Lucas shook his head impatiently. Time was running out. The Goodwin trial only had a couple of weeks to go, and as Charlie had said he had no use for his witchwork, it could take several more weeks, months even, before Lucas got a chance of infiltrating the Wednesday Coven. The trial would be over and his father would haul him home long before that . . . with nothing to show for himself, and no options left. 'I appreciate it's a long shot, but I still want to follow it up. Will you help?'

"Course. I want to see the bloodsucker nailed even more than you do.'

He nodded – apparently not firmly enough. 'What?' she said, bristling. 'Don't you believe me?'

'Absolutely. And I need your help. It's just – well, it's such a huge risk you're taking –'

'Listen here: my mum was brought up with Charlie and his brothers like their own sister. And they killed her in cold blood, just 'cause she got in their way. They'd do the same to me if it suited them. So I'll see them rot in hell if it's the last thing I do.'

Lucas had seen Glory angry before, but this was hate. He felt scorched by the strength of it.

Then she gave herself a shake and she looked different again; young and uncertain, her make-up smeared like a bruise around her eyes.

'Never mind. It'll be over soon. We just need to get through . . . keep going . . . get past the crap, you know?'

He nodded.

'Come on, then. There's a night bus we can take – the short cut's through here.'

Glory's route to the bus stop lay through a deserted market-place. By day, Talbot Road market was full of bustle, its stalls heaped with colourful foods and eccentric fashions. At night, the only signs of life were the rats that scurried among the crates. The maze of walkways between the stalls was pockmarked with oily puddles. Plastic awnings sagged from their frames.

Glory and Lucas had just reached the drinking fountain that marked the centre of the square when a man stepped out of the shadows, blocking their path.

The main road was not far away. Lucas wondered if they should make a run for it, but Glory, in her teetering gold platforms, wouldn't get very far. Instinctively they moved a little closer, held themselves a little straighter.

The man gave a hoarse chuckle. Five others emerged from the ranks of empty stalls.

All wore hooded tops. Nonetheless, Lucas recognised their leader. The sleeves of his white tracksuit were pushed up to reveal the tattoos on his sinewy arms: crucifixes, angels, crowns of thorns. He was the man Gideon had been talking to in the club.

Glory knew him too. 'Striker,' she muttered under her breath. 'Crap.'

The tattooed man took out a box of long-length matches from his pocket and set one alight. He made a low hissing sound.

The five men behind him did the same. Their matches struck and spluttered into life. Sssss . . .

'What do you want?' Lucas demanded.

The gold cross around Striker's neck glinted in the firelight. The gold tooth in his smile glinted too. 'To save your souls,' he said. His companions laughed.

Striker turned to Glory. 'Fooling around with

witch-boys will only end in tears, Gloriana. I've heard the Devil's Kiss is catching.'

'You've got it wrong. I'm not –' Lucas began.

But Glory got there first. 'So you know who we are. Congratulations. That means you know who my family is. Uncle Charlie don't take kindly to your kind of crackpot – specially when you start running riot on his turf.'

'The Wednesday Coven may have the Devil in their pocket. But me and my boys are God's own soldiers, and we know where witchkind belong.' With a flourish, Striker lit a second match and grinned his gold-toothed grin. 'For "all shall have their part in the lake which burns with fire and brimstone: which is the second death."'

Lucas felt the hairs prickle on the back of his neck. Glory, however, laughed insolently.

'Nice line. Bet you've got it tattooed across that puffed-up chest of yours. Keep navel-gazing long enough, and maybe you'll learn how to read.'

She'd gone too far. Striker sprang forward to grab a fistful of her hair, and held his burning match to its tip. Before she or Lucas could react, both were seized from behind by Striker's henchmen, who clamped their hands over their mouths.

'Word is,' Striker spat, 'the Wednesday Coven is going down. And when that happens, the hags they've been shelter-ing will go down with them. There'll be nowhere to run to then.' Giving Glory's hair a savage yank, he turned to Lucas, and pushed the still burning match up to his neck. Lucas had to twist his head away to avoid the flame. 'So consider this a warning, witch-boy. Three strikes and you're out.'

A car revved noisily, and jolted over the kerb into the marketplace. It was a silver Mercedes.

Lucas would never have imagined he'd be so glad to see Troy Morgan. His and Glory's captors immediately let go, slinking back into the maze of stalls. Only Striker held his ground.

Though thick-set, Charlie was not a tall man. His son was. Troy towered in the headlights' glare.

'Messing about with matches again, Striker?' he said. 'Remember, kids who play with matches get burned.'

'You think I'm scared of you?'

'You should be. You know who I am.'

Striker sneered. 'Daddy's boy.'

'Yes,' Troy said. 'I am my father's son. That's one of the many reasons why I'm stronger and smarter than the likes of you. I own these streets. I own you.' Casually, he moved back to the car. 'And if you get in my way again, hell itself will be a mercy.'

In the car, Lucas and Glory both tried to speak – to say thank you, to explain, to exclaim over what had just happened. Troy cut them off angrily. 'I don't want to hear any of it. Shut up and let me drive.'

They obeyed. For the next ten minutes, Troy drove in silence. The night-time streets slid past, slick with rain.

Then the car phone rang.

'Hi . . . Yes – just had to take a slight detour . . . No, of course you should go, Mum. They need you . . . Mm . . . We'll be fine. Promise . . . OK. Love to Auntie Ness. Bye.'

The silence broken, Glory began to ask something

about Kezia. 'Keep your nose out of it,' Troy snapped. 'This is a family matter.' Then his exasperation got the better of him. 'What the hell did you think you were doing, running round Talbot Road market at this time of night? It was a total fluke I drove past when I did. Bloody idiot kids.'

It had been a long and stressful night, and both Lucas and Glory were feeling the aftershock of their recent ordeal. Hysteria mounted. Troy's Angry Dad act was the final straw. Back in the passenger seats, they caught one another's eyes, and shared a terrible urge to giggle.

CHAPTER 23

Glory dreamed of the Burning Court again. This time Striker was there, holding a lit match to her throat. Her own eyes stared out at her mother's reflection, and saw a second face in the glass: a boy with blue eyes and a streak of silver in his black hair. He was frowning at her. She woke up with a heart-thudding wrench. The dream always left her with dread but it was more intense today, like an omen.

Get over it, she told herself as she kicked aside the tangled sheets. Her sleeping brain had simply overreacted to the events of yesterday, as well as the problems ahead. Harry had told her that he'd seen Striker talking to an inquisitor in the club. It was not that surprising the Inquisition was supporting the vigilantes on the sly. There had always been rumours to that effect. Since the police weren't doing much about the lynchings, it was going to have to be up to the covens to impose order. But, Glory thought uncomfortably, that wouldn't be easy in the middle of an Inquisition crackdown.

When it came to getting people's fear as well as respect, the trick was to make them believe you were capable of anything. What was Troy capable of? He'd been a little kid when Edie Starling was killed, but as coven heir he should know about the bodies, and where they were buried. He had told Striker that he was his father's son, and he had faced him down with his father's menace. Yet the way he'd spoken to his mum in the car had been so anxious, affectionate . . .

Right now, Glory had her own responsibilities to attend to. Nate, jealous that she'd been the one to introduce Harry to the Morgans, had reasserted his authority by taking his protégé to an illegal dog-racing track on Sunday morning. It was up to Glory to do the recce for Charlie's assignation in the Radley.

She had waved Harry off with a commiserating smirk. After last night, they finally felt like co-conspirators – allies, even. Holding his own with all three Morgans must have taken a lot of nerve. Then there was his spur of the moment hijack of Kezia's listening talisman. It was just the sort of thing Glory would have tried. Imagine if he ever found out what she could do . . . ! The frustration of not being able to use her fae left her restless and twitchy, like having an itch she couldn't scratch.

Auntie Angel was less impressed with their night's activities. 'I don't wonder Charlie's not rising to the bait,' she said at the end of Glory's report. 'Harry's getting above himself – all this bad boy posturing's gone to his head. Behind that glamour, I shouldn't be surprised if he's just some nerdy clerk. That's how the government likes to keep its witches, see: downtrodden and repressed.'

Glory kept quiet. Whoever the real Harry was, he didn't

have the appearance, let alone the manner, of an office drudge. But she wasn't ready to produce his undone amulet. She was enjoying the novelty of keeping a secret from the old bossyboots.

'Striker, now, is a menace,' Angeline went on. 'And one you'll have to deal with once the Morgans are out of the way. It's a pity really . . . He'd be a useful lad to have around, if only you could knock some sense into him.'

'He's a *maniac*, Auntie! A witch-lynching loon –'

'He's an excitable young lout who needs a cause. People like that change loyalties quick as others change their underwear.' Angeline pursed her lips. 'Now, I reckon this Radley rendezvous will be more trouble than it's worth. But wild goose chase or no, you'd best play along with it. Harry needs to believe he's the one calling the shots.'

'Right,' said Glory wearily.

Angeline gave her a consoling pat. 'We'll soon be rid of him,' she said. 'Him and Charlie both. In the meantime, grit your teeth, and remember you're a Starling.'

The Radley building was part of a strip of decaying offices and warehouses in the outer reaches of Hallam. With the extension of the City East train line, the area had become a prime site for redevelopment. A local firm had made an early bid to knock down the existing complex and replace it with an upmarket apartment block. Unfortunately for them, the Wednesday Coven had seen its potential too. The coven had bribed members of the construction crew to sabotage the work, and leaned on investors to cut the funding. When the original owner went bust, the coven was able to snap up the site at a knock-down price. They were now leading the development scheme.

Glory arrived just after one. The vacant lot across the road from the Radley was an unofficial dumping-ground, and she found a good surveillance spot among the piles of rubbish and rusting fridges.

As yet, the new phase of building hadn't begun. The ground floor was little more than an empty shell. The metal beams of the unfinished upper storeys stretched skywards like the fingers of a monstrous skeleton. The ramp down to the basement looked as if it led to a bottomless pit. Even in daylight the place was menacing. Little traffic passed this way, and even fewer pedestrians.

It was hard to think of a more isolated spot for a rendez-vous. Whoever Charlie was meeting must be a trusted source as well as an important one; someone who could demand an out-of-hours meeting in an out-of-the-way place, without the usual coven defences.

At least there were no iron bells on an abandoned building site. The only security was a man with a dog. Since there was nothing worth stealing, Charlie must have posted them here ahead of his meeting. They'd be check-ing for trespassers – junkies looking for a place to shoot up, tramps for somewhere to doss in . . . or snoops looking for trouble. The guard had a bulge in his jacket that Glory was pretty sure was a gun, and the Alsatian was almost as mean-looking as its owner. Although she didn't know his name, she recognised him as one of Charlie's senior henchmen.

When she arrived, the guard and dog were just finishing a patrol. The guard stood on the threshold, and unleashed the animal so that it could sniff around. Afterwards, it trotted out of the building, and snuffled about for a few minutes longer, before cocking its leg over a pile of sand heaped by the road. Its master called for it impatiently. Duties done, he retreated to a trailer parked in the forecourt. The dog was chained up nearby.

Glory weighed up the options. She and Harry would need to get past the guard to position themselves inside the building ahead of Charlie's arrival. The main entrance was just a hole in the wall, but the meeting would no doubt take place in the basement, away from the gaze of a scrying-bowl. The dog was the biggest problem. Unable to reveal her fae, her own contribution was limited to supplying the raw material for Harry's witchwork. Luckily, she had a good idea of what to use.

She retreated to the back of the vacant lot, and took a roundabout route to emerge a few hundred metres down the road from the Radley. The dog watched with ears pricked, as she approached its territory. She was dressed like a jogger and wearing the wig from the diamond heist tied back in a ponytail, as well as a baseball cap to hide her face. Pretending to retie a shoelace, she knelt down by the sand heap at the edge of the road and used a stick to scoop out a urine-soaked clump. The dog let out a low growl but Glory paid no attention as she poked the wet sand into an empty crisp packet. Anticipating Harry's reaction, she grinned. Dog-piss was a lot better than the alternative.

*　　*　　*

Harry did indeed turn up his aristocratic nose at her offering. However, once they got down to the practicalities of the stake-out he put his squeamishness aside. He was certain Charlie was meeting one of the tribunal members from the Goodwin trial. Glory, who knew the Wednesday Coven relied on all kinds of corrupt officials and informers, wasn't quite so convinced. Even so, whatever got discussed was sure to be incriminating.

Since evidence obtained by witchwork wasn't admissible in court, Harry was going to film events with a tiny spy-cam disguised as a button. He hadn't risked smuggling any gadgets into the coven and so had arranged to collect the camera from a WICA drop.

This didn't mean there was no call for witchwork. The dog would be dealt with once they were on site, so Harry started with their elusions. Glory was interested to see that he used a map instead of a compass as the base for his amulets, tearing out a random page from an A to Z of London, then using a mix of ink and spit to draw along the road markings in a crazy maze.

To further protect them once they were inside the Radley, Harry assembled the materials for a shroud: a pocket mirror, black felt, and two little totems to represent himself and Glory. For these, he used a sliver of each of their thumbnails, wound in a strip of cloth torn from their pillows. Glory donated hers reluctantly. It was a big step, handing over a piece of yourself for another witch's work. But they were partners. She had to trust him.

Glory was increasingly tempted to ask Harry how he'd been recruited to WICA, and what kind of training he'd had. She also wanted to know what had put the grey in his hair, whether he'd left school yet, what other operations he'd been involved in . . . But all these questions were too personal. It wouldn't be good policy to feel like she knew him or to wonder if, in different circumstances, they might have been friends. Still, it was a shame that WICA had got to him so early. Whatever Auntie Angel might think, Harry Whoever-He-Was had the makings of a fine coven witch.

By six, their plans were in place. Harry went out to collect the spy-cam, as well as a few supplies. Luckily, Nate had bumped into some mates at the racetrack, and was off boozing somewhere. Angeline was at the bingo. Since they wouldn't have to leave until eight, Glory thought she might as well get some rest.

She lay on her bed and tried to relax. No chance. Although she was nervous about tonight's expedition, she was excited too, and impatience made her restless. Her thoughts whirled and fizzed. In search of distraction, she turned to the stack of magazines that Patch had nicked from the hairdresser's. They were a couple of months out of date, but better than nothing.

Glory liked to read about celebrity gossip and her favourite TV shows. These magazines were a different kind of glossy, showcasing clothes she couldn't afford, parties she wouldn't be let into, and people she'd never heard of. The *Tatler* even had a 'social diary' at the back, filled with snapshots of posh people at cocktail parties and polo matches. Some of them were Glory's age.

Like the two pretty girls, Miss Beatrice Allen and Miss

Davina Henderson-Holt, posing arm in arm with Harry Jukes.

Except he wasn't called Harry, of course. Glory had already seen the face behind the glamour; now she read the name behind the alias. Mr Lucas Stearne.

Her heart skipped a beat.

Stearne. The name was almost as familiar as her own. Everyone knew about the Stearne family, but witchkind knew them the best. Or worst – ever since Bloody John, sidekick to Matthew Hopkins, had marched forward to take his place in history. Hopkins, the first Witchfinder General, had been an enthusiastic amateur. John Stearne, however, made witch-hunting into a profession. When Oliver Cromwell made him Witchfinder General after Hopkins' death, Stearne had persuaded parliament to formally establish the English Inquisition and enshrine it in law.

From then on, all Stearnes had been the same: hunting witches, imprisoning witches, torturing witches. Burning witches. Through every generation, right up to the reign of Ashton Stearne, king of the Inquisitorial Court, Chief Prosecutor of the Goodwin trial. And his son . . .

His son and heir.

Lucas. Harry Whoever.

Lucas Hexing Stearne.

Lucas Stearne was in her own home, plotting the destruction of another coven. And she was helping him.

A bitter nausea rose in her throat. Glory had found ways to resist the shame of collaboration, to reason it away. But to ally herself with a Stearne took her treachery to a whole new level. It didn't occur to her that Lucas might be just a distant relative of the Chief Prosecutor. The resemblance to his father was too strong. In fact, she wondered how she could have failed to spot it before. Her cheeks flamed with humiliation. How quickly she'd let down her guard, allowed herself to imagine that maybe they weren't so different after all.

What a gullible fool he must think her!

She let out a little moan. Then she began to pace up and down the room, arms wrapped around her chest, trying to think.

So a High Inquisitor's son had turned witchkind . . . that must've set the cat among the pigeons. And yet it clearly hadn't done Daddy any harm. The man was still there in court, still lording it over witchkind. Well, the Inquisition had many nasty little secrets. They must have decided to turn this latest one to their advantage. Lucas was the ultimate weapon: half inquisitor, half witch.

She bitterly regretted not telling Auntie Angel about undoing the glamour. If Angeline had seen the boy's true face, she might have made the Stearne connection from the first. They could have planned a new strategy together, found some way to turn it to their advantage. Maybe they still could. But not now. There was no time.

Harry's – Lucas's – motives were clearer than ever. Where, though, should Glory's loyalties lie? Charlie Morgan, in partnership with his brothers, had murdered her mother. Yet Lucas's family had been murdering her kind for centuries . . .

Someone knocked at the door. Lucas Stearne was standing there smiling, his eyes treacherous and blue.

'Are you ready?'

CHAPTER 24

Something was up with Glory. Her attitude towards Lucas had definitely relaxed over the last couple of days, to the point at which they could share a joke as well as plot a strategy. But now she'd retreated into her former hostility. Hunched and pale, she barely spoke to him on the way to the Radley. When he nudged her at the bus stop, she recoiled as if she had been struck.

Perhaps Glory was more frightened of her Uncle Charlie than she let on. Or maybe she was suffering from delayed shock, after her face-off with Striker. But Glory wasn't the nervous type. Most likely she was just having one of those inexplicable strops that girls went in for sometimes. Philomena was expert at them.

It was annoying, because Lucas already had more than enough on his mind. He was filled with jittery anticipation of who he might see tonight and what he might learn. But there was something else bothering him. On his way to collect the spy-cam from the drop – a DVD rental store – he'd called Zoey from a payphone. She was alarmed about his stake-out plans, and tried to get him to meet with her first, to discuss contingency measures and back-up, even though both of them knew there wasn't time.

Lucas finished the conversation by mentioning his suspicions of Angeline. Her activities in Cooper Street made a mockery of the poor-little-old-lady act she'd put on for the Inquisition.

'It's not a concern,' Zoey told him crisply. 'She's a proven source. Her relationship with the Inquisition goes back twenty-eight years.'

What kind of relationship was it? But either Zoey didn't know or she wouldn't tell him.

Lucas wondered if Glory knew the extent of her great-aunt's informing. He'd got the impression that Glory, like himself, thought Angeline's collaboration was a recent development. He couldn't ask her, though, even if she'd been in a better mood.

The Radley was on the edge of a busy if run-down neighbourhood, but on a Sunday night the place felt like a ghost town. Hulks of empty warehouses and abandoned offices loomed on every side. Glory and Lucas, dressed in dark clothing, elusion amulets worn next to their skin, made their way through the shadows to the rubbish dump across the road.

The glow from a street lamp was enough to see the guard pacing up and down on the Radley's forecourt, Alsatian at his side. Although the dog was in some ways the bigger threat, animals were easier targets for witchwork than humans.

Lucas settled down behind a rusting fridge. Keeping

his target in view, he took out a wad of brown modelling clay and set about crafting a poppet. Since natural materials responded to the Seventh Sense better than synthetics, he blended some earth into the clay, as well as a good sprinkle of the urine-soaked sand, kneading his fae deep into the mix.

Soon he had a little model dog in the palm of his hand. He breathed on the miniature head with its pinched-out ears and snout, the dimples for eyes, then ran his thumb down its muddy back. The real dog pricked up its ears and whined a little.

Suddenly, the air was ripe with rich stinks. Lucas felt new and agonising appetites tug him in all directions. Every hair on his body seemed to be standing on end. The sensation didn't last for more than a few seconds, but left him shaken. He mustn't get too close: he needed to guide the animal's thoughts, not enter its mind.

It was hard to concentrate with Glory so close by. Although his animal senses were already fading, the scent of her flesh and breath had been tantalisingly strong. He forced his mind back to the task, stroking the poppet gently from head to tail, as he nudged a warning into its living counterpart's brain. Something dangerous, some-thing exciting. Somewhere else . . . around the corner . . . far back . . .

The dog raised its head. It whimpered, then growled. Lucas growled himself, soft and low. He continued to nudge the animal: pushing its attention away from the entrance-way, round the back of the building. Soon it was straining at the leash. Muttering, the guard followed his dog's lead. His hand was inside his jacket, resting on the gun. The pair turned the corner and went out of sight.

Still holding the poppet, Lucas darted across the road and into the Radley. Glory followed him. Her torch, its light partly dimmed by her sleeve, revealed a soaring bare space interspersed with steel pillars set in concrete. Their destination, however, was the dank basement below. Wooden planks had been laid to make a crude floor cover, littered with coils of wire, boards and chunks of rubble. A sheet of rusting iron was propped over the doorway.

There was a workman's bench close to a wall and they crouched behind it, pulling down some plastic sacking over their heads. It was a very makeshift sort of hiding place, and without witchwork they would have been dangerously exposed. As it was, there was precious little time to assemble the shroud. Lucas put the two totems – his and Glory's thumbnails, wrapped in scraps of their pillowcases – on the pocket mirror. He breathed on the glass, fogging it over, then wrapped it in black felt before the mist could clear. Finally, he scattered it with grit and wood-shavings from the floor. A fog to lose them, blackness to hide them, earth to cover them . . . Even when crafted with fae as strong as his, a shroud wasn't very reliable. They couldn't move away from where it had been placed on the ground and it wouldn't make them invisible, just hard to notice. Used with the dog-poppet, however, they should have enough witchwork to keep them safe.

Moments later, the sentry and his Alsatian arrived and a searchlight's powerful beam swept across the interior. As the dog started snuffling about, Lucas pressed his thumb down on the poppet's pinched-up ears. 'Hear no evil,' he whispered, before squashing down the clay snout, the dimpled eyes. 'Smell no evil, see no evil, speak no evil.' The poppet's head was a shapeless lump of mud. The real animal's mind was also muddy and formless; its senses functioning, but slowed. Lucas was its master now.

The guard came further in, shining his light into the corners. After two or three anxious minutes, he satisfied himself that all was well. He went back up the ramp. But before Lucas and Glory could get their breaths back, voices were heard, and Charlie Morgan himself tramped down.

He came alone, and carried a hurricane lamp that he set down on an upturned crate. His stocky bulk was swathed in a camel-hair coat, from which he took out what Lucas expected to be a cigar, but was in fact a nicotine inhaler. He sucked on it irritably. He looked at his watch, also irritably. Ten past nine. Whoever he was meeting was late.

Lucas switched on the tiny pin on the button-camera, and shifted fractionally to get a better view. Glory tensed up in response to his movement.

A moment later, the iron sheet over the entrance was scraped back. High heels click-clacked over the rough floor. A woman. Ruth Mackenzie. It must be. Tribunal member, civil servant and –

It wasn't Ruth. This woman was smaller and slimmer. She was wearing a full-brimmed hat, pulled low, a dark coat with the collar turned up, and a scarf. When Charlie saw her, he picked up the lamp and held it in front of him, squinting suspiciously.

His visitor opened her coat and loosened the silk scarf.

Lucas caught his breath. The lamp shone on an ugly iron collar that encircled her neck. Lady Serena Merle.

'Don't worry, Charlie.' The little-girl voice wasn't as breathy as Lucas remembered. 'I'm still trussed up like a dog on a leash.'

Tonight there was nothing glassy about her eyes, or vacant in her smile. She looked tired, though. Her face was thin and strained. 'Long time no see.'

'Indeed. How's Rose?'

'About the same, thank you. No worse.'

'That's good to hear.' He nodded. 'All right. We both know this isn't a social call. What have you got for me?'

'Trouble,' she said bleakly. 'The worst kind. It's about the witchcrimes. They – they're not what people think. You see . . . I found out . . . well, my – my husband's behind them. And other people at the Inquisition.'

Lucas felt Glory stiffen beside him. His blood turned to ice.

Charlie, however, gave a low chuckle. 'Well, well, well. The pyros must've got themselves a pet witch. Someone they're paying or someone they're forcing to do their dirty work?'

'Forcing, I think – there's been some "disciplinary" issues, apparently. I don't know the details. I only got wind of it on Wednesday night. Godfrey had been at his club, and drinking . . . he's not used to it, really . . . Then he said something as I put him to bed. I didn't have to pretend not to understand. Later I heard him – with Silas Paterson, on the phone. So I did some digging. There's a government minister, Helena Howell, who's helping in some way, and they have back-up at the Inquisition. The police too. I don't know how far up it goes.'

'Hmm. Trying to provoke a witch-hunt, are they?'

'It's cleverer than that.' She twisted her hands. Her rings glittered in the lamplight. 'It's Jack Rawdon they're after. They hate him and what he's trying to do with WICA. They're going to produce evidence he did the whistle-wind and plague and so on himself. They'll say that when he was working against Endor all those years ago, he got turned. That he's been one of the terrorists all along.'

'Very neat. Yes, that's a nice little stitch-up.' Charlie sounded almost approving. 'In fact, the only thing I don't understand is why you've brought it to me.'

Lady Merle widened her violet eyes. 'So you can put a stop to it, of course. You'll have to be quick. There's going to be one more attack, later this week, which is when Rawdon will be arrested. But this witch they're using – they've got them locked up in one of the Inquisition's hidey-holes. If you get to him or her first, make them testify, or . . .' There was a catch in her voice, and she put out a hand in appeal. 'Please. I've always given you good information, haven't I? With your contacts and resources, you're the only person who can help. The only one I can trust.'

Charlie laughed.

'You always did make a good damsel in distress. Such charms might've worked on poor old Vince back in the day, and any number of eligible bachelors since. But I'm made of sterner stuff.' He leaned back against a pillar and regarded her narrowly. 'You're a capable girl, Reeny. You've got this far without anyone suspecting you've a brain or a backbone. Why not make the most of it, and put the world to rights yourself?'

'I can't. I *can't*. If Godfrey found out I'd gone behind his back, spilled his secrets . . . It's not me I'm worried about – it's Rose. Ever since the accident, she's been helpless. She's only his stepdaughter. He or his friends would find some way of avenging themselves on her. I know it.'

In her agitation, the cut-glass accent had slipped and roughened. Her eyes welled. 'If Godfrey and Silas bring Rawdon down, it'll be the end of WICA and any other institution that gives witchkind a role and rights. Don't you see? After that kind of scandal, the Inquisition will be able to do whatever it likes –'

'It's a sad story, Reeny. It really is. Just the kind of villainy those two-faced pyros go in for. But let's face it, I'm no fan of Jack Rawdon. My life would be much easier without his gang of witch-snoops poking their noses into my affairs.' He grinned humourlessly. 'If there's a backlash, the covens will ride it out. We always do. Besides, desperation is good for recruitment. All those poor persecuted witches with nowhere to run, and no place to hide . . .'

'You're a cold-hearted son of a bitch.' This time there was no emotion in Lady Merle's voice. She wiped her eyes and began to button up her coat.

'So everyone keeps telling me. And now's not the time to turn soft. Kez is away, there's Bradley Goodwin getting ready to mouth off in court, and to top it all, I got word this afternoon there's a traitor in the ranks.'

Lucas felt all the breath squeeze out of his body.

'I'm sorry, Reeny,' Charlie said, as she turned to go. 'But this ain't my battle.'

* * *

Charlie stayed nearly fifteen minutes after Lady Merle left. He looked deep in thought. Then he began to type something into his smartphone. Just when the cramp in Lucas's leg got to the point where he thought he'd have to stretch it out or scream, the guard reappeared.

'Car's here, boss.'

'OK.' Charlie sighed heavily. 'You might as well push off too. There'll be no more business here tonight.'

He and the guard stumped out and away. The rev of an engine could be heard. Lucas and Glory held their position for another agonising five minutes before emerging from the shelter. Glory switched on the torch. In its thin grey glow, her face was ghostly. Her eyes glittered.

'Should've known. The Inquisition and every pricker in it – born and bred scum.'

Lucas was almost too dispirited to reply. He felt sick and hollow. 'The Inquisition's a vast organisation. A few corrupt officials –'

She was already marching out of the basement into the main building. When he caught up with her, she turned on him savagely.

'Don't you *dare* make excuses. You've got it on bloody film. You can't trust none of them. Not the government, not the pyros, not the police. The whole stinking gang is rotten to their bones.'

'Charlie Morgan's just as happy to sell witchkind out as Silas Paterson.'

'Charlie's an evil sod. Nothing new there. And we ain't a jot closer to giving him what for.'

'And now he knows there's an informant in the coven.' Lucas bit his lip.

'Huh.' She propped the torch against a pillar. 'The Inquisition probably gave him the heads-up on that and all. One less witch-agent for them to worry about.'

Lucas shook his head but couldn't bring himself to deny the possibility outright. He crumbled the remains of the dog's poppet between his hands, feeling the fae bleed away. He had to face the fact that Silas Paterson had Inquisition support. There were plenty of officers who shared his views, and some of these must be working with him. People like Gideon Hale, perhaps . . . The idea sickened him. For the conspiracy wasn't just a crime – it was a betrayal of everything the liberal reformers had achieved. The Inquisition's reputation would take years to recover. So much good work would count for nothing.

'To terrorise their fellow citizens . . . People they've sworn to protect . . . how can they *live* with themselves?'

Glory made an exasperated sound. 'Very nicely, I'm sure. So you can quit the hand-wringing. You'll only give yourself another bunch of grey hairs.'

He would have thought it was just a figure of speech. But then he saw Glory's eyes flinch. She knew that she'd let something slip. Though she recovered quickly, it wasn't quickly enough. They stared at each other and the space between them hummed.

'My God.' He felt stupid with shock. 'You can see past the glamour. You're . . . you're a witch too.'

For a moment, it looked as if she was going to try to face it out. Then she laughed, defiantly. 'As good a witch as you, or better. Next time, find a safer place to hide your amulet. Or put stronger fae into its crafting.'

He swallowed hard. 'Does this mean you know who I am?'

She didn't answer. There were two spots of colour high on her cheeks.

'Do you?'

Her lip curled.

'*Do you know who* I *am?*'

He stepped towards her.

Anger and fear drummed through him. Their faces were so close they were almost touching. Both were breathing hard.

Suddenly Glory struck out at his chest, pushing him away. She drew herself up to her full height. 'Yeah. I know you, all right. Lucas Hexing Stearne.'

A terrible thought came to him. Glory must have only recently learned his name – that was why her behaviour towards him had suddenly turned. And that afternoon, Charlie Morgan had been told there was an informant in the coven. 'Were *you* the one who warned Charlie about the mole?'

'Don't be pathetic,' she spat. 'I hate the Inquisition and every pyro in it, but I hate Charlie just as bad.'

This time her gaze didn't waver.

'All right,' he said stiffly. 'I shouldn't have doubted you. I guess we've both had some surprises today. You've learned my name, and I've discovered you're a witch. We're quits. Now we need to –'

'Quits! Mab Almighty . . . don't you know nothing

about my world? There's some who say turning snitch is the worst crime of all – worse'n murder even. But I ain't just helped Auntie bring a spy into the coven. I've betrayed it to a *High Inquisitor's son*.'

The gutted building loomed around them, dark and cavernous. Thunder rumbled distantly.

'Are you saying that if you'd known who I was from the start, you'd never have helped me?'

'I'm saying that everything's changed. This ain't the Inquisition against a corrupt coven boss. This is the Inquisition against witchkind. And . . . and I don't think even you can be sure which side you're on.'

Perhaps she was right. The idea infuriated him. 'Hex you, then. You say I'll never understand your world. What about you understanding mine? In your world, they roll out the red carpet for witchkind. Well, that's not how it works where I come from. You think it was easy for me, telling my father what I'd become?' He glared at her in the torchlight. 'And I have just as much reason to distrust witches as you have inquisitors. Some hagbitch murdered my mother. With a bane.'

Lucas hadn't meant to say this. It felt like a cheap shot, but some of Glory's sharpness immediately softened.

'Oh,' she said. 'Christ.' Then, with effort: 'I'm sorry. Because I can . . . I mean, I do know how . . .'

Poor motherless witches, the pair of them. 'Yeah. So it turns out we actually have two things in common.'

It wasn't funny, but for some reason he wanted to laugh. To his surprise, Glory's mouth twitched too.

It was then that the sirens began to wail.

Flashing lights pulsed in the cracks around the boarded-up windows and entranceway. Several police cars, ambulances and a fire engine were racing down the road outside.

This time it was Lucas's sixth sense that kicked into action. He knew, somehow, who those sirens were for. Glory guessed it too. Before he could stop her, she hurried out of the building.

CHAPTER 25

That far-off rumble hadn't been thunder, but an explosion. When Glory and Lucas reached the shabby high street at the end of the Radley's block, some people were already stumbling away in panic, while others, like them, pressed on – drawn by a desire to help or witness, to sniff out the blood. They followed the commotion through a housing estate, until they came to what should have been another unremarkable road.

The police had already cordoned off the area. Acrid smoke hung in the air. It came off a wreck of twisted, blackened metal, shot through with flames. The remains of Charlie Morgan's BMW.

Lucas thought, before he could stop himself, of his mother.

Glory could think of nothing at all. Her mind was a roaring blankness.

The car-bomb had exploded outside an off-licence. Its windows were blown out, the interior in shreds. A woman was sitting on the kerb, a bloody rag pressed against her head. Another bystander lay in the road, surrounded by paramedics. One ambulance had already gone and frantic activity could be glimpsed inside the other two. A crowd had already gathered.

'. . . it'll be a political target,' somebody was saying. 'Some government bigwig the witches don't like.'

'Just like Endor, all over again,' said his friend.

Glory's face was dazed and white.

'Here you go, luvvie, have a tot,' said the elderly man standing next to her and Lucas. He handed her a hip flask. She took a swallow of whisky and coughed, spluttering. 'That's right – put some colour in your cheeks.'

'Did you see what happened?' Lucas asked.

'I seen it all.' The old man spoke with relish. 'I was waiting for me bus, just over there. Then a car pulled up and this bloke – big, important-looking – got out the back. He went into the offie for a packet of fags. But as soon as he opens the car door again . . . *kaboom!* The blast threw him halfway across the street. Poor sod looked in a bad way. Still, at least he was alive when they put him in the ambulance. His driver didn't have a hope.'

Perhaps there had been a problem with the detonator. Thanks to a trick of timing, Charlie Morgan had – possibly – survived.

A policeman was taking down names and asking for statements. The old man moved towards him eagerly. Lucas took Glory by the arm. 'Come on,' he muttered. 'We shouldn't be seen here.'

Because he didn't know where else to go, he led her back in the direction they'd come from, and the desolate row of abandoned buildings.

'Not the Radley,' Glory told him, rousing herself a little. 'The Wednesday Coven crew – once they hear – they might come looking –'

A disused office block provided an alternative shelter. Someone had already cut the wire fence across the entrance and they climbed inside a smashed window on the ground floor. Glory's torch picked out a sleeping bag and syringe lying in the corridor, and couple of half-melted candles stuck in jam jars. All the items were filmed with dust.

They moved on to a windowless room furnished with a couple of beaten-up filing cabinets and a pile of filthy curtains. Glory propped the torch on a cabinet and sat on the curtains. Her legs still felt a little wobbly. It was only now, looking at Lucas in the torchlight, that she thought back to the confrontation that the sirens had interrupted. It already seemed faded and far away.

She had wanted Charlie punished, and thought she would have rejoiced to see him dead. Yet she couldn't get that smoking, bloodied heap of metal out of her head. The image alternated with one of Charlie topping up her glass at dinner the other week: bragging, swaggering, invincible.

'All right . . . who d'you think done it?' she asked, trying to keep her voice firm. *Grit your teeth and remember you're a Starling.* 'Paterson and Merle?'

Lucas was relieved by her businesslike tone, and did his best to match it. 'I don't see how killing a coven boss fits into the plot to frame Jack Rawdon. And what about the timing? They'd need to prep an insider, wouldn't they, for access and so on. I'd think it more likely one of Charlie's associates or rivals decided to take him out.'

'All right. Maybe you ain't the only snitch on the block. Maybe somebody else just got their cover blown.' Glory sighed. 'We'd better hope so, anyhow. 'Cause if Charlie found out you're a WICA mole, he'll have spread the word. Me and Auntie A will be under suspicion, along with anyone else who's been within a mile of you in the last week.' She got out her phone. 'I need to warn Auntie.'

But Lucas stopped her hand. 'Let her know we're safe. Say we were following Charlie, saw the explosion, and that we're hiding out till we know what's what. But don't tell her what we heard from Lady Merle.'

'Are you cracked? We need all the help we can get.'

This was tricky. Lucas didn't want their recent accusations and recriminations to flare up again. He paused, searching for the right words. 'How long has your great-aunt been an informant for the Inquisition?'

'Coupla months.'

'Are you sure about that?'

''Course. Why?'

'According to my handler at WICA, Angeline's been informing for decades.'

Glory smacked a filing cabinet in frustration. 'More crappy Inquisition lies! Auntie Angel's no snitch.'

'Er, you both are, remember? For good reason, of course,' Lucas added hastily. 'If Angeline *did* get in touch with the Inquisition thirty years ago, I'm sure there's an explanation for it. But I don't think we should risk getting her involved. Not until we know exactly what she's been telling them, and why. And why she hasn't told you.'

'Thirty years, you said?'

'Twenty-eight, to be precise.'

Glory felt her whole body lurch. It was like missing a step on the stairs. The big event of twenty-eight years ago was Granny Cora's return. After five years on the run with Edie, she'd telephoned her sisters, and arranged for them to meet. But the Inquisition got to her first. Someone had tipped them off.

Don't go there, she told herself fiercely. The Inquisition lies, everyone knows that. They want to make you paranoid. They twist things, and people, to suit their own ends. If Auntie Angel ever went to the prickers, it would have been to try to bargain with them, to ensure her sister's release . . .

In which case, though, why hadn't she ever told Glory about it?

Lucas, sensing his advantage, pressed on. 'Even if my cover's safe, we won't get any help from the covens. Charlie made that clear to Lady Merle. We can't risk going back to Cooper Street and WICA won't be much safer – the Inquisition monitors everything. So I need to get word to my handler in secret.'

'You trust him?'

'Her. Yes, I do. She's WICA, and loyal to Rawdon. She'll find a way to warn him.' As he spoke, he realised there was someone else he could go to. Zoey was under surveillance, but Senior Witch Warden Jonah Branning wasn't. The man might be irritating but he wasn't corrupt. That freckled face practically shone with honesty. 'But if we're going to put a stop to this conspiracy, we'll need proof.'

'On that film you took, all you got is accusations. A chat

between a mobster and some high-class bimbo ain't evidence. It'd be laughed out of court.'

'I know. That's why we need to speak to Lady Merle ourselves. She may have more information for us. The key to all this is the witch that the conspirators are using. We have to find out who it is and where they're being held.'

'Hmm.' Glory eyed him thoughtfully. 'If we're going to play detectives, then I'll need a drink.'

With a flourish, she brought out a hip flask from her jacket pocket.

'I don't believe it! You nicked it from that old man!'

'What else d'you expect? Light-fingered chav like me.' She smirked. 'Actually, he went off so quick I forgot about it. But don't have any if it'll offend your delicate morals.'

Lucas took a swig, just to prove her wrong. The raw alcohol hit the back of his throat and he winced. He realised he hadn't had anything to eat except a sandwich, five long hours ago. Investigation of his own pockets produced a chocolate bar he'd forgotten about. Better than nothing. Glory, meanwhile, was trying to compose a text message to Auntie Angel. The difficulty of deciding what to write was made worse by having to convey the message in code.

The glow of the phone's screen reminded Lucas of the candles left by the earlier intruder. His witchwork supplies included matches, so he was able to light both candles and place their jars on the floor between them. He put out the chocolate bar too.

Glory raised an eyebrow. 'Candles, booze, chocolate . . . are you trying to seduce me, Mr Inquisitor?'

His face set. 'You know I'm not an inquisitor. I never will be.'

When he had interrogated her in the Radley, demanding that she tell him what she knew, Glory had felt an instant of real panic. It was an atavistic response, the fear felt by generations of her ancestors responding to the threat made by generations of his. As he had loomed darkly over her, eyes burning with their own pale fire, he had seemed a High Inquisitor in his own right.

She recognised that she had to get past this. It wasn't as if the Inquisition had specially bred him to be its own fae-powered witch-hunter. He was a witch by accident, not design. Glory had once known how the Chief Prosecutor's wife had died. But she'd either forgotten or ignored the fact, and that made her ashamed. The power in Lucas was the power that had murdered his mother. Small wonder he distrusted it.

Almost as if Lucas knew what she was thinking, he said abruptly, 'Getting the fae was the worst thing I could imagine. Yet I didn't ever imagine it; the idea was too impossible. And when it happened, my dad . . . Well. Maybe it was even worse for him. I know you won't believe it, but my father's a good man as well as a good inquisitor. They do exist.'

He looked down at his hands. 'The crazy thing is we both know that if I'd committed some crime, or got a girl pregnant or started taking drugs . . . that kind of stuff, we could have dealt with it. Got through together. But the fae changed everything.'

Glory didn't know what to say to this. Instead, she asked

him how he had first got the fae. His answer was as hesitant, and awkward, as her question. It was then they discovered they'd become witches on the same day. From there, Glory moved on to all the other questions she'd been storing up. What his training had been like. What kind of witchwork he liked best. Whether he'd ever tried sky-leaping... Before long, Lucas was asking his own questions back.

Whatever was waiting for them in the outside world, they would face it tomorrow. The two of them sat on grubby piles of curtains, passing the chocolate and hip flask between them, exchanging their stories. For this one night, their defences were lowered, blurred by tiredness and whisky and the smoky flicker of the candle flames.

'What about the rush?' Glory asked him sleepily, towards the end. 'The witchwork high?'

'I don't trust it. I know the thrill would be the same if I was doing harm or hurting someone with my fae,' Lucas replied. 'And yet I want to keep feeling it, in spite of everything. In spite of the stain. Because that's what witchwork is: mud and sweat and blood... a kind of fever...'

Glory pulled down the neckline of her jumper, exposing the velvety pinprick under her collar bone. She touched it, feeling the fae's dark flush.

'Look,' she told him. 'Look.'

Reluctantly, he raised his head, facing her through the haze of light and shadow, as the Devil's Kiss bloomed beneath her skin.

'It can be beautiful too.'

CHAPTER 26

Glory woke up first. She was stiff and cold, and smeared with dirt from her nest of curtains. Her mouth tasted vile. There hadn't been much whisky in the flask, but on an empty stomach, at the end of a long and tumultuous day, it had been more than enough. She squinted at her watch. Nine twenty. They'd overslept.

Lucas was still asleep. He was lying face upwards, his black hair falling back from his forehead, frowning in his dreams. In spite of the frown, the vulnerability of his unconscious form disturbed her, and she turned away.

The water supply had been turned off along with the electricity, but Glory managed to find a scoop of rain water in a tub in the backyard. She splashed her face, rinsed her mouth out and chewed on a wad of gum. It didn't touch her thirst. Squatting behind a rubbish skip to pee, she reflected that if she'd known she was going to camp out in a derelict building, she'd at least have packed a toothbrush. And some mascara. Her reflection in the window was dismal, unkempt hair straggling around her grey face.

Lucas was up when she got back. Tersely, she directed

him to the water. Both were wondering if they had revealed too much last night. They avoided each other's eyes. However, when Lucas returned, he had a spring in his step. He was holding a small twist of paper, which he proceeded to rip apart with relish.

'The amulet for Harry's glamour,' he explained. 'If the Wednesday Coven do suspect Harry's a mole, then I'm safer as myself.' He looked at his hands affectionately. 'It's good to be back.'

Glory also ripped up the undone amulet she'd been carrying. It felt symbolic of something, though she wasn't sure what. At any rate, some of the awkwardness faded.

At quarter to ten, they set off for the local tube station, where Glory remembered seeing an internet centre. They had decided to start their investigations via the web. Their first stop, however, was a café round the corner. After using the washroom, and ordering bacon sandwiches and tea, they both felt slightly more human.

Glory had turned her phone off at night to save the battery, and also for safety, in case it could be traced. In the optimistic light of morning, this seemed like taking things to extremes. She found she had a curt voicemail from Troy ('Call me', received at 2 a.m.), several missed calls from Auntie Angel, one from Nate, and a garbled message from Patch. Word of what had happened to Charlie had spread quickly. There was nothing from her dad. He probably hadn't even realised she'd been gone for the night.

In the end she sent another text to Auntie Angel to ask her to keep covering for them, and promising to be in touch soon. Then she switched off the phone again. She was determined not to give another thought to the allegation that Angeline was a long-term snitch. Still, better safe than sorry.

Lucas asked if any of her messages had been important.

'Troy wants to speak to me. It don't mean he's on to you, though. Poor sod probably just wants to give me the heads-up on his dad.' Charlie had made plenty of people widows and orphans, but Glory couldn't get any satisfaction from the thought of his own family gathered tearfully by his bedside.

'What's the deal with you two anyway?'

'How d'you mean?'

He didn't quite have the courage to repeat Nate's insinuations. 'I just, um, wasn't sure how close you are.'

'Not very, considering I'm his future missus.'

Whatever he'd been expecting, it wasn't this. She was tired and dishevelled, and she should have been plain. Yet when he looked at her face, the strong bones and stubborn mouth, he found himself thinking that she was prettier than he'd realised. Striking, at least. Troy must have seen this too.

'Makes business sense,' Glory explained. 'If I was to marry into the Wednesday Coven, Charlie'd be able to keep me and my fae under his thumb. He might not know I'm a witch, not for definite, but he's making plans all the same. He'd like me to be a good little wifey, see, breeding witch-babies for the Morgan empire.' She tried to sound flippant, but it didn't quite come off. 'It turns out there ain't many options for coven girls. Even the witchkind ones.'

'That's . . . awful.'

For some reason, his pity annoyed her. 'Oh, stop gawping. I'll bet marriage-fixing goes on in the Inquisition too. Ain't that the best way to keep the fae and other riff-raff out?'

Lucas remembered his father with Marisa in the study, reassuring her about Camilla's witch-free background. I *did the usual checks: her pedigree was impeccable.* It had never occurred to him that his parents' marriage might have been arranged. He pushed the idea away.

'If so, it didn't work, did it? Look at me.'

Once in the internet centre, they found a quiet corner away from the other customers. The first thing Lucas did was download the file of the recording he'd taken at the Radley from the miniature spy-cam. Then he set up two new email accounts, and sent the film as an attachment from one account to the other. It was now saved in cyber-space.

Next, he logged on to an online news archive his school subscribed to. They were going to use it to search for background on Lord and Lady Merle.

The first item of interest was from the website of the Meadowsweet Children's Hospice. The charity announced that its patron, Lady Serena Merle, was hosting a fundraising ball on the Easter bank holiday Monday.

'That's tonight,' said Glory. 'Could be our lucky break. A big party like that should be easy to gatecrash.'

Lucas had lost track of time and dates. It had only been a week since he'd arrived at Cooper Street, yet his old life seemed to belong to another person, long ago and far away. Now he remembered that today was Ashton and Marisa's wedding anniversary. They were away in Paris for the long weekend. Otherwise, they might even have attended the ball. Marisa had campaigned for the same charity.

The only real news story they found was about seventeen-year-old Rose Merle's horse-riding accident last December, though the details of her disability were vague. It seemed that Serena Merle kept a low profile after her bridling and subsequent marriage. Before that, Serena Drew, model and actress, had been a regular in the gossip columns. One photo showed her in an embrace with a still-famous rock star. Her smile was radiant, her throat bare.

Lucas peered closer. 'Hey – isn't that Vince Morgan behind her?'

Glory leaned in too. The mobster's craggy profile was unmistakable. 'I know where that photo was took. It's the Morgans' club on the Strand. So that's where she met Charlie and co.! Did you notice her accent stopped being so la-di-dah when she was talking to him?'

'Whatever her origins, she moves in high-powered circles these days. No wonder she's been a good source for the coven.'

They turned their attention to Godfrey Merle and the Cardex News Group. Its dominance of the media was controversial, but remained unchallenged. No doubt it helped that Lord Merle was a major donor to the government.

The scope and purpose of the conspiracy was

becoming clear. The arrest and trial of Jack Rawdon would be led by Paterson and his cronies at the Inquisition, aided and abetted by their government and media contacts. Rawdon's demise would be followed by a general clampdown on witchkind rights that the public, already fearful of a return to the dark days of Endor, would back all the way.

In fact, the only remaining puzzle was Godfrey Merle's motives. Silas Paterson was a militant inquisitor of the old school, the kind who thought all witches were the enemy and should be treated as such. His ally in government, the minister Helena Howell, was a right-wing Christian evangelical who had made a career out of anti-witchkind campaigning. But Lord Merle himself had made no public gestures or statements to suggest a personal animosity towards witches. After all, he was married to one.

The last website they visited was the BBC news, which had the assassination attempt on Charlie Morgan as its headline. Charlie was described as a 'prominent business-man, with alleged links to organised crime'. His condition remained critical. They followed a link at the bottom of the webpage to witchcrime updates and the Inquisition. The main story here was that Commander Josiah Saunders had been taken seriously ill. Silas Paterson was now acting head of the Witchcrime Directorate.

'We have to move fast,' Lucas said. 'The next attack, and Jack Rawdon's arrest, will take place later this week. We need to get hold of some real evidence to show the authorities, so they can stop this thing in its tracks.'

'Authorities?' said Glory suspiciously.

'WICA and the police. Sir Anthony Brady will also have to know.'

'The Witchfinder General! Mab Almighty, ain't you learned *nothing*?'

'He'll do the right thing. No, really – Sir Anthony encouraged the Inquisition's cooperation with WICA in the first place. He's an honourable man.'

Glory wasn't convinced. Still, they could argue about it later. 'OK, so I was thinking . . . this party tonight. It's at the Merle mansion, the charity said. Now, Lady La-di-dah reckons whoever the prickers have been using to do the witchcrimes is locked up somewhere in the Inquisition. But what if the captive witch is closer to home? Posh pile like that must've loads of hidey-holes.'

Lucas was sure Serena Merle would have thought of this herself. All the same, it was worth a try.

'We can poke around His Lordship's study too,' Glory added. 'If his wife's been snooping for Charlie, she can probably give us her hubby's PIN numbers and private papers and suchlike. We'll need to get her on side first. But it's not like she don't want to help.'

'Good idea. The other place that needs searching is the Inquisition's HQ at Outer Temple. There are cells immediately below ground, but lots of people have access to them. The catacombs, however, are a different matter. You can't get down there without a key.'

'And you've got one?'

'No, but I know a man who does. That's why it's best if I take the Inquisition, and you go to the party.'

Glory began to protest, but he cut her off. 'Listen. I can

get into Outer Temple without any trouble. Everyone knows me there. It will be a different matter for you; much more dangerous.'

'I don't need protecting, thank you very much!' She glared at him. 'I'm being practical, OK? Splitting up is a stupid idea. If something goes wrong, and we're on our own, we'll be shafted.'

'I agree. That's why we need to get back-up. My warden, Officer Branning –'

'No prickers. No way.'

The ensuing argument took them out of the café and into the street. The fact that it was conducted in whispers and hisses didn't lessen the strength of feeling involved. Lucas explained that the Inquisition had such a heavy presence in WICA that if he contacted his handler himself, the enemy might intercept his warning. Jonah, as an inquisitorial officer, could get round the surveillance restrictions. But Glory utterly rejected the involvement of anyone from the Inquisition. None of them were trustworthy, all were corrupt. As soon as this Officer Branning suspected she was a witch, she'd be registered and bridled and bang to rights. And so on.

They were so caught up in the row that Troy Morgan burst upon them as if from nowhere.

In a few brutal seconds, Lucas found himself seized by the scruff of his neck, dragged down an alley, and slammed against the wall.

'Who are you? Who sent you? *Tell me your hexing name.*'

Lucas was too breathless to respond, even if he'd wanted to. Dumbly, he shook his head.

Troy hit him across the face. It was a sharp smack, rather than a violent one, but Lucas had never been struck in his life.

Glory, meanwhile, was tugging on Troy's arm with one hand and thumping him with the other. He ignored her. His hard green stare was fixed on Lucas.

'*Don't make me force it out of you.*'

Lucas opened his mouth, but again no words came.

'He's got nothing to do with the car-bomb.' Glory's voice was scratchy with panic. 'Troy, I swear it. I swear –'

'I know that,' Troy snarled. 'But he's still going to tell me what I want to know. You both are.'

He took out a pair of thick iron handcuffs from his coat and locked Lucas into them. Then he frogmarched him back to the main street, opened the boot of the Mercedes, and bundled his captive into it. Lucas barely had the chance to struggle before the door slammed shut. A passer-by looked at them doubtfully, but Troy held up an impressively shiny badge. 'Inquisitorial street patrol. Nothing to concern yourself with, ma'am.'

Then he took Glory by the wrist and, ignoring all squawks of protest, hustled her into the front passenger seat.

'Right,' he said. He put his hands on the dashboard, making a conscious effort to restrain himself. His voice was like iron. 'For the first time ever, you're going to sit in this car and talk to me without lying.'

The first lie Glory told Troy was that she'd only discovered that Lucas was a WICA agent last night. The second lie was the purpose of Lucas's mission; Glory said he had been sent to the covens to investigate the recent witch-terrorism attacks. The third lie was that she had helped Lucas spy on Charlie at the Radley because she was afraid he'd report her as a witch to the Inquisition.

Even so, she told him more of the truth than she'd wanted to. This included the fact that she was a witch, and Lucas's real identity.

She expected Troy to react explosively to both. Instead, he gave a twisted smile. 'I've got the Chief Prosecutor's kid in my boot? Mab Almighty . . . this day is getting more surreal by the minute.'

As for her fae – 'Like I didn't see *that* one coming.'

They were parked in a side street only a block away from where Troy had picked them up. Glory did her best not to get too distracted by thoughts of Lucas's welfare. She needed to concentrate on making her story fluent, the lies persuasive. She didn't know how much Troy believed, but at least he heard her out.

'How did you find us anyhow?' she ventured.

He produced a pocket mirror and a wad of black felt from his pocket, plus two slivers of fingernail. The materials from the shroud.

'I got the details of Dad's meeting from Uncle Frank at the hospital. Then I went to take a look around the Radley. As soon as I found this little lot, I set one of the Wednesday witches to a scrying-bowl.'

Scrying could be done with any personal item up to half a day after it had been taken from the target. It had been horribly careless to leave the materials of the shroud behind. However, to scry on somebody, you also had to know who you were looking for. The witch must have been told who the fingernails belonged to. 'How –' Glory began. But Troy was already giving her the answer.

'I'd asked Nate to keep tabs on the pair of you, and though he's a feckless idiot, he did at least spot that you were both away from home last night.' He grinned, enjoying her discomfort. 'So I told the witch who I expected to see, and showed her both of your mugshots. Then she described the result of her scrying. Imagine our surprise when your partner in crime showed up as someone else entirely! Now, it was *possible* you were in the company of a different boy to Harry. But since your little pal's a witch, it wasn't hard to imagine he'd had a makeover. Just like he did for the Blake Gordon business.

'Lucky for us, my scryer could see the shop front behind you clear enough. Once we'd identified that, it didn't take long to track you down.'

Glory bit her lip 'You said you know Lucas weren't responsible for the car-bomb. How come?'

His face darkened. 'Because we found out who was. Jonesy, in security. You might have seen him at the Gemini: built like a tank, shaven head, bad teeth.'

This description applied to most coven muscle. She made a non-committal sound.

'He's been with us for nearly seven years. The tip-off came too late. Uncle Vince caught up with him early this morning but Jonesy'd already put a bullet in his head. Apparently he'd been blackmailed into it. Someone had got hold of his kid – this sweet little three-year-old called Tess. She was returned to Jonesy's ex this morning. Neither of them can tell us anything.'

Glory knew the only UK outfit to rival the Morgans' was the Craven Side Coven, up in Manchester. 'Could it've been the Cravens?'

'Maybe. Or one of the Russian gangs. They've been trying to muscle into UK turf for a while. Either way, we need to find out – fast.'

'And how . . . how's your dad doing?'

As far as Glory could tell, Charlie and Troy had a good relationship. But she had never seen any demonstrable gesture of affection between them. From the look of Troy now, unshaven and with bloodshot eyes, it was clear he'd been up all night. But he was tired and angry, not distraught.

'It's pretty bad. If he does pull through, God knows what state he'll be in. Mum arrived this morning. She and Skye and the uncles are at the hospital now. Which means the thorny issue of what to do with you and your snitch-pal is my responsibility.' He looked at her soberly. 'And I've got to tell you, Glory, this is one hell of a mess you're in.'

Glory's mouth was very dry. 'Y'know, before you take any decisions, you might want to have a look at the film what Lucas made at the Radley.' She had not yet told Troy what, exactly, the two of them had learned from Lady Merle.

'Dad's last meeting . . . Yes, I should see it.'

Glory waited. Troy was staring out of the window at the wall in front, one hand tap-tapping on the wheel. 'I just thought I'd have a bit more time,' he said at last, very quietly.

'Time? For what?'

'Nothing that you'd understand.' He looked at her with impatience, and a kind of envy. 'You're big on inheritance, aren't you? The Starling Girl Destiny . . . Must be nice and simple for you.'

Before she could respond, he opened the car door. 'All right. Let's go chat with Little Lord Fauntleroy.'

Lucas had been locked in the boot of the Mercedes for nearly half an hour. He was very hot and cramped when he came out, the discomfort of his confinement intensified by the dizzying effect of the iron cuffs. These stayed on when Troy shoved him into the back seat.

Glory turned around from the front. 'I told him how you was sent to investigate the witch-terrorism,' she managed to say before Troy cut her off.

'Stay put and shut up,' he told them.

Although Lucas didn't really think Glory would rat on him, he felt a flood of relief. He had spent most of his time in the boot agonising about what she might reveal, and boiling with frustration that he couldn't be there to hear whatever cover story she came up with. At least this took his mind off all the things that Troy might be planning to do to him.

Troy's destination was a run-down office block behind Kings Cross. There was a private gym in the basement that was used as an informal drop-in centre for the lower coven ranks. Nobody was there now. The air was thick with stale sweat and aerosol spray; treadmills and weights gleamed dully under the fluorescent lights. Troy marched them through the fitness suite into the office behind.

It was only then that he released Lucas from the cuffs. 'Glory seems to think the meeting you snooped on last night is something I ought to know about. So before I decide what to do with you, I want to see what you've got.'

With nervous hands, Lucas attached the tiny spy-cam to Troy's laptop and pressed the playback button. WICA's equipment had not let him down: the picture was clear, the sound crisp. Troy watched the discussion between his father and Serena Merle in grim silence. He didn't say anything afterwards either.

'You have to understand,' said Lucas, as the silence stretched on, 'that the only reason I came to Cooper Street was because WICA thought a coven witch was responsible for the terrorist attacks. Now I know differently, what goes on in the coven doesn't matter to me any more – it's the corrupt inquisitors I'm after. I haven't got anything on you, let alone your organisation. I'm not any kind of threat.'

'Threat! Don't flatter yourself.' Troy's voice dripped scorn. 'Do you want to know why you're still here, still breathing? Because you're not just a kid, you're *incompetent*. An amateur.

'I don't care how fancy your fae is. You didn't spot I had Nate checking up on you. You left traces of witchwork all over the place. You either didn't bother to remake your elusions, or you forgot. WICA must be in a bad way if they're putting untrained schoolboys on the job.'

Lucas flushed resentfully. 'If they're in a bad way now, it's only going to get worse. We have to look at the bigger picture. This is a matter of national –'

'It's a matter of an evil stinking pyro plot,' Glory interrupted. Lucas's lord-of-the-manor air would do nobody any favours. 'What d'you reckon, Troy?'

'You heard my dad,' he said slowly. 'Whatever we might think of the situation, it's not the Wednesday Coven's business.'

'That was then. This is *now*,' Glory replied. 'With Uncle Charlie on life-support, everything's changed. You said yourself that car-bomb could be the start of something bigger – a turf war, even. So whether your dad recovers or not, the Wednesday Coven is going to face one hell of a mess. It'll be a coven blood feud on one side, and a witch-hunt on the other.'

Troy didn't respond.

Lucas took a deep breath. 'Look. I went to Cooper Street with a lot of preconceptions about the coven world. Some of those ideas were wrong. I didn't appreci-ate that the covens came into being to protect people, by giving witchkind opportunities and rights they didn't have elsewhere.' He wasn't sure he believed in what he was saying. It was part coven propaganda, part myth. But myths were powerful things, and sometimes there was truth at their core. 'That's why so many witches still trust them. That's why they give them their loyalty, and why the Inquisition and the police find them so hard to break. Maybe a witch-hunt's good for recruitment, like your dad says. But if people find out you guys had a chance to stop the lynching and the burnings, and didn't . . . Well. Doing nothing – it's not that different from collabora-tion, is it?'

Glory tensed. She wondered if Lucas had gone too far.

'You told me you trusted this boy before,' Troy said to her, his expression unreadable. 'He was lying to you then.

He might be lying to you now. Or you're both lying, and always have been. What do you think?'

'I think this thing is bigger than any of us.'

'Hmm. And what do the pair of you intend to do about it?'

Hesitantly, they explained about Glory going to find Lady Merle at the ball, and Lucas searching the Inquisition's HQ.

'I'm sure you'll be right at home,' Troy remarked. 'In fact, I'm curious as to why you've not yet run to Daddy Dearest. Unless, of course, you suspect the Chief Prosecutor's mixed up in this.'

'My father's not corrupt.'

'Oh yeah? He's a High Inquisitor who's spawned a witch but kept his job. I would've thought there was something in the rules about that.'

'There is. He's going to resign at the end of the Goodwin trial. In the meantime, my . . . condition isn't widely known. That's why WICA recruited me.'

'That still doesn't explain why you haven't asked him for help. Or aren't you on speaking terms, now you're an out and proud witch-kid?'

'It's nothing like that. I need to get proper evidence first.'

'Your dad won't believe you without it?'

'Of course he would. But he'd insist on doing things by the book. By the time he went through the protocol, and got search warrants issued and witnesses subpoenaed, it might be too late.'

'If the conspirators suspect we're on to them,' Glory

chipped in, 'that witch they're using is as good as dead. They won't risk keeping him or her alive to tell tales.'

Lucas nodded. 'Supposedly, only a handful of top-ranking people at the Inquisition know I'm a witch. However, as soon as we make our accusations the truth will come out. The enemy'll be quick to turn it to their advantage, so that Dad's credibility is damaged as well as mine. Getting him involved could backfire.'

This wasn't the whole truth about why Lucas wasn't ready to ask his father for help. He might have failed to infiltrate the Wednesday Coven, or keep the Goodwin trial from collapse, but now he had a new opportunity to prove himself – to stop an even greater crime, against even worse odds. He would use his fae to purge the Inquisition of the enemy within. He would be a Stearne worthy of the name . . .

But Troy was laughing to himself. 'I see. You don't know when or what the next witch-attack will be, where the witch responsible is being held, or how to bring the guilty parties to justice. You can't trust any of the authorities. And you want start your crusade by gatecrashing a high-society ball.' He leaned back on his chair, fingers laced behind his head. 'OK . . . First, you need to get Glory on to Lady Merle's guest list. This isn't a school disco – you can't just turn up and hope for the best. You'll need to look the part and have an escort, as well as a nice fancy invitation card.'

'An escort?' Glory repeated.

'If you'll do me the honour.' He gave a mocking little half-bow. 'And preferably wash beforehand.'

So they'd won Troy over! Glory felt a rush of optimism. Lucas wasn't sure whether to be relieved or alarmed. But perhaps any help – even the criminal kind – was better than nothing.

Ironically, Lucas's best hope of infiltrating the Inquisition would be to play the part of his father's son. Most of the guards and officials there knew who he was, but hardly anyone knew of his condition. His records would be kept under a false name until the Goodwin trial was over, just in case an over-zealous inquisitor learned of his condition, and insisted that Ashton Stearne stand down. This evening, he explained to Troy and Glory, he would simply turn up at the gate and explain that he'd come to collect some paperwork for his dad.

'I'll need to stop off at home first,' he said. 'My father and stepmother are away, and I know where Dad keeps his keys to the catacombs. But once I'm in the Outer Temple compound, I'll be able to wander about undisturbed.'

It was not, in fact, quite so simple – although Troy and Glory weren't to know any different. Lucas had indeed visited his father at the office and in court on plenty of occasions, but he would still need a good reason to be there unsupervised at night. The Inquisition was a 24-7 organisation. Even though it was a bank holiday, there would still be people about, and strict security controls.

Luckily, Lucas had the perfect cover. He'd had the idea in mind ever since he'd thought of searching the catacombs. His way in would be through the Hammers: the members of the young inquisitors' club who met at St Cumanus's church. Lucas wasn't an official member. But last Christmas, at some Inquisition event, one of the younger officers who was keen to ingratiate himself with Ashton Stearne, had offered to take Lucas along to a social. 'Come as my guest,' he'd said. 'Any time you like. Just give me a call.'

Now was the time to take him up on the offer. The Hammers met on Wednesday nights, but they also marked religious holidays – Christmas, Balefire Night and Easter. Tonight would be a big event.

I'll say I've got over my illness and want to celebrate, Lucas thought. *I'll get one of those hooded robes they wear, and a bottle of booze, and if I do get caught somewhere I shouldn't, I'll just be a drunken idiot who got lost en route to the party. If the worst comes to the worst, they'll only phone my dad.*

Since Lucas's arrangements seemed to be in hand, the three of them got down to the practicalities of attending Lady Merle's ball. Although the tickets were sold in benefit of the children's charity, and the Merles were hosting the event, the actual organisation was done by a professional party-planning service. Troy used his IT skills to hack into the files. They discovered Silas Paterson was on the guest list, presumably to support his good pal Godfrey Merle.

'Even though it's sold out, I can still add us to the list,' Troy said. 'There's a picture of a ticket on the website, so you can knock up fakes with a fascination.'

'What about the Morgan name, though?' Lucas asked. 'That might set off alarm bells.'

'My family are major charitable donors,' Troy informed him coldly. 'It happens that Dad gave an endowment to the Meadowsweet Children's Hospice earlier this year. Besides which, I'm a fine upstanding citizen without a stain on my character.' He turned to Glory. 'You should maybe think about a glamour, though.'

'I ain't so sure. If we're going to persuade Lady Merle to trust us, I don't reckon we should hide behind witchwork.'

When she left for the toilet, Lucas felt suddenly vulnerable. Sure enough, as soon as Glory had closed the door, Troy leaned across the table and fixed him with his red-rimmed glare. 'I *know who you are and where to find you*,' he said. 'Don't ever forget it.'

'Er . . . OK.'

'Now,' Troy continued, 'it's true my organisation can't afford a witch-hunt, not with our boss down and a blood feud in the offing. It may be that provoking war between the covens is part of Paterson's plan, and so he arranged the car-bomb to frame one of our competitors. If that's the case, then I need to know about it.

'However. That doesn't mean I like you or I trust you. So if anything bad goes down tonight, I and my coven will hunt you down, and make you pay. You and Paterson both. Understand?'

Lucas nodded.

Troy pinched his cheek, in a parody of affection hard enough to leave a bruise. 'Good boy.'

Soon afterwards, it was time for Lucas to leave. Arden House, Lord Merle's country pile, was a forty-minute drive outside London, and Troy and Glory would have to set off around quarter to seven. Lucas aimed to get to the Hammers by seven thirty, but he had to stop by home first. It was already half past three, and there was a lot of preparation still to do.

When it was time to say goodbye, he felt constrained by Troy's presence. Glory seemed constrained too. She was uncharacteristically quiet, arms folded tightly across her chest, eyes on the floor. Lucas was gripped with foreboding. None of them really knew what they were doing and how it might end. Then he remembered the night in the Gemini, just before going to see Charlie, and Glory's warm breath in his ear. 'We'll be OK,' he told her softly, and touched her on the hand. 'They're greedy murdering scum but we're better than them. I know you can do this.'

Glory smiled a little, crookedly.

'Look after her,' Lucas said to Troy.

What an idiotic thing to say, he thought as he left them.

CHAPTER 27

Look after her.

It was an idiotic thing to say. But Glory didn't feel as insulted by it as she ought to be. She stared at the door. Lucas's words had been so . . . final.

'Quite the little gentleman,' Troy observed. 'Or are you sticking to your original estimation of him as a "pillock"?'

'He's only a pillock some of the time. And he's doing his best.'

Troy rolled his eyes. 'Don't tell me. The pair of you had an all-night pyjama party, bonding over your dysfunctional family life and the Joy of Fae.' Then his expression turned serious. 'You need to watch yourself, Glory. Lucas might be a witch, and he might be on our side – for the moment. But he's got twelve generations of inquisitor in his blood. He's not our kind.'

Glory resented this on a number of levels. 'I don't care what "kind" he is or he ain't. I just want him to get his part of the job done, and for us to do ours. That's all. Then we can get on with our lives.'

'Our lives have changed,' Troy said, and looked more serious again.

*　*　*

Since Troy had already added them to the guest list for Lady Merle's ball, the next stage of their preparations mostly involved shopping. They needed the materials for the fascination Glory intended to craft, and a dress, make-up and a wig for her to adjust her appearance.

First, however, Troy hired a car under a false name, in case his Mercedes was being tailed. The next stop was his flat. This was in a discreetly plush apartment complex near Tower Bridge. Glory was made to wait in the hall outside while he picked up his tuxedo and other bits and pieces.

As Troy opened the door, she glimpsed a big light room, with lots of books on the shelves and, intriguingly, two wine glasses on the table. There was a kicked-off pair of women's heels underneath it.

'Why can't I come in?' she complained. 'You afraid I'm going to lower the tone or something?'

'This is my private space. It's got nothing to do with the coven, and nothing to do with my family. And I'd like to keep it that way.'

Troy closed the door on her, re-emerging a few minutes later in a clean shirt and carrying an overnight bag. Glory was dying to ask who the shoes belonged to, but didn't quite dare.

In spite of everything, she was looking forward to going on a spree with Morgan money. But here too Troy proved a disappointment. He only let her look in one boutique and rejected her first three choices of dress: leopard print, scarlet and sequins. 'You don't want to stand out. You want to disappear into the background,' he told her, before presenting her with a selection of outfits that were as plain as they were pricey.

'Frumpy,' she pouted.

'Classic,' he retorted. 'And don't go mad with the heels. You might need to move fast.'

In the end they compromised on a dark purple cocktail dress and black slingbacks. Anything was better than Glory's current get-up. She felt like an urchin, with her grubby black clothes and unwashed hair. The snooty sales assistant clearly thought that Troy had picked her up in the street, and handled his platinum credit card as if it had been dipped in manure. This provided pretty much the only amusement of Glory's day.

Perhaps to avoid similar censure, Troy chose a distinctly downmarket hotel for their base. They would only be using the place for a couple of hours, to make their final preparations and consolidate their plans. The receptionist looked them over wearily, with the air of someone who's seen it all before.

Glory went to use the shower while Troy made phone calls to the hospital and various coven contacts. She returned to find him typing on his smartphone. 'What's the latest?'

'Dad's in intensive care. He's suffered forty per cent burns, but his condition's stable, at least.'

'I'm sorry.' Well, she was sorry for Troy, at least. 'I'm sure you must want to be with your family right now.'

'Dad's not the type who'd appreciate me snivelling by his bedside. Not when there's work to be done. Mum understands that too. Uncle Vince's team are shaking down the usual suspects, trying to find out who Jonesy's blackmailers are, and once we know that, I'll set about dealing with them – whether they're connected to the Inquisition or not. But in the meantime . . .' He shrugged. 'I might as well kick some bad-guy butt with you.'

While Troy took his turn in the bathroom, Glory set about crafting their tickets. She had already looked them up on the charity's website, and seen how they were designed as personalised invitation cards. Now she carefully copied out the text on to two plain white postcards. She used gold ink, and reproduced the style and layout as accurately as possible. They'd decided that disguising Troy's identity would be more trouble than it was worth, but that she should change her name to match her subtly-altered appearance. The name on her ticket was Elizabeth Brantly.

Glory's method was close to the one Lucas had used to replicate the diamond necklace, since both objects represented similar things. Before enfolding the cards in the cashmere stole she would be wearing to the party, she drew a picture of Lord Merle's coat-of-arms (found on an internet heraldry site) and pasted a twenty-pound note (courtesy of Troy's wallet) on to the back of each. The fascination of luxury, money and privilege were now all represented in the witchwork.

As she was wrapping up the cards, her mobile beeped. It was a text message from Lucas, with a mobile number. *ZConnor, in case of emergency. Good luck.* She was just saving the witch-agent's number when Troy came back from the bathroom. She felt guilty hiding it from him but maybe Lucas was right. Better safe than sorry.

'Here you go, Cinders,' she said, handing the fascination over to Troy to uncover. 'Your fae-godmum says you *shall* go to the ball!'

He took out the tickets and examined them carefully. 'I knew you had talent,' he said. 'But this is really impressive.'

Glory glowed. It felt great to be witchworking in the open. It was also good to be on friendly terms with Troy. Once again, she wondered what he knew about her mother's murder and, if he knew, what he thought about it. But to ask him would raise his suspicions about her motives for helping Lucas. She couldn't take the risk.

Looking out of the bus, Lucas viewed his home neighbourhood with a stranger's eye. The squares were leafy, the streets quiet, the paint on the walls as smooth as cream. The people strolling on the pavements didn't have a single tattoo or tracksuit among them.

He got off the bus one stop early to hunt for a payphone. Out of habit, and superstition, he looked around to check that he was unobserved. Troy's threats were not to be taken lightly. But Lucas knew that if things went wrong, somebody in a position of authority would need to know the full story. He would start with Witch Warden Branning.

The call didn't begin well. Officer Branning was angrier than Lucas would have thought possible. Since learning of the assassination attempt on Charlie Morgan, Lucas's father had been phoning Jonah every hour on the hour, asking for news of his son, and demanding that Lucas be recalled from duty. He had threatened to go to Jack Rawdon himself.

Jonah had only managed to put him off after speaking to Agent Connor. She'd expected to hear from Lucas following the surveillance operation at the Radley, and had taken the emergency step of contacting Angeline after news of the car-bomb broke. The old lady confirmed that she'd heard from Glory that she and Lucas were alive and well, but were now out of contact. This news went only part-way to relieving the general anxiety.

Lucas was ashamed. It had honestly never occurred to him how the attack on Charlie, and his own lack of communication, would affect the people responsible for protecting him. Yet he disliked being treated like a foolhardy kid, even if he had behaved like one. Besides, there were much more important things to worry about – as he told Officer Branning the moment he could get a word in. 'It's a matter of national security,' he said, an unconscious note of hauteur creeping into his voice. 'You'll understand the seriousness of the situation when you see the recording I made.'

'What situation? What recording? What –'

Lucas explained that he'd saved the film of Charlie's meeting in the Radley in an anonymous email account. It was something Agent Connor needed to see as well, but he couldn't risk alerting the team at WICA because he didn't know what kind of surveillance they were under. 'I'll text you the log-in and password for the account in a couple of hours. But there's something I need to do first.'

Jonah made various exclamations of protest, exasperation and alarm.

'I'm sorry,' said Lucas at the end of them. 'I really can't tell you anything more for the moment. Once you've seen the film, make sure Agent Connor sees it too. Don't worry; I'll be in touch soon.' Then he hung up.

*   *   *

There was, in fact, nothing stopping Lucas from letting Jonah access the film right then and there. But that would set in motion a train of events he wasn't ready for. It wasn't that he was afraid of Troy and Glory's reaction if he brought the authorities in behind their backs. It was that he was sure they were on the right track. They just needed a head-start, to get on with the job without any outside interference.

Lucas had learned from Jonah that although his father and stepmother had planned to return from Paris early that afternoon, France was gridlocked by a transport union strike. Even if they had tried to come home earlier, they wouldn't have got past the blockade. They would certainly be away for a few hours more. Since Philomena was spending the Easter weekend at her dad's, the coast was clear. He got past the guard, camera and access code at the Stearne residence's gate, then went up to the front door and put the key in the lock. He could hear Kip barking inside. The dog rushed up in a slobbering frenzy of enthusiasm, as if he'd been away for a year.

He kept away from the portraits, though. All those generations of Stearnes, with their unsmiling mouths and proud eyes, would be the witnesses to his burglary. There was no other way of describing it, even if the end did justify the means. His father would be implicated in the plot if it succeeded, for it would be his job to convict Jack Rawdon of witch-terrorism and treason, and send him to the Burning Court. But Lucas had to remind himself that when – if – the case came to trial, his secret would be out, and the Stearnes in disgrace. A new Chief Prosecutor, probably one of Paterson's cronies, would conduct the trial.

He couldn't worry about that now. It was time to make his second phone call of the day. He switched on the mobile he'd left in his bedroom, ignoring the accumulated text messages, voicemails and missed calls, and dialled the number for Rory Dixon.

'Rory? Hi. Lucas Stearne here. Yeah . . . Really good, thanks . . . Actually, I've got a bit of a favour to ask . . .'

Rory was more than eager to oblige. He was a junior lawyer in the Office of the Inquisitorial Court, who calculated that making pals with the Chief Prosecutor's son would be a smart career move. However, there was a problem. 'The thing is, Lucas, I've got quite a lot on. I wasn't actually planning to go to the Hammers tonight.'

Lucas's voice swelled with disappointment. 'But you did say come *any* time . . .'

And somehow, Rory found himself promising to visit the Inquisition that evening, and process the application to bring Lucas Stearne in as his guest.

Lucas rewarded himself with a shower in his en suite bathroom. It was as if the squalor of Cooper Street was steaming out of his pores. His clothes felt like old friends. Here was his proper self: the same but different. Irrevocably so. His right hand rested on his left shoulder blade, the one with the Devil's Kiss. He saw Glory again, leaning towards him through the candlelight, the dark stain waxing and waning under her skin.

He blinked the image away.

From a trunk in the attic, he pulled out the

inquisitorial cloak that had belonged to his grandfather. It was made of heavy black wool with a lining of scarlet silk, faded with age. He stuffed it into a rucksack, collected black gloves and a small torch from his bedroom, and headed downstairs. Getting into Ashton's study was easy enough. Lucas knew a spare key was hidden in the Chinese porcelain vase in the library. Moments later, he was pulling away the set of *Encyclopaedia Maleficia* from the bookshelves to expose the safe behind.

His father had shown him how to access the safe in case of emergency. The numbers on the combination lock were the date of Camilla's death, in reverse order. The safe contained various legal documents, such as the deeds to the house and Ashton's will. Lucas wasn't interested in any of these. His target was the two iron keys tucked at the back.

One of the keys' handles was marked with a tiny cross, the other with a sword. They were too small and plain to look like anything special, yet were one of only four pairs that provided access to the Inquisition catacombs. The only way to get down there was through the crypt of St Cumanus's church. A couple of times a year, the catacombs were opened up for historical tours. Otherwise, they were out of bounds. Ownership of the keys was a matter of prestige, rather than practical use. Apart from the Witchfinder General, only three inquisitorial families had a personal set: the Stearnes, the Hopkins . . . and the Patersons.

Lucas slipped them into the rucksack with the cloak. They were iron, but the quantity of metal was too low to cause him any discomfort. Carefully, he closed the safe and replaced the encyclopaedias. Then he turned to his father's computer. With the industrial action in France, he still had a good hour before Ashton and Marisa were likely to return, and before he needed to set off for the Hammers. He knew he might never have an opportunity like this again.

Getting started was easy. He'd seen his father log on enough times to know that his password began with a 'G' and was eight characters long. Lucas guessed the G was for Grantham, the name of the historic Stearne house that been sold in the nineteenth century. Sure enough, 'Grantham' got him in.

He immediately brought up the National Witchkind Database. There were four access levels. Level One recorded the names of anyone suspected but not proven to be a witch. Level Two provided basic information on all proven witches whose identity wasn't classified. Level Three gave access to their personal files. Level Four contained summarised reports on all witches whose identity was secret or sensitive. To read their complete case histories you had to apply directly to their warden, or whichever state official was responsible for their supervision.

Only senior inquisitors could use Level Four. Lucas knew the individual access codes for this were changed every week, and sent to the relevant personnel via an encrypted file. As long as Ashton had logged on to Level Four within the past seven days, Lucas had a good chance of recovering the sequence. His principal tool would be dust.

House dust is primarily composed of airborne pollution, human skin and hair. This was his father's private room, so it would mostly be his father's dust. Although the housekeeper would have been in over the weekend, to look after Kip and put things in order, she didn't have a key to the study. Even so, the surfaces were fairly clean, and it took Lucas some time to sweep the thin film of dust lying over the desk and windowsill on to a piece of paper. He had better luck with the top shelves of the bookcase, behind volumes that were rarely consulted. The dust was quite thick there.

Materials gathered, Lucas clicked on the log-in page for Level Four of the witchkind database. He sat for a while in his father's chair, fingers spread out on his father's keyboard, visualising Ashton at his desk. Then he held the paper layered with dust over the keyboard and blew, very gently.

The dust did not fall. It hung above the keys in a greyish-beige mist. Lucas's breath had sent his fae into this mist, and now it worked its way into the particles of his father's skin and hair, the fibres of his clothes. For a second or two, the fae-dust floated before his eyes, before hazy trickles of it began to float down to the black keys, one trickle after another.

The first key the dust landed on was P, where it left the faintest of blurs, like a fingerprint. Then 5. Then 9. The ?/ key. J, Q, A. With a final puff, 6.

Lucas typed in P59, and stopped.

The fourth symbol could either be ? or /, depending on whether he used the shift key or not. Suddenly, everything was in doubt. He didn't know what letters, if any, should be in caps, and whether the numbers should be symbols instead. He would only have three chances to type the code before the security system was alerted and the database shut down.

Lucas stared at the smudgy keys again. Was he imagining it, or was the dust somewhat heavier on the ?/ key, the J and the 6?

He typed in p59?Jqa^, and held his breath.

Access Confirmed.

A guilty thrill ran through him. This was his chance! As a precaution, he began by typing in his own name into the search engine, and was relieved to see that nothing came up. His identity was still protected by a false name. He could now move to the real object of the exercise: finding out what the Inquisition had to say about Angeline Starling.

It was very straightforward. Up popped Angeline's profile, along with a photo. Quickly, he scanned the notes. Her first encounter with the Inquisition was at the age of twenty, when she had been witch-ducked and pricked under suspicion of witchwork. The results were inconclusive. She had been taken in for questioning by the police and Inquisition on three subsequent occasions, and each time she was released without charge. Lucas guessed this was in conjunction with the Starling Twins' activities. But twenty-eight years ago, Angeline had presented herself at the Witchcrime Directorate and 'volunteered information pertaining to the whereabouts of a known witch-criminal'.

Cora Starling. It had to be. Lucas could see that the dates matched, and felt foolish for not making the connection before. It also explained why Glory had become so agitated when he told her the year when Angeline was alleged to have started informing. She must have turned in her own sister to the Inquisition! Where she was witch-ducked, and drowned . . .

Lucas thought of the Starling Girl shrine in Angeline's room in Cooper Street, and how the old lady was always droning on about the sacred memory of her beloved sisters. Then there was the way she doted on Glory, and hated the Morgans. Her betrayal made no sense.

He read on. Angeline had never been formally tested or registered, but her fae was estimated to be a lowly Type B. Presumably that was why she hadn't been bridled: they knew her to be a witch, but she was more useful to them as an informant. Her Current Status read: *Operation Echo. Active.* Operation Echo was the mission to place Harry Jukes in Cooper Street. To learn about Angeline's activities in more detail, he would have to submit an application to Commander Josiah Saunders or another name that he didn't recognise.

Lucas pressed 'print'. He knew it would hurt Glory to see this, but she needed to know, even though she'd no doubt find some way of dismissing it as yet more Inquisition propaganda.

He saw there was a list of reference numbers at the bottom of Angeline's page. They were links to more Level Four files, probably those relating to her sisters. The other Starling Girls might be dead but their records were still classified. Lucas clicked on the top one.

It took him to Edie Wilde, nee Starling.

Glory's mother. Charlie's victim. Alleged witch.

He had read all this in the Cooper Street file, which had been compiled by the Inquisition and supplemented by WICA. According to this, she was an unregistered low-grade witch who'd probably got the fae in her early twenties. Yet the version of Edie Starling on the database seemed like a different person entirely.

Firstly, Edie was Type E, not Type A. Type E was the highest known ranking – the same as Lucas's. By her own admission, she had turned witchkind at the age of thirteen, though it was not until the age of twenty-seven, when her daughter Glory was three years old, that Edie was formally tested and registered. This was the same year that she disappeared. Yet there was no mention of a feud with the Morgans or a coven hit. And now Lucas understood why Edie Starling was unbridled, and had a fake profile in the Cooper Street file – she too was an undercover agent. Not for WICA, though. She was working directly for the Witchcrime Directorate.

Current Status: *Operation Swan. Missing in Action.* The last sighting of her had been five years ago.

Lucas stared disbelievingly at the screen. It was impossible, but true. Glory's mother was – just maybe – alive. The photograph of her didn't much resemble her daughter. She looked to be a natural blonde, with thin, fine features and startled eyes. He scrolled down to the names of the officers supervising her case, and his heart almost stopped. One of the four was Ashton Stearne.

There was no time to absorb the impact of this discovery. Something at the corner of his eye tugged his attention away. The monitor at the door, which was currently trained on the entrance gate, showed a blonde struggling with a suitcase. Marisa and Ashton had returned.

Lucas didn't think he'd ever moved so fast in his life. He shut down the computer, brushed off the dusty keyboard with his sleeve, and grabbed the printout of Angeline's profile, all in less than twenty seconds. Then he sprang out of the room and locked the door behind him. A few moments later, the key was back in its hiding place and the printout stuffed behind a sideboard. Meanwhile, Kip was barking. 'Oh shut up, you stupid mutt,' said a familiar petulant voice. Not Marisa, but Philomena. Lucas waited until the banging in his ribs had calmed, counted to ten, and walked into the hall.

'Hi, Philly.'

She gave a theatrical start. 'Lucas! What are you doing here?'

'A flying visit. I just had to collect some . . . stuff.' He picked up the rucksack with the inquisitor's cloak and keys.

Philomena edged around him, hugging the walls as if he was suddenly going to blast her with a thunderbolt.

'When are you coming back?'

Good question. 'Soon, probably.'

'Well, it's been absolutely horrid here. Your dad's in a permanent grump and Mummy's not much better. There's no one to talk to about what I'm going through.'

'I'm sorry if you've been suffering.' He couldn't keep the sarcasm from his voice.

'God. Why doesn't anyone take me seriously? It's still all about *you*. How *you* must be feeling. What *you're* going to do. Same old, same old.'

Lucas moved to the door. 'When you see my dad, will you tell him I'm fine? And . . . and I'll talk to him later.'

'I'm not a bloody answering machine.'

'Just do it, Phil.'

She stared at him. 'You cause all this trouble,' she said, 'and yet you still think you're so hexing special.'

CHAPTER 28

Mindful of Troy's instructions about blending into the background, Glory kept her make-up to a boring minimum. Mascara, eyeliner, clear lipgloss, a touch of blusher. Sighing, she pulled on the shoulder-length brown wig. Just because it was close to her real hair colour didn't mean it suited her. At least she was coming round to the dress. The deep purple was nice, and the material clung in all the right places. She was rather disappointed when Troy's only comment was 'Good'.

Troy wore his tuxedo in the same effortlessly casual way he wore his suits. He accessorised it with a gun holster under the jacket. She watched him adjust the shoulder straps and wondered what he'd used it for before.

'You think we'll need a gun?'

'I think it's best to be prepared. Witchwork can only get you so far.'

They spent the drive out of London with the radio on, each lost in their own thoughts. However, they paid more attention when it came to the news. The police had made a statement that no witchwork was suspected in Charlie's car-bomb. All bar two of the Roma migrants who'd escaped from their detention centre had been found. Another top footballer had been caught in a sex and drugs scandal. Another witness had withdrawn from the Goodwin trial. But the focus was mostly on Helena Howell's efforts to rush a raft of new witch-terror legislation through parliament. Her gratingly sweet voice sounded entirely reasonable as she outlined why Britain was 'on the brink of a public emergency that threatened the life of the nation'. Troy switched the radio off with a snap.

'Are you nervous about tonight?' he asked Glory.

'No,' she lied.

'You should be. We don't know how Lady Merle will react to us or what might kick off. This isn't nicking a flashy necklace out of a shop window. We're meddling with matters of state.'

'Yeah, well, that's why me and Lucas asked you to help. You're good at meddling.'

They had reached the turning for Arden House. The mansion rose up at the end of a tree-lined drive: three storeys of worn rosy brick, the entrance sheltered by a portico on two round columns. Glory almost laughed. It was very similar to Charlie Morgan's house on Cardinal Avenue. Just bigger, older, grander. The real thing.

Their first setback was the discovery that the event wasn't actually taking place in the house. Instead, a pavilion marquee had been erected on the front lawn. Both the entrance to the marquee and the house were supervised by men who looked less burly than the bouncers Glory was used to, but nonetheless had a forbidding air about them.

Taking a look around the place was going to be even harder than anticipated.

'Them tickets cost three hundred a pop. And they're fobbing us off in a tarted-up tent!' she grumbled as she got out of the car. 'I thought this was meant to be a ball, not a night at the circus. Hey – what are you doing?'

Troy had taken the keys to his hired car and casually scratched a long line in the paint along the passenger side. He grinned. 'You never know when we might need to cause a diversion.' Then he keyed his neighbour's Porsche too.

A group of polished young women were waiting to check tickets and direct guests to the cloakroom facility. Their desk was adorned with tasteful black-and-white photographs of the hospice kiddies who would benefit from the money raised. 'Oh dear, Mr Morgan,' said their ticket girl. 'Your and Miss Brantly's names don't appear on my list.'

'But we have our invites,' said Troy, presenting the fascinations.

The girl typed into a laptop. 'Well, yes; you're certainly on the database. I'm so sorry. It must be some glitch in the system.'

'No problem at all,' Troy said smoothly.

Glory had to admit the marquee was impressive inside. The ceiling was swathed in gold and purple awnings from which chandeliers twinkled, and there was a working fountain in the centre of the parquet floor. Floral arrangements of irises and yellow roses continued the colour scheme; the grandest display was a gilded tree from which jewel-coloured Easter eggs hung. Glory peered this way and that, hoping to catch sight of their hostess.

'Stop goggling,' Troy told her. 'She'll be here soon enough. No doubt there'll be speeches and so on before things really get under way.'

It wasn't just their task that was making her twitchy. The whole set-up was unnerving. Glory thought Troy could have been less of a spoilsport about her outfit when she surveyed the other ladies, who were dripping in jewels as well as all sorts of unlikely furs and feathers. Everyone had the same way of talking as Lucas did. This was his world, she realised suddenly. People like this. Houses like this. Parties like this. She looked at one of the few guests near her own age, a brunette in a backless peach silk gown. Her face was peachy too, and she had a sweetly tinkling laugh that set Glory's teeth on edge.

Waiters glided through the throng, bearing champagne and platters of canapés that were flourishes of garnish, and not much else. Glory tried a tiny biscuit topped with a curl of pink mousse. She expected it to be sweet, but it tasted fishy and horrible and, when she thought no one was looking, she spat the remains into one of the flower arrangements.

To wash away the taste, she helped herself to some champagne. Troy promptly confiscated the glass and presented her with an orange juice instead.

'Dear me, that's not the way forward,' a balding, red-faced man remarked to him jovially. 'There's nothing like a spot of bubbly to soften the ladies up! Half a bottle, and she'll be all yours.'

Troy gave him the Morgan stare. 'That is a disgusting insinuation.'

Red-face got redder, and moved on. The next moment

Lady Merle arrived, and took to the stage at the far end of the marquee, where the band was sitting.

She was wearing a billowing violet gown the same colour as her eyes. Her curves were billowy too. The dark bridle looked more of a mutilation than ever against the pale skin. Lucas had described his first meeting with her to Glory, but she still found it hard to reconcile this person with the desperate yet focused woman in the Radley basement. Her voice was slurred and her face slack.

As far as Glory could make out, the gist of Lady Merle's speech was that they were wonderful, wonderful people for supporting this wonderful cause. There would be a charity auction later, full of wonderful, wonderful gifts. She hoped they all had a wonderful time.

Lord Merle then said a few words about being delighted to be able to welcome people to his home. He did not look delighted. He looked bored and contemptuous. Glory thought he had the appearance of a fat speckled toad.

'Did you know Serena was one of your dad's sources?' she asked Troy, under cover of the party's social roar.

'I knew of her, but not her identity – only her code name. The Pearly Queen.'

'Why d'you think a babe like her got hitched to a pig like him?'

'Money. Connections. Desperation. Whatever.'

Glory watched Lord Merle fondle his wife's waist with a pudgy hand, and shuddered. Not all the mansions in the world could make up for that.

Troy had seen the shudder. 'Marriage is a contract like any other. As long as both parties know what's expected of them, and agree to stick to it, there's no reason they can't make it work.'

'I bet that ain't the kind of marriage you'd want for yourself,' she said unthinkingly.

'Well, that would depend. On you . . . as it happens.' He turned and looked at her, eyebrow cocked. 'How about it?'

The world stood still. 'Mab Almighty. Is this is a *proposal*?'

Troy laughed. 'I'm no cradle-snatcher. You've got a hell of a lot of growing-up to do first.' He spoke with the effortless assurance of someone who had always looked and acted much older than his age. 'Several years of it, in fact. C'mon, Glory – I can't believe this is a total surprise. The idea must have crossed your mind before.'

But to spring this on her now, at such a time and place! Torn between outrage and incredulity, all possible responses stuck in her throat.

'But – but you've already got a girlfriend,' she said at last, clutching at straws.

'So? That's hardly an issue now.'

'It might be later.'

'Not if we both set some ground rules. I'm not a hypocrite. I've seen what works in my parents' marriage, and what doesn't. We're the next generation, we can do things our own way. I want an equal partner at home as well as at work.'

'At work . . . in the coven?'

'Obviously.'

Anger flared. 'And *obviously* we wouldn't be having this conversation if I weren't a witch.'

'Ah, but you've always wanted to be a witch, haven't

you, Glory? A head-witch in a powerful coven. It's in your nature and it's in your blood. But talent can only get you so far. You need connections as well. I can give you all that.' Troy smiled, an easy, rather charming smile that she hadn't seen before. 'Who knows? I think you're a pain in the butt now. I'm sure the feeling's mutual. But with time, we might even find ways to like each other.'

The first time Glory had got wind of the Morgans' marriage scheme, the idea had repulsed her in every possible way. But she was beginning to see that there was more to Troy than she'd realised. He had made her a fair offer.

She tried to consider it practically. Even if Charlie survived his hospital stay, his recovery would be slow and difficult, and Kezia would have to devote herself to looking after him. Vince Morgan was a feral thug and Frank a prissy old pen-pusher. They'd let Troy run the Wednesday empire how he liked. And if – *if* – he was serious about wanting Glory to be her own person, and an equal power in the coven, then she could find other ways to make Charlie pay. Maybe the saying was true: 'living well is the best revenge'.

'There's no hurry,' Troy said softly. 'This is a long-term plan. I'm just asking you to think about it. Because we both know it makes sense.'

It did. Like any good business deal.

Glory looked around at the elegant crowd. The air smelled of roses, the champagne sparkled, the fountain splashed. The band had just struck up a waltz. Most people would think it a dream setting for a proposal. The brunette in the peach dress whirled by, going to kiss her boyfriend. Her eyes were shining, their embrace carefree. Glory felt a tightness in her chest, something sharp and squeezing, that also pricked at the back of her eyes. *I'm not living in a fae-tale*, she thought. *Those stories are never about girls like me.*

Troy touched her arm. 'Look – Lady M's on the move. Now's our chance.'

CHAPTER 29

Lucas approached Outer Temple with an ache in his chest. For as long as he could remember, the historic headquarters of the British Inquisition had been as much a part of his future as his family's past. The stately buildings loomed behind the iron wall, their aged stone warmed by the glow of Victorian street lamps. The windows of the surveillance block glittered high and bright. All through the night, inquisitors would be at work there, watching and listening to keep the nation safe. Or so Lucas had always believed.

At the security check, the guard's face split into a grin of welcome. 'Stearne the Younger, as I live and breathe! It's been a while since we've seen you round here – they've been working you too hard at that school of yours, I reckon.'

Jeff Buller's father, uncle and grandfather had also guarded the gates of the Inquisition, and he took a personal interest in all the staff there, from the lowliest assistant groundskeeper to the Witchfinder General himself. It wasn't Jeff's fault that he was about to let loose an unregistered Type E witch on the premises.

'I've been ill,' Lucas said. 'So no school for me. Would

you mind paging Rory Dixon? He's supposed to be taking me to the Hammers.'

Jeff checked the computer for Rory's application for a visitor's pass for Lucas Stearne, and compared it with the printed documents in his file. 'Here you go, young sir,' he said, passing Lucas a form to fill in. 'Got your ID with you? That's right. Look straight into the camera. And a thumbprint, if you don't mind. Better safe than sorry, eh?' He chuckled.

The Home Office's Identity and Passport Service was responsible for issuing national ID cards and collecting biometric data. Lucas's was stored under the name of Harry Jukes for the duration of his cover. In recent months, however, the Home Office's system had been plagued by technical glitches and security scares, and so the Inquisiton had decided to issue its own cards and collect its own data for staff and regular visitors to the Inner Temple compound. As a result, this was the only security check in the UK where Lucas's thumbprint and iris-scan wouldn't show up as Harry's.

'Now, you take it easy tonight,' Jeff told him 'Some of those Hammer shindigs can get a bit rowdy for my liking, though I know their hearts are in the right place. Raised over two grand in their last fundraiser, bless 'em.' He patted the collection tin on his desk. It bore the badge of the Inquisitorial Widows and Orphans fund.

Lucas shoved in a couple of quid. 'By the way, is Jonah Branning on duty?'

When he'd spoken to Jonah, the warden had been at home. Still, he'd like to be sure.

'Let me check the log . . . No, Officer Branning's on leave today. Did you have a message for him?'

'I'm actually trying to avoid him, to be honest.' Lucas lowered his voice conspiratorially. 'Dad's nagging me to set up some work experience in the Assimilation Bureau.'

'Work? In the "Hug a Harpy" gang? Dear-oh-dear. I'm sure we can find you something a bit more exciting than that.' This was from Rory, who was striding importantly towards the gates. His face was pale and baby-fattish, with a smile as oily as his hair.

'Hello, Rory. Awfully good of you to let me tag along, especially at such short notice.'

'No worries at all. We'll make a night of it, eh?'

While Rory finished off the paperwork, Lucas composed a text to Jonah. *Here's the info u need. Pls make sure Z sees it. G and I will find out more tonight. Spk later.* Then he typed in the email account and password that Jonah needed to access the Radley recording. He pressed 'send', deleted the copy of the text in the sent messages folder, and switched his phone to silent.

Job done, Lucas put on his cloak, and sent his rucksack through the X-ray machine. He had already added the keys to the catacombs to his set of house keys, which he dropped into the tray for pocket items, along with his wallet, mobile phone and watch. His possessions passed through the scanner without alarm, and so did Lucas. He walked into the heart of the Inquisition.

The cloak was musty and heavy, and Lucas had to keep hitching it up so that it wouldn't drag on the ground. But the hood was a comfort, hiding his face from view as they crossed Kindle Yard. Even if Jonah did turn up, he was very unlikely to spot him.

'You're in for a treat,' Rory told him. 'It's a bit of a special occasion, what with Easter and so on. There's going to be a trial.'

When the Hammers weren't collecting money for widows and orphans, they liked to recreate famous inquisitorial trials, reading from the court transcripts and playing the parts of witchfinders, witnesses and witchkind alike.

'Great,' Lucas said, forcing as much enthusiasm into his voice as possible.

'It'll be the Berwick. What a pity it's not one of the Stearne specials! Otherwise, we could have roped you in to play your own great-grandad or whatever, ha, ha. By the way – I asked around to see if Gideon Hale would be attending. I know you're old school pals. But I'm afraid to say he can't make tonight.'

'That's a shame.'

Lucas's show of regret was as insincere as his enthusiasm. He had no evidence that Gideon was involved in Paterson's schemes. In any case, he was confident his condition remained a secret, and there was no reason for Silas Paterson or any of his allies to suspect him of acting against them. But Gideon's presence would have been a complication he was relieved to avoid.

The Hammers were starting the evening in one of the reception rooms to the side of the Great Hall. Rory lead the way. On arrival, he knocked on the door in a complicated sequence of taps. It opened a crack.

'*Maleficae dictae a maleficiendo* –' began the person on the other side.

'– *seu a male de fide sentiendo!*' Rory whispered throatily back.

This exchange gained them entry into a candlelit room full of young men and women wearing black and scarlet hooded cloaks over their suits. Several wore ornate crucifixes. They were drinking wine from silver beakers, and complaining about overtime.

Rory introduced Lucas to whoever he thought would be impressed by the Stearne name. Various people presented Lucas with various drinks. Since pretending to get drunk was part of his cover, Lucas needed little encouragement. There was a lot of laughter and mutual backslapping. As he furtively tipped his wine into somebody else's beaker, he wondered how Glory and Troy were doing.

The room got increasingly hot and crowded, the laughter more raucous. There was a flurry of excitement with the entrance of an attractive brunette in an extremely short white shift. Lucas recognised her as Gideon's companion at the witchcrime lecture; Zilla, he thought her name was. She must be playing the part of the witch in the trial. Shortly after her arrival, a high, bright chime rang through the room, and silence fell. The society's president had struck a bell with the silver hammer that was their emblem.

Everyone stood to attention for the toasts. One to the Queen, one to the Witchfinder General. The third was 'To Twenty-two Eighteen!' Lucas bit down on the rim of his beaker. It was a reference to the Book of Exodus, chapter twenty-two, verse eighteen, and the former motto of the English Inquisition. 'Thou shalt not suffer a witch to live.'

The bell was struck again. With a cheer, everyone surged out of the room and towards St Cumanus's Church. The pretend witch got a piggyback ride from the president. A night-shift worker on the way to his desk stopped to let them pass, muttering resentfully under his breath.

Lucas stumbled along the cobbles. He kept on tripping over the hem of his cloak, which at least added to the impression that he'd had a few too many. Rory, who'd been increasingly distracted by all the other people he wanted to impress, eyed his protégé nervously. Ashton Stearne would be less than pleased if his son got drunk and disorderly on Rory's watch.

There was a queue for the stairs down to the crypt. When they got to the bottom, Lucas hung back. 'I'm not feeling so good,' he mumbled to Rory. 'I think I'd better push off.'

'Golly, are you sure? Shall I walk you out? Or –'

'No, no, no. I'm fine. Honestly.' He hiccupped. 'I mustn't spoil your evening. 'S'OK – I'll get Jeff whatsit to call me a cab. Dad's not home tonight.' Lucas clutched Rory's arm and looked at him with drunken solemnity. 'Thank you, though. He's always wanted me to be a Hammer.'

As a matter of fact, Ashton Stearne thought that the Hammers were a glorified frat-house, and it was high time someone got them under control. But Rory wasn't to know this. He gave Lucas a hearty handshake, and moved on.

Lucas stepped back to let the others pass into the body of the crypt. It was a large and surprisingly airy space, presided over by the tomb of St Cumanus, the fifteenth-century inquisitor who gave the church its name. For the Hammers' meeting, a red velvet drape had been slung up between the pillars. It was for purely theatrical effect, but very useful for Lucas. Now everyone was gathered behind the curtain, both he and the door to the catacombs were hidden from view.

The door was iron-plated, and when he touched it the cold of the metal brushed down his spine. It couldn't actually hurt him, or even block his fae – not unless he kept in physical contact with the metal. Still, he felt the threat it represented. It served the same purpose as the wall around the inquisitorial compound. *Keep Out.*

The Hammers' president was making another speech. Under cover of the applause, Lucas fitted the key marked with a cross into the lock. He didn't know the purpose of the second key, but the sign of a cross was appropriate for a church door. With a protesting creak, the door inched open and Lucas slipped through. He was careful to lock it behind him.

The catacombs pre-dated the church. According to legend, a religious order of medieval witchfinders had been the original settlers of the site, and had built the catacombs for their rituals. Over the centuries, they had been used as a burial place, prison and storage facility. Primarily, though, it was a place of refuge. Inquisitors had taken shelter here during the Great Plague (started by the witch Ambrose Vellum, and spread by his coven) and again during the Great Fire, when a spate of balefires got out of control and set London alight. People had also slept here during the Blitz.

Although the catacombs didn't cover a large area, the series of small stone cells was dense and maze-like. It was an ideal place for a secret captive.

The burial chambers had been cleared in the nineteenth century, and their contents moved to the Inquisitorial cemetery in Brompton. There were still a couple of urns in the alcoves, but the main visitor attraction was the wall paintings. They were very old, and apocalyptic in nature, showing lakes of fire and hideous beasts from the Book of Revelations. There were also pictures of witches at work: conducting orgies, sacrificing infants, and dancing with the Devil. Although the colours were faded and childish, the lines crude, the intensity of the artist's vision was undimmed.

Snarling faces flared briefly into life as Lucas's torch skimmed the walls. During a tour last year, he had found the place strange and spooky, but not sinister. He had underestimated the difference it would make coming here on his own and in such circumstances. It didn't take long to pass beyond the official tour circuit. The further he walked, the more oppressive the silence and darkness became. The weight of earth seemed to crowd around him, ancient fears and hates sweating out from the stone. His inquisitor's cloak dragged on the floor. He tried not to think about what had been done down here when the place was a prison.

Most of the cells were open and empty, but he found one with a broken bed frame and a chamber pot. The door had a grille at the top and there was a bag of workman's tools on the floor; perhaps someone had been going to fix the place up. If so, the project had long been abandoned. The bag and bed were covered in cobwebs. It was time to admit defeat: the catacombs were as lifeless as the graves that had once filled them.

Lucas prepared to retrace his steps, following the chalk crosses he'd made along the way. He swept his torch around for one last look at the tunnel-like passage ahead of him, and it was only then that he saw the stairs. The passage did not lead to a dead end after all. The steps were very steep, and very worn, leading up to a squat iron door.

It was hard to keep track of direction and distance below ground, but Lucas calculated that his explorations had taken him north-west of the church. That meant he was somewhere in the vicinity of the Witchcrime Directorate. The building had been extended and heavily remodelled over the years, but the original structure was an old one, and odd corners of it survived. Lucas remembered something about a historic cloister. It was possible that these stairs were connected to it.

He looked at the key marked with the sword. The cross and the sword . . . the two ancient weapons of the inquisitor.

The second lock was much stiffer than the first and he had to put all his weight against the iron to push the door open. It could not have been used for a long while. The metal ached through his shoulder and arm. A lesser witch might not have been able to withstand it. But he got the door open at last. It took him into a covered walkway. When he looked through the colonnade, he saw a window he recognised. Or rather, he recognised the sundial in the courtyard outside it. The BBC news website had illustrated its witchcrime report with a photograph of Colonel Paterson at his desk; a sundial could be seen through the window behind him.

Below ground, a mounting sense of failure had added to Lucas's claustrophobia. Up in the fresh air, he was filled with new determination. He couldn't and wouldn't fail – not after coming this far. Especially since one of the few useful things he'd learned at Cooper Street was Nate's how-to guide to breaking and entering.

He hung back in the shadows of the cloister, thankful for the protection of his black cloak and hood. It was nearly nine o'clock. There were no lights on in any of the windows overlooking the courtyard. At this time of night, and on a bank holiday, the only people in the building would be a handful of night-duty officers. The inquisitorial guards would be making their usual patrols through the grounds. But they wouldn't bother with this courtyard. It was enclosed on all sides, and the only exit or entrance was through the main building – unless, of course, you came through the catacombs.

The opportunity was too good to resist. Silas Paterson's office had a box sash window, which was the kind Nate said was the easiest to open from the outside. The iron shutters weren't even drawn. Once more, Lucas rehearsed his cover story. He'd been drinking with the Hammers and thought it would be a laugh to explore the catacombs. He'd got lost. He didn't want to get in trouble. He was only trying to find a way out . . .

Lucas returned to the catacombs, and the cell with the bag of abandoned workman's tools. It seemed like fate when he found a small hacksaw. He put on his gloves, and went back up the stairs. He crept along the cloister, under cover of the shadows and his cloak, until he reached Paterson's window. His heart was pounding so hard his body felt like it was vibrating, yet he realised he was enjoying himself. Maybe once he'd finished spying he'd take up burglary. He slid the thin blade of the saw between the upper and lower sash, in the centre where the latch was. Mindful of Nate's instructions, he jiggled the blade up and down until he got it against the latch, then forced the latch back. He heaved open the window and climbed through.

It was much more nerve-racking inside the office than when he'd been trying to break into it. The enormity of his actions suddenly hit home. He had to pause, waiting for the jitters to calm. The room was dark and peaceful. So was the yard outside. He had disturbed nobody and nobody would disturb him.

Silas wasn't head of the Witchcrime Directorate just yet, but you wouldn't know this from his office decor. His desk was antique mahogany, and a Persian carpet adorned the floor. There were no family snapshots on his desk, just framed photographs of Paterson looking grave and statesman-like alongside the US Ambassador, the Prime Minister and a minor royal. Lucas opened the top right-hand drawer to find a bottle of single malt whisky.

The other desk drawers were locked. So were the filing cabinets, though he found the key stuck on a lump of Blu-tack at the back. He wished his gloves weren't made of such thick wool, as they slowed him down as he flipped through the paperwork. None of the budget sheets, management reports or minutes from departmental meetings seemed particularly interesting, let alone incriminating.

Time was running out. If he didn't check out at the security gates at a reasonable time, alarms would be raised. That meant he had to leave either before or with the Hammers. If he bumped into Rory, he could always say he'd fallen asleep somewhere, or gone to the canteen for coffee. He looked at his watch again, and decided he could afford another ten minutes.

Lucas eyed the computer. That was where the secrets were kept. Something in the emails, a special folder . . . He'd need Paterson's username and password to logon – and he knew how to get them.

There hadn't been anything dangerous about hacking into his father's computer. This was different. His story about being drunk and lost wouldn't fool anybody if he got caught committing witchwork. And he'd have to take off his gloves, so his prints would be all over the place. But if he didn't give it a go . . . Well. Who knew what Glory might or might not learn from Lady Merle? This could be their only chance.

Taking a deep breath, Lucas switched on the computer. When he removed his gloves, he realised how grimy his own hands had become during his explorations in the catacombs. He wasn't sure if mixing dust from different sources might corrupt the witchwork in some way. All he could do was wipe his hands on his cloak, and hope for the best. He set about gathering the office dust on to paper; looking under the Persian rug, around the bookshelves and along the top of the curtain rail.

He was standing over the keyboard, sheet of dust in his hands, when he heard brisk footsteps in the corridor outside. He froze, waiting for them to pass.

The feet didn't pass. They stopped outside. Keys jangled, the door opened. And Lucas made his first serious mistake.

His only instinct was to get out of there – back through the window, across the yard, and into the catacombs. But there was no time to think anything through. The fae, already unspooling through his body and brain, was at his fingertips. It took a hold of him. And as the door opened, he backed away in the direction of the window, and blew the dust he'd gathered – the dust of Silas Paterson's office, and the grime of the catacombs – into the air.

He'd had some muddled idea about covering his retreat. The result exceeded all expectations. The fae-blown dust was suffused with the alarm of the moment, the dread he'd felt in the catacombs, and the grime of their ancient cells. The small grubby puff gathered into a vile-smelling fog that rolled in billows across the room.

Under cover of the cloud, as the unknown inquisitor cursed and flailed, Lucas dived for the window. He might even have made it, if he hadn't stumbled over the wastepaper basket and got tangled in his cloak. The inquisitor blundered through the room after him, and made a grab for his sleeve. Both of them fell to the floor, thrashing about blindly in the toxic dust. Coughing and choking, Lucas's captor dragged him to his feet.

In his worst-case imaginings, Lucas had wondered what he'd do if Silas Paterson returned early from Lady Merle's ball. The reality was almost as bad. He was staring into the face of Gideon Hale.

CHAPTER 30

About the same time as Lucas took his first steps into the catacombs, WICA Agent Connor was sitting in Senior Witch Warden Branning's car in a deserted car park. The film that Lucas had recorded in the Radley was playing on Jonah's laptop.

Zoey's face as she watched it was a blank, taut mask. It was Jonah's second viewing of the material but, if anything, his horror of it had only increased. When the footage came to its end, a dull flush spread under his freckles.

'On behalf of . . . that is . . . as an inquisitor, I feel I should – that it is my responsibility to –' He swallowed painfully. 'There are no words. But I want you to know I am truly sorry. This must confirm all your worst suspicions of us.'

'I judge people as I find them,' Zoey said at last, and with effort. 'But I don't judge a community only by its criminals. Witchkind's history has shown us the danger of that.'

Jonah didn't think of the Inquisition as a community, but perhaps that was because he didn't feel like he fitted in. It was a vocation, though, and his faith in that vocation had been badly shaken.

'Do you know where Lucas is now?' she asked him.

'No. He's cut off all contact. I can't get hold of Glory either. I'm worried the two of them have taken matters into their own hands.'

'Well, Lucas was right to be cautious about contacting me. The Inquisition has too heavy a presence in WICA for us to make use of its resources without alerting the enemy.'

'Can you find a way of warning Rawdon?'

'Jack's been away at a conference but he's due back tomorrow. I'll get word to him. It would help if we had some idea of what the next target is likely to be.'

She logged on to her smartphone. After accessing Rawdon's schedule, they agreed the most likely target was a parade in Windsor for troops returning from peace-keeping duties abroad. The Director of WICA would be there to highlight the role of witch-soldiers in the armed forces. The event was taking place tomorrow and would attract large crowds. It would be the perfect opportunity for a terrorist outrage, followed by a spectacular arrest.

'I'll tell Jack to cancel all public engagements,' Zoey said. 'In the meantime, we need to deal with our teenage runaways. I know they're trying to help, but it's likely they'll just make things worse. And get themselves into a hell of a lot of trouble along the way.'

Jonah rubbed his face tiredly. 'At a guess, they'll try to get in touch with Lady Merle. That would be the obvious place to start. But Lucas has a lot of insider info about the Inquisition. I'm worried he might try to act on it, without really knowing what he's dealing with.'

Zoey was just about to respond when her phone rang. 'Hmm. Not a number I recognise.'

She hit the answer button. 'Connor,' she said crisply.

'Hello? Hello?'

'Who is this?'

'It's Glory. Glory Starling. Lucas gave me your number – I didn't –' Her voice was a raw whisper. 'I didn't want to call you. But it's an emergency. We're at Lady Merle's country place. It's all kicked off. She – he – I think he's dead. We're going to –'

The line cut out. When Zoey called back, it went straight to voicemail.

'You were right,' she told Jonah grimly. 'Lucas and Glory must have gone to see Lady Merle. And now they're in trouble. We need to get to them, fast.'

CHAPTER 31

Troy and Glory had followed Lady Merle out of the marquee to a small and inconspicuous door at the side of the house. They strolled arm in arm, trying to look as if they were merely admiring the grounds. But this entrance also had a staff member hovering nearby, ready to usher guests away from the family's private quarters.

'What shall we do?' Glory whispered, as they backtracked round the corner.

'I'll get him distracted so you can sneak in. You're the witch-damsel in distress – Lady M's more likely to respond to you. I'll catch up with you in a bit.'

Troy strode across the grass. 'Look here,' he said to the footman or bouncer or whoever he was, 'I went to get something from my car, only to find some git's keyed it. The car next to ours too. I thought I saw a kid skulking in the drive, but when I yelled at him he ran off.'

The flunkey was flustered. 'I'm terribly sorry, sir. Would you mind coming along with me to show us the damage?'

As soon as their backs were turned, Glory nipped along the terrace and through the door that Lady Merle had used.

She found herself at the foot of the back stairs. They took her up to a corridor, lined with paintings covered in dark varnish and lit by small hooded lamps. The doors along it were all closed. It was dim and warm and utterly silent. Her wig was itching, and she took it off and bundled it into the cashmere wrap. She wanted Lady Merle to see her as her real self, roots and all.

There was a second set of stairs at the north end of the corridor, steeper and pokier than the last. She climbed them too and found herself on a small landing, with a bathroom to her right and another door in front of her. She hesitated, straining to hear sounds of life. Had she lost Lady Merle already? She'd thought she'd heard voices on her way up the stairs, but all was quiet.

When she opened the door, she found herself in a long low attic. It had been converted into a bed-sitting room, comfortably but sparsely furnished. The furniture that was there was soft and padded. Sitting in an armchair in front of a folding screen was a girl of about seventeen. When she saw her, Glory came to a confused stop. Hair like fire, skin like snow, eyes the colour of violets . . . It was like looking at a picture in a fae-tale.

'Um, hi,' said Glory.

The girl turned her head, very slowly. Her eyes were wide and unblinking. Glory realised that she wasn't so perfect after all. The skin on her right hand was shiny and puckered, like a scar that had healed badly.

'I . . . don't . . . know . . . you,' the girl said at last. There was no alarm or curiosity in her voice, or on that frozen, lovely face. She spoke in an empty monotone.

But Glory knew who she was: Rose Merle, the girl in the riding accident. 'It's OK,' she said. 'I'm looking for your mum.'

'Who are you and what are you doing here?'

It was Serena Merle herself, who had come in from an adjoining room. She didn't appear as wasted as she had in the marquee, but she didn't look well either. Her eyes wandered and her hands twitched.

''Scuse me for the interruption, Your Ladyship, but my name's Glory Starling and –'

'Starling?'

'That's right. I really need to talk to you. It's about what you told Charl–'

'No.' Serena put her hands over her ears. 'No, no, *no*. I don't want to hear any of it. It's too late. Too much has happened.'

There was a knock on the door, and a mild-faced woman in a nurse's uniform entered the room. 'The car's here, milady.'

Serena shot Glory an agitated look. 'I don't care who you are or what you're here for. None of that matters any more. My daughter is leaving, and I have to – to –' She took a deep breath, and made a visible effort to pull herself together. 'I have to say goodbye.'

She went over to Rose, and helped her out of the chair. 'You're going to go and stay in a safe place,' she told her. 'The people there will look after you much better than I can.' Then she took Rose by the shoulders, and looked searchingly into her blank eyes. 'Remember how much I love you, always. Try to understand. Try to remember.'

336

'Always,' Rose repeated tonelessly. 'Always.' Her expression didn't change. She moved in stiff, precise movements, like a wind-up doll. The nurse took her by the hand and gently led her down the stairs.

Serena watched them go with such anguish on her face that Glory had to look away. But the next moment, the woman rounded on her. 'How *dare* you invade my house? On this night of all nights!'

'I didn't have no choice! I heard about your talk with Charlie in the Radley, and the plot what you discovered. Somebody's got to act. So I'm working with Charlie's son Troy, and we've got help from WICA. I'm not giving up. I can't. I'm – I'm a witch too.'

'A Starling, you said.' Serena suddenly softened. 'Like mother, like daughter . . . Did you see my Rose, how beautiful she is?'

'Er, yeah.'

'Talented too. And so popular! Rose was destined for great things. All the lovely, lovely things I never got to do because I turned witchkind.'

Her eyes had glazed over again. She'd definitely been drinking, Glory decided. Or taking pills of some kind. 'Because I was going to be a star, you know. Everyone said so. But nobody wants a bridled witch on their sets and screens. Or in their centrefolds. The fae stole all that away from me.

'So when Rose – my beautiful, talented Rose – when it happened to her . . . I was ready to try anything. *Anything.* Whatever it took.'

'Rose is a witch?'

'Not any more.'

'But . . . once you turn witchkind, the fae's a part of you. For ever.'

'Well, we cut it out.' Her voice was brittle. 'There's a clinic that does it. Experimental psychosurgery.'

'I don't get it.' The idea was too appalling to be true. Glory was increasingly disorientated by Lady Merle's abrupt changes in manner. It was like talking to three or four different women at once. 'The fae ain't a piece of your brain. There's more to it than that.'

'Like a "ghost in the machine", as the philosopher said? Maybe so. But the US Inquisition conducted research on witch-brains, back in the fifties. As did the Nazis, in their camps. And in witches, they found a difference . . . a different kind of neural connection . . . "abnormal circuitry", they called it. I read the research papers, I heard the testimonials. But there wasn't much time. The surgeon told me the procedure only worked if the fae was caught early. We had to do it quickly, and secretly, before Godfrey found out.'

She was twisting her hands, as she had when making her appeal to Charlie. They looked red and rubbed.

'It was my idea, but later I began to be afraid. Rose wasn't, though. She begged me to let her do it. If she was a witch, her life would be ruined, just like mine. How could I refuse? And then when she came out of the operation, and her fae had gone, we were so happy we cried. Imagine that! We thought we'd beaten it. We thought we were safe. And then . . .'

'Then . . . ?'

'Then one morning, out in the garden, Rose collapsed. She was unconscious for only a few minutes, but afterwards . . . she was blind. Blind, deaf and dumb. This lasted for twenty-four hours. And although she recovered her three main senses, her memory had gone. She can't hold a thought for more than a few minutes at a time. Perhaps it's a mercy, considering what she has become . . .

'You might have seen the scar on her hand. It's from when she put her hand into boiling water and didn't realise it. Rose, you see, has lost the ability to feel pain. She could bleed to death and never notice. That's why she has to be watched every minute of every day. My daughter is never hurt or scared, but she doesn't feel anything else either.' All Rose's lost emotions flooded into her mother's voice. 'When we cut out the fae, we cut out the heart of her. I betrayed my daughter. I betrayed our kind.'

Glory's body crawled with horror. She wanted to get away from this wild-eyed woman, the memory of the ruined girl, away from this mausoleum of a house. But she had a job to do.

'Is that why you started helping the covens?' she asked.

Serena's hands twisted and turned. 'I didn't plan it that way, but soon after Rose's . . . after Rose . . . I crossed paths with Charlie Morgan. I'd been friends with him and Vince once upon a time. Far away and long ago . . .'

'More than just friends, I reckon.' It was Troy, who'd been standing unobserved in the doorway. 'I saw Rose down in the hall. She's Uncle Vince's kid, isn't she?'

The red hair, Glory thought. Charlie had even hinted at something of the sort, back in the Radley.

'She's not Vince's, she's mine. My crime. My guilt.'

'You're not the criminal,' said Glory hotly. 'It was the crooks what did the experimental psycho stuff.'

'Speaking of crooks,' said Troy, 'I'd like to have a chat about His Lordship.' He shut the door, and moved towards Serena. 'Circumstances have changed since you went to my father. The Wednesday Coven is ready to offer you its support. But when it comes to identifying the guilty parties, we need more than just your word for it.'

'We're out of time.' Her eyes darted to the clock on the wall. It was quarter to nine. 'I already told Charlie all I knew.'

Troy wasn't about to back down. 'You did your own investigating, didn't you? There must be some kind of paper trail. This witch they've imprisoned –'

'Don't worry, darling.' Serena gave an off-key laugh, and ran her finger around her iron collar. 'The only captive hag around here is me.'

'I don't see why Lord Merle married you, if he hates witchkind so much,' said Glory.

She laughed again. 'He hates witchkind because he envies us. Ironic, isn't it? Godfrey's got prestige, wealth, influence. But he hasn't got the fae. The one power he doesn't have! It eats him up, the bitterness. It's his obsession. He's even got a collection of witchwork objects. He keeps them in his den: all polished up, under lock and key. Just like his wife.'

Suddenly she gripped Glory's wrist, breathless with urgency. 'Don't trust them. They hate us, and they want us. They fear us even as they despise us. That will never change.'

Glory shrank back. She didn't know if Lady Merle was

talking about non-witchkind, or men in general, but she was frightened by the mad light in her eyes.

Troy had had enough too. 'All right. Tell us where your hubby's office is, and how to get into it. Then we'll go.'

'So masterful!' Serena mocked. 'Just like your father. In the old days, mind you, it was Vince who had the sex-appeal . . . I always had a weakness for dangerous men. But really, you mustn't worry. Silas won't get away with it, and neither will Godfrey.'

'What d'you mean?'

'I mean that I've made my plans. You'll understand later. That's why you have to leave – it's for your own good.'

But when she went to open the door, she reeled back. Lord Merle was glowering at the top of the stairs.

'Godfrey! You're – you're early. I asked you to meet me at nine.'

'It's my own damn house. I'll come and go however I please. Besides, you're the one who made all the fuss about saying goodbye to Rose. Pointless as that'll be.' He shouldered his way past, and saw Troy and Glory for the first time. 'Who the hell are you?'

'They're nobody, nothing,' Serena said agitatedly. 'Just some guests who wandered up here by accident. They're leaving now.' She tried to smile at him. 'Please, Godfrey. Have a seat. The clinic collected Rose earlier, but . . . I . . . I still need to talk to you.'

Lord Merle turned back to Troy. 'Do I know you? You look familiar.'

'I don't think we've met,' Troy said impassively.

Godfrey looked from him to Glory to Serena again.

Serena was white-faced and twitching. Glory was staring at the floor. From the folds of her cashmere wrap, which she'd put down on a side table, a hank of brown wig was showing. His voice sharpened. 'What's going on?'

Serena took Troy and Glory by the arm and tried to hustle them out of the room. 'I warned you already. Go.' She turned back to Lord Merle and smiled brightly. 'See – they're leaving! Just like you wanted! Everything's fine!'

'I don't agree. In fact, I'm calling security.'

He marched to the door.

'No,' Serena burst out. 'Don't – you mustn't!'

She turned to Troy, and threw her arms around him. 'Make him stay,' she pleaded. 'You have to.'

Troy tried to push her off. She clung on, babbling.

Her husband stared at her in disgust.

'Get a grip of yourself, for Christ's sake. Or take another damn pill. Maybe then you'll turn into as much of a vegetable as your daughter –'

Crack.

Glory didn't understand what had happened at first. Even when Lord Merle fell to the floor she didn't quite believe it. Then she saw the gun Serena had pulled from Troy's holster, and the blossom of red on Lord Merle's shirtfront.

'Oh God,' said Serena. 'Oh God oh God.' She began to shudder all over. Quickly, brutally, Troy wrested the gun out of her hands and shut the door. Then he knelt by the body.

'Is he dead?' Glory asked, forcing all her strength into her voice to keep it firm. She mustn't be weak. Troy mustn't know.

'Almost.'

Serena collapsed into Rose's chair. She put her face in her hands.

'Should we get a doctor . . . or . . . ?' Glory asked.

'It's too late for that. Still, we might be able to get something out of him.'

Troy put his hand on Lord Merle's shoulders and shook him. The dying man made a clotted, choking sound. A bubble of blood oozed from his lips. Glory had to look away. 'Jesus, Troy,' she muttered.

'This isn't the time to be delicate,' Troy snapped, putting the gun back under his jacket. 'Go outside and check no one heard the commotion. We can't have anyone coming up here.'

Glory took a final look at the scene. Serena was quaking and gasping. Troy had blood on his hands and shirt. He shook Merle again. 'Look at me,' he hissed. '*Look at me.*' Merle groaned. There was a faint, acrid smell of gunpowder.

At least there were no sounds of alarm or activity from the rest of the house. Out on the landing, all Glory could hear was her own heart, banging against her ribs. She closed her eyes. Then she got out her mobile.

There was little or no reception in the attic. She had to go down to the shadowy corridor below before she got a signal. In one of the bedrooms off the hall, she dialled the number Lucas had given her.

'Connor,' said a voice the other end.

'Hello? Hello?'

'Who is this?'

'It's Glory. Glory Starling. Lucas gave me your number – I didn't – I didn't want to call you. But it's an emergency. We're at Lady Merle's country place. It's all kicked off. She – he – I think he's dead. We're going to –'

She froze. Someone was climbing the back stairs. A voice called out, 'Serena? It's Silas. Am I going the right way?'

CHAPTER 32

Gideon snapped iron cuffs around Lucas's wrists and yanked him to his feet. They stared at each other through the swirling dust. Gideon's pale eyes were cold, amused.

'Well,' he said. 'This is interesting.'

Lucas gathered together the shreds of his story. He began to say something about the Hammers, about having a few too many, taking a wrong turn –

'Indeed you have.' Gideon smiled with real pleasure. Then he spoke into his earpiece. 'Alpha One to Alpha Two. Protocol Six security breach in one-oh-nine, requesting back-up.'

The fae-dust was already fading away. Soon there would be no trace of it. Lucas knew, however, that there was no hope of denying what Gideon had witnessed. It was witchwork of a very high order. He cast around for an explanation, however hopeless.

'There was an intruder in the office,' he said. 'I saw them from the courtyard. I wasn't thinking clearly but I thought I should . . . y'know . . . chase them off. But as I was coming through the window, the dust appeared. I think whoever it was must've been a witch. I mean, that fog stuff wasn't normal, was it? Anyway, I never got a proper look at the person. As I was trying to get in, they fought to get out. Then you arrived – it all got confused – and –'

'So how did this other intruder get in and out?'

'Um, the same way I did, I guess. Through the cata-combs. I found the door in the cloister already open. You know, someone should probably go and search the place.'

There was a knock on the door. Lucas was relieved. If he was lucky, it would be an officer he knew. He must stick to his story until the proper authorities took over and his father or Jonah were brought in.

But the newcomer was not an inquisitorial guard or even a directorate worker. It was Zilla, the inquisitor playing the witch at the Hammers' mock-trial. She was wearing her costume under her coat, but there was no sign of the flirta-tious party-girl of before. If this was 'Alpha Two', then Lucas was in serious trouble.

'Watch him,' Gideon told her as soon as she arrived. 'And check this.' He tossed her Lucas's rucksack, then made a call on his phone. 'Hello? It's Hale . . . I'm sorry to disturb your evening, sir, but there's been a break-in at your office . . . yes . . . I think so . . .' He glanced at Lucas. 'There's something else . . .' He went out in the corridor and shut the door.

It didn't take long for Zilla to find and confiscate Lucas's torch, phone, keys and gloves. She had brought along gloves of her own and an evidence bag. The hacksaw went in along with the rest.

Lucas watched from a chair. He tried to look tipsy and

346

confused, a guilty schoolboy who'd been caught where he shouldn't be, but he knew it was probably too late. The call to Paterson was a bad sign. The correct procedure was to summon the officer of the watch. They should all be in the custody suite, filling in paperwork, by now.

'Good news,' Gideon announced, when he returned to the office. His phone call had taken some time. 'The Colonel has authorised us to make further enquiries and you, Lucas, are going to assist me. Together, we're going to get to the bottom of who broke into this place. Maybe we'll even find the witch responsible. I'm sure you'll find it very enlightening. I know what an eager student of the Inquisition you are.'

'Sure, yeah, I'm ready to make my statement. If you'll take me along to the guard room –'

'Let's not get ahead of ourselves.'

Zilla hauled him to his feet.

'Where are we going?'

'Somewhere we won't be disturbed,' said Gideon. 'We can't be too careful: there are witch-terrorists on the loose.'

Lucas licked his dry lips. 'OK, it's just that people are going to wonder where I am. Jeff Buller knows I'm here, and Rory Dixon. Then there's my dad, of course. If I don't sign out soon, they'll start to worry.'

'There's nothing to worry about, Stearne. Colonel Paterson and I have been working together *very* closely, you see. I have his full confidence.'

Gideon was smiling as he stepped forward, his hand flicking out to pull down something that had been hidden against his wrist. Lucas jerked away from Zilla's grip, but it was too late. He could already feel the sting where the syringe had pierced his inquisitor's cloak, driving through to his skin.

Lucas tried to kick, to wrench himself free. Instead, he sagged. His body was like that of a puppet whose strings had been cut. He tried to shout that Gideon and Zilla were traitors and criminals; that the integrity of the Inquisition was under threat. But when he opened his mouth, the only sound to come out was a drooling bray. 'Wha – wha – whaa –'

Zilla and Gideon took him between them and half carried, half pushed him down the corridor, and out through a side entrance. His limbs were ridiculously floppy. His sense of direction had gone too, but he could feel the cobblestones of Kindle Yard underfoot. A couple of Hammers were walking ahead, on their way home. Zilla returned their banter.

The trio approached the security gate. It wasn't Jeff Buller on duty. Gideon's voice was confident, capable. 'I'm afraid young Stearne's taken the celebrations a bit too far.'

The guard tutted. 'These young lads just don't know when to stop.'

'It's nothing a few pints of water and an aspirin won't cure. Don't worry; Zil and I will see he gets home safely.'

With monstrous effort, Lucas tried to work through the drug, forcing his tongue to retrieve the shape of words. All he came out with was a garbled slur. Even looking the guard in the eye was impossible, when his own were rolling all over the place. There was more laughter, and remarks about the morning after. Gideon's arm squeezed him fondly.

The three of them walked out of the Inquisition, Lucas with legs of rubber and a head full of fuzz. Locked in the other two's supportive embrace, he was taken along the street and round a corner to where an unmarked van was waiting. And for the second time that day, Lucas found himself cuffed in iron, and bundled into the back of a moving vehicle.

CHAPTER 33

Silas Paterson reached the corridor just as Glory switched off her phone. He didn't seem in a hurry. He opened the first door he came to in an exploratory sort of way. While his attention was turned, she darted out of the bedroom and back up the stairs. She shut the attic door as gently as possible. 'Silas Paterson is on his way,' she said. She was light-headed with the unreality of it all.

Troy was staring down at Lord Merle's lifeless body. Serena was still collapsed in the chair, rubbing her hands and rocking. But when she heard Glory, her face lightened. 'Silas! Oh good. He's right on time.' Her hysterics were over almost as quickly as they'd begun. 'Quick,' she said. 'Over here.'

She hurried over to her husband's corpse and, with Troy's help, dragged him behind the folding screen. Glory pushed a rug over the blood smears on the carpet. Heavy steps could be heard on the stairs outside.

Serena grabbed Troy by the arm. She spoke in an urgent undertone. 'I'm sorry. Godfrey turning up early – well, it unsettled me. It wasn't the plan. The two of them should have got here at the same time. But it's all right. I can improvise.'

There was a tap on the door. 'Serena? Are you in there?'

'You wouldn't believe me before,' she whispered. 'So believe me now. You *have* to go.'

Somehow, Troy and Glory allowed themselves to be pushed into the adjoining room, the one Serena had originally entered from. It was the connecting corner room between the west wing of the attic where Rose had her quarters, and the south which ran the length of the main house.

'There's a set of stairs at the other end,' Serena said. 'From there you should be able to get away. Be quick.'

Troy began to protest but she shut the door on him and turned the key. 'Just a moment, Silas,' her voice said brightly.

Glory and Troy looked around them. They were in another bedroom, but its furnishings included a medicine cabinet, and various scans and charts pinned to the wall. The second door opened on to a corridor, and a series of small rooms that must have once belonged to servants.

'The woman's cracked.' Troy muttered. 'What the hell is she up to?'

'We'll find out soon enough.' Glory pointed to a TV monitor in the corner. Serena had said that Rose needed to be watched all the time, in case she injured herself without realising it. This room must be for her private nurse. She pressed her ear to the wall, and was gratified to find the partition was thin enough to listen through. She kept her eyes on the screen.

Godfrey Merle was a bully. Glory was used to men like him. Silas Paterson, however, was a different kind of crook.

351

Apart from Officer Branning, he was the first inquisitor she'd seen at close hand. He looked much more how she imagined such a person to be: tall and lean with a silvery, sinister elegance.

Lady Merle had undergone another of her transformations. 'I'm so sorry to have kept you waiting, Colonel,' she was saying, all a-flutter with charm.

'I've never had a secret assignation in an attic before. Your note was most mysterious. I confess I wasn't sure what to make of it.'

She laughed mischievously. Her bosom billowed over the violet dress. She went behind him and shut the door to the stairs. 'Maybe I just wanted to have you all to myself.'

'And what would Godfrey have to say about that?'

'He'd probably tell me to stop being so theatrical.' Serena took out a packet of cigarettes from her bag. 'And he might have a point . . . However, I wanted to talk to you somewhere I knew we wouldn't be disturbed.' She lit a cigarette and inhaled pleasurably. 'Mm – *mm*. I know that you and Godfrey are behind all these witch-attacks, you see.'

Troy and Glory exchanged looks. How would this end?

Silas Paterson, however, didn't look alarmed. 'Do you now?' He settled into the armchair. 'How interesting.'

'I thought so, yes.'

'And how did you find out, might I ask?'

She smiled, breathing out a stream of creamy smoke. 'Pillow talk.'

'Oh, Serena.' Silas shook his head indulgently. 'I'm sure there was more to it than that. I've always thought Godfrey underestimates you . . . And come to think of it, I suspect that you've done some talking of your own. Only twenty minutes ago, I had a call from one of my associates. He's just apprehended an intruder in my office. A friend of yours, I assume?'

Glory bit her lip, so hard she tasted blood. Lucas. It had to be.

'I don't have any friends, Silas darling. Even my admirers are getting thin on the ground.'

The Colonel brushed a speck of dust from his sleeve. 'No matter. We have arrangements in place for just such a contingency. The situation is under control. I'm curious, however – what did you hope to achieve by bringing me up here? Are you going to beg me to see the errors of my ways? Make me an offer I can't refuse?'

'Actually, I'm here to give you a present.' Her left hand traced, teasingly, the curve of her iron collar. 'You like balefires, don't you, Silas? You like to watch witches burn? Well . . . this is your lucky night.'

She tossed her lit cigarette in the direction of the door. It lay smouldering for no more than a second or two, before the carpet and door panel combusted with a *whoosh!*

Troy and Glory, watching events on the little screen, recoiled in shock. Silas leapt to his feet.

'You crazy bitch – what the hex are you doing?'

'Toasting my success. It's pure alcohol, sweetie; no smell or stain. The room's been soaked with it. So are the stairs. They'll be alight already.'

He got out his phone, saw there was no signal, and swore.

Oily plumes of smoke were already rising from the

doorway and up into the corners of the room. Flames fluttered after them.

The attic windows were too small to offer any hope of escape. Silas lunged towards the only other door in the room, behind which Troy and Glory were standing. Of course it was locked. 'Open this door. Now.'

Serena watched him calmly. 'I couldn't possibly. I threw the key out of the window. Don't worry,' she added, 'the smoke will get to us before the fire. We won't feel a thing.'

The inquisitor continued to blunder about as the flames muttered and scurried along the floor and up the walls. He kicked over the screen, exposing Lord Merle's bloodied corpse, and gave a cry of horror.

'You'll burn in hell's own balefire for this!'

'I deserve it,' Serena said. 'And so do you. Have a little dignity, Silas.'

It was a big room but half of it was already ablaze. The lens of the camera was obscured by smoke; shortly afterwards the screen went dead. Troy turned to Glory. 'Time to get out of here.' He opened the door to the rest of the attic.

'But we can't just leave them –'

'Why not? She's mad and he's evil. With Merle already dead, I reckon that's quite a few problems solved.'

'It won't change nothing! Paterson and Merle have associates. They'll carry on without them – this'll just be used as more proof of how wicked witches are!'

He hesitated.

'And besides, you heard what the bastard said. His goons have got Lucas. We have to find out what they've done with him. C'mon, Troy. Please.'

'All right. Whatever.'

Troy checked the door handle. The metal was still relatively cool to the touch. He stood back, then ran to slam his shoulder against the door.

Silas shouted from the other side. Troy tried again, again with no success. Smoke was seeping around the edges.

'Keep back,' Troy yelled, and got out his gun. He shot repeatedly at the lock. Moments later, Silas Patterson stumbled through, and collapsed on the floor.

It was astonishing how quickly the fire had taken hold. The room was a flickering cavern of heat, the curtains and drapes peeling off in flakes as they burned.

Lady Merle was on Rose's bed, trying to heave up her husband's body beside her.

Troy and Glory ducked down low, raised their arms over their noses and mouths, and lurched towards her. By crouching low to the floor, where the air was clearer, they managed to escape the worst of the fumes. Glory tried to pull Serena away, but the woman fought back, kicking and scratching. Troy wrestled her down at last and began to drag her towards the exit.

'No, no, I won't,' she choked out. 'You're wrecking everything. Let me *go* –'

'What about Rose?' Glory pleaded.

'She's better – off – without me. I've made my – my bed and – now – now I'll lie in it –'

Serena wrenched herself free and ran back into the flooding heat. Glory stared with streaming eyes as white skin, violet silk, were swallowed by smoke.

'Leave her,' Troy shouted. 'We can't save them both. For God's sake, Glory! *Move!*'

They plunged back through the burning doorway. Silas was collapsed on the floor the other side, his body racked by coughs. The air was poisonously thick. Glory felt as if there was an animal scrabbling to get out of her chest, its hot black fur clogging her lungs. All she wanted was to lie down, to close her eyes, just until she could recover her strength. But Troy's hand was on her back, pushing her on, and together they staggered through into the further reaches of the attic, hauling the inquisitor along with them.

CHAPTER 34

There was more space in the back of the van than in the boot of Troy's Mercedes, but because of the drug, Lucas couldn't sit upright and he lolled helplessly, jolting about with the motion of the vehicle. Perhaps the drug was of some benefit: he was too confused to be truly afraid.

Soon, far too soon, the van came to a stop. The doors slid open and Gideon and the driver, a pinched-faced young man Lucas thought he recognised from the inquisitorial guard, pulled him out. They were in a street of big dirty-white townhouses, of the kind that had once been impressive homes but were now eking out a living as hostels and cheap hotels. Their particular destination had chipped cornicing and broken steps that were sprouting weeds. The upper storeys had been converted into flats; through the sagging curtains of the ground floor window, Lucas glimpsed a woman sitting at a table with a little boy. He was colouring with crayons. The light was peaceful, warm.

As he was hustled towards the basement steps, Lucas willed the woman to look out. Even if she couldn't tell what, if anything, was wrong, he wanted her to see his face, for her eyes to connect with his. But of course her attention was on the child. The little boy laughed, and Lucas felt an anticipatory constriction in his chest. The muddling effect of the drug was already wearing off. Nobody knew he was here, nobody could stop what was happening. This was real.

It became even more real in the room they took him to: windowless, with an iron door, and lit by a bare bulb. Gideon and Zilla faced Lucas across the table: real grown-up inquisitors doing a real grown-up interrogation. In spite of their grave looks, they were excited about it, Lucas could tell. Gideon probably practised this sort of thing in front of the mirror. Zilla's severity sat uneasily with her pouty, posh-girl looks, like badly applied make-up. *What are we doing here?* Lucas thought. *We're all amateurs. None of us knows how this will end.*

He tried and failed to sit up straight. He was drugged and dirty, in iron cuffs. He looked at Gideon in his well-cut suit, his sleek hair slanting over his brow. The clear eyes, the easy smile. He was everything Lucas was supposed to be.

Lucas cleared his throat. 'This is illegal. Kidnap, drugging and assault.'

'I'm disappointed, Stearne,' Gideon said. 'I would expect a swot like you to have studied the small print of the 1997 Witch-Terrorism Act. You like quoting rules and regulations, don't you? So let me remind you of Clause 9: in times of national crisis, the British parliament can vote to impose special short-term measures for the prevention of witch-terrorist attacks. Which they did only this afternoon. Emergency powers are now in effect.'

'OK. Before you go any further, you should know that I'm working for WICA –'

Zilla actually giggled. 'A boy detective! How *thrilling*.'

'That's why I'm off-record. My case file is classified.'

Gideon folded his arms across his chest. 'How convenient. Because you certainly don't appear on any register I've ever seen.'

'Well, since you're a glorified intern, not a High Inquisitor, that's not exactly a shocker.' Finally, Lucas felt ready for a fight. 'That must be why Paterson recruited you to his crackpot scheme – he knew you'd be vain enough to think that being his henchman is some kind of promotion.' Gideon's face tightened, and Lucas knew he was right. He let the anger rise, pushing out the fear. 'So yes, I know all about Paterson and Lord Merle, and that awful Howell woman. I know what you're up to. You're framing witchkind for your own crimes, so you can return this country to the golden age of a balefire on every corner, and a witch-hunt twice a week.'

'A general crackdown is in the national interest,' Zilla said coldly. 'We have intelligence that Endor is regrouping. We need to be ready for them, to have the necessary powers and procedures in place.'

Now it was Lucas's turn to laugh. 'Seriously? You're *seriously* going to give me the whole "the ends justify the means" crap?'

'If we're going to talk about clichés,' Gideon retorted, 'let's start with the liberal ones. All that whining about witchkind rights, the endless hand-wringing over so-called persecutions . . . And people actually fall for it! It's retreat after retreat. Concession after concession.' He spoke with a passion that had been missing from his performance in the school hall. 'They have insinuated themselves into all aspects of public life. The rise of Jack Rawdon is a case in point – we've put national security in the hands of the people who pose the greatest threat to it! For wasn't that Endor's mission, in the first place? A world run by witches. Ten, fifteen years down the line, the offices of the Inquisition will be little more than a heritage theme park.'

Lucas saw a flash of Glory's face, bright with outrage. The thought warmed him. 'Pity the poor oppressed inquisitors! How lucky they've got you as a champion.'

'I don't pretend to be a hero,' said Gideon. 'But I'm not afraid to do what has to be done, however unpleasant. Somebody has to be prepared to get their hands dirty.'

There was a tap on the door. It opened to reveal a shaven-headed young man in a white tracksuit. When he saw the prisoner he rolled up his sleeves in a gloating sort of way, and Lucas once more stared at the angels and crosses, blood and thorns, entangled on his skin. But, course, the man didn't recognise him. He'd only seen Harry Jukes.

'Lucas, I'd like you to meet Mr Striker. He's one of our most valued colleagues.'

Striker nodded in satisfaction. 'We must "stand against the wiles of the devil,"' he intoned, fingering the crucifix around his neck, '"for we wrestle not against flesh and blood, but against principalities, against powers, against the rulers of the darkness of this world . . ."'

Gideon and Zilla exchanged slightly weary looks. They must have had their fill of Bible-bashing by now. Still, fanatics made good foot-soldiers.

'That's the spirit,' Zilla said.

Lucas did not try to resist, let alone wrestle, when Striker took him out of his chair and marched him out of the door. Gideon followed, leaving Zilla behind. He was taken to a bare concrete room. There was an iron tank bolted to the centre of the floor. A pock-marked mirror hung on one wall.

Lucas's pulse pounded in his throat. He looked at Gideon. 'You know there's no reason for this. My condition is registered, and so is my position at WICA. Commander Saunders, Officer Jonah Branning and the Witchfinder General himself can all vouch for it.'

'Mm. You always were good at name-dropping, weren't you? I think that's part of your problem, Stearne. Delusions of grandeur, leading to paranoia and fantasy. Frankly, I can't trust a word you say.' Gideon went over to the tank, and stirred the water lazily with his fingertip. 'Are you a witch, a spy or a pathological liar? Either way, I'd like to find out.'

Lucas swallowed. Witches died in these tanks. What had Paterson's instructions been?

Cold water, held in iron, drew out the mark of the fae. The problem was, it wasn't just non-witches who emerged stain-free from the tank. If a witch hadn't used their fae recently, the stain would be very faint, or not appear at all. In theory, a stain-free ducking was proof of innocence. In practice, frustrated inquisitors would sometimes push the process to the limit, thinking that if they kept going for long enough, the fae would eventually emerge. This was why people sometimes drowned, and why the process was now strictly regulated. No doubt these regulations were another of Gideon's grievances against the bleeding-heart liberals who wanted to bring the Inquisition to its knees.

'Are you going to get out the needles too?' he asked.

'Don't be melodramatic. This isn't personal.'

'Crime is always personal. What about Jack Rawdon? An innocent man you're framing for murder. Christ, Gideon – somebody *died* in your witch-attacks.'

'A tragic error. Casualties have been kept to a minimum. That wouldn't be the case if it was real witch-terrorism. The British public have forgotten the scale of the danger we face. They've grown complacent, relaxed the rules. They need to be taught a lesson.'

Lucas remembered Gideon saying something like this at the Charltons' party, with Nell Dawson bridled at his feet.

'Lessons? Rules? We're not at school any more.'

'No,' said Gideon. 'Unfortunately for you, we're not.'

Because there was nothing else he could do, Lucas stripped to his underwear. He undressed himself slowly and scornfully. He was not going to fight; there was no point. He would not give the satisfaction. He felt quite calm and detached, as if he was looking at himself as a stranger would, from far away. This was how Glory's grandmother Cora had died, he remembered. Angeline too had been ducked on several occasions. Funny to think of that nasty old woman, standing in a room like this, all those years ago.

Striker held him by the shoulders and pushed him towards the tank. It was just under a metre high, a metre wide and about one and a half metres long, filled with icy water. An iron seat was fixed on the top of one end. There was a lever at one side that, when pushed down, tipped the seat and its occupant backwards into the tank, at such an angle to ensure the face and upper body were totally submerged.

Lucas had seen the diagrams of how this worked. He remembered the little stick-man in the textbook as Striker strapped him into the seat. The leather bindings were worn and old. They must have tied down many witches. He was shivering already from the chill coming off the damp concrete, and tried to brace himself against it. He didn't want Gideon to think he was trembling.

Striker loitered by the lever, drawing out the anticipation, waiting for the nerves to take hold. His gold tooth glinted. Lucas started to count in his head to steady himself, to keep his breathing slow and sure. He had got to twelve when the lever jerked down, and his body plunged with it, deep into the water's bite.

It wasn't just the cold. It was the iron containing it. Nausea rushed up his throat, his head crackled with static. All the muscles of his body struggled against his bonds. It was impossible not to try to fight.

The first ducking was short and sharp, to wind him. His heart crashed in his chest. His skin felt flayed. When he came up, the fingers of both hands shook uncontrollably. He gulped and gasped, and before he could even blink the water out of his eyes, he was smashing down into it again.

This time he was kept there. Water and metal became one, squeezing his lungs in an icy fist. They were dragging the witch-stain out of him. It was burningly, bone-crackingly cold. Just as he thought his chest and skull were at bursting point, Striker brought him up. The concrete room, the figures of the watching men, ran and smeared, as if they too were underwater. Through the flood, he thought he saw his father standing by the door. The vision dissolved into streaks, like tears.

He went down unprepared and sucked in water. It broiled around and inside him, scorching his lungs. He knew he was going to die. He thrashed about, first desperately, then limply. Blackness sparked behind his eyes. The darkness spread. He wasn't even aware he'd been hauled out of it, until he felt the blow on his stomach. Striker's fist forced him to spew out the water he'd swallowed, to open his eyes and wince against the light.

He coughed and retched. Over and over. In the midst of it, Striker undid the straps and pulled him upright, so that he faced the mirror on the wall.

'There it is.' Gideon's voice was rich with satisfaction. 'Your stain.'

The Devil's Kiss had spread. It was no longer confined to the spot below Lucas's shoulder blade. It was bleeding out of the corners of his eyes, seeping from his nostrils and his ears, inking his fingertips. The fae was claiming him: the purple shadow that spread like ancient blood, like midnight, like the rivers of the underworld.

Gideon was standing very close. Slowly, he ran the tip of his finger along Lucas's brow, the bridge of his nose, the curve of his cheek.

'Look at you,' he said softly. 'Look at the dirty hag.'

Lucas, dripping, gasping, shuddering all over, looked back into Gideon's pale eyes. They were light as glass. He felt his dark secret self, beating and pooling beneath his skin. He remembered the first time he'd seen the blot on his shoulder blade, and how the needle had thrust through to the bone. There had been blood, then, and tears. And though he was even more afraid now, in the grip of true disaster, he felt, behind it all, a strange and separate peace.

CHAPTER 35

Silas Paterson was slipping in and out of consciousness. When Troy tried to get him moving, he could only crawl drunkenly along the floor. In the end, Troy and Glory half carried, half dragged the inquisitor along the south wing of the attic. It was slow progress. 'This pricker had better be worth it,' Troy said through gritted teeth. Dark air rippled after them; Glory looked behind to see a lick of yellow flames.

Finally they came to the stairs and stumbled down into the main body of the house. The air here tasted fresh and cool, and they sucked it in gratefully. After the insidious hiss and sputter of the fire, the silence was a balm; if the place did have a fire alarm, Lady Merle must have found a way to disable it. It was hard to believe that an inferno was raging somewhere above and behind them. Smoke had soaked so deeply into their skin they barely noticed the stench.

They reached a gallery that surrounded three sides of the square entrance hall. From the shadows, Glory looked down to the doorway, where the last few staff were being ushered out by a health and safety official in a fluorescent jacket. The fire had been discovered in good time; it looked like an orderly evacuation.

Meanwhile, Troy had propped Paterson against the wall, and was tying his hands behind his back with the inquisitor's handkerchief. A search of Paterson's pockets revealed nothing useful; his phone must have been lost during the scramble through the attics.

'Who are you people?' he mumbled.

'Your guardian angels,' said Glory. 'And don't you forget it.' If she wasn't so knackered, she'd have given him a kick.

'It's just as well we found our own way out,' she told Troy. 'I don't see nobody rushing to go pull people out of the fire.'

'We should head for the back of the building, try to sneak out through the kitchen or whatever.' Troy wiped his sooty face with his sleeve and surveyed their prisoner. 'Then once the three of us are somewhere nice and private, we'll see what the Colonel has to say for himself.'

For the moment, Paterson was saying nothing. He'd blacked out again.

'OK. But as we're here, we might as well take a quick look around, right?'

'The fire brigade will be here any minute. We need to get back to the coven.'

'It won't take long.'

'We've got a hostage inquisitor! What more d'you want?'

But Glory had had enough of accusations and

suspicions and threats. They needed more. She began to hurry along the gallery, opening doors at random.

'Goddammit, Glory!'

'I'm nearly done –'

The final room on the left-hand gallery overlooked the avenue. From the window, she could see the huddle of party refugees. It was hard to believe there had been a ball going on, all this time. She wondered if and when the guests had realised their hosts were missing.

However, it was the room itself that caught her attention. As soon as she'd opened the door, she'd felt her Seventh Sense stir. The walls were lined with glass-fronted cabinets and display stands. She skimmed the labels. *Ceremonial Persian Scrying-Bowl, seventeenth century. Witch's Bridle, German, circa 1815. Gris-gris Amulet, from the grave of Marie Laveau.* Over the door hung a portrait of the crowning glory of Lord Merle's witchwork collection: his wife. Her painted eyes stared out above the exaggerated band of her bridle. Their calm was haunting. Later, Glory knew, she would have to think about those last searing moments in the attic, the frenzy and flames.

But now was not the time. Paterson's conspiracy had afforded Godfrey Merle the perfect opportunity to indulge his fetish, by using a captive witch to commit witchwork on his behalf. He'd surely want to keep some memento of their triumph. He'd be too arrogant not to.

Glory began to open cases and rummage through drawers. Troy shouted at her to stop whatever the hell she was doing and *get out*. He could hear sirens. The fire brigade were on their way.

'Just a sec!'

The lower compartment of the cabinet nearest the window was locked. Thank Hecate she'd managed to hold on to her evening bag. Her ticket for the cloakroom was a small square of laminated plastic, not unlike a credit card. She slid it into the crack between the door and the frame. After a few swift wiggles and a final jerk, it popped open.

All that the cupboard contained was a small cardboard box. She opened it up to find a jumble of oddments. A sparkly red whistle, a plastic horse, a doll with scribbles over her face, and a model train. They had bits of dirt and hair attached to them. Glory thought about the witch-attacks, and how neatly these objects fitted into them. 'Gimme a break,' she said as Troy came into the room, hauling Paterson along by the scruff of his neck. 'I think I've got something.'

'Great,' Troy started to say. 'Then let's –'

He didn't get any further. Paterson had suddenly sprung into life. He had worked his hands free of his bonds, and now he seized the Persian scrying bowl from its stand and smashed it against Troy's head. It was made of bronze and made a clanging sound as it struck.

Troy staggered, then fell to the floor. The Colonel snatched up Troy's gun.

'Put that box down, girl,' he told Glory. 'Whatever that is, I'm sure it doesn't belong to you. It will be better for you to give it up, and yourself with it.'

Glory relinquished the box. She had no choice. The inquisitor's eyes were bloodshot, and his cough was hoarse.

But he wasn't overcome with smoke or exhaustion. He looked very alert indeed. He must have been shamming all this time. In the world outside sirens blared, and the night flashed black and blue.

'Serena Merle was a vicious maniac, with connections to the criminal underworld.' Paterson spoke slowly, carefully, working things out. 'The three of you lured me and Lord Merle up to the attic, where you –'

'We saved your life!'

'You took me hostage. A coven slut and a two-bit hood.' He looked at Troy. 'Like father, like son. It appears to be a bad week for the Morgan family.'

'It was you behind that bomb, weren't it?'

Paterson smiled. 'Charles Morgan is a very unpopular man. There's a long line of people waiting to give him his just deserts. I merely . . . encouraged . . . the operation. Morgan Senior got lucky. You two won't be quite so fortunate.'

'Let's not get ahead of ourselves.' A small dark-haired woman Glory had never seen before was standing in the doorway. She too was armed. Officer Jonah Branning was behind her, holding up his inquisitorial badge. They were both breathing hard. 'Put the gun down, Colonel,' the woman said.

Paterson turned around. He looked more irritated than alarmed, and when he saw Jonah, he visibly relaxed.

'Wait . . . I know you . . . Branston, isn't it? What are you doing here? Well – never mind. Your timing is perfect. I've apprehended a pair of dangerous criminals, and I'll need you to radio ahead for back-up.'

'I'm afraid I can't do that, sir. I have a warrant for your

arrest from the Witchfinder General, on a charge of high treason.'

Silas Paterson's silvery features turned iron grey. 'That is impossible.'

'Nevertheless, sir, I'm going to have to ask you to surrender your weapon and come with us.'

The small dark woman advanced towards the room. Her face was intent, and her aim didn't waver. Disdainfully, Colonel Paterson put down the gun.

Glory seized the box of witchwork, and went to Troy. He stirred and groaned and, to her immense relief, managed to sit up. 'I knew you were trouble,' he mumbled.

'You are making a grievous mistake,' Paterson was saying, as the woman put him in cuffs. 'And you'll live to regret it, just as soon as my colleagues –'

A radio crackled, and a man called up from the hall below. The fire brigade were on their way. Paterson smiled. He knew he had the real authority in the room. Quick as a flash, the female agent slapped a piece of adhesive tape across his mouth. His eyes bulged.

'New operational procedure,' she explained, as she proceeded to pull a black cloth hood over his grunting, tossing head. 'Clause 9 of the Witch-Terrorism Act came into effect this afternoon.'

She propelled her now anonymous captive out into the gallery. Jonah helped Glory get Troy to his feet, and the five of them moved towards the stairs. A firefighter met them there. He looked at them uneasily.

'Is everything all right, sir?'

'Yes,' Jonah answered briskly. 'And thank you for your

cooperation. Agent Connor and I are now going to escort the suspect to a secure detention facility. These two will accompany us as witnesses.'

Silas Paterson shook his head furiously and made a kind of strangled bellow. Jonah ignored him. 'As I explained to you when we arrived, this is an issue of national security. Special measures are in force. The Inquisition expects your utmost discretion.'

It was not the place of the Fire and Rescue Service to question the diktats of the Inquisition, or its officers. 'All right, fine. But I have to ask you to leave immediately. We need to evacuate this building.'

Jonah nodded. As soon as the firefighter had moved on, he turned to Glory, and his composure slipped. 'But where's Lucas?'

CHAPTER 36

Zilla came into the ducking-room with an armful of blankets. She stared at Lucas with impersonal curiosity. The witch-stain was already fading from his skin, but the shakes had set in. He was sitting against the wall, arms wrapped around his body in a futile attempt to keep in the warmth. His shivers were hard and merciless, the muscles contracting in mechanical jerks. His teeth rattled like loose stones. She threw the blankets at his feet and he crawled into them with animal relief. *I'm alive*, he thought. *It's done.* For the moment, he didn't care about anything else.

'Have you heard from the Colonel?' Gideon asked.

'I left a message but he's not answering his phone. How'd it go in here?'

'Fine – I even managed to get some photos for the file. Really, it went like clockwork. Much better than the demo.'

'Lucky you. What do we do with him now?'

'Keep him here until further notice, I imagine. It'll all be wrapped up by tomorrow night anyway.'

'In that case, I'm going to check on . . . well. You know. Then I'll try the Colonel again. He'll want an update.'

Zilla left, and Striker went to stand guard outside the door. For the first time since coming here, Lucas wondered about the witch they'd been using for the attacks. Was he or she locked up in this basement too? Was that who Zilla was checking? Yet he could not summon the energy for real interest. He wound the blankets about him more tightly. They were smelly and itchy, but thick wool. After a while, the shudders became shakes, then trembles. He concentrated on breathing in and out, slow and sure.

Gideon, meanwhile, sat on a chair nearby and fiddled with his phone. Maybe he was sending urgent communications to the other conspirators. Maybe he was posting the pictures of Lucas's ducking on his Facebook page.

'People will be looking for me,' Lucas said eventually. His voice was scratchy and thin, and hard to steady. 'My father, my warden, WICA . . . they won't rest until they know what happened.'

'That's simple enough,' Gideon drawled. 'You were caught breaking into a High Inquisitor's office, where you used witchwork to attack an inquisitorial employee. You tried to feed us some garbage about being a secret agent, yet there's no record of you in any official file. Your detainment and interrogation is entirely legitimate. Really, Stearne, you've only yourself to blame.'

'Keeping me down here won't do any good. Someone on your team has already leaked the plot to the Wednesday Coven. WICA have the details; the Inquisition too.'

'Funny. You're so full of righteous certainty, you say you have all this support . . . and yet you decided to burgle the Inquisition by yourself. That seems pretty desperate to me.'

Gideon tilted back on his chair. 'Besides, the covens aren't in any position to cause trouble. Not after Charlie Morgan's unfortunate accident. And, as we know, WICA's credibility is about to be shot to pieces.'

'Not all inquisitors are like you,' Lucas said quietly. 'They'll know something's up. They'll start to ask questions.'

'I'm sure they will. Such as "what strings did the Chief Prosecutor pull to keep his witch-spawn off the register?", for example. You see, it's starting to look as if the Stearne family have cut a lot of rather dangerous corners. Important security procedures have been breached. The fact that a handful of Inquisition officials have colluded in this only confirms how deep the corruption goes. Once Colonel Paterson and his team have swooped in to arrest Rawdon and save the day, I think a lot of people will be calling for regime change.'

Lucas was finding it increasingly difficult to keep up. He looked at Gideon tiredly. 'How long, really, have you known I'm a witch?'

'Ah . . .' Gideon pulled a sorrowful face. 'Let's just say that your stepsister has been having a very difficult time. Poor Philly feels that no one ever listens to her.'

Philomena. Of course. Not that it had made any difference in the end. Gideon was right: he'd brought this on himself. Lucas closed his eyes, let the world fade.

He might even have dropped off for a moment or so. Sheer exhaustion had overwhelmed everything else. But he snapped back to wakefulness when he realised Striker was in the room.

'Fine,' Gideon was saying. 'I'll talk to her. Stay here, and keep an eye on our friend.'

Striker squatted down on his haunches and regarded Lucas. His lean, bony face had a hungry look. 'Sssssss,' he whispered, and sucked his gold tooth. Lucas kept his eyes on the floor. He was trying to listen to Zilla and Gideon's conversation on the other side of the door.

'. . . Helena on the line . . . There's a problem . . . blaze . . . Can't . . . get hold . . . Nobody's seen . . . I'm sure . . .'

But then they moved away, and he couldn't hear anything more, except for Striker's soft hiss.

After only five minutes or so, Gideon returned. He didn't look quite so sleek, or so sure. Something was wrong. Lucas felt a flicker of hope. Then he saw what Gideon was holding.

'Zilla and I have some business to attend to, so we'll have to say goodbye for now. Striker here will look after you. I'm sorry about the bridle, I really am. But we can't afford you trying any witch-tricks while we're gone. As an inquisitor's son, I'm sure you'll understand.'

He passed the witch's bridle to Striker. It was the same one he'd used to muzzle Nell Dawson.

Lucas lifted his head. 'Aren't you going to stay and watch? That's what you really like to do, isn't it, Gideon? Isn't that why you took my photograph?'

If Gideon felt his contempt, he didn't show it. He paused at the door, and smoothed down his hair disdainfully. 'I like to see justice done. That's what the public wants too. Once the Inquisition's powers are restored, we'll start to see more punishment, less witchcrime.'

Once Gideon left, the room felt even colder. It was not the witch's bridle that Lucas was most afraid of. It was being alone with Striker.

The fire in the west wing of Lord Merle's mansion had spread from the attic to the upper floors. As Glory followed the others out of the main entrance, she could see thick red flames gushing like blood from the side of the house. The mill of firefighters, medics and gawping onlookers reminded her of the aftermath of Charlie's car-bomb. But with all the activity and excitement, their own exit passed relatively unnoticed. A black van was waiting for them outside the door with its engine running. Without further ado, Colonel Paterson was bundled into the back and she and Troy clambered into the passenger seats, next to Jonah. Agent Connor sat up with the driver.

Jonah was already on the phone to the Inquisition. 'They say Lucas left about an hour ago,' he told Glory. 'He'd been drinking apparently – was in quite a state. An old school friend by the name of Gideon Hale was taking care of him. It sounds like a set-up to me.'

Glory looked at her watch. The meeting between Silas and Serena, the fire and their escape, the confrontation in Merle's collection room . . . it had taken just over half an hour. And all this time, Lucas had been in the hands of the enemy.

'How d'you get here so quick?' she asked, as they sped out of the avenue and back to the city.

'We have Matt to thank for that.' Jonah indicated the driver. 'He works for the police, in the armed response unit. We sort of . . . well, requisitioned his vehicle.'

'Jonah is my sister's witch warden,' said Matt, a middle-aged man with a stocky build and quiet manner. 'She's bridled, and last year some yob threw a stone at her in the street. It missed Stacey, and hit her little girl instead. Blinded her in one eye. It was Officer Branning who brought the man to justice.' He shrugged. 'Breaking a few traffic regulations is the least I can do.'

Agent Connor turned round from the seat next to him. 'Sorry. There hasn't really been time for introductions, has there? I'm Zoey,' she said. 'We spoke on the phone.'

'Yeah, we've met before.' This, then, was the true face of the redhead who'd accompanied Lucas to the safe house. 'Um, thanks for the rescue.'

'Don't thank us yet,' she said crisply. 'We've illegally abducted a High Inquisitor. Our troubles have hardly started.'

Glory had wanted to get straight to the Lucas issue, but this brought her up short. 'I thought you got a warrant?'

'Not yet. Jonah has informed the Chief Prosecutor of the situation. He's on his way home from abroad, and is in contact with the Home Secretary and Police Commissioner, not to mention the Witchfinder General. But in the meantime, we're operating outside the law.' Zoey shook her head. 'It's damn lucky we found you when we did. We had no idea what we'd be dealing with . . . How's your friend doing, by the way?'

Troy had his eyes closed. His red hair was rusted

with blood from where the rim of the scrying-bowl had cut him.

'I'm fine,' he muttered. 'Bit of a headache, that's all.'

'Looks like a nasty blow,' Jonah said. 'You should see a doctor.'

'I said I'm fine.' Troy's mutter deepened to a growl. Glory could sympathise. A road trip with an inquisitor, a policeman and an WICA agent would give any Morgan the jitters.

Glory looked down at the box she'd carried out of Lord Merle's collection. It had seemed so important at the time, but away from the witchwork display, the contents could have been any old junk. 'We need to find Lucas,' she said. 'Now the prickers know we're on to them they're probably chucking out all the evidence. Even if we get warrants and suchlike, it'll be too late.'

'Paterson won't cooperate,' said Jonah. 'He's tough, he's clever, and he knows his rights. Until he sees a warrant, we won't get anything out of him.'

'We'll see about that,' Troy said.

'No.' Jonah frowned. 'I won't sanction any physical coercion.'

Troy laughed weakly. 'That must be an inquisitorial first. You're in the wrong job, mate.'

Zoey shook her head. 'Jonah's right. No more violence. Too many lines have been crossed already.'

Glory still didn't see why a witch would choose to work for the government, and against the covens. She almost felt like saying, 'See? See where it's got you?' She wanted Agent Connor to spit and swear, to pound her fist in rage. Her cool professional front wasn't something Glory could understand.

'I can get Paterson to talk,' she said abruptly.

'And how will you do that?' Jonah asked.

'Feminine charm.'

Troy laughed again.

But Agent Connor had turned round from her seat, and was regarding her seriously. Perhaps she'd already guessed what Glory planned, and what it meant. In response to the question in her eyes, Glory gave a very slight nod. Face to face . . . witch to witch.

'Let me try,' she said. 'I know how to get through to him. No aggro, just chat. I promise.'

Agent Connor looked at her again. Another silent understanding passed between them.

'OK,' Zoey said. 'Five minutes.'

The van pulled up in a lay-by. Glory went round to the back. The inquisitor, hooded and gagged, was attached to one of the built-in benches by the cuffs on his wrist, and a second set around his ankles. Matt the policeman stood on guard outside as Glory got in and closed the doors behind her. Then she pulled off the prisoner's hood and – with a satisfying rip – the tape.

He didn't look afraid; she'd say that for him. Instead, he let out a sigh of weary scorn. 'Is this where you bring out the knuckledusters?'

'Oh, I'm just a coven slut, remember. I'm sure there ain't nothing I can do to scare a big strong inquisitor like yourself.'

She leaned across and brushed the shoulder of his suit. 'You've got dandruff,' she told him. Then she sat back on her heels, and unwrapped the wad of tissue she'd brought with her. It contained a scoop of earth from the side of the road. A tiny grub wriggled in it, which she carefully removed and put aside on a scrap of paper.

Colonel Paterson was already pale, but he grew paler.

'Do you know what I'm doing?' she asked, casually rolling the ball of mud and dandruff back and forth in her hands. The grub squirmed on its paper nest.

He didn't answer.

'Ain't you guessed yet? Ain't you worked out what I am?'

He swallowed. 'This,' he said, 'is exactly why I and my colleagues have been forced to take the action we have. If tonight's events prove anything at all, it's that witchkind are as irredeemably unstable and vicious as we've always feared.'

'Well, seeing as you're such an expert on us,' said Glory, 'I'm sure you know what I'm crafting.' She spat on her palm and began to shape the mud into a little figure of a man. 'I'm a strong witch, you see. One of the strongest. And I know how to hex a bane that lasts. You understand?'

He didn't say anything. He was absolutely still, mesmerised by the lump of mud in her hands.

She made her voice gentle. 'So I'm going to put a worm in your brain. No one but you will know it's there. Only you will hear it, as it whispers and gnaws . . . only you will feel it slither through your skull . . . It'll grow bloated in there, and rotten. Your brain's going to rot too. And there is nothing, *nothing* in the whole world that can help you.'

She cocked her head at him and smiled. The trick was to make people believe you were capable of anything.

'. . . Unless, of course, you can tell me what you've done with Lucas.'

CHAPTER 37

The bridle wasn't as painful as Lucas expected. As the metal curb closed on his tongue, and the iron clenched his skull, he felt a rush of weakness. Pins and needles prickled all over. But after a while the iron's effect was merely numbing. All his senses were deadened. His vision was dimmed, his hearing muffled. Even his thoughts slowed. He was cold, cold to the bone. It felt like he had been cold for ever. He didn't notice it much now.

Time passed. He didn't know how long. He was vaguely aware of Striker moving about but he wasn't particularly worried. He drifted in and out of a disembodied limbo.

Something flickered into the haze. His bleary eyes took a while to identify the brightness. Not matches, this time, but a lighter. Striker was flicking it on and off, up and down. The spark of it danced in his eyes.

'You've soaked up a lot of water, witch,' he murmured. 'Maybe it's time to dry you out. Maybe it's time to heat you up again . . . to shine some light . . .'

He began to hiss.

'Sssssssss . . .'

* * *

Glory was adamant they shouldn't pass on the information she'd got from Paterson to the authorities. Lady Merle had said the police were implicated in his plot. The five of them had to get to Lucas before anyone else did. They couldn't risk the enemy alerting his captors. However, Jonah insisted that Ashton Stearne be informed. He phoned as they entered the outskirts of London. It was a necessarily brief conversation; Ashton was on a call to the Witchfinder General at the time.

They parked in a side street a little way down the road from the address Paterson had given them. Since the place wasn't an official Inquisition facility, they hoped the security measures would be minimal. In fact, Number 26a looked to all intents and purposes like a normal residential flat. The basement area beneath it was boarded up and the building as a whole had a neglected air. Glory wondered if Paterson had lied to them after all. This was not the setting for the high-tech evil inquisitorial lair of her imagination.

Zoey did the initial reconnaissance, and reported that there was a second entrance to the ground floor flat via the back of the building. It was agreed that Troy and Matt would cover the main door, in case any escape attempt was made, while the other three went in through the back. Paterson, meanwhile, would remain locked up in the van.

A builder's skip eased their scramble over the wall. In spite of everything, Glory felt a shiver of excitement as she dropped down into the enclosed yard. The overlooking windows were dark and silent. Zoey had clearly had more experience than Troy at breaking down doors, for she despatched it in three swift kicks, driving the heel of her boot into the area just below the handle. Jonah stood behind her, covering her with the gun.

No inquisitors lay in wait. No alarms were activated or weapons deployed. They found themselves in an ordinary if dilapidated kitchen. Underwear dripped on a clothes rack, dishes soaked greasily in the sink. In the inner doorway a woman with a thin sallow face and tousled hair was standing in her dressing gown, hand on heart. A child squirmed at her side.

'Please,' the woman said in a thick Eastern European accent. 'I have visa.' Her voice trembled. 'Papers, visa. Everything. The man say. He promise.'

Her little boy had a snotty nose and big brown eyes. The broken lock, the night awakening, the hard-faced strangers with guns . . . It was how Glory had imagined the Inquisition coming for her. But he stared back at them solemnly, unafraid.

'We're not from immigration,' said Jonah, showing his badge. 'We're the Inquisition.'

The woman seemed, if anything, relieved. At any rate, she nodded vigorously. 'Yes. British Inquisition. Yes, they who promise. They have our papers. They arrange all.'

The child wriggled away from his mother, and ran towards the front room. The carpet was sprinkled with coloured pencils, and lines of toy soldiers arranged on the floor.

'This is the witch,' Glory said slowly, wonderingly. Jonah and Zoey turned to scrutinise the woman again. 'No,' Glory said. 'The kid.'

Lord Merle's box of witchwork made a new kind of

sense. The red whistle, the toy train, the doll with scribbled spots on its face, the plastic horse . . . They were playthings turned into weapons; childish props for adult nightmares. It was the toy soldiers that made her see it. Zoey had talked in the car about the army parade that Jack Rawdon had been going to attend.

The boy's mother shook her head. Her eyes darted, fearful and quick. 'No understand. No possible.'

'Not possible,' Jonah echoed, though he knew that it was. He guessed too who these people were. They were the last of the detention centre runaways, the missing Roma who'd broken out in hope of a better life. The words of his boss came back to him. *Juvenile witches can be a valuable asset.*

'Where is he?' Glory demanded. 'Where's Lucas? What have you done with him?'

The woman stared hopelessly. *No understand.*

But Zoey had already pushed ahead into the hall. There was a door at the end, down to the basement. Glory started after her, though Jonah tried to pull her back. 'Wait,' he said. 'It's not safe. Let me –' She twisted free and ran down the stairs. She saw a man in a white tracksuit, sprawled on the floor with Zoey on his back and a cigarette lighter by his side. She saw a tank. A puddle of water. A boy, caged in iron.

Crashes and shouts sounded all around. Armed officers had arrived. Troy and Matt came with them, the Chief Prosecutor was close behind. Glory barely noticed.

Lucas's skin still had a faint stain around his eyes and mouth, the tips of his fingers. Not a bruise, but a bloom, paler than violets. When she lifted the bridle off, she felt the cold of the metal pass through her, like an echo of remembered pain.

What did Lucas know of it? A smell of burning, and the bright flare of Glory's hair. The smoke on her skin, the salt of her tears. Her light and fire.

And afterwards, his father, bursting through, picking him up like a child, holding him in his arms. *My son. My son.*

CHAPTER 38

Glory did not go home that night, or the night after. She got a message to Cooper Street that she had gone to visit her Morgan cousins, to offer support in Charlie's hour of need. In fact, she was staying at Troy's flat. He himself returned to the family house in Cardinal Avenue.

With the arrival of the team from Special Branch, the professionals had taken over. Lucas was immediately whisked away in an ambulance with his father, but at one point Glory thought she'd have to stay in the basement all night. Men in uniform swarmed everywhere: shining lights, taking photographs and collecting samples, barking codes into transceivers. Officer Branning and Agent Connor did most of the talking. Somehow, they managed to keep the details of Troy and Glory's involvement to a minimum. Glory made the most of acting dazed and confused; Troy, at least, had his head wound to excuse him. Eventually, they were allowed to leave. Formal statements would be taken later.

That was when Troy took her to the flat. 'You need a breathing space,' he said as he left. 'Take your time.'

Afterwards, Glory barely remembered crawling into bed, her body still rank with sweat and smoke. She was afraid the smell would haunt her dreams, taking her to the Burning Court, or the attic with Lady Merle. But the night was quiet, her sleep deep enough to drown in.

She stayed in the flat all of the next day. She spent two hours getting soap scum and water all over Troy's immaculate and expensively accessorised bathroom. Then she ransacked Troy's immaculate and expensively stocked fridge. Browsed his bookshelves, rummaged through his drawers, pilfered a pair of cashmere bedsocks. She kept the TV on, partly because the background noise was comforting, and partly because she was waiting for news of the scandal to break. So far, the only part of the story to come out was 'tragic blaze at media tycoon's mansion'. The report was mostly speculation. Glory thought of Rose Merle, sitting quietly in some hospital room, her perfect face as blank as her thoughts. Perhaps Lady Merle had been right to call her memory loss a mercy.

Zoey Connor came around in the afternoon. She was tired but upbeat. She said that all of Paterson's accomplices, including the MP Helena Howell, had been taken into custody, and were cooperating with the police. The Roma mother and her son were under guard in a safe house, while the authorities tried to decide what to do with them. They'd already bridled the boy.

'It turns out that one of the Witchcrime Directorate's informants found them, and alerted Paterson. I'm not sure how they discovered the boy's fae. I think the mother was perhaps planning to use it in her appeal for asylum. But

Paterson offered a different kind of deal. A new, legal life in Britain for her and her son, in return for their help with some clandestine government operations. It's still not clear how much the woman understood. The little boy obviously didn't know what he was doing.'

Glory nodded. That was why he would be beyond suspicion. A six-year-old witch was so unlikely as to seem impossible. 'Paterson weren't ever going to hand over a couple of shiny new passports and a council flat, was he?'

'No. Once the job was done, I'm sure the plan was to ship them off on the quiet.'

'Or dump their bodies in a ditch. Why ain't none of this stuff on the news?'

Zoey seemed a little uncomfortable. 'There's a media blackout, until all the facts are known. A story as big as this requires careful management.' She didn't quite meet Glory's eye.

On Wednesday morning, Glory went shopping with the money put out for the cleaner. When she got back, Jonah telephoned with the news that Lucas was back at home. He was asking to see her.

They met in the WICA safe house where Glory had first been introduced to Harry Jukes. Jonah let her in, and she surprised both of them with the warmth of her greeting. He showed her up to the small bare kitchen where Lucas was waiting, but didn't go in.

Lucas got up from his chair when Glory arrived, and this unsettled her. She wasn't sure what to do. Shake his hand? Give him a hug? She felt clumsy, and unprepared.

He looked OK, she thought. Not much paler than

usual anyway. The shadows under his eyes reminded her of the witch-stain. He smiled at her and the shadows lightened. For some reason this confused her too.

'How are you doing?' she asked abruptly, to cover it.

'I'm fine,' he said. 'They kept me in hospital overnight as a precaution. But there was no need. It was . . . it was only water, after all.'

Unconsciously, he moved one hand to touch the chafe marks on his wrists. Glory could see the red lines from the leather straps. She sat down in the seat opposite him. She cleared her throat.

'They got the bastards what done it. Striker, and that Gideon creep and his girlfriend. Zoey told me.'

'So I heard. They and the other accomplices have made full confessions, Patterson and Howell too. It means that you and Troy probably won't even have to be called as witnesses.'

'But you'll have to testify.'

'Yes. My identity will be protected, though. The trial is going to take place in a closed court.'

'Closed?'

'It's when the public and press aren't allowed access, so that classified evidence –'

'I know what it is. It's what happens when there's a cover-up.' Heat rushed to her cheeks, and she gave a bitter, constricted laugh. 'Mab Almighty! Nothing changes, does it? The people in charge are going to sweep their muck under the carpet, just like they always do.'

'They can't,' Lucas said – dismissively, Glory thought. 'The story's too big, and too many people are involved. Jack

Rawdon and the Witchfinder General are going to make a joint statement to the press this afternoon.'

He frowned a little. 'I thought you'd be relieved about the trial. It's good, isn't it, that you and Troy won't have to be cross-examined? It'll keep the business with Harry Jukes and Cooper Street out of things. You'll be able to stay unregistered, and out of the spotlight, and the guilty parties will still get what they deserve.'

Glory certainly did not want to go to court, and she would have done her best to get out of it. But Lucas was so damned sure about the matter – so coolly casual in the face of her outrage. She could feel the same old conflict, thickening the air between them.

Lucas must have sensed it too. 'Anyway, I don't want to argue. I want to thank you. I owe you . . . everything.'

His eyes, the blue of them, were too intense. She looked away. 'You can save the speeches. I was lucky, you weren't.'

'It's more than that. Everything that was discovered, and achieved, is down to you. If you hadn't found me when you did, I don't know what would have happened.'

'That weren't your fault. It was all a load of accidents. We were making it up as we went along.'

He was still looking at her. She could feel it.

'What are you going to do?' he asked.

Now, today? Or for the rest of her life?

'Go back to Cooper Street, I guess.'

'It won't be the same, though.' He spoke as if to himself. 'It can't be. Too much has happened. I don't think I even want my old life back, even if I had the chance.' For the first time, he looked a little shy. 'You know, WICA doesn't just work on coven crime. There's industrial espionage, and government security, and international terrorism –'

'Lucas Stearne!' She widened her eyes theatrically. 'Are you trying to recruit me?'

He flushed. 'I'm hardly in a position to make job offers. I'm not sure what my status is at the moment. Nobody quite knows what to do with me. But if I get a chance, I want to stick with it. I think – well, I think this kind of work is worth doing, that's all.'

This time, she looked at him seriously. In her pocket, the crisp edge of the card Agent Connor had given her was poking through her jeans. She waited before she replied, trying to get it right. 'I can see that WICA does an important job,' she said. 'I guess there are some inquisitors who do things right too. With Paterson and his gang put away, maybe the good guys will have more of a chance.

'There are some things, though, that won't never change. Like with this trial – it's just more secrets and scheming . . . more deals behind closed doors.' She shook her head. 'I ain't saying the covens have the answer. They've got their own problems. But it's as important to have good people in the covens as it is to have them anywhere else.

'You people think that if you make enough rules, fill in enough forms, then you'll make things safe. It's not enough. Lady Merle shouldn't have done what she did. Not to Rose, not with the fire neither. But desperate people do desperate things. There'll always be people like her, and they'll always need a way out – somewhere outside the rules and the forms.

'So I need to stay on the outside, Lucas. It's where I fit.'

* * *

Glory's words made Lucas immensely tired. He knew that some of what she was said was right – more than she knew, in fact.

A face-saving strategy was already in place. The uncovering of the conspiracy was being rewritten as an official joint operation between WICA and the Witchcrime Directorate. In this version of events, Lucas – known only as an anonymous WICA agent – had been recruited by Commander Saunders to monitor the activities of his deputy, who was already under suspicion of malpractice. There would be no mention of Cooper Street or Harry Jukes, or the Morgan family. Privately, the Chief Prosecutor had admitted that Gideon and Zilla would get off lightly. They would present themselves as naïve young idealists, whose patriotism and zeal had been cynically exploited by the real villains of the piece.

Lucas did not like this. He accepted it, though. The government, Inquisition, even WICA, agreed that it was in all of their interests to minimise the fallout. It was in the public interest too. An aggrieved and hostile witchkind community was bad news for everyone. Lucas understood this. Glory wouldn't. Part of him respected her for this. Part of him resented her for it. She was always so certain, of everything.

He hadn't known what it would be like to see her again. He was half afraid to, unsure of what kind of memories she would revive. The crashing weight of water, the rub of the bindings, iron's echo and throb . . . To look back on what had happened, even now, was to feel it in pieces. Like trying to find one's reflection in shattered glass. Yet as soon as

Glory had walked through the door, he knew it would be all right. Whatever had been broken would come together again.

That was why he couldn't entirely trust his motives for what he was about to do.

Lucas got out the piece of paper he'd pulled from behind the sideboard that morning.

'I have something you need to see. I found it on Monday, when I was trying to hack into the Inquisition files.'

He passed her Angeline Starling's profile from the National Witchkind Database.

In seconds, Glory had skimmed the page. Her face hardened into a mask, china white. Her cosmetics stood out as brightly as paint.

'Is it true?' she asked him. Her voice had become artificial too: tinny and distant.

'Yes, I think it is. I'm sorry.'

The breath went out of her and for long seconds did not come back.

'OK.' Her hands plucked at the paper, twisting and fidgeting. 'I have to talk to her then. I have to see – to hear –'

'There's something more.' Right up to the last possible moment, he wasn't sure how to do this, and now the words stuck in his throat. 'The report on Angeline's . . . it's from a database . . . there were updates on the rest of her family . . . and your mother . . .'

'Yes?'

'According to the record, your mother was last seen five years ago.'

'A – alive?'

'Yes.'

'Where? What was she doing? Who was she with?'

'It didn't say. There was no other information.' He looked her straight in the eye. 'We can't be sure your mother is still alive. But she wasn't killed by Charlie Morgan. At least, not the way that Angeline said.'

Lucas knew that Glory needed to be told that Edie Starling had been working for the Inquisition when she disappeared. But it wouldn't be fair to burden her with it now, not when there was so little real information. I'll see her again, Lucas reasoned. I have to. Then I'll tell her the full story. I just need to get the facts straight first.

Unless, that is, my father was responsible for her mother's disappearance. Or worse. Because if that's true, she will never forgive me.

He had suppressed the knowledge, but now it cut and crackled, like broken glass. He knew his face must have sharpened with it, because Glory reached across and grasped his hand. She had mistaken the nature of his hurt.

'Thank you, Lucas. For telling me.'

He smiled back at her, foreseeing his treachery.

'Thank you for finding me.'

CHAPTER 39

Glory returned to Cooper Street in the late afternoon. It had turned warm again and a moist green smell hung in the air, mingling with the traffic fumes. The same skinhead kids dawdled in the shadow of the tower block; chewing, gobbing, blagging, cussing. When she walked by, one whistled and the others jeered.

Patrick was sitting on the steps of Number Eight, peering into the hand-held games console Patch had swiped for him last Christmas. His thin hair puffed up a little in the breeze.

'There you are, Glory.'

'Hello, Dad.'

She went to sit beside him, and leaned against his shoulder. *Plink, plink, bleep* went the console. He was still in his dressing gown. She remembered the Chief Prosecutor, storming into the basement with a squad of armed men. How he'd sunk on to the puddled floor and cradled his son in his arms. How fierce his tenderness.

'I was sorry to hear about Charlie,' Patrick said, eyes fixed on the screen. 'Nasty business, that. How's the family bearing up?'

'Not too bad.'

'And what about, er, Harry? Is he with the Morgans now?'

'No. I . . . I'm not sure we'll be seeing much more of him.'

'Oh, dear. He seemed like a nice lad.'

'I s'pose. Turns out we had more in common than I thought.' Glory wearily got to her feet. 'I need to talk to Auntie Angel.'

Patrick looked up at her at last. He gave a cough. 'Ah. Hmm. You know, you spend an awful lot of time with your great-aunt. Sometimes I worry she has a bit too much influence over you.'

'Do you? Really?' Her voice trembled. 'And you never thought to say before?'

His face clouded with puzzlement. Before it could turn to hurt, she managed a smile. 'Never mind, Dad. It doesn't matter. I – I love you.'

'Love you too.'

Plink, plink, bleep.

She went a little way down the street and knocked on the old lady's door.

'Glory! I've been worried sick. Why ain't you returned my calls? Keeping me in the dark – what do you think you're playing at? Downright rude, I call it. Ungrateful too. D'you have any idea how many people've been looking for you, missy? And what's this I hear about you running around with Troy Morgan? Where's Harry? There's all sorts of rumours flying, I can tell you . . .'

She rattled on for a while. Glory didn't hear any of it.

She stood very still in the room she'd been raised in. She knew every fringe and tassel and candy-stripe, every scrap of newsprint, every black and white smile. The Holy Temple of the Starling Sisterhood.

Angeline had run out of breath for scolding. Or maybe Glory's silence had got to her. 'Come on, girl,' she said gruffly. 'Speak up.'

Glory unfolded the piece of paper Lucas had given to her and passed it to her great-aunt.

'I know it's true.' She sat down on one of the overstuffed chairs. 'Now you tell me why.'

Glory had seen Angeline do her frail old lady act before. This was different; a stripping down, not a putting on. Her great-aunt's face grew patched and grey, and when she lowered herself into a seat, her flesh shrivelled and her hands shook. But her voice stayed firm.

'You want the Starling Girl story, do you?'

'The real one. Yeah.'

'All right,' Angeline said, with a kind of ragged defiance. 'All right, then. I'll tell you how it was with my sisters and me.' Her mouth convulsed. 'I'd blowed their noses and wiped their arses ever since I were old enough to stand upright. Then after our ma and pa was gone, I scrimped and slaved to keep us together and off the streets. I got married to Joe, even though he were a drunk and a thug and fifteen years older'n me, so they'd have a roof over their heads, and because our family owed it to the coven. And as soon as they could, they skipped off to seek their fortunes. Didn't ever look back.

'Well, I should've known. Everyone said they'd grow up to be heartbreakers. The adorable Starling Twins! Sweet enough to charm the birds off the trees, sharp enough to steal the coat off a drunk's back.

'They got riches, lovers, power, their picture in the papers. I didn't begrudge them, I were proud. All I wanted was to be allowed to help – to be a little part of the legend. Maybe my fae weren't as dazzling as theirs, but they still used it, and me, whenever it suited. I covered for them. I witchworked for them. I got poked at with needles, and ducked in tanks.

'I loved them girls but they only loved each other. Not any of their fancy men, nor even their own children really. They was each other's whole world . . .'

There was a film on her eyes. Glory hardened herself against it.

'I see. You loved my granny so much you turned her in to the Inquisition.'

'It weren't a *plan*. I hardly knew what I was doing. I was half crazy, at the time. When Cora called, I'd just got home from burying Old Joe. The police and prickers was swarming over Cooper Street; we was up to our eyeballs in debt. And there was my little sister on the phone, laughing and prattling away like she'd never left. Five years she'd been gone, and never a word. "Oh, I got such adventures to tell you," she said. "So many stories! And how are you?" she asked. "How's poor old Ange?"

'Cora weren't ever frightened of nothing. A right wild one, she was. Careless of everything and everybody. Just once, I wanted her to know how it felt. To be powerless and humiliated and afraid. I wanted her in those tanks, yes. But I never . . . I never wanted her to drown . . .'

'But she did.'

'Yes, she did.' Angeline sniffed loudly. 'God forgive me, she did. And I tried to make amends by raising her child. But Lily took Edie away from me; said I'd never been a mother myself, that she knew what was best for her precious twin's girl. And it were only when Lil died and your ma was on her own again that she remembered Cooper Street, and her poor old Auntie Ange. Ha. A right comedown it must have been for her.

'Still, I was so pleased. So happy. Everyone could see Edie was special. God only knew who her father was, but she had her mother's talent, all right, and her own steadiness. The makings of a great witch. She'd give Cooper Street what it needed, what I deserved. Together we'd be unstoppable.'

'So what happened? You shopped her to the Inquisition too?'

Angeline looked confused.

'You can cut the crap, Auntie. I know Charlie didn't kill her. She was seen five years ago. Alive.'

'But how d'you –? Where –? It can't be . . .'

'It is,' said Glory roughly. 'Because we both know there was never a grave in Dunstan Woods, or a burial amulet. My mum really did leave. She'd had enough. Just like her note said. What did you do to her, to drive her away?'

The old woman smiled sourly. 'Edie was more like Cora than I knew. The kind that always leaves, never looks back. I didn't see it till it were too late.'

'Shut up. You lied before and you're lying now. You manipulated me so I'd turn snitch, become a traitor like you. The Morgans –'

'The Morgans have made plenty of widows and orphans, girl. Don't you forget it.' Angeline's bright black eyes stared into hers. 'And I never lied about your inheritance. I want you to be a great witch, Glory. I want you to make this coven the biggest and the best there ever was. That's why I taught you everything I know, that's why I'll fight for your rights till there's no breath left in my body. I've put my love in you, and my hopes. I've made you my own.'

Glory looked around the room. The faded headlines. The three laughing girls. The shabby old woman before her.

'I ain't yours. I never have been, and I never will be.'

Angeline gave a small dry sob. Then she bared her yellowed teeth. 'You think you can go crawling to the Morgans, I suppose. You reckon if you pout nicely enough, Troy'll sweep you off your feet. Or maybe you'll cosy up to the Inquisition instead, now you and the pyros are such pals?'

Glory got to her feet.

'Goodbye, Auntie.'

'Go on, then. Leave me, just like all the rest.' She staggered upright. 'Ungrateful little bitch.' Her voice rose, hoarsely, to a shriek. 'Get out and don't ever come back. Because it'll be too late then – too late –'

Glory shut the door. She breathed in the cool damp air. A wash of crimson flooded the sky behind the tower block.

Through the window of Patrick's bedroom she could hear a *bleep, bleep, bleep*. Music pounded from Number Seven; next door, the bull terriers howled. On the steps of Number Eight, Nate smoked and lounged.

'Hello, girlie,' he said as she walked past him. 'Troy's been looking for you.'

She didn't look round.

'Where're you going?'

'I don't know.'

I am Gloriana Starling Wilde. I am fifteen years old. I am a witch.

I can do anything.

She walked further, faster. She put back her head, and laughed. She spread out her arms. She began to run.

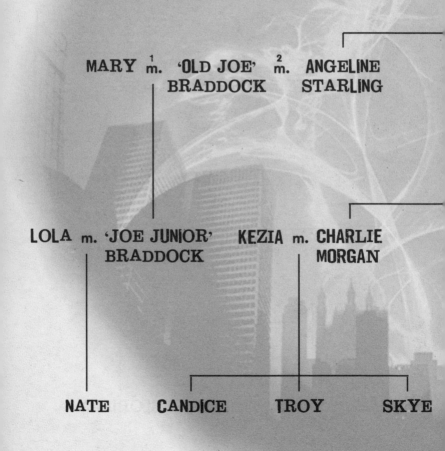

MARY m.¹ 'OLD JOE' m.² ANGELINE
BRADDOCK   STARLING

LOLA m. 'JOE JUNIOR'   KEZIA m. CHARLIE
BRADDOCK   MORGAN

NATE   CANDICE   TROY   SKYE

THE STARLING FAMILY TREE

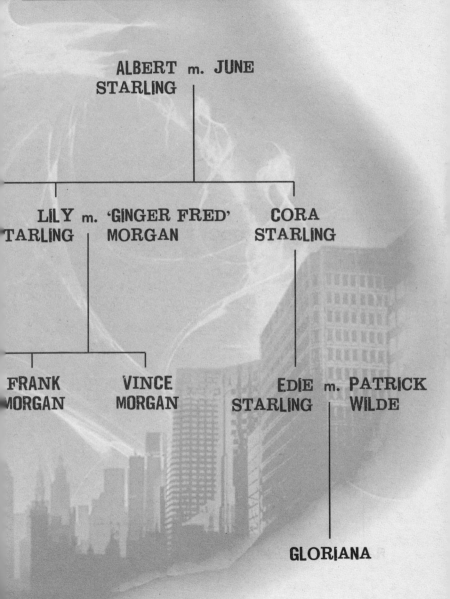

ALBERT m. JUNE
STARLING

LILY m. 'GINGER FRED'   CORA
STARLING   MORGAN   STARLING

FRANK   VINCE   EDIE m. PATRICK
MORGAN   MORGAN   STARLING   WILDE

GLORIANA

Author's Note

A belief in witches is common to nearly all cultures through-out history. The Hebrew Bible, the New Testament and the Koran all warn against witchcraft and prescribe punishments for it. The Roman Catholic Inquisition sponsored witch-hunts on the grounds that witches entered into a pact with the Devil and bore his mark.

The age of widespread witch-hunts in Europe and North America lasted from about 1480 to 1700. It is estimated that between forty and sixty thousand people were killed. Contemporary witch-hunts still occur in sub-Saharan Africa, India and south Ghana.

There has never been a British Inquisition but Matthew Hopkins, self-styled 'Witchfinder General', was a real person. So was his colleague John Stearne. They and their fellow witchfinders used pricking, ducking and witch's bridles on their victims.

My witches' work is inspired by the African-American magical practices known as hoodoo and British folklore. There is an old tradition that bells warn of witches, and water and iron guard against them.

Acknowledgements

No Dark Arts were used in the writing of this book. I didn't need to because of the following people: Emma Matthewson and Isabel Ford at Bloomsbury, Sarah Molloy at A M Heath, Sarah Lilly, Luke Staiano and Lucy Wilkins. Together, they have employed the zeal of an inquisitor, the cunning of a mobster and the creative pluck of a whole coven of witches. I would like to thank them all very much.

Brien Ō Keeffe of the London Fire Brigade kindly advised me on the events in Chapter Thirty-Three. Although the final-version scenario is somewhat different to the one we discussed, I am very grateful for his help. Any errors are due to my ignorance alone.

www.laurapowellauthor.com